I0762538

BY RUTA SEPETYS

I Must Betray You

The Fountains of Silence

Salt to the Sea

Out of the Easy

Between Shades of Gray

The Bletchley Riddle

You: The Story

A Fortune of Sand

A Fortune of Sand

A Fortune of Sand

— A NOVEL —

RUTA SEPETYS

BALLANTINE BOOKS
NEW YORK

Ballantine Books
An imprint of Random House
A division of Penguin Random House LLC
1745 Broadway, New York, NY 10019
randomhousebooks.com
penguinrandomhouse.com

Hardcover ISBN 979-8-217-09324-3
Ebook ISBN 979-8-217-09325-0

Printed in the United States of America

1st Printing

FIRST EDITION

BOOK TEAM: Production editor: Kelly Chian • Managing editor: Pam Alders • Production manager: Richard Elman • Copy editor: Kathy Lord • Proofreaders: Allison Lindon, Jennifer Abella, Frieda Duggan, and Megha Jain

Book design by Ralph Fowler

The authorized representative in the EU for product safety and compliance is Penguin Random House Ireland, Morrison Chambers, 32 Nassau Street, Dublin D02 YH68, Ireland. https://eu-contact.penguin.ie

For the Motor City

Where the wheels of history keep turning.

A Fortune of Sand

1927

GROSSE POINTE, MICHIGAN

1

ALWAYS WATCHING

"Trees, they're always watching."

The officer stares at Marjorie, confused. "Have you been drinking, Miss Lennox?"

The cramped booking area of the station echoes with a clack of typewriters beneath rings of flickering light. Marjorie sits, her small frame lost beneath the folds of an oversized police shirt. A chestnut bob frames her wide eyes edged in smoky kohl. She watches as the officer's expression fades from confusion and settles into the familiar judgment. She's not drunk; she's a dotty rich girl. A velvet brat, indulged by preoccupied parents. Marjorie quickly leans forward to object. "Officer, this is a misunderstanding."

Halos of summer sweat bleed through the armpits of the deputy's uniform. The wheezing fan perched on a chair in the corner brings no relief, just sways the sticky yellow flypaper dangling above the desk.

"A misunderstanding. Right."

He reaches for his cigarettes, and Marjorie's eyes dart to the open file folder on the desk. She spots the names of her three siblings, listed in a descending row. Oh, dear. Did the groundhog story travel? She looks at his name badge.

FOOT.

There are many types of feet. Bare, socked, bunioned—and this man? Marjorie regards the officer and nods with quiet certainty. Socked. Wide and flat. Short toes. Practical more than philosophical. She must take that into consideration.

He exhales a ghost of smoke and resumes the conversation. "So, trees. Care to elaborate, Miss Lennox?"

"Yes, allow me to explain. Trees—they're companions, a silent witness."

"You're not making a lick of sense."

"Nature doesn't make sense. It's wild and expressive."

"Well, what you call 'expressive,' the Hardwicks call indecent. Now see here, that artistic crap might fly downtown, but this is Grosse Pointe, not Detroit."

A clap of commotion pierces the room as a woman enters the booking area.

"Chet!" exclaims Marjorie.

A young woman with unruly brown hair and a smear of peach lipstick yanks at the vacant chair next to Marjorie and sits down.

"This is my sister Chet," says Marjorie.

"We've met," mutters the officer.

"Yes, you called me a grave lurker." Chet thrusts her arm across the desk for a handshake. "Charlotte Lennox. Good to see you again." She surveys the desk and points to a paperweight. "Say, that's new. I like it. It's an entombed beetle, right? When you die, I'll buy it at the estate sale. Your kids will need the cash."

The officer sighs, shaking his head. "Ah, the Lennox clan. Titans of windshields."

"Titans of glass," corrects Chet.

"Right, the self-proclaimed dynasty of Detroit." He glances at the file in front of him. "I met your brother—drunk in the fountain at the golf club. And now your younger sister. Is the entire family bat-crackers?"

"Depends on your definition." Chet points to the officer's cigarette. "You mind?"

"Help yourself," he nods. "How many smart alecks are there?"

"Four siblings," says Chet through a drag of smoke. "Technically, Marjie's a half. But here's a hot tip. Our oldest sister, Cecile, is a gangster in the making. Do the world a favor and ship her to Sing Sing."

"Be nice, Chet," sighs Marjorie. "It's not Cecile's fault. Every litter has a favorite." She turns to the officer. "As noted, I'm a half-sibling. The youngest."

"Yeah," says the officer. "I was new on the force when the first wife died. Tragic puzzler."

Chet stiffens. "We can skip the overture. Care to fill me in here?"

"It's Helen's birthday," explains Marjorie. "Last month, a storm destroyed a beloved sugar maple in her backyard. As I was trying to describe to Officer Foot, the tree was her watchful companion, and she was absolutely bereft to lose it. So, as a gift, I wanted to replace her tree for a day." Marjorie stands and throws the large police oxford from her shoulders. She's covered in leaves.

Chet shrugs. "My sister's here because she's a tree?"

A sultry whistle sounds from across the room.

"She's here not only because she's pasted with leaves but because her breasts are exposed."

"Oh," nods Chet. "I didn't notice."

"Of course you didn't," says Marjorie. "They're mushroom caps on the trunk of the tree. And—with all due respect, Officer—I'm not 'pasted' with leaves. I'm wearing a tailored tunic, 'covered' in leaves. I created it myself." She sits down.

"My sister's an aspiring designer," nods Chet.

"Well, the Hardwicks feel she's an aspiring nudist and the charge should be indecent exposure."

"Charge?" says Marjorie.

"Yeah. And you have priors," says the officer.

"Priors?" Marjorie's eyes flash. "Whatever do you mean?"

"Prior incidents. Prior complaints to the police," says the officer. "How do you think I know about your family?"

"That's ludicrous," laughs Chet. "I'll wager your paperweight that you have nothing."

"Oh, yeah?" The officer lifts the file folder. "Let's see. Your beloved sister was reported for riding a pony through the front door and up the interior staircase of an estate on Lake Shore Road."

Marjorie nods. "Of course I did. Judith was very ill, bedridden, and missed her pony. What are friends for, right, Chet?"

"You have to understand," says Chet to the officer. "Marjie is a very loyal friend. I just wish her 'friends' were as loyal to her."

"Well, the animal wasn't loyal either. Judith's parents filed a report that the pony dropped a gift on their prized Persian rug," says the officer.

"Oh, please," says Chet. "They needed paperwork for an insurance claim." She gives a wave of her hand. "You have nothing."

The officer looks at the two women. "Oh, yeah? What about this one—the calamity with the Detroit Institute of Arts."

Chet winces. Marjorie looks to her lap. "Oh, the Peter incident. Poor Peter."

Peter. Yet another misunderstanding.

Marjorie takes a breath and slowly raises her gaze. In misunderstanding her, they underestimate her.

A voice calls across the din of the police station, summoning the officer. He rises, gesturing with the file. "Stay put. I'll be right back." The women watch, craning their necks to see the silhouette of the officer speaking to a tall, dark figure behind a milky glass window.

Marjorie stares at the shape of a man behind the glass. Her brows arrow. "Who's he talking to?"

"I don't know," replies Chet. "You're lucky I was home when you rang up. And Gramps was there too. It's probably Gramps out there."

"No. It's too tall and slender to be Gramps." Marjorie wrings her hands in her lap. Her voice dims. "My dress. It's just a tunic, Chet. I thought it would make Helen happy."

"How can you consider Helen a friend? She allowed her parents to call the police."

"Does my mother know?"

"No, Lilah was still at tennis when you called. But this is bad. After the pony and Peter incidents, Dad's been ranting that his tolerance tank is empty. He claims you need discipline and structure."

Marjorie rolls her eyes and plucks the cigarette from her sister. "I've explained repeatedly that I'm not college material."

"Not college. A convent."

"A convent! That's noble, but they'd never take me. I look ghastly in black, and life without champagne sounds positively unholy. Oh, Chet, our father mustn't find out about this—about my mushroom caps. I can be structured and disciplined. It's just terribly boring."

"Speaking of boring, tonight's the annual 'June boom' dinner at the club."

Marjorie grimaces at the thought. Lobster thermidor laced with argument.

The dark figures shift behind the glass. The door opens and the officer's head appears. "Miss Lennox. You're free to go."

"See? Dynasty of Detroit!" shouts Chet to the officer. She stands. "Well, Gramps must have pulled his strings."

Marjorie takes a slow breath, looking toward the hallway for her grandfather. But the retreating figure she spots isn't Gramps. She could swear it's . . . No. Impossible. It couldn't be him. Could it? He hasn't been seen in more than a year. But if so, it might explain the mysterious item that recently appeared in her bedroom. A thrill stirs within her. The figure disappears, but like a drop of sap from bark, something else emerges.

Hope.

Chet inspects the beetle imprisoned in glass. "Exquisite. Its dead legs curl slightly under, as if it braced for the blow." She turns to Marjorie with a grin. "Officer Foot, he's alright. But I do hope he dies," she says. "I really want this paperweight."

2

A DIVERSION

Marjorie sits, tucked into the tall window seat of her bedroom, smoking and gazing out over the sprawling grounds of Glen Arden, the family estate. The imposing baronial mansion was the enchanted vision of her grandfather. It looms, protected by tall wrought-iron gates and shrouded at the end of a tree-lined drive bearing the family name.

A gray limestone manor with ivy-covered windows, the house has thirteen chimneys and a tiered roofline that stabs at the clouds. It boasts a dozen bedrooms across three levels, a grand staircase with a galleried landing, a ballroom, a formal dining room, a staff wing, and a large library with bookshelves that part to reveal an illegal liquor room. At the rear of the estate, a glass atrium—forever smudged and impossible to keep clean—casts a distorted view of the grounds beyond.

Marjorie first came to understand that the house was unique when Cecile's friend Delphine Dodge refused to spend the night, claiming the walls whisper.

"Who cares what Delphine thinks," said their father.

"But what on earth could she be referring to?" questioned her mother.

Marjorie's friends avoid Glen Arden. But her brother, Graham, often has a parade of chums lazing on the sun terrace or spilling onto the lower lawns to cocktail near the tennis courts and the small summerhouse.

Adjacent to the main driveway is a car park and garage hangar to house the family's collection of automobiles. Marjorie watches Atchison, the family's longtime butler, exchange words with a telegram courier on the loop of the gravel drive. Atchison was originally hired to serve their grandparents when they built Glen Arden. As the family expanded, so did his purview. His narrow build and silver hair radiate elegance, but his intensity kept the siblings from pulling childhood pranks on him as they did with the other servants. Atchison and Slorah, the head housekeeper, are not to be trifled with.

Marjorie's four-poster room is in its usual state of chaos, littered with silk stockings, sketches of bare silhouettes, and chocolate tins overflowing with jeweled buttons.

"You shouldn't smoke, Miss Marjorie," says Ina, one of the family housekeepers. "Your grandmother says smoking is dangerous for young girls."

"Granny's probably right," nods Marjorie. "She's right about most things."

"Like when she told you it would be a mistake to jump in the Detroit River," says Chet.

"Yes, but it was so invigorating," replies Marjorie. "Worth the rash. And sometimes we just need to take a leap, don't we? Smoking isn't a leap, but I do like the way it makes my voice sound. Deeper, more mature."

"Let me have a drag." Chet flops her hand off the edge of Marjorie's bed, reaching for the cigarette. Marjorie hops from the window seat and surrenders the Chesterfield to her sister.

Ina exits the room just as Graham enters, dressed in a black dinner jacket with satin lapels, a matching bow tie, and his signature eye patch—an unfortunate party favor from last year's celebration.

"This room. It's like a fairy tale met a brothel," he says.

"I imagine brothels have damp sheets," replies Chet.

"Depends on the brothel. Where have you two been?"

"At the police station," says Chet. "The Hardwicks called the cops on Marjie."

"What for?"

"A lack of imagination," replies Marjorie.

"Old Man Hardwick griped because the dress she made flashed her headlights," says Chet.

Graham flops down on the bed next to Chet. "Is that why Dad's in a rage?"

"He knows?" gasps Marjorie.

The voice of Duncan Lennox booms outside the door. Marjorie shoots a panicked look to her siblings. She slips behind her dressing screen as the door whips open.

"Where's your sister?" bellows their father.

"We were about to ask you," replies Chet. "We're waiting for her."

"What's wrong, old boy? Your face has that cardiac glow," says Graham.

"What's wrong? Your sister was seen in the back of a patrol car."

Chet sighs. "She probably just needed a ride."

"Well, mark my words. I'm going to give her one—straight out of this house. And the sooner the better. She's a liability!" He throws up his hands. "She told Henry Joy's wife that I'm in a feud with your grandfather."

"You are," shrugs Chet.

"That's private! Airing our dirty laundry's bad for business!"

"So wash your socks and speak with Granddad about a compromise," says Graham.

Duncan's face fires with anger. "I don't want a compromise. I want Marjorie to keep her damn mouth shut." He looks at Chet and Graham, splayed on the bed in their dinner finery. "Am I the only one in this family who actually works?"

"I work," objects Chet. Graham gives her a silencing elbow.

"Petting horses isn't work," scoffs their father.

"The investors at the polo club would disagree," says Graham.

"Dad," sighs Chet. "Shouldn't you get dressed for the birthday dinner?"

Their father stomps from the room and slams the door.

Marjorie reappears from behind the dressing screen, draped in a stunning sheath of ivory silk. "Graham, be a dear and button me up, would you?" She turns her back, exposing a long line of pearl buttons descending from her neck to her buttocks. "Dad's voice. Goodness, so stormy. His face was pink?"

"More like crimson," says Chet.

"Oh, dear. I'll drive separately and meet you at the club," says Marjorie. "I'm running late. Have you seen my suitcase?"

"I used it as an infirmary for the groundhog, remember?" replies Chet.

"Oh, that's right."

"Why do you need a suitcase?" asks Graham.

Marjorie applies a sweep of lipstick and breezily diverts. "Ooh, speaking of luggage, did you see that Hudson's now offers a Vuitton steamer trunk? It's very handsome."

"Yeah. I feel a kinship with Louis Vuitton," says Chet. "His mother died when he was ten. He disliked his stepmother, so he set out on foot and walked nearly three hundred miles to Paris."

"Poor chap. He should've designed a car, not a suitcase," says Graham.

Chet sits up. "Are you heading to the equestrian series? Is that why you need a suitcase?"

Marjorie doesn't reply. She's still unsettled by the anger she heard in her father's voice. Despite her efforts, he's always annoyed with her. Marjorie smiles softly. No matter, she has a plan. Yes, she'll need a suitcase. She'll also need a ride out of town.

And she'll need something else.

To slip away without her parents knowing.

3

DRY TONGUE

The Lennox family sits abreast at a long table of white linen. Six warped reflections wink back through crystal glasses. Waiters rush about the club, taming billowy curtains and securing doors to the veranda. Darkening skies and distant thunder creep closer, upstaging the waltz of a string quartet.

Marjorie loves storms. And when she was younger, she loved the collective birthday celebration at the club. But since her father waged war with their grandfather about building a new glass factory, the family façade has fractured. Cormac Lennox no longer appears in public beside their father, leaving a marked absence and a shift in decorum.

When their grandfather was at the table, no one dared interrupt. But with their boisterous father now at the helm, a stream of Detroit's automotive well-wishers sashays by. This time it's Myrtle Branley, self-appointed community sleuth and starchy cousin of the Fisher family. Chatelaine in widowhood, her timeworn dowager's ensemble has faded from black to charcoal from overpressing. Her wiry gray hair and sepia teeth speak more of October than June.

Marjorie leans, whispering to Graham, "Mrs. Branley's hair would make a wonderful nest for a family of crows. I must sketch it. It could be quite beautiful."

"Even more beautiful if they crap down her face."

Mrs. Branley stops at the head of the table. "Duncan. Lilah. Good evening. I'm happy to run into you. I'm enlisting neighbors for a citizen patrol. Would you like to volunteer?"

"I'm sorry, Myrtle. I don't think we'd have time. We're quite busy," says Lilah.

"We're all busy. But this rash of burglaries and jewel thefts must be stopped. I'm tired of sleeping in my pearls."

Marjorie smiles. "Ooh! Many ways to interpret that."

Graham calls down the length of the table, "Have you considered buying a revolver, Mrs. Branley?"

"I beg your pardon?"

"Pocket steel. Cold thunder," nods Chet. "To beat gangsters, it helps to become one."

Mrs. Branley lifts the spectacles from her bosom and surveys the siblings. "How old are you children now?"

"Let our father answer that," says Graham. "Go ahead, Dad. How old are we?"

The four children look to their father, who's well-oiled and glistening with sweat. He pauses, as if to reply, then laughs. He pistols his thick fingers as guns for no discernible reason, then promptly drains his gin rickey.

"Careful, cowboy. Would be a shame if you choked," says Graham.

"Indeed," replies their father, wiping a hand across his mouth. "Who would pay for Yale?"

Lilah smiles, her fake stepmother smile baring too many teeth, and stands quickly to reply. She waves a hand toward the children, as if unveiling the new Ford Runabout. "Cecile is twenty-five. You were at her wedding."

"Yes, of course. But where is the husband?" asks Mrs. Branley.

"Lou is . . . indisposed this evening." Lilah clears the annoyance from her throat and continues. "Charlotte—Chet—is twenty-four. Graham is twenty-one, and Marjorie is twenty."

"I remember Graham. He wrote a wonderful obituary for my late husband."

Chet stifles a laugh, spluttering champagne back into her glass. Graham kicks her under the table.

"And Marjorie, of course," says Mrs. Branley. "You were friends with Peter Howell. He had such a tidy reputation until it unraveled. I do wonder what he's up to now."

"Probably thirty to life," sneers Cecile, glaring at Marjorie.

"Poor Peter," says Chet.

Their father eyes Marjorie and shakes his head with disgust.

"Tell me—how are Cormac and Finola?" asks Mrs. Branley. "It's none of my business, of course, but I do agree with Cormac. Detroit has enough factories. We must economize. Make use of what we have instead of building more."

A tremble of thunder sounds beyond the French doors of the dining room. Wind mews, trapped by the shutters.

"Shots fired," whispers Graham, rubbing his palms together. "Here we go."

Lilah rests a silencing hand on her husband's shoulder. "Cormac and Finola are fine. Enjoying retirement."

Their father stabs into his prime rib, releasing a pool of blood onto the plate. He snaps his fingers for another gin rickey.

"Well, such a shame they're not here for the annual birthday celebration. How entirely unique that all of your children were born during the first week of June," says Mrs. Branley.

No one replies. Silence stretches until Lilah releases a fake laugh and begins to chatter about nothing.

A chorus of thunder rolls. Louder. Closer.

"Unique," murmurs Graham. "What a snide bluenose."

"Oh, but she loved your obituary," grins Chet. "Her husband—Harold, wasn't it?"

"Well done, Chet," nods Marjorie.

"You're such pigs," scoffs Cecile.

"*We're* pigs? Why can't people just steer clear of us?" whispers Graham. "They call us nouveau riche—and so many other things—behind our backs. And please, it's not *unique* that three of us were born in June. Our birth week is exactly nine months from our father's birthday, the only day he might possibly guilt a woman into his bed."

"Graham, stop!" hisses Cecile. "You're so crass. You're making us look bad." Their eldest sister grips her butter knife. "And you're aggravating my headache."

A crack of lightning sets the electricity flickering.

"Cecile," says Marjorie softly. "You might enjoy being on display here at the club, but it's difficult for some of us."

"Thank you, Marjorie," says Graham.

A year prior, at the annual birthday celebration, Graham lost an eye by way of one of their father's rocketing champagne corks. The incident was reported on the society page of *The Detroit News*. His black eye patch is an ever-present reminder.

"Quit whining. It was an accident," says Cecile.

Marjorie lifts her pale eyes toward her sister. Her voice is gentle. "But was it really, Cecile? An accident, I mean. He pointed the bottle at Graham's head."

Cecile thumps the base of her knife on the table. A reprimand to Marjorie for saying unspeakable things—something she is known for.

And at that moment, their conversation ceases. Lilah has pulled a dramatic breath, strategic in distraction. "Really?" She touches Mrs. Branley's arm, her voice escalating in volume. "Where did you hear that?"

"Why, here. They said Bonafante returned a few weeks ago. He was seen at the yacht club with the Algers."

"YES!" shouts Marjorie. So she hadn't imagined it. He was at the station.

Mrs. Branley looks to Marjorie. The family looks to Marjorie. The black-walnut chair dwarfs her wisplike frame. Candlelight flutters, dancing soft sparkles across her brown bob and Cleopatra bangs. Amidst the growing darkness, she appears almost pearlescent.

"Well, yes," she begins. "I heard Mr. Alger was at the yacht club and—"

"Thank you, Marjorie," interrupts her mother. She returns to Mrs. Branley. "And what are Mr. Bonafante's plans for the summer?"

"Well, no one knows, of course. Do we ever know what he's doing? Someone mentioned that he's reinvested in his arts program. Arts program—" Mrs. Branley clucks a dry tongue. "A residency program. For women only. Quite dubious, if you ask me."

"We didn't ask you," mutters Graham.

Thunder claps. Rain unleashes on the roof of the club, pounding like fists. The string quartet has abandoned their instruments in favor of bootleg gin from Windsor.

"So nice to see you, Mrs. Branley," calls Graham, waving from his end of the table. Mrs. Branley takes the hint, gives a pinched smile, and walks away. Graham grips his throat, gagging. "I can't stand her. She's such a gossip."

"Her nostrils are different sizes," says Chet.

"I think she might be lonely," says Marjorie.

"My head," says Cecile.

"She's a gasbag," says their father through a mouthful of meat. "But you can't blame her for doubting the motives of a guy like Bonafante."

"Why?" asks Marjorie. "Have you ever spent time with him?"

"No. But a daydream and doodle program for young ladies? Kittens should chase husbands, not asinine escapades in the arts."

"Calling women 'kittens'—now, that's asinine," says Chet.

"Won't you stop yammering?" shrieks Cecile, now brandishing her steak knife. "I have a goddamn headache!"

"You always have some kind of ache," says Chet. "Probably guilt. Too many secrets."

"Or maybe she's being eaten by cancer," says Graham.

"Could be," nods Chet in agreement.

"You're horrid!" says Cecile. She stands and storms off.

Their father slaps down his fork. "Dammit, Graham. Leave her alone. She doesn't feel well." He stands and goes after Cecile.

"Please!" says Lilah. "Can't we enjoy one dinner like a normal family?"

"But we're not a normal family," says Chet.

Lilah sighs, tosses her napkin on the table, and stands. "I'll be at the bar." She pauses, then says, "Marjorie, the dress you made for this evening is beautiful, dear. Ivory silk brings out the warmth of your hair. But the plunging neckline, it's not quite respectable." Lilah walks off.

Marjorie looks to her plate.

"Your neckline is fine," says Chet. "Lucky she missed the mushroom caps. You have real talent, Marjie."

"Thank you, Chet. I do feel strongly about fashion design and women in the arts." Marjorie smiles. "And one of you must too. That would explain how the information on Mr. Bonafante's program appeared in my room."

Heads turn. Brows arrow. "What?" says Chet.

The siblings stare at Marjorie. The light telescopes amidst the thunder. She feels she's on the stage. Marjorie stands, sets her chin, and adopts a clear, performance voice.

"Four weeks this summer. An immersive residency with structure and discipline to pursue artistic passions."

"Artistic passions? Sounds inappropriate." Graham grins. "Scandalous."

"Perhaps," says Marjorie, raising her flute of champagne, her eyes strangely alight. "Wish me well, won't you? I've applied and been accepted. I leave tomorrow."

Dear Coco,

The birds, they flutter so strangely.
Hovering.
Whispering.
Perhaps weather.
Best to prepare.

4

POOR PETER

Marjorie reclines in the slender niche of her bedroom window. The sky is now a pure, crisp blue, nature's peace offering after the holy wrath of the prior night's storm. The snip-snip of clippers floats through the yard as gardeners tame tumbles of colorful peonies vying to escape their neatly edged beds. Marjorie hates the clippers. Flowers should be crawling and wild. She looks to Chet, who is sitting on the bed, smoking, and scribbling on a writing tablet.

"Is Dad still sick?"

Chet shrugs.

Ina, their housekeeper, dusts Marjorie's prized glass rabbit, which is dressed in a tutu of shredded telegrams. "Your father will be fine. Just a bit of bottle flu."

"Exactly," says Chet.

Marjorie hops from the window, sits at her vanity, and stares into the mirror. "If I moved to New York or Paris, would you miss me, Chet?"

"I don't know."

"Well, that's not a nice thing to say," says Ina.

"I disagree," says Marjorie. "It's nice to speak the truth. And Chet always speaks the truth to me."

"Almost always," says Chet, exhaling a scarf of smoke toward the ceiling. "By contrast, you speak the truth to everyone. It's problematic."

"Oh, don't criticize me, Chet. Life is short, but the sting of unkindness is long. If anyone should know that, it's you. Who are you memorializing in that flutter of papers?"

Chet pulls a lungful of smoke, pauses, then gestures with the cigarette while exhaling. "Mr. Theodore Kolansky. Cardiac arrest. Aged seventy-five when he was promoted to the upper chambers. He was a wig salesman."

"Wigs," says Marjorie, twisting her bangs. "I wish they were popular. You can create an entirely new persona with a wig. Have you ever thought of that?"

Although she pays no attention to her own feral hair and freckled face, it's likely that Chet *has* thought of that. She's thought of everything. Chet writes obituaries for *The Detroit Times,* the city's splashy newspaper, an assignment that originally belonged to their brother, Graham. In an attempt to become financially independent from their father, Graham briefly had the notion of making a quick buck penning a salacious novel before heading off to Yale. He felt a summer job in the obituary department would provide fodder for stories. So despite the family's abhorrence of journalists, their grandfather pulled strings to get him a part-time job at the paper. Graham quickly lost interest, but Chet became invested and scolded him.

"This is someone's life!" she'd wailed, clutching the deceased's paperwork. "They've endured a journey and must be memorialized."

"If you're so passionate about this sorry sap, then you write it," said Graham.

And she did.

And the editor loved it.

And she wrote more.

And more.

And she gave them to Graham and he presented them to the newspaper as if they were his own. Which suited them both, because it would be highly improper for a young woman from a wealthy automotive family in Detroit to be a journalist. So Chet wrote the obituaries, Graham split the money with her, and the editor bought the ruse that Chet was delivering work that Graham had dictated through a costly wire from Yale—including the glowing obituary of one Mr. Harold Branley, deceased husband of the perennial mourner, Myrtle Branley, who crashed their birthday at the club.

And the most shocking aspect? Their distracted parents believed the ruse too. They criticized Graham for his supposed interest in writing but labeled Chet their "most compassionate child" because she attended so many funerals.

A knock sounds and Graham appears. He shuts the door and notices the housekeeper. "Oh, hello, Ina. Might I ask you and your duster to disappear?"

"My pleasure. I have eight more bedrooms to clean."

"Take your time, old gal. I don't give a whip about the cleaning. You work too hard as it is. But I need to discuss something unsavory with my sisters. I'd hate for you to be implicated in our plotting and get sacked. Best for you to remain unaware." Graham swipes the cigarette from Chet and assumes Marjorie's spot on the window seat, waiting for Ina to leave. He sits in profile in the window. His deeply tanned face, mussed brown hair, linen trousers, and monogrammed mint socks make a handsome portrait. And he knows it.

The heavy oak door closes with an audible click.

Marjorie jumps from her vanity and pulls the suitcase from beneath her bed. "Are they gone?"

"Yes," replies Graham. "Dad's downtown, and your mother just drove off for tennis."

"Tennis? Please," sneers Chet.

"I know." Graham points to his eye patch. "I'm rolling my eye." He pulls a deep drag on the last of the cigarette and flicks it out the window.

"You shouldn't do that," says Marjorie. "You could start a fire."

"If we're lucky. You ready to go?"

"Yes." Marjorie pulls on white summer gloves and places a lavender felt hat on her head. She tucks her short hair behind her ears. "Graham, you're such a dear for offering to take me. Chet, you won't tell anyone about the residency, will you? Please, be a good sister."

Chet stares absently at the ceiling. "Will you be a good sister?"

"Of course I will."

"I imagine good sisters are understanding. Forgiving."

"Yes, that's my definition of a good sister too," says Marjorie. "Like when I told you that sometimes a silk dress needs a good nipple. You didn't tease me, you understood me."

Graham shakes his head. "Don't say such things aloud, Marjie."

"But I'm talking about fashion. Fashion is art. It's not unsavory, Graham. Chet understands me. And good sisters confide in each other. Speaking of confiding, just tell my mother I'm at the cottage."

"Alright," he nods. "So, this residency program is Bonafante's? You really think you'll meet him? I've never met him. Gramps is the only one who has."

Marjorie lifts the suitcase but keeps her head down. Just the mention of Bonafante brings a flush to her cheeks.

"Our sister," announces Chet, raising a finger. "Cecile is not a good sister."

"Cecile is a complicated sister," says Marjorie.

"How can you be sympathetic after the incident last summer?" replies Chet. "Poor Peter. She double-crossed you both."

The previous summer, Marjorie had dated Peter Howell, an expressive young artist working in advertising. Just as the Lennox name symbolized a fortune in glass, the Howell family had built a fortune in steel. They had also built a reputation of respect. A match in family fortunes, Marjorie and Peter were also a match in creativity. Peter's outlandish wardrobe often rivaled Marjorie's creations. He loved jewelry and made his own designs using glittering chips swept from the floor of the Lennox glass factory.

Their father had detested Peter's flamboyance and scorned his family's success. So Cecile took great pleasure in ratting to their father that Marjorie's beau had been questioned in conjunction with a jewel heist at the Detroit Institute of Arts—a heist that involved dozens of unique and valuable gems. Peter's potential affiliation with a crime was bad enough, but the newspaper reports had gone further, including mention that his sweetheart was a girl from Grosse Pointe.

Their father exploded over the media mention, insisting that Marjorie's connection to Peter had stained his reputation. Graham and Chet argued that you can't stain something that's already dirty. Cecile insisted that Marjorie aided and abetted. The whole episode confused and upset Marjorie. Peter hadn't been arrested, just questioned. But she was forbidden from further contact with him. Although her mother had defended her, her father didn't budge. The family quarrel escalated and is now referenced simply as "the incident," with occasional refrains of "poor Peter."

"Peter was a friend more than a boyfriend. I still don't understand what happened, but I don't hold a grudge against Cecile," sighs Marjorie. "She suffers. She's Father's favorite, but she's imprisoned by pain. I feel so fortunate to be free of those burdens." Marjorie releases her suitcase, twirls a hand to the sky, and begins reciting. "I'm free but not empty. I'm innocent yet brave. I'm curious and romantic. Show me yourself so I might see . . . myself!" She pauses, then breaks into a delighted smile. "Ooh, that was a good one."

Chet turns and looks searchingly to Graham.

Graham sighs, running a hand through his hair. "Alright, brave sister. Let's go."

5

SOURING CITY

Graham maneuvers the hunter-green Nash Touring down Woodward Avenue.

"A residency, for women only. And run by a man. Still don't know what to make of that. Do you have any cash in case you need something?" asks Graham.

"A bit," says Marjorie. She thinks of the money she pinched from the play fund. Her mother keeps cash in a secret compartment in her vanity. Lilah refers to it as her "play fund" but has no idea that Marjorie discovered its hiding place when she was a child and that over the years she's pilfered from it. She and Peter once lifted a few bills to finance an impromptu trip to Chicago to see a Ziegfeld production at the Illinois Theatre. Her mother never noticed. But when Marjorie visited the drawer this time, there was more than money. Tucked beneath the play fund was a sheet of paper—a love note from her mother's "tennis" partner, addressing her as *my darling angel.* It was too upsetting to read.

She changes the subject. "I feel terrible not telling Granny or Gramps about the residency."

"You'd have to answer a million questions. And Gramps knows everyone in Detroit," says Graham. "He's probably familiar with the exact building you're going to. And unlike our father, he would care about your safety."

"True. But, Graham," says Marjorie softly. "Why is it that our father doesn't care?"

Graham laughs. "Why doesn't he care? He's distracted, obsessed with the new auto game. He's ruthless, competitive, and greedy, not to mention shallow. Our family business is windshields, Marjorie. Glass. An entire fortune built on sand. There's a deep irony there."

Marjorie doesn't see the irony. She sees her grandfather's hard work. His journey from Scotland to Detroit, his many years of working sixteen hours a day, camped out in the evenings at the Pontchartrain Hotel to haggle with Louis Chevrolet and Henry Leland of Cadillac. She sees Gramps's passion. His quiet creation of a dynasty and his patience in building their estate in Grosse Pointe. Their father enjoys the spoils of Gramps's hard work. But in lobbying for a new factory, he's been quick to criticize and push for change.

And things have changed. Several years ago, the Pontchartrain was leveled. Now the Statler and the Detroit Athletic Club are the preferred spots for the new, postwar automotive men—men like her father who are determined to transform Detroit from "the Paris of the Midwest" to "the Motor City."

"Do you know who's courting our father?" asks Graham.

Marjorie shakes her head.

"Death. Mortality. His appetite, for all things, is beyond gluttony. He makes Henry the Eighth look like an amateur. Have you seen the sores?"

"Goodness, no. Does he have syphilis? Chet has a list of famous people who died of syphilis."

"I don't know if it's cock rot, but convincing himself he's still young and virile just might kill him. He tried to keep up with our brother-in-law last week and ended up so blotto that he defecated in bed."

"Oh, dear. So that's why Slorah was burning the sheets."

"As much as he infuriates me, I'm concerned. We've seen how these auto men can go down in their early fifties."

Marjorie reflects on her brother's words. The tragic, threaded deaths of brothers John and Horace Dodge had shaken middle-aged men like their father. If death ever came knocking, it was assumed that the rowdy, indestructible Dodge brothers would beat it back in a brawl of honor. They were giants, men of endurance who slept on shop benches rather than waste time going home. Rumors swarmed that they died from drinking Prohibition liquor, poisoned by federal authorities. Dying of influenza while caring for each other on a sickbed was a fate altogether too human.

The day before Horace Dodge died, Slorah, their head housekeeper, reported hearing screams of the bean-nighe, the Scottish omen of death, coming through the walls of Glen Arden.

"The screams, though. They weren't for a person," whispered Slorah. "Not just Horace Dodge, ye ken. They were for the city. An omen for the whole of Detroit."

Construction on the Dodge estate—planned as the most magnificent home ever to grace Detroit—was abandoned. John Dodge had brought more than ninety stonecutters from Scotland to create his ancestral manor. The 110-room mansion with underground tunnels sits unfinished, a haunted crust of a dream, now home for nesting ravens and whistling winds.

The city is souring. Prohibition has brought the rise of crime and illegal business. "Detroit the Dynamic" and "Detroit the Wonder City" is under transformation. Since the guns fell silent and the Great War ended, it's been nothing but change. If the Dodge brothers died in their fifties, others might too. Good men, older men like her grandfather, are now stepping aside to let the younger, hungry generation—like her father—step up. But Marjorie grasps the truth:

Younger and newer isn't necessarily better. Sometimes it's dangerous.

And truly successful men—they're known but not often seen.

Like Charles Bonafante.

Bonafante owns his own Grosse Pointe mansion, behind tall gates on Windmill Pointe. The auto barons bow to him, the women adore him, the children idolize him. They whisper that his aura is so striking that when he passes, people step back without realizing it. His prolonged absences create speculation, and a rare Bonafante visit to his estate on the Pointe sets the community into a frenzy. But why? The six-foot-two bachelor with leading-man looks has never hosted an event or invited others into his home. He receives stacks of invitations but never attends. His only companions are his elderly valet and his dog, a Doberman reportedly named Daisy. His glistening yacht is moored not at the yacht club with those of the elite families but waterfront at his own estate. And when he sails, it's with crew only. He sails alone.

He is watched. He is whispered about.

Marjorie wouldn't normally bother with such chatter.

But she met him once.

She met him for herself.

It was several years ago. The last night of the Pontchartrain Hotel before its demolition. She was the only family member to accept Gramps's invitation and joined the old gang of automotive power brokers, emerging rumrunners, and dignified gangsters who decided to hold one last private banquet in the grand ballroom that once saw seven U.S. presidents and royalty of the arts and sciences. Unlike Marjorie's parents, Gramps never drank alcohol. He was pensive and sober when he joined the other men in deciding that a bonfire was the only logical and befitting end to the Pontch. Marjorie remembers the waiters, the hat-check girl, and the entire staff agreeing. Chairs, tables, and other contents were piled into the center of the ballroom. Toasts and prayers were raised. The band began to play.

And the pile was lit on fire.

Song after song, the large crowd danced around the fire. Some laughing, others crying. Marjorie twirled and danced, leaning dangerously toward the blaze to light her Chesterfield. More items were piled on. The flames rose and spread.

And that's when he appeared.

Charles Bonafante stepped through the smoke toward Marjorie and set a hand on her shoulder. "Not so close," he said, quelling a cinder on her dress and steering her a step from the flames. They stood next to each other, silently sharing the cigarette and taking in the music, the dancing, and the fire, until across the smoldering ash they spotted Gramps. And once she was guided safely back to her grandfather, Bonafante nodded and walked away. But then he stopped and turned—to look back at Marjorie. He smiled. She returned the smile.

And then he disappeared.

And she's relived the moment in her mind countless times.

Marjorie told no one of the encounter. There was nothing to tell, really. Yes, he was handsome. Yes, he was quiet. But for all the things that people whispered of Bonafante, she had never heard what she herself had experienced.

He was kind.

6

THE NIGHTINGALE

Graham turns down a narrow, tree-lined street and parks in front of a building.

Three-story. Gray stone. An ornate black door framed by two flickering gas lamps.

"What lovely ironwork around the windows," says Marjorie.

"Nice. And smart. Bonafante's no dummy. This is Detroit City, not Grosse Pointe. He's housing female artists for a retreat. Can't have them being burgled, now, can he?"

"Burgled?" says Marjorie, intrigued. "Do you think there might be burglars?"

"Wise up, Marjie. This is the city." Graham opens the trunk of the Nash and pulls out her suitcase. "You packed light."

"The instructions were very specific. Anything I might need will be provided here. I'm only to bring a few outfits and my personal sundries. I imagine I'll sew new designs and wear whatever I create. It's so exciting."

Marjorie and Graham stand on the sidewalk, looking at the building.

Marjorie clutches her armload of books and fashion magazines and sighs. "Hello, Nightingale!"

"Is that what it's called?"

"Yes," replies Marjorie. "See the word etched within the stone? Such a lovely old building. I think it's beautiful."

Graham shakes his head. "You think everything is beautiful." He walks to the front door and examines the posted roster of residents. He presses a buzzer. A curtain flutters on the front window. A pale hand appears on the glass, then disappears.

Graham shifts on the stoop. "If at any time you feel uncomfortable or homesick, you can leave. I can be here within the hour. Or Chet will come."

"That's so kind of you, Graham. But this is an exploration. And often, explorations are uncomfortable. That's the point of growth. I just worry about the wrath of our parents."

"You leave them to me."

The door opens and a stout balding man smiles widely. He wears a plaid bow tie, crisp khaki trousers, and holds a clipboard.

"Miss Marjorie Lennox, I presume. Welcome."

Graham takes a step forward, and the man quickly raises a protesting hand. "It's Miss Lennox who has been granted the residency."

"Oh, no arguments there. But see here, old pal. I've dodged my parents and grandparents on this adventure. And if you think I'm going to leave my baby sister on some random doorstep like a foundling, you've got another think coming. I'll see her into her lodgings or I'll take her home right now."

"Graham, no!"

"No, indeed, Marjie. I'm at least inspecting your . . . room . . . or whatever this is."

The balding man blinks quickly. "One moment, please." He shuts the door.

"Graham," breathes Marjorie. "I understand this might seem strange to you. You're fiscally minded, not artistically minded. But an insular community, a bohemian atelier—this is the way of the arts."

"Fine, be insulated. But I'm not leaving you here without seeing where and how you'll be living." Graham stands tall, gripping his sister's suitcase.

"Well, that's very fine of you, Graham. I won't forget this. I'm sure all will be well."

The door whips open and the man reappears. "Alright. You may bring your sister into her apartment, but then you must leave, as you weren't granted an artist's residency."

"Trust me," says Graham. "I'll be doing a turn and burn." He pushes into the building.

The man shuts the door behind them.

"This front door is to remain closed and locked at all times. Is that understood, Miss Marjorie Lennox?" Marjorie nods. They stand in a long strip of hardwood hallway, punctuated by four doors of different colors. Blue. Green. Red. Gray.

"You'll be first on the left. The green door. I'm Dockery, by the way. Everyone calls me Dock."

"Hello, Dock. I'm Marjorie. I apologize for my brother's behavior. My family's a bit overprotective."

"No trouble. No trouble at all," says Dock. He opens the green door and steps aside for Marjorie and Graham to enter.

It's a compact apartment, with a small sitting area, a bedroom, bathroom, a desk, and a kitchenette. But the furnishings, decorations, and drapes are not bohemian. They're overly traditional, if not old. Marjorie passes her books and magazines to Graham. She runs her hand across peeling wallpaper, a scuffed rocking chair draped with a pink crocheted afghan, and an enamel-top dinette with wooden legs. She stops in front of bookshelves housing sun-faded volumes and small paintings depicting what appear to be religious scenes.

"Looks like you'll be living at the bottom of Granny's purse," laughs Graham.

"Yes, I thought it might be . . . more modern," whispers Marjorie.

"You're a fashion designer," says Dock, looking at his clipboard. "I believe they'll be swapping out the desk for a sewing machine and a cutting table."

"They?" asks Marjorie.

"The boss," replies Dock.

"And who is the boss?" asks Graham.

Dock falls silent.

Marjorie elbows Graham. "The boss," she whispers.

"Why are we whispering? For God's sake, just tell me who's in charge here."

"Bonafante," says Marjorie.

Dock nods.

"Wait. You're telling me that Bonafante himself will oversee the refitting of my sister's apartment for her costume-design work?"

"Well, things are delegated to me," says Dock. "Bonafante funds the program, but I run it." Marjorie's shoulders sink with disappointment.

Graham eyes Dock with suspicion. "Oh, yeah? And which room are you in?"

"My apartment is in the basement. If your sister needs me, she can call down the stairs at the end of the hall. The only thing that might take some getting used to is the city noise." Dock motions to the windows. "It's an old building and we've no air-cooling, of course, so at times it's necessary to keep the windows open to the night air."

Marjorie smiles. "My sisters tell me that I snore something awful. The alley cats might lodge a complaint. So no need to worry about me."

Dock laughs. "Well, aren't you delightful, Miss Marjorie Lennox!"

"Yes, she is delightful," says Graham. "And that's why we cherish her so. Don't you forget that." He gives Dock a glare and then turns to his sister. "Well, Marjie, I'll be heading out, then."

Graham makes his way to the apartment door and opens it. Standing across the hall in front of the blue door is a woman wearing a bright red scarf with lips to match. She's taping a piece of paper to her door. Her platinum hair and bodacious curves bring French cabaret designs to Marjorie's mind. Something deliciously risqué.

"Well, hello there," says Graham.

Marjorie pushes by her brother.

"Hello, I'm Marjorie."

"Hi there, Marjorie honey. I'm Ivy." Her words slide slowly, in a boozy crawl. "So nice to meet you. Is this your husband?"

"Goodness no, this is my brother, Graham."

Ivy gazes at Graham, looking him up and down, pausing on the eye patch.

"Hello, Graham. I'm so sorry that something has happened to your eye. Hope you don't have to endure too many pirate jokes."

Graham laughs. "Thanks for mentioning it. I wish people would just acknowledge the patch, but it seems to make most folks uncomfortable."

Ivy raises her thumbs and forefingers, placing Graham's face in a frame. "I think it's dashing."

"Okay, time to go," says Dock, flapping his hands at Graham.

Graham winks at Ivy. "Your warden here is strict." He pauses, looking at the sign on her door. "One hundred and eighty-three. What's that?"

Ivy smiles, tongue caressing her square teeth. "Why, the days until Christmas, of course."

"Mr. Lennox, I must insist that you take your leave. You were not—"

"Granted an artist's residency," they all finish in unison.

"Yeah, yeah. I'm off. See ya, Marjie. Have a swell time." Graham exits the front door of the building and pauses on the stoop. "Remember, if you get homesick, just drop a line and I'll come get you."

"No, no. I'm afraid that won't be possible," says Dock. "This is an immersive residency. Early departures are not allowed. Goodbye."

Dock shuts the door in Graham's face.

He locks it.

7

FINE PRINT

Ivy smiles. "Your brother sure seems nice. Does he enjoy Christmas?"

"Christmas? I think so," replies Marjorie.

"Miss Lennox," says Dock. "If we could proceed into your apartment. I need to go over a few important details and procure your signature on some forms."

Ivy leans against her door. "Give a knock after you've pledged your creativity and we'll get to know each other, Marjie."

"That sounds wonderful."

Marjorie follows Dock back into her apartment. He gestures for her to have a seat in the rocking chair. It's the only chair in the small sitting area, so she obliges. When was the last time she sat in a rocking chair? Marjorie can't remember. The chair feels too large and the worn wood feels oddly cold. And she is not inclined to rock. Not inclined at all.

"Might I request a different chair?" she asks.

"No, you may not. But we're so happy to have you with us, Miss Marjorie Lennox. Congratulations on being granted this residency. Only the most talented are chosen, so you must be quite extraordinary."

"Are you responsible for choosing the candidates?" she asks.

"Well, no." Dock pauses. "Selection is . . . by committee."

"Am I to meet the committee?"

"No," says Dock. "The purpose of your stay here is not to socialize but to have uninterrupted time to explore your artistic ideas." He consults his clipboard. "You will be provided with a worktable and a sewing machine. Fabrics and notions of your choice will be refreshed weekly. Do you sketch, Miss Marjorie Lennox, or do you create from visual impressions?"

Marjorie pauses. "I create . . . from emotional impressions. From feelings. It's a multisensory approach, really. For example, a certain emotion or intuition presents itself in a color and type of fabric. That's what I get first. And then I sketch a—"

"Do you need papers or an easel?" interrupts Dock.

"A large sketch pad, please."

"Scissors?"

"I've brought mine. I'm partial to my own scissors."

"I see." Dock scribbles onto his clipboard. "And are you able to render your creative visions yourself or will you require a seamstress to assist?"

"Oh, I construct and assemble on my own. But I've always longed to work with someone who excels at embroidery and beading."

"We can arrange that," says Dock.

They'll provide a needlewoman to assist?

"How lovely," says Marjorie. "Also, a dress form would be helpful. In France they're using something called 'mannequins' now. Lifelike models made from wax."

"You'd like a lifelike human made of wax? I will consult the boss."

Fabrics and notions refreshed at whim? Assistance with finish details and possibly a mannequin? Marjorie looks about the aged décor. "Dock, please understand that I always speak plainly. Here's what I see. I need light. Absent large windows, I need several lamps. Odeon glass would suit. A chaise, as I often recline while sketching. Potted ferns for oxygenation. A few gilt frames for my paper-doll designs. And perhaps a large rug of rabbit fur. Warmer on bare feet."

Dock makes a final note and lowers his clipboard. "Unlikely, but I'll do my best."

"Thank you," says Marjorie. "That's very generous of you. Very generous of Mr. Bonafante," she says. "Rather than bother you, I'd be happy to ask him myself."

"It's no bother at all. I've made note of your preferences. And now all that is left is for you to sign the lease."

"The lease?"

"Yes, that's what we call it. Staying in this apartment—it's a lease, if you will. And it's important that we respect the premises. I'll just run down the quick rules of the lease."

"Retention isn't my strong suit. Perhaps you can discuss the details with my brother?"

"No. Your brother wasn't granted a residency." Dock clears his throat. "As this document outlines, Miss Marjorie Lennox, while here you will abide by the following rules of the lease:

"You will not remove or modify any of the contents of the apartment. Everything must remain as it appears now, on your move-in date. The arrangement has been noted and there will be inspections weekly.

"You will make sure, *at all times,* that the front door of the building and your own door are locked and bolted."

Dock looks at her. "I repeat: locked, *at all times*. Morning, afternoon, and night.

"You are free to socialize with the other three women who have been granted residencies, but you will remain on this first floor at all times.

"You are not permitted to ascend or descend the staircase.

"You will not speak of your residency to anyone outside the building. Ever.

"You will not open your door to anyone but myself and the other three residents.

"You will be assigned a job—"

"A job?" says Marjorie.

"You will be expected to contribute," says Dock. "We must all pitch in."

"Yes, I've read that's how an artistic commune works."

Dock nods slowly, then returns to his clipboard.

"Smoking is permitted, of course, but there shall be no smoking or candlelight in bed."

Dock's eyes pull from the clipboard to Marjorie. "The goal of the residency is to ascertain what might be inspired and created while in the same space for an extended period. If you must take a walk or leave the premises briefly, the limit is thirty minutes and the curfew is nine P.M. All doors will be bolted from the inside promptly at nine and will not be reopened. Is that understood? I don't mean to frighten you, but Detroit has one of the highest murder rates in the country. We're responsible for your safety while you're here, and we take that seriously."

"My family would appreciate that."

"Now, let's talk about meals. Staple groceries will be delivered each week for you to keep on hand. But we understand that every artist has their own meal preferences. Tell me about yours."

Marjorie efforts to keep up. "In the morning, Ina or one of our housekeepers pulls the drapes, then brings me coffee and sweet rolls in bed." Marjorie stops. "Oh . . . now that I say that aloud, I realize how terribly spoiled I must sound. I'm sorry."

"We're not judging, just trying to gather information to best keep you fed."

"Well," says Marjorie, "I'm afraid that culinary arts aren't a talent of mine. But perhaps one of the other residents is talented in the kitchen and we can trade services?"

"I'm afraid not," says Dock. "You are a fashion designer, and we have a painter, a playwright, and a modern-furniture architect."

"Oh, how interesting!"

"Might I suggest that you request a hamper to be left on your doorstep—one in the morning that contains breakfast and lunch, and then a separate hamper for dinner."

"And mealtimes?"

"You determine your own mealtimes," says Dock. "Would you like the hampers?"

"Do we dress for dinner?"

"That's up to you." Dock points to the chipped enamel table. "You will be dining at that table, here in your apartment. Would you like the hampers?"

"There is no dining room in the building? Or perhaps I can pop down to the Statler for a meal?"

"No, my dear. As I said, the goal of the residency is to ascertain what might be inspired and created while in the same space for an extended period. The hope is that you will be so engaged in your work that you will not notice the time. Again, if you must take a walk or step out for air, the limit is thirty minutes. Our curfew is nine P.M. Doors will be bolted from the inside promptly at nine P.M. Is that understood?"

"Yes," says Marjorie. "You mentioned that."

"Would you like the hampers?"

"Alright. I'll opt for the hampers, I guess."

"There are two entry doors on this floor—the front door you came through and a back door at the end of the hall. Both must be locked at all times. Your job will be to pick up five newspapers outside the front door each morning and distribute them to each of the residents. No later than seven-thirty A.M. You will leave mine at the top of the basement stairs. Well, I believe we've covered everything. I'll just need your signature in the two places indicated on this paperwork."

Dock hands across a few sheets of paper. Marjorie looks at him, hesitant.

"The lease," says Dock. "You must sign the lease. And I do ask that you read the fine print as well."

Marjorie nods slowly. It all feels quite official. Would Graham object to her signing something? Her parents would object, of course. They don't find fashion design respectable. Her father would be enraged at the idea of her conducting any sort of official transaction.

Marjorie's pulse begins to tick. She knows how they whisper about her, as if she's some fragile sugar butterfly. But this will provide the structure and discipline that her father claims she needs. And she's entirely capable of making decisions on her own. Did Anna Dodge consult with someone when she gave away Catherine the Great's million-dollar pearls? Certainly not. Women of automotive families are perfectly able to think for themselves. And the same with the arts. The Folies Bergère didn't ask permission to put their dancers in nude body stockings. Paul Poiret didn't hesitate to design dresses without corsets. They were free to make their own decisions, and freedom is likely a central tenet to the artist residency and to this lease. And then the thought occurs to her.

"Dock, does our program sponsor know about this document?" she asks.

"Why, yes," he says with a nod. "Bonafante was involved in creating the lease."

Marjorie smiles, signs the papers with a flourish, and hands them back to Dock. He gives her a ring with two keys. He exits the apartment and then she realizes.

The fine print he mentioned. She didn't read it.

Dear Coco,

I heard you laughing.
What has filled you with delight?
Your laughter brought me such joy
That I almost laughed myself.

TICK TOCK

Within seconds there's a knock. Marjorie turns the knob and peers out.

"You didn't lock your door," says Dock, clutching the clipboard dejectedly to his chest. "You signed the lease, which stipulates that you agree to keep your door locked at all times. And you opened the door without asking who might be knocking." He shakes his head.

"Oh, goodness. I'm sorry." Marjorie blinks, flustered. "Let's try that again."

"It's the gold key," says Dock.

Marjorie closes the door and locks it. In addition to the gold key, there's a silver key on the ring. "And this silver key?" she asks loudly.

Dock's muffled voice sounds from the hallway. "Have a lovely afternoon, Miss Marjorie Lennox!"

Marjorie turns slowly, resting her back against the door. A wooden wall clock volleys a steady yet dismal rhythm.

Tick tock. Tick tock.

She's here.

Tick tock. Tick tock.

She's really here. She's been selected to take part in an artistic residency, a residency created by Mr. Bonafante himself. She'll be given fabric and whatever else she might need to create her designs. And she has complete independence. How shameful that she's never locked a door or been responsible for meals. Her family has always relied on Atchison or Slorah for such things. Her family has fortune and freedom, but they are not independent.

Marjorie takes in the apartment. The lease stated that she will not remove or modify the contents. But it didn't say anything about adding contents. The parochial space begs for light. And ambience. She walks through the living area. Could she use the rocking chair as a fabric holder? Surely that wouldn't be considered modifying something. She has to have somewhere to put the fabrics.

The kitchenette is miniature, like something from a dollhouse. She inspects the hot plate, cupboards, and drawers. Two plates, two glasses, one fork, two spoons, and four knives. A teakettle. Various kitchen sundries. She'll sew some colorful napkins and placemats to brighten up the table. Such a shame that she can't change the curtains. They're quilted and a horrid shade of moss.

Marjorie pauses at the bedroom door. The little windowless room is what she imagines a convent to look like. Spartan, with just a narrow bed, small dresser, and nightstand. No closet or wardrobe. Although the mattress is cracker thin, the bed frame is interesting. White metal with large globe finials at each of the four ends. She'll design a coverlet for the bed that will transform the room. But how will she play off the terrible acorn wallpaper?

The bathroom is equally stark. It's very clean, and rare to have an en suite in a unit such as this, but the weak light makes the bathtub and sink look dreary. The mirror's surface is fogged with age and scratches. She steps toward it and removes her lavender hat. The scars on the glass—are they scratches? She runs her index finger along the marks on the edge of the mirror, following their path. A series of peaks and circles.

She squints, focusing on the mirror. Is that why they created the lease? A prior resident defaced some of the items in the apartment? As she looks at the scratches, a pattern emerges, resembling the repetition of a word. One repeating word: *No.No.No.No.No.*

9

A DEADLINE

Graham pulls down the long gravel drive. Freddie, the family's auto steward, appears from the garage.

"How'd she run today, Mr. Lennox?"

"Freddie, how many times must I ask? Call me Graham. Please. Mr. Lennox is my grandfather. I work hard to be irresponsible. Too irresponsible to be a mister to anyone."

Graham knows the truth. His grandfather deserves the respectful form of address but would never require it. His grandfather goes by his first name, Cormac. Their father, by contrast, rarely uses Duncan, his first name. He refers to himself as "Lennox." A servant or employee referring to their father as anything other than "Mr. Lennox" or "Sir" would be grounds for immediate dismissal.

"She ran well," says Graham. "The new tires are quieter. But if my father leaves the Cadillac this evening, I'll take that instead of the Nash."

"Certainly. And by the way, did you leave a case in the trunk of the Packard? I think you were the last to drive it."

"What kind of case?"

Freddie shrugs. "Looks like a suitcase."

Graham follows Freddie into the garage, weaving through the rows of gleaming motorcars in candy-apple red, shiny black, and deep-indigo blue. They arrive at the Packard. Freddie opens the trunk, and sitting squarely in the back compartment is a brown leather suitcase. Graham's never seen it.

"Thank you, Freddie," he says with a smile, politely dismissing the mechanic. Once Freddie steps away, Graham pops the latches on the suitcase.

And he's confused.

It's full of old shoes. Baby's shoes. Infant-sized and so small that a pair could fit in the palm of his hand. Lambskin Mary Janes, high button boots, knitted booties with pearl buttons. There are countless pairs and a variety of styles. But he doesn't recognize them as belonging to his family. Is Cecile pregnant? Even if she is, why would she need twenty pairs of old shoes? He shuts the case and closes the trunk.

"I'll leave that for now," he calls through the garage to Freddie.

Graham crunches across the gravel drive to the wide stone steps of Glen Arden. The familiar static crawls across his arms. Most of his friends admire the sweeping mansion. Marjorie adores it. But Graham detests its eerie elegance and cold stone walls, tucked far from the road like some ghostly charm school. Atchison opens the almond-shaped doors before he reaches the top step.

"Good afternoon."

"Hiya, Atch."

"Just a reminder that Mr. and Mrs. Fletcher will be joining for dinner this evening."

"Oh, I forgot. Say, Atch, doesn't it feel odd to call Cecile 'Mrs. Fletcher'? I'm still not used to it."

Atchison shakes his head. "It is not odd. She is married now. She is a Fletcher."

Lucky Cecile, being able to shed the Lennox family through marriage. If only he could be so fortunate. But as his father's sole male heir, he'd often been the object of his grandmother's romantic plotting.

Chet meets Graham in the dark front hall.

"I saw you pull in. How did it go?"

"Shh." Graham pauses until Atchison disappears around a corner. "Fine. Apartment's a little dowdy, but she was excited."

"Was Bonafante there?"

"What do you think? Of course not," Graham whispers. "There's some sort of houseman overseeing the program."

Chet gnaws at a cuticle, squinting across the constellation of freckles on her nose. "So, I've been thinking. What if this is a huge mistake?"

"Oh, now you're thinking? Great, Chet. Where were your sisterly concerns this morning when we agreed that it's actually quite convenient to have Marjorie away?"

"The timing is awfully helpful. And it might allow her to prove herself once and for all. But something feels off."

"Well, it's too late to change course. The houseman was all too happy to rush me out. And he immediately locked the door behind me."

"Well, that makes sense. It's Detroit. But what if she gets lonely and wants to come home?" Chet whispers.

"I told her to send word if she gets homesick. I acted like we would come and get her. But she insisted that discomfort is part of the exercise, or some nonsense. Look, Marjorie's delicate physically, but she's not fragile. There's a difference. She's strong-willed, spends hours and hours alone, lost in her designs. She'll become entranced in her art. Want to make a wager on it?"

Chet's face twists with disgust. "You're despicable. This is our sister, not a horse."

"Spoken by the woman who prefers groundhogs to people."

"The groundhog, that was ill-conceived butchery and you know it," objects Chet. "The neighbors could have seen. I gave it a proper burial."

"Sure, and now my childhood sandbox is haunted." Graham stretches. "So, where are we on the latest tribute? Deadline's tonight, right? Deadline—such an apt term in this line of work. What's the name?"

Chet lifts the paper she's been holding and hands it to him. "Kolansky. Theodore. Went by 'Ted.' "

Graham scans the page. "Wig salesman?"

"Yes. For diphtheria patients and others who lost their hair from illness."

Graham's lips move silently as he reads. "Loved pierogies?"

"Makes him human, salutes his Polish homeland."

The mention of food distracts Graham from the obituary to thoughts of the impending dinner. The Lennox family has complicated relationships with food. He and his grandparents enjoy meals. His father overindulges, Lilah's a picky eater, and Cecile only pretends to eat, succumbing instead to her long-harbored addiction of sucking postage stamps. When teased about her gluey breath, she scoffs, insisting she enjoys the taste of money in her mouth.

After their mother died, Chet ate very little. But as the years progressed, her appetite emerged during the graveyard hours. She'd wake Graham and Marjorie and herd them down to the kitchen in their pajamas, where she would proceed to play the part of "Knödel," the murderous fictional chef of Kaiser Wilhelm, and invent new recipes, using every pot and pan in the kitchen. The cook always suspected their father and was too fearful to complain of the mess, so they got away with it. Marjorie once insisted that they invite their eldest sister to join their midnight mayhem, but Cecile rebuffed them, preferring to spend her evenings masked in radium-infused facial mud, talking to herself in the mirror while wearing Granny's jewelry, and penning letters to the U.S. Postal Service, promoting her ridiculous idea of creating holiday postage stamps.

One winter night, while downy drifts of snow feathered in the corners of the windows, young Marjorie insisted she must taste the experience of smoking a pipe. So they all sat on the kitchen counter in their pajamas, passing Gramps's pipe until he himself wandered down, climbed on the counter, and joined them. The kitchen escapades began as childhood mischief and evolved into tradition, especially over the Christmas holiday. As they got older, Knödel's murderous cooking sprees involved pinching good bottles from the secret liquor room, getting sozzled, and gossiping until sunrise. The memories are a comfort. Graham wishes they could return to those days, before everything became so tangled and secret.

"Graham?" says Chet, piercing his thoughts.

"Pierogies, yes. Salutes his Polish homeland."

"Right. The boss loves details like that."

"He does?"

"Yes. And I think you need to deliver this one. Since you're home for the summer, you should go in from time to time. It'll buy us some breathing room."

"Breathing room? Who needs breathing room?" Their grandfather's deep Scottish accent booms through the corridor.

Chet and Graham freeze.

Gramps. How much has he heard?

10

CROOKED STRAIGHT

"Graham. A word, please?" calls their grandfather. Chet shrinks into the shadows of the grand staircase.

Graham makes his way into the oak-paneled sitting room accented with tartan plaids. His grandparents sit on the sofa, reading the newspaper together—their custom for over half a century of marriage. Next to his grandmother leans Nero, one of her many umbrellas. Her collection is vast, all black with ornate handles, and all named after tyrants and mad monarchs. To outsiders, his grandparents might simply appear as a gray-haired elderly couple. The kind who enjoys walking a border collie or reading a cozy mystery. But beneath the geriatric exterior are two brilliant and devious minds. Leagues ahead of his father.

"Hello, dear."

"Hi, Granny. Granddad."

"You just missed Myrtle Branley," says Granny. "She stopped by—uninvited, of course—trying to recruit your grandfather for some sort of citizen patrol force."

"She did the same to us at the club."

"Poor old duck. Widowhood has left her hunting for purpose," says Gramps. "But can't she find something more matronly than policing and investigation?"

"Why should she? Women have sharp instincts, Cormac." Granny peers at Graham from over her glasses. "What is that paper you're holding?"

Graham lifts the sheet. "Have to deliver an obituary to the paper."

"I'm glad you've been so reliable with that little job. Builds character." Granny smiles.

Granddad lowers both his voice and the paper. "I saw you carting Marjorie off this morning. Everything okay?"

"Yeah, fine." Graham smiles but avoids looking at his grandfather. Does Gramps suspect that he has secrets with Chet?

"Marjorie's a smart girl," says his grandfather. "Smarter than most realize."

"And she's a sweet soul," adds Granny. "Like a little fairy. A truth fairy."

Graham smiles at his grandmother's play on words. It's accurate. When she was a young girl, Marjorie's outbursts of observation could be funny. But now that she's older, her weak filter can be problematic.

Granny sits up. "Graham, dear, Myrtle Branley mentioned that a doctor who specializes in prosthetic eyes is giving a lecture in Cleveland. Why don't we go and have you fitted while we're there?"

Graham walks toward the window seat. "I'm sorry, Granny, but I'm not ready. Carrying around a glass eye in a box is almost as creepy as telling people how I lost my eye."

"It was an accident!" huffs Granny. She makes a show of rising easily from the couch before grabbing Nero. She pounds the umbrella with a "Hmph!" and exits the room.

Graham releases the breath he was holding.

"She's trying to protect your father," says Gramps. "A mother wants to protect her children."

His grandparents have two other children, both younger than his father, both living outside of Detroit. Their daughter, Finny, married into banking money. Jamie, their youngest and "spare" son, defied expectation and made his own fortune in the Caribbean. "But who's going to protect you?" whispers Graham. "Do you ever think about that?"

"Of course. We both know that your father has a talent for making things disappear. I saw Dr. Boyce last week for a full cognitive exam. Filed the report with my attorneys just to make sure your father can't trolley me off to some asylum to get me out of the way. We know he's not above that. Unfortunately for your father, my mind is even sharper than my conscience. I'm covering all my bases."

"Any letters from Uncle Jamie?"

"Yes. The new house is nearly finished." His grandfather's eyes twinkle as he removes a small envelope from his pocket. He proudly shows Graham a photo. A sweeping coral stone villa framed by tropical palms and poised by the sea. Jamie stands beneath a breezeway arch, framed within a spill of light. "I'm so proud of him. My youngest boy has made quite a mark in the West Indies."

"It's certainly a far cry from Detroit," nods Graham. He looks about the room at the eclectic mix of polished antiques, leather books, fresh flowers, and parasols with gilded handles, all offset by his grandfather's moth-eaten cardigan and gum boots. He gazes out the window of the sitting room and sees black-clad Slorah trudging toward the side door, gripping a chicken by its snapped neck. Slorah volunteers to break and chop the necks of poultry for the cook. She claims it's soothing. Graham shakes his head. His question rides atop a whisper. "Granddad, what sort of family are we?" he asks.

"A crooked one," replies his grandfather. "And it's hard to bend a crooked straight. Speaking of crooked, your sister and Louis are coming for dinner tonight."

The suitcase of shoes appears in Graham's mind. Will Cecile be making an announcement? He turns from the window, back to his grandfather. "Do you think Cecile knows about Lou working with the Purples?"

"Probably. Wives often know everything."

"Did Granny know about your secret?"

His grandfather nods. "She was the first to figure it out."

11

POOR DADDY

A list. She needs to make a list.

Marjorie retrieves a piece of paper from her purse and tries to remember everything that Dock mentioned.

Curfew at 9:00 P.M. Lock the doors. No smoking in bed.

Goodness, what else was there? And where did he say his apartment was?

Marjorie takes her key ring and heads into the hallway. A large picnic basket sits in front of her green door. The meal hamper? Already? It's quite heavy, so Marjorie decides to simply drag it over the threshold. She can't resist a look. A loaf of bread, some sort of dried meats. She lifts a jar of what appears to be soup.

"You disobedient girl. You're not supposed to keep your door open."

Marjorie looks up to find Ivy draped against her doorframe. Her neighbor wags a reprimanding finger, then breaks into a laugh. "I wondered what was taking you so long. Lock your door, darling, and come over."

Marjorie shoves the hamper aside and locks her door.

"Your sign is gone," says Marjorie. "The days until Christmas."

"Dock removes it each day. Claims I'm altering the door. He's a dear, but he's overly concerned with rules. And rules are just tedious, aren't they?"

Marjorie steps inside the apartment and Ivy locks the door. Spatially,

Ivy's apartment is identical to hers but with a reverse layout. Stylistically, their apartments are nothing alike.

Ivy's apartment is painted white, with sky-blue curtains. A chandelier floats theatrically from the center of the ceiling. Its outstretched arms dangle crystal lozenges that throw sparkle about the room. Against the wall are several easels covered with drapes.

"Oh! Dock mentioned that one of the residents was a painter. That must be you."

"Well, I know you're the fashion designer. You're the last to arrive." Ivy lights a cigarette and offers her gold case to Marjorie.

"How long have you been here?" asks Marjorie, taking a cigarette.

Ivy reclines on the couch, as if posing for a boudoir photo. "Just over a week. From what I can tell, the residencies are on some sort of rotational basis, with people coming and going. The gal who was in your apartment left the day after I arrived. Didn't get to meet her. But I saw several pair of ballet slippers outside her door, so I assume she was a dancer."

"A dancer? The apartment isn't big enough for a dance routine."

"Who knows. Did Dock give you the boring lecture that the goal is to create within our own space? Maybe she was a dance contortionist."

Marjorie laughs.

"Is that funny, honey? You've never met a contortionist?"

"No. But I've heard they can smoke with their feet, which sounds very convenient. And, yes, Dock told me the same thing about creating within our space. But I'm envious. Your apartment is so light and bright. Much more cheerful than mine. And you have a sofa and an armchair too. I just have an old rocking chair and a table that should be in a butcher shop."

"But what am I to do with blue?" laments Ivy. "Blue is not my color. Red and green are my colors." Ivy sits up. "Oh, Marjorie, be a darling and whip up something red or green for me. I asked for red candles, but Dock claims candles are a fire hazard. But without red or green, I'm just not myself." Ivy shivers as if she's got a chill. She inhales a deep pull on her cigarette. A snake of ash dangles from the glowing tip. "So, where are you from? Tell me about your family," she says.

"We're part of the automotive set. Lennox windshields. We live in Grosse Pointe."

"The Lennox empire. Everyone knows of your family, sweetie. My family's in rubber. Tires. We just built a house in Palmer Woods. How many siblings do you have?"

"I'm the youngest of four. We're half-siblings. My father was a widower before he met my mother. And you?" asks Marjorie.

"I'm an only child," says Ivy. "But I've always longed for siblings. I ask Santa for them each year."

Marjorie looks at Ivy, trying to reconcile her burlesque appearance with the youthful comment.

"Your face, darling. It's all over your face. You find me eccentric. But aren't all artists eccentric?"

"Of course," says Marjorie. "That's what I try to explain to others but am often dismissed. I just turned twenty. And you? The fatigue of your brassiere signals somewhere near thirty?"

"Oh, my. Sweet, but so bold with your words. Hmm . . . I'll linger somewhere in my early twenties, I think," says Ivy. "I've finally grown into my figure, but I've looked like this since I was thirteen." Ivy waves a hand around her bustline. "Can you imagine? Poor Daddy."

"Your family, do they know you're here?" asks Marjorie.

Ivy's brow quirks with confusion. "Of course they know. Your family doesn't know you're here, darling? That handsome boy—Graham—he's not really your brother?"

"Oh, Graham is my brother, and he obviously knows that I'm here. And my sister Chet knows. I suspect Chet's the one who slipped the residency information into my room. But my parents, my grandparents, and my oldest sister, they don't know I'm here. They think I'm at the family cottage. They don't approve of women in the arts."

"That's unfortunate. It's just Daddy and me. My mother was a painter. She died when I was six, and I think Daddy's intrigued that I've followed in her footsteps. We have a lot of fun, especially when I wear Mother's clothes. So, would you like to see my work?"

"I'd love that!"

Ivy sets her cigarette in the ashtray and saunters toward the four easels. "Do you know the origin of Tuesday?" she asks.

"Tuesday?"

"Yes, the word 'Tuesday' is derived from the Norse god Tyr. Thor's forgotten half-brother."

"Mythology," nods Marjorie, flicking the tip of her cigarette against the ashtray.

"Exactly." Ivy pauses and sniffs. She purses her red lips, then pulls the curtain off each easel in dramatic succession.

Marjorie looks at the paintings. She blinks. She steps closer.

Four paintings. All in the same color scheme. All on the same theme. Not mythology. Not Thor. Or Tyr.

Christmas.

"You were thinking of Christmas?" asks Marjorie.

"I'm always thinking of Christmas. This particular series is called *Tuesday Christmas*."

"Tuesday Christmas."

"Yes, it's an exploration of Christmases that fall on a Tuesday. Quite deep."

Marjorie looks at the paintings. Each has some representation of Tuesday—a calendar on the wall, a newspaper with a date, a diary-entry page. They're not particularly unique, but they're cozy, like a scene from a dime-store holiday card.

"Do you think a museum will buy them, darling?" she asks. "Would you like to buy them? Five hundred apiece. I can hold them until you procure a bank draft. Which one do you think Graham would like?"

"Hmm. Graham might be more of a New Year's man. I'll give it some thought."

"Please do, and please give thought to whipping up something fabulously red or green for me. I know I must seem terribly odd and demanding, but I now understand why people say they're 'blue' to express feeling down. Blue just does that." Ivy picks up a paintbrush and dabs at one of the paintings.

"Thank you for sharing your work," says Marjorie. "I think I'll go introduce myself to the others."

"Oh, you won't meet the playwright. She's apparently on deadline and won't open her door. But do say hello to Bernice, the furniture designer behind the gray door. She's fabulous. Her family's in lumber, and they live in a lighthouse on the Keweenaw Peninsula." Ivy suddenly gasps and turns wide-eyed to Marjorie. "Well, silent night! Why didn't I think of that before? I should paint a Christmas lighthouse."

"Do you paint anything besides scenes of Christmas?"

Ivy throws her head back with a laugh. "Of course not, darling. Why on earth would I do that?"

12

SILVER GHOST

Marjorie walks to the playwright's room and knocks on the red door.

No reply.

She leans in, speaking toward the doorframe. "Hello. I don't mean to disturb you. I'm Marjorie Lennox. I just arrived and wanted to introduce myself. If you ever feel inclined to chat, or if you should need anything, just give a knock on the green door."

Silence.

And then the clackety-clack of a typewriter sounds from inside the room. Louder, faster, typing up a fury.

Oh, dear, thinks Marjorie. I truly am disturbing her. She knows how annoyed Chet becomes if she's interrupted when she has an obituary to deliver. "I'll leave you be," she calls through the doorjamb.

Marjorie knocks on the gray door.

"Yep, yep. Coming!" she hears. The door whips open, nearly jerked off its hinges. "Ahoy there!" bellows a young woman. She's a head taller than Marjorie and wears what looks to be a white pharmacy jacket over a gray cotton dress. Her dark-brown hair hangs in two thick plaits. Pencil behind her ear, bright-hazel eyes, and full lips with no lipstick. Marjorie spots a tape measure and a screwdriver peeking from her pockets.

"Hello, I'm Marjorie Lennox. I've just arrived and wanted to introduce myself."

"Perfect timing," says the young woman. "I'm waiting for some varnish to dry. Come in!" She steps aside for Marjorie to enter. The woman closes the door and locks it. She holds up her key ring. "Mine locks with the gold key. What about yours?"

"Same," says Marjorie.

"Do you know what the silver key is for?"

"No, I was wondering."

"If you find out, let me know. Such a mystery. Well, you came to introduce yourself and here I am talking about keys. I'm Bernice Tessin." Bernice thrusts out a hand.

Marjorie accepts her hand and is taken aback by the grip. "How do you do, Bernice. Marjorie Lennox."

"How do I do? I'm doin' dandy. Hope you are too."

"What an enchanting accent you have, almost Canadian."

"North Woods. Tip of the Upper Peninsula," nods Bernice.

"Yes, Ivy told me. That's quite far."

"Yep. Took me a few days to get here. Down the rails through Green Bay and then over from Chicago."

A large drafting table is positioned in the corner. Once again, Marjorie is surprised by the similarity of the space but the difference in décor.

"And you smell lovely," says Marjorie. "A mix of pencil shavings and coffee. Perfectly aligned with your style."

"Ha! I'll take that as a compliment."

"Please do," says Marjorie. "I mean it as one."

"Coffee in the morning, tea in the afternoon, and the good stuff at night, right? I've got the kettle on. Would you like some tea?"

"Oh, that sounds lovely," says Marjorie.

Bernice moves to the kitchenette. "You're in the ballerina's apartment?"

"Yes, but it's quite different than this. I love your cream walls and—" Marjorie gasps. "Look at that chair! Oh my goodness, did you *make* that chair?"

Bernice grins. "I did. What do you think?"

"I love it! I've seen nothing like it. Very experimental."

The chair is crafted of pale-blond wood, with a curved backrest cascading directly into a seat. It resembles the shape of a banana.

"I'm glad you love the look of it, but I hope you love the feel of it. Milk or sugar?"

"Just a little milk, please. Ivy said you're from a lumber family. Did that inspire your interest in wood design?"

"It did. My gramps was in lumber. As a kid, I used to experiment and gathered all sorts of tricks. I learned that if I heated plywood, I could mold, bend, and shape it. That's what I've done here. I'd let you try it, but I just put a coat of varnish on."

"It's entirely unique."

"Thank you. Most assume that as a woman I'm interested in designing bedroom interiors or department-store windows. No interest. Doors. Beams. Furniture. The way a man looks at pretty women? That's how I look at houses. And I'm absolutely batty for chairs." Bernice hands Marjorie the cup of tea without a saucer. "Dock says you're a fashion designer. Who are some of your influences?"

"My influences?" Bernice was speaking to Marjorie of craft in a way no one ever had. She was taking her seriously. "Well, Fortuny is brilliant, and I love Erté. He designed costumes for Mata Hari. The clothing and costumes he creates aren't just designs, they're innovations. Sinewy yet geometric, nothing traditional, and probably nothing acceptable to stores here in Detroit."

"I love the sound of that. Are you working on a specific project during your residency?"

Marjorie caresses the teacup, warming her fingers. "Well, this is the first opportunity I've ever had, outside of making a few outfits for myself or my family members. Two of my siblings know I'm here, but my parents don't. They feel that a career in the arts is scandalous. I briefly dated an artist last summer and, unfortunately, he confirmed their bias. They feel I should find a reputable husband."

"Sorry about that. I know a lot of parents feel that way." Bernice hoists herself up on the counter in the kitchenette. "There's a wealthy family near me that shipped their daughter off to England to hunt for a duke. This is a gal, mind you, who loves loggers. The whiskery the better. But you should give some thought to what you'd like to accomplish while you're here. Make your mark. We might not have another opportunity like this. I live in a lighthouse up in mining territory and don't have access to materials and mentors like the ones available here. Speaking of, do you know who's sponsoring this program?"

Marjorie nods without saying the name.

"And have you ever laid eyes on him? Wowee. That's a smooth drink of water. Aren't many like that where I'm from in Copper Country."

"You've met him?" asks Marjorie.

"Not yet, but I've seen him. Several times. He lives upstairs."

Marjorie's head snaps to Bernice. Her tea sloshes. "Here? No, he lives in Grosse Pointe."

"Well, maybe he's got a place there as well. Your apartment faces the front sidewalk." Bernice points to the window in her apartment. "Mine faces the parking area. I've seen him pull in and head upstairs at night. There's a separate door back there. He seems to entertain a lot."

"Entertain? Are we talking about the same man?"

"Charles Bonafante. Have you seen his car?"

Marjorie nods. "A Silver Ghost."

"Right. That's some automobile. And the clothes?" Bernice gives a thick whistle.

"Bespoke suits. Double-monk shoes from William Lobb," sighs Marjorie with distraction. Her mind is buzzing. Mr. Bonafante entertains? Since when?

"So what's he all about?" asks Bernice. "Why's a dashing gent like that sponsoring an arts program for women? And the lease, did you sign it?"

"I did," says Marjorie. "But, Bernice, I made a terrible oversight. Dock mentioned the fine print, but I neglected to read it."

"Well, I read it. It said that once we sign the lease, we can't leave until the residency is deemed over. And if we break the rules, we'll be required to . . . compensate. I wasn't sure what 'compensate' implied, you know? When I asked Dock, he said not to worry, that it's not financial and it's determined on a case-by-case basis. Sounded very odd."

"Well, I did notice some damage, small defacements in my bathroom. Perhaps one of the previous residents defaced the property, so they added that compensation clause to the lease?"

"Maybe. Anyway, I figure it can't be as challenging as living in a lighthouse. Here I'll have dedicated time to experiment with my own line of chairs. I can work the hours I want without worrying about keeping the light, and I'll have an endless stream of supplies. So if that means I have to lock my door and be in by nine, so be it."

Marjorie feels confused yet oddly excited. Mr. Bonafante lives at the Nightingale? She moves toward Bernice's window and shifts the curtains. Just a few empty parking spaces out back. No sign of the Silver Ghost. "Well, I best go back to my apartment and get settled. Thank you for the tea. I'm so happy to meet you, Bernice."

"I'm happy to meet you too. Think about what I said. Use this valuable time to make a statement."

Marjorie walks down the hall, her mind a flurry of thoughts. Bernice is so focused, so businesslike, but she's also a true artist. And she's right. Instead of sewing placemats and bed linens, she'll come up with a plan, a series all her own.

Marjorie enters her apartment and locks the door, feeling proud that she remembered. And then she notices a sheet of paper on the floor near the hamper of food. Someone must have slid it beneath the door. She bends to retrieve it.

Dear Miss Lennox,

I'm sorry I wasn't able to meet you. I'm on deadline for my draft and have promised myself that I won't become distracted. You were so kind to make the effort to introduce yourself that I feel obliged to return a kindness. So I shall share this:

This building is lovely. But this building is haunted.

Dear Coco,

The thunder becomes louder.
Creeps closer.
Some storms last all night.
But I am not afraid.

13

POISSON D'OR

Evening light slants through the windows as Graham enters the family drawing room. Ice cubes tinkle against a crystal tumbler, and Poochie, Granny's obese lime parakeet, squawks from a cage in the corner.

Graham leans toward Chet. "Are you up for a wager?"

"I told you, I'm not making a bet on our sister."

"Not on Marjorie, on Cecile."

Chet's brows flash. "What about Cecile?"

"Whether she's pregnant."

Chet sighs, annoyed. "Just because she had a headache at the club doesn't mean she's pregnant. Her headaches are fake, just a ploy for attention."

"So you'll take the bet?"

"I will. If Cecile isn't pregnant, you'll fork over the entire next check from the newspaper."

"You're on. And if I'm right, I keep the whole check."

Their parents enter the drawing room and deliver empty pleasantries. Their father wears a navy dinner jacket and his perpetual blood-pressure sunburn. Lilah dons her staple accessory—a grimace of annoyance. Their pace quickens as they both head for the sideboard and the bottle of gin.

"Perhaps keep it to one drink, Duncan. You're putting on more weight. You don't want to look like your mother's pig of a bird."

"You don't seem to mind when our pig of a bank account puts on weight, Lilah."

Chet raises a glass. "Aren't they wonderful?"

"To the happy household," toasts Graham.

Cecile and Lou make their entrance, guided into the room by Atchison.

Graham laughs. "Did you forget the layout of the house, Cecile? You need Atch to guide you, help you make a grand entry?"

"What kind of greeting is that?" She turns to her husband. "You see? This is what I'm always telling you. They're so unkind to me."

"I'm not unkind," says their father. "Come here, sweetheart." He hugs Cecile and shakes Lou's hand.

"Spoiled pet." Chet sneers.

Graham looks at his older sister and her husband. They're attractive people but not necessarily an attractive couple. Cecile inherited the classic beauty of their mother, their father's first wife. Blond, slender, with a long neck to showcase her ever-rotating necklaces and pendants. But despite her Tiffany & Co. appearance, Cecile can be unpredictable, hostile. A fist in haute couture.

The book of Lou sits on a different shelf. Muscled, dark hair slicked with an over-dip of pomade, a perpetual grin, and mischievous gray eyes. Instead of replying, Lou will often chuckle, lifting the left side of his mouth in what could be a sneer or a grin, leaving those in the conversation unsure if he agrees or disagrees. Lou worked the boxing circuit until he realized that he could make significantly more money lending muscle to the Lennox auto aristocracy. Their grandparents initially opposed the match with a retired pugilist from the bookie beat. But Lou has the humid sex appeal that Cecile favors and the type of intimidating muscle their father favors.

On Cecile's wedding day, Marjorie had posed a question to their eldest sister.

"Cecile, tell me what you love most about Louis. What about him inspires you?"

Cecile turned a dead face to Marjorie. "The sex. The man can hold his fizz as long as I want. You'll come to learn how important that is."

"Let's count the lies Cecile spits out tonight," says Chet. "These days, her stories rotate as often as her jewelry. I don't know how Marjie can be so forgiving of her."

Cecile now sifts her way over to Chet and Graham. "What sort of evil are you two concocting?" she asks.

"I'm considering taking out his other eye," says Chet. "Just to make the night interesting."

Graham laughs.

"You're such a savage, Chet. No wonder you adore animals. You are one." Cecile takes a sip of her drink. "I thought you were going to bleach your freckles."

"Chet didn't want to bleach her freckles," says Graham. "That was your idea."

"Along with taming my hair."

"Your hair?" asks Graham. "What's wrong with your hair?"

"According to Cecile, it's too bushy."

Cecile rolls her eyes. "I didn't say bushy. I said bristly. Your hair is wiry. No one in our family has hair like that, not on their head anyway."

"I'm inclined to spit on you, Cecile," says Graham. "But instead I'll ask—what's with the family dinner? You and Lou have an announcement to make?"

Cecile's eyes snap to Graham. "What have you heard?"

"Nothing, just seems strange to have a big dinner on a weeknight."

Atchison announces that dinner is served, and Cecile quickly departs.

They make their way down the dim paneled hallway into the dining room. Their grandparents have already arrived, standing at opposite ends of the long oak table. Their grandfather's moth-eaten cardigan has been replaced by a double-breasted dinner jacket. His white hair and beard are respectably finger-combed. Being that it's summer, the five-foot stone fireplace stands dark; instead, the mullioned windows hinge open between the green brocade curtains. A pair of thistle silver candelabras, each holding five lighted tapers, wave pools of light across the intricate plasterwork ceiling.

"It's so damn hot. Do we really need candles?" grouses their father.

"Of course we do," replies Granny. "A candle burns the curse of darkness."

Unlike at the club, where their father holds court, Glen Arden is still the domain of their grandfather. They report to their usual chairs, and Gramps motions for everyone to be seated.

"Where's the little troublemaker?" asks Cecile.

"I'll get you a mirror," says Chet.

"Marjorie's at the cottage," replies Graham. "Attending the equestrian series."

"I wish she would have told me," says Lilah.

"You were busy with tennis." Chet smiles. "Handle some good balls today? How was your game?"

"Fine," their stepmother replies.

The servants step forward, laying bowls of soup in choreographed motion.

"I saw Myrtle Branley in the Village," says Cecile. "She said there's a nickname circulating for Marjorie."

"Will someone please hit Myrtle Branley with a bread truck?" scoffs Graham. "I'm sick of hearing about her."

"What's the nickname?" asks Chet.

"Poisson d'or," says Cecile.

The parakeet squawks from down the hall.

"What the hell does that mean?" asks their father.

"The goldfish," replies Chet. "Why the goldfish?"

"Perhaps because of her pocketbook," suggests Granny.

Marjorie has a beloved wicker purse shaped like a fish. She had it special-ordered from Scotland. It's entirely bizarre, which delights Marjorie to no end.

"Goldfish. I think that's a sweet nickname," says Lilah.

"No, it's not," says Chet. "Goldfish are captive victims of cruelty. Someone thinks Marjorie's a prisoner?"

"Oh, spare us the parlor psychology," says Cecile. "I just brought it up because nicknames can be damaging."

"Do you know yours?" asks Graham. Lou chuckles.

"Can't be as bad as yours. The men downtown call you a dandified dimwit," says Cecile.

"I prefer the pirate nicknames for Graham," says Chet.

"Speaking of pirates and Myrtle Branley," says Granny, "I told Graham that Myrtle heard of a specialist in prosthetic eyes who's coming to Cleveland."

"I told you, Granny. I'm not interested in a glass eye. And I certainly don't care what Myrtle Branley has to say."

"Imagine Myrtle Branley in the bath," says Chet.

The entire table recoils with disgust.

"We're eating!" protests Gramps.

"What on earth would make you say such a thing?" gasps their stepmother. "That is not appropriate dinner conversation . . . or any conversation."

"Chet's a savage," sneers Cecile.

Graham sets down his spoon and turns to their eldest sister. "Why do you pretend to be so refined? This is Detroit, not England."

"Thank God for that," says Gramps.

"Oh, forgive me," feigns Cecile. "You're a Yale man now. Detroit must feel so base."

"Theodore Roosevelt didn't wear a glass eye," says Chet.

"Enough!" booms their father, pounding a fist on the table. The room falls silent. He lifts his wineglass, as if to make a toast. "Myrtle Branley can choke on her own lace collar for all I care. Before we eat, I believe Lou and Cecile have something to share."

Graham kicks at Chet beneath the table.

Cecile smiles, jaw clenched.

"Yeah," says Lou. "Well, we're real excited."

Granny clasps her hopeful hands.

"Cecile and me . . . well, we're moving," he says, followed by an awkward chuckle.

Granny's shoulders sink.

"Moving?" says Lilah. "Where?"

"The Detroit Golf Club," says Cecile.

Chet turns to Graham, smug. "The next check. Thank you very much."

"The Detroit Golf Club?" says Graham. "You're leaving Grosse Pointe?"

"It's not far," says Lou. "More central. New development."

Graham leans back in his chair. "New development? There's new development right here in Grosse Pointe. Edsel Ford's breaking ground around the corner."

"Yeah, I heard," nods Lou. "Might be nice to have some distance from the Ford crew. There's a lot runnin' around them."

"What does that mean?" asks Chet.

Cecile jumps in. "You're welcome to visit. Seven thousand square feet. Six bedrooms."

"Plenty of room for babies." Granny smiles.

"And plenty of room for you and Gramps," replies Cecile.

"Oh, I see where this is going," says Gramps. He leans forward, setting his forearms on the table. "Your father can stay with you. I built Glen Arden and I'll die here."

"What a coincidence," says their father. "Hell called this morning. Your table is ready."

"Stop it, you two," scolds Granny. "I'm sick of your fighting."

"Wait, how can you afford a mansion in the golf club?" asks Graham.

"Graham! Don't be so uncouth," says Lilah. "Lou does very well."

"Indeed he does!" agrees their father. He smiles and lifts his glass. "Well done, Lou. Congratulations, Cecile. And get ready, because I'm gonna throw you one helluva housewarming party!"

14

THAT HANK

Graham races the Cadillac down Jefferson Avenue, weaving in and out of traffic.

"The Detroit Golf Club? A housewarming party? What the hell is Dad scheming? And Cecile looked so damn smug."

"I know. And poor Granny and Gramps. Did you see their faces? Slow down. The deadline's not until nine-thirty. We still have time," says Chet.

"We have plenty of time. Ted Kolansky, the wig salesman, is dead. Doesn't matter when the obituary runs."

"It does matter. His family chose the *Times* exclusively for the obituary. They could have given their money to the *News* or the *Free Press*."

Chet's right. The newspaper war is in full swing in the city of Detroit. Six years ago, William Randolph Hearst bought the flailing *Detroit Times*. In a short period, it's been transformed into "the paper with a personality" and now poses a serious threat to the other media outlets. Competition for breaking news, advertising, and even obituaries is bloodthirsty.

"Your commitment to the deceased is truly admirable," says Graham.

Chet smiles. "Admirable. And enjoyable. You know I find the dead more lovable than the living."

Graham turns onto Bagley Avenue and parks in front of the building.

"I wish they'd keep this old, rat-infested office instead of building a new one," says Chet. "I've heard they're going to call it 'Times Square.' How original." Chet exits the passenger side of the long, elegant vehicle.

"Gosh, Dad's Cadillac sticks out like a sore thumb here. I bet it gets stolen."

"One can hope," says Graham. "Shall we leave the key on the hood?"

He looks at the car. The blue Cadillac 314 Cabriolet Imperial glistens beneath the streetlight. The epitome of American luxury, the seven-passenger, extended Fisher-Bodied sedan has the same wheelbase as a funeral vehicle. It features spoked wheels wrapped in whitewall tires and a custom Cadillac Court Trumpeter hood ornament. The little silver mascot wears a herald's tunic with the Cadillac coat of arms.

"Why didn't we think of that?" groused their father while sauced one night. "I love that trumpet tooter. We could have etched the Lennox coat of arms into our windshields."

"We don't have a coat of arms," said Graham.

"We could make one up. We're a Detroit dynasty, for Christ's sake."

"Oh, yes, with an eponymous driveway," said Chet.

"That leads to a dead end," laughed Graham.

"You're a waste of space, Graham. Why can't you be more like Harley? He ditched Stanford and joined his family in the auto business. He's making a fortune, and you're writing one-eyed, bullshit death stories for a useless rag."

After ditching Stanford, Harley Earl returned to Detroit and was brought on as a designer at Cadillac. He quickly became known as "the pretty picture boy," and his shop was referred to as "the beauty parlor." Soon after, Cadillac began offering hundreds of color and upholstery combinations.

Graham sneers at the hood ornament as he passes.

"You could shoot the tooter," suggests Chet. "Or have Slorah decapitate it."

They make their way into the building and up to the editorial department, which bustles under scalding lights like a medical triage unit. Men in white shirts, vests, and black ties dash frantically with notepads, while lines of typewriters issue strings of stutter like miniature machine guns.

Chet gives Graham a refresher. "Joe Hogan. Obituaries editor. He owed Gramps a favor of some sort. That's why he hired you. He's still sore that we didn't get the lead on Houdini's death in Detroit."

"Right. When was that?"

"On Halloween."

"And who got the lead?" asks Graham.

"The *Free Press.* They were camped out at Grace Hospital. Ran a front-page feature. But Houdini's wife is planning a séance. I suggested attending to request that Houdini dictate his own death notice from the afterlife."

"That's disgustingly creepy, Chet."

"I told Hogan it was your idea. He loves it. He'll probably mention it. Here, take the Kolansky write-up."

Graham takes the typewritten sheet of paper from his sister. They approach the small, smoke-stained office and knock on the open door.

"Well, well. The Yale man returns!"

Graham approaches his desk. "Hello, Mr. Hogan. Yes, I'm home for the summer, so I thought I'd come by and deliver this one myself."

Mr. Hogan takes the paper and removes the pencil from behind his ear. "Bet Chet's happy about that. She's been quite the little secretary for you. Better be careful or one of my guys might steal her away and buy her a shorter skirt. Lots of coffee to make here."

Chet's slow intake of breath is audible. Graham presses his arm against hers.

Hogan scans the paper, ticking off lines with the pencil as he reads. He crosses something out and Chet cranes her neck to see. He finishes reading and nods. "Love the pierogi mention. Lotsa Poles in Hamtramck. We need 'em as subscribers. Well, once again, fantastic job."

"What did you cross out?" asks Chet.

"Small thing. There was a misplaced modifier."

"No there wasn't," she says.

"Your sister's pretty protective of you and your work," laughs the editor. "She fought like hell to get you the Kehoe obits." Hogan whistles. "I was hesitant. Too awful. Too soon. The wife, okay, but why should we give ink to that Michigan monster? But, man, what a profile that was. Did Chet give you the letters sent in from readers?"

"Kehoe . . . yes," says Graham. He looks to his sister.

Chet nods. "Bath School massacre. I agree. You did a great job on that one. Everyone was writing about the forty schoolchildren who were massacred or the fifty injured in the attack. But the way you captured Kehoe's psyche and what he did to his wife before blowing up the school, it really was chilling, Graham."

"I'm still getting letters about her charred remains and questions about why the jewels were positioned around the milk cart," says Hogan.

Graham looks to Chet in disbelief, his one eye wide.

"Now, your idea about Houdini's séance? That's bloody brilliant," says Hogan. "You sure you're up for that?"

Chet smiles contentedly. Graham turns again to Hogan. "The séance, yes," he says. "But actually, I'd like to speak with you about a wage increase. Our partnership is productive, but it's challenging to constantly find new takes on such harrowing content."

"Challenging? What's challenging is explaining why one of my writers who receives a paycheck isn't at a desk here daily," says Hogan.

A man bursts into the office. "Sorry to interrupt, but I need a file. I've got a ferocious cub reporter who swears he's onto something big and needs an obituary to reference."

Hogan crosses his arms. "Oh, yeah? What's the story?"

"Some mysterious rich bachelor from Grosse Pointe. Bonasante, Bonafante, or something like that. My undercover cub, Hank, swears the guy is into something foul."

"Wait," says Hogan. "Your undercover reporter is Hank? Chief editor's son?"

"Yeah, *that* Hank."

"Shit. Take whatever you need." Hogan points to the row of file cabinets. "Say, Graham, you're from Grosse Pointe. Ever hear of a rich bachelor named Bonafante?"

Graham stands silent. He blinks. Swallows.

"No," Graham finally replies. "Never heard of him."

15

DEEP SLEEP

Quibbling. Arguing. Her father raises his voice. And then pounds.

Pounding on the table? He does that during dinners.

No. This sounds like a knocking.

Marjorie rolls over on her cot of a bed amidst a dream. The windowless bedroom is pitch black. Beautifully conducive to deep sleep.

Yes, she wants to sleep. It was difficult to fall asleep. Too early to wake.

But then she hears it again. A knocking.

She sits up, gathers herself, and feels her way toward the bedroom door. She swings it open and a sweep of light washes over her. She squints. The room is so hot.

And then she hears it again. The knocking. It's coming from the window. Is it a bird? Cardinals sometimes bang into their windows at Glen Arden. Slorah's the only one who can make them stop.

More knocking.

"Quiet, little bird. I'm trying to sleep," calls Marjorie. But the knocking continues.

Marjorie pads from the bedroom in her nightdress, still drunken with sleep. She yawns and pulls the curtain to chase the bird away. "Birdie, birdie. Enough now, I—"

A face pushes toward her. A man in a gray cap is crouching, peering through her window. She jolts back, about to scream, when he points to an armload of newspapers.

"Newspapers," he says loudly.

Goodness. The newspapers. That's what she forgot to write down. Her job is to deliver the newspapers each morning. She signals to the man in the window to wait a moment and disappears into the bathroom. She turbans a towel around her head, splashes water on her face, and pulls on the prior day's dress.

She stumbles to the window and opens it. The young man speaks through the screen.

"I'm supposed to deliver five papers. Prior delivery boy said it was important, that someone in the front left flat would be waiting for them before seven."

"Yes. I'm sorry. I believe I've overslept. What time is it?"

"Eight-thirty. I dropped them early, but on my way back I noticed they hadn't been picked up, so I was concerned."

Eight-thirty? She was supposed to deliver the papers to each door by seven-thirty.

"I'm terribly sorry. I'm new here, and a windowless room plunges one into a whole new depth of sleep."

"No trouble. Shall I return them to the stoop?"

"Yes, please. I won't oversleep tomorrow. I just need to make myself decent and I'll be out to get them. Thank you for waking me . . . what is your name?"

"Hank."

"Thank you, Hank. I'm—" She stops. Per the lease, can she share her name? "I'm grateful you woke me."

"Alright. I'll drop the lot again tomorrow."

Marjorie pulls the curtains for privacy and leans against the enamel table. Goodness, what a deep fog of sleep. After receiving the neighbor's message about the building being haunted, she initially laughed and thought it could be fun to meet a ghost. But as night crept in, she became unsettled by odd knocking noises. She made some tea from the cupboard and then must have fallen asleep. And now she's terribly tired, but Ina isn't around to open the drapes and bring her coffee and sweet rolls. Marjorie looks to the kitchenette. She doesn't need Ina. She's independent. She can do this. How shameful that she's never interacted with a delivery boy.

Marjorie fills the kettle and sets it upon the hot plate to boil. She dresses quickly, makes a cup of coffee, applies nothing but a dab of lipstick, and combs her hair without fuss. She'll be in her apartment all day. It's liberating living with artistic women. More relaxed.

She heads to the door to get the papers. The keys. She remembers the keys.

Marjorie exits her apartment, locks the door, and opens the front door of the building. She retrieves the stack of papers, closes the front door, and locks it.

Goodness, the rules of a lease are fatiguing. Is that why her grandfather insisted on buying his own land and building the Lennox glass factory without debt? So he didn't have to follow rules or answer to a landlord? She glances at the top stories on the stack of papers. The bridge to Canada is under construction, but the race to build a tunnel isn't far behind. A Ford story catches her eye.

**DOCTORS REPORT FORD RECOVERING.
DEATH PLOT RUMOR DISCREDITED**

Rumors ran riot through Detroit this week that the accident experienced by Henry Ford Sunday night near the entrance to his estate was an attempted death plot. Mr. Ford was sideswiped by a hit-and-run driver and thrown over an embankment. He is now at Henry Ford Hospital, recovering from his injuries.

Ford and his security team report the incident was an accident.

Each day the papers shout with tragic headlines. The glamour of old Detroit is now eclipsed by the grit of its underworld. Slayings, kidnappings, and the Milaflores massacre. And recently, a young woman from Detroit was hacked up and shipped to New York in a steamer trunk.

Just to make a point.

The media is always quick to blame a batch of thugs they dubbed the Purple Gang, a group of gangsters known for bootlegging and extortion.

But Chet argues that the paper is taking the easy way out. The Purples can't be behind everything.

Marjorie fans herself with the papers. It's already quite hot. She sets a newspaper at each of the apartment doors. Should she knock and announce their arrival? Best not—perhaps the other women are sleeping deeply, just as she was. At the end of the hallway she sees the steps to Dock's basement apartment and peers down. Blackness.

She places Dock's paper at the top of the stairs. She's about to return to her apartment when the back door catches her eye. Sturdy, black, with a large brass handle and a thick bolt lock. Marjorie creeps toward the door and places her fingers on the cold handle. She slowly unbolts the door and turns the knob. Sunlight streams in from the back lot, illuminating her face and hair. The sun feels so good on her skin. She squints, peers out, and that's when she sees it.

Bonafante's Silver Ghost. It's parked out back.

16

SO INCOGNITO

Graham walks through the upper corridor, past the row of Scottish paintings. He spots Ina, the housekeeper, oiling the balustrade of the gallery landing.

"Morning, Ina. Chet still around?"

"Good morning! Yes, she's in her room."

Graham spies the door ajar and enters. Chet spins from the mirror. "Nice of you to knock."

"What are you all dressed up for?"

"None of your business."

Graham flops onto the bed. "Got a date?"

"Maybe I do."

"Really? With who?"

"Nice grammar, Yale man. With 'whom.' "

"Don't change the subject. With whom will you be carousing in such a lovely dress? Still sneaking around with the meat inspector?"

"No. This is a business breakfast." Chet takes the cloche hat from the edge of the bed and pulls it over her frizzy hair.

"Business breakfast. Hmm. Gravedigger?"

"Mortician. He's new in town. From Cincinnati," says Chet.

"Makes sense. I'd say Detroit's got more dead folks than Cincinnati does."

Graham reclines on the unmade bed, looking about the room. Tattered books stand in wobbly rows beneath the leaded windows. Chet's passion for reading and learning was inherited from their grandfather. She endured a semester at Rockford College and was deeply homesick. She came home for Christmas and simply never returned. It wasn't until February that the family realized she should have been back in Illinois. Chet argued and produced a letter from the college reinforcing that *her social graces make for a better fit within a factory setting than an academic institution.*

Above Chet's small desk and typewriter are shelves crowded with glass domes helmeting faded flowers and other dead mementos. The leather collar of Colonel Winfield, Chet's dearly departed beagle, is buckled around her desk lamp. A framed photo of their mother playing in the garden with four-year-old Chet sits on her nightstand. Graham was an infant when their mother died. Unlike Chet, he has no true memory of her. Next to the sterling frame is the old rosewood metronome.

When the children were young, Lilah wanted Marjorie to play the piano, but she was hopeless. Instead of putting her hands on the piano keyboard, Marjorie insisted the ivory keys felt better upon her bare feet. When adults weren't around, they'd position a chair at the end of the piano to see who could dash across the narrow keys barefoot without falling off. Chet would set the metronome and time them, titling the cacophony of each run.

"*Allegro Digitorum Pedum*. Three seconds for Marjie!" she'd shout. "*Cadenza Crawl.* Five-second disaster for Graham."

Chet hated the piano but loved the metronome. She still does. Graham often hears it swinging behind her closed door but can't figure out what particular situations call her to use it.

"So, what have you decided about Hank, the cub reporter?" asks Chet.

"I've decided he's a pain in the ass. Like I said last night, this could throw a wrench into everything."

"That's an understatement. I tossed and turned all night. What does this guy have on Bonafante—and what about Marjorie? Is this a huge mistake? We should check on her. The last thing we need is our sister's picture in the paper."

"I know. Imagine Dad's reaction. I had an idea. What if we contact this Hank fella, give him fake names, but tell him we know Grosse Pointe and that we might be able to exchange some mutually beneficial information.

We arrange a meetup, give him shite for info, but shake him out and see what he knows."

"Fake names? Because a gent from Grosse Pointe with an eye patch is so incognito. I have another idea," says Chet. "Despite his abhorrence for the media, Gramps is the one who pulled a favor at the *Times* to get the job in the obituary department. He knows people there."

"He also knows Bonafante."

"Exactly. Gramps might like to know that some reporter is sniffing around about people from Grosse Pointe."

"That's a good idea. Gramps won't get directly involved, but he'll have someone from his side check it out."

"And in the meantime, we check on Marjorie. Tell her not to talk to anyone, or Lilah might find out she's at the residency."

"I'll stop by," says Graham, rising from the bed. "After I pick up our check at the paper."

"A check you will promptly sign over to me, since you lost the bet. And while you're there, pick up the next assignment."

"You don't want to do that? Fight the boss to feature some mass murderer like Kehoe, who sprinkles his victims with jewels around a milk cart?"

"I'm going to be late." Chet grabs her purse and heads toward the door.

"Say hi to your mortician," smiles Graham. "And, hey—ask if he can embalm Myrtle Branley."

Chet laughs. "Anything for you, dear brother."

17

SMALL REMNANTS

Marjorie stands, frozen, staring at Bonafante's car.

How long has he been here? She considers placing a hand on the hood to determine but quickly remembers her hair and how she's dressed. Chatting with Charles Bonafante in a simple day dress? No, that will not do.

Marjorie runs back to her apartment, unlocks and locks the door. She applies her makeup with a full complement of rose lipstick. She brought such minimal clothing—what should she wear? She certainly can't overdress. There's nothing worse than a woman who's trying too hard with her wardrobe. Better to be underdressed and avant-garde than overdressed. Marjorie opts for a simple crêpe de chine dress. She wets and combs her bobbed hair and finishes the look with a white bandeau headwrap, a style made popular by the scandalous tennis star Suzanne Lenglen and her designer, Jean Patou. She's reaching for the ring of keys when a knock sounds at the door.

No. It couldn't be him. Could it? She scurries to the door and then remembers the rules.

"Who is it?" she calls brightly.

"Well done, Miss Marjorie Lennox! It's Dock."

Marjorie releases the breath she was holding. She unlocks and opens the door.

Dock stands, gripping the clipboard just beneath his green bow tie.

"Good day! I'm glad to see that you're awake and looking so sprightly. I commend you for remembering the security rules. But, unfortunately, you have earned your first demerit."

"A demerit?"

"Why, yes. You signed the lease, and the lease stipulates that you have a job. A job you failed to perform this morning."

"You are correct, Dock. I am entirely at fault. But after the playwright behind the red door told me that the building is haunted, I stayed awake in anticipation of meeting a ghost. I made myself some tea and then, when I finally dozed off, I overslept. I'm terribly sorry."

"You drank tea waiting for a ghost." Dock makes a notation on his clipboard.

"Yes, I hope that's okay. The tea was in the cupboard. I assumed that was permitted? Using items in the cupboards wasn't mentioned in the lease. Oh . . . but removing things from the apartment *was* mentioned in the lease. Dock, is drinking tea considered removing it?"

Dock breaks into laughter. "Oh, aren't you delightful, Miss Marjorie Lennox! A true artist. Of course you may use the items in the apartment. We'll discuss your demerit later. Are you ready for your delivery?"

"Delivery?"

"Your supplies. It's important for you to get started right away. The point of the residency is to create!" Dock waves a hand, and two deliverymen in white coveralls appear from the direction of the front door, carrying an ornate wooden cabinet.

Marjorie gasps. "Oh, my goodness, a Singer in tiger oak!"

"You recognize the unit?"

"Of course. The sewing machine is nested inside the cabinet. It's very practical, especially in a small space such as this. When not in use, the top can be closed, and one can use it as a cocktail bar."

"Do you cocktail while sewing, Miss Marjorie Lennox?"

"Not usually. Alcohol and sharp objects can be unpredictable for me. But once Chet and I secretly got tippled and she gashed her knee. We didn't want my mother to know, so I sewed her up. But a medical stitch is quite different from a fashion stitch, isn't it? And I just realized that I failed to ask for champagne, so unless it's in the hamper, we won't have to worry about me getting tippled." Marjorie smiles.

The men stand in the hall, still holding the heavy cabinet.

"Oh, my apologies! Please put the cabinet against the wall beneath the window. A bit of fresh air and street noise might be inspiring while I'm working."

The men enter the apartment, followed by a parade of similarly uniformed men, all carrying armloads of different items.

"Heavens, so many people. And what lovely lamps!" says Marjorie.

"Odeon glass fringe, as you requested." Dock nods, making a tick on his clipboard.

In addition to the lamps, there are two expressively large ferns on podium stands, three ample baskets brimming with brightly colored threads and notions, a worktable, a stack of large sketch pads, a small cream brocade chaise with a detached pillow roll, several gold frames, and a hand-carved mahogany sculpture that features a fainting swan.

"What a lovely swan. Are you sure this is intended for me? I didn't request it."

"Everything is intentional. You mentioned frames for your paper dolls," says Dock. "Did you bring paper dolls?"

"No, I create the dolls when I'm birthing a new design. Oh, Dock, I forgot to request cardstock to make the dolls."

"We assumed you might need it. It's in the stack with the sketch pads."

"We?" says Marjorie.

"Yes. But the lifelike human made of wax that you requested, that will take a few more days."

The two men lift the sewing machine, while another unfurls a white rabbit rug to place beneath it. The string of deliverymen march out the door as quickly as they entered.

"Well, I believe that's everything. I'll leave you to get settled."

"How wonderful. But I do beg your pardon—what about the fabric?" asks Marjorie.

"What about it?" Dock points to a rumpled paper sack on the floor. "It's in the bag."

Marjorie walks to the lonely bag and peeks inside. "Oh, I'm sure it's lovely, and I don't mean to sound ungrateful, but these are small remnants." She removes a bundle of rolled fabric. "I was rather hoping for larger bolts?"

Dock backs away toward the door. “I’ll see what I can do. In the meantime, happy creating!” He smiles and shuts the door.

Marjorie stands, holding a small roll of fabric.

“Miss Marjorie Lennox!” calls Dock from the hallway.

“Oh, yes, yes.” Marjorie runs and locks the door.

“There we are. Happy creating!” sings Dock.

18

A MONOGRAM

Marjorie sits at the enamel table with a pad of paper and five small rolls of fabric stacked before her.

The five fabrics are all beautiful, but there's only a half yard of each. She recognizes a viridian Bianchini silk from a recent issue of *Vogue* and a piece of knitted jersey that has to be Rodier of Paris. In addition, there are pieces of canvas, satin, and linen. And suddenly, a thought occurs to her. Beautiful things don't have to be large. Sometimes it's the small gestures that make all the difference. Inspiration cascades over her, and she immediately has a direction for the remnants. Her pencil moves and she's lost to her designs.

The steady tick-tock of the wall clock marches on, but the time it keeps is now nothing but static stirred with noise from the Detroit streets. How much time does she have until evening? She's so immersed that she doesn't hear the voice addressing her.

"I'll try that again. Hello in there!"

Marjorie looks up from the sewing machine to find her brother at her window.

"Graham! I'm sorry. I didn't hear you."

"Clearly. You were jockeying that machine so fast it looked like you were at the track."

"I'm just so inspired. I'm trying to meet the challenge of the residency."

"Shouldn't you pull your curtain? I could see right in. And what's going on in your apartment? It looks more crowded than yesterday."

"Indeed. My deliveries arrived. But when I sat with the fabrics, a fountain of inspiration bubbled over and I set to work right away. I'll have time to arrange the room later." Marjorie's posture tightens. "Is everything okay? I didn't expect you here."

"Yeah, yeah. All's swell. But after leaving yesterday I started to worry about you, and since I was nearby at the newspaper, I thought I'd check in. Everything okay?"

"How very considerate of you, Graham. Everything is fine. A little peculiar, but of course you know I love that."

"Oh, really. What's peculiar?"

"Well, four artistic women all pursuing our creative passions. It's quite exciting. And yesterday one of the women informed me that the building is haunted."

"What?"

"Oh, just some odd noises. Knocks and groans."

"Could be the plumbing. Do you feel safe?"

"Entirely. Oh, Graham, please don't worry."

"Well, you know I do. And say, Chet heard that the paper's got a reporter sniffing around Bonafante and his ventures. Obviously Bonafante isn't here, but be careful. Don't speak to anyone. The last thing we want is your picture showing up in the paper. Imagine the family's reaction. Lilah thinks you're at the cottage. If she discovered the truth, she might haul you home."

Marjorie nods slowly. Yes, her mother would be livid to discover she lied and escaped to the residency without permission. Her father might revisit his convent scheme. And Graham is so overprotective, he might become concerned if she mentioned that Bonafante lives upstairs and that she signed a lease. She clears her throat.

"You have nothing to worry about, dear brother. As you can see, I'm tucked in this nest of an apartment, working diligently, and speaking to no one. But tell me, why is a reporter so curious about Bonafante?"

Graham laughs. "Well, aren't we all a little curious about Bonafante?

Maybe the reporter heard talk of the residency program and wants to write about it."

Oh, dear, thinks Marjorie. People in Grosse Pointe know about Bonafante, but if a story is written about him or the residency, every woman in Michigan will be chasing him.

"How are things at home?" she asks.

"Fine. Helen Hardwick rang for you."

"To apologize for the dress incident?"

"No. She wants to borrow a necklace for a dance at the yacht club."

Marjorie rolls her eyes.

"I told her you were at the cottage. Cecile and Lou came for dinner last night and dropped a bombshell that they're moving to the Detroit Golf Club."

"Oh, how wonderful! A bit of change will do Cecile good. Get her mind off sex and the headaches. Speaking of sex and illness, how is our syphilitic father?"

Graham shakes his head. "Marjie, don't go saying that our dad has syphilis. It's probably just gluttony. Too much rich food and booze."

A knock sounds at Marjorie's door. "Someone's at the door. I should go."

"Who would be knocking at your door? Is it the ghost?"

"Graham, step away from the window."

"Why?"

"I'm not supposed to have visitors."

The knocking sounds, louder.

"Then who the hell's pounding?"

Marjorie steps to the door. "Who is it?" she calls.

"It's the bogeyman. Open the door, darling."

Marjorie recognizes Ivy's voice and opens the door.

Ivy pushes past her without waiting for an invitation. "My, what a dreary pile of an apartment you have. Messy too. Can you believe what was in my afternoon hamper? Maraschino cherries. Bless Dock for trying. Yes, they're red, but they've got nothing to do with Christmas. It's so frustrating." Ivy stamps a foot, then clutches her breasts. "Don't worry, girls, we'll find some tinsel."

Marjorie's eyes shoot toward Graham. Ivy tracks her gaze.

"What's this?" Ivy saunters to the window. "Oh, my, your husband of a brother is here! You naughty girl. Breaking the rules again. Well, hello there, Graham. Do you like big lighthouses?"

"Why, sure. I love big innuendos too."

"Graham, you must leave," says Marjorie. "I have to get back to work."

"Oh, Marjie, you sound like Dock." Ivy leans toward the windowsill. "Come and shop at my window, darling. I'm just across the hall." She blows a kiss and departs. "Don't forget to lock up, Marjorie honey."

"I'm sorry to run you off, Graham, but I really must finish here."

"I'm happy you're content. And I'm proud of you, Marjorie."

"Proud? Why, thank you, Graham. I'm excited to be here. Please give Chet my love. Assure her that I'm following discipline and structure." Marjorie smiles at her brother. "And, Graham, you really have nothing to worry about. I'm completely safe here."

Marjorie locks her door and walks back to sit at the sewing machine. Safe *and* well cared for. That's what she should have told Graham. She runs her palm over the black-and-gold Singer sewing machine. Her hand stops, and for the millionth time she traces her fingers over the letters:

ML

It's a monogram. Her initials. They've been engraved into the Singer.

Dear Coco,

I chose the red dress today.
I feel like wearing red.
But I know I should wear black.

19

ICE BUCKET

Graham pulls down the long gravel drive of Glen Arden and rolls the Packard to a stop in front of the garage. Freddie steps out to greet him and wipe down the car.

"I'm sorry for your loss," says Freddie.

"My loss?"

"Well, your grandmother's loss is yours as well."

Wait.

Gramps? No.

Graham runs from the garage, up the stone steps, and bursts through the doors of Glen Arden. A warble of weeping echoes throughout the shadowy front hall. He bounds down to the sitting room, following the sound. He enters and sees his father, Lilah, Chet, and a cluster of people. He brushes by Slorah and Atchison and spots his inconsolable grandmother.

With Gramps sitting next to her.

There's a tug at his sleeve and Chet pulls him aside.

"What the hell's going on?"

"Poochie died," she whispers.

Poochie. Their grandmother's parakeet. Graham's shoulders sink with relief. "I thought it was Gramps. Who cares about the damn bird."

"Our grandmother cared. And so did I!" says Chet.

"How'd it die?"

"Choked on its own vomit. I warned her, but Granny insisted on feeding it lobster."

"Oh, for Christ's sake."

"Did you see Marjorie?" asks Chet.

"Yes, she was locked up in that hole of an apartment, sewing things. Happy as Horace Dodge in his workshop."

"Did you bring her flowers?"

"No. Why would I bring her flowers?"

"I thought I told you. She always has them in her room. She might become unsettled without flowers, Graham."

"Well, I'm sorry, I didn't think of that. But I did warn her that a reporter is sniffing around about Bonafante. I told her not to say anything and that if her picture somehow wound up in the paper Lilah would know she isn't at the cottage. That seemed to register and concern her." Graham pours himself a slug of whisky from the sideboard. "How was your meeting with the new mortician?"

"Good. He's interesting."

"So that means creepy and disgusting?"

"Maybe to you. He has no sense of smell. Did you know that embalming fluid and formaldehyde destroy your sense of smell? I could have postal breath like Cecile and he'd never know it. We talked about human composting. I had a club sandwich."

"Okay, that's enough."

"Did you stop by the paper?"

"Yes, I got your check." Graham pulls an envelope from his pocket and hands it to Chet. "Don't blow it all on embalming fluid, okay?"

"And the next assignment?"

"Hogan said it's in the envelope."

Their grandfather walks toward them. "Poochie." He throws up a hand. "We normally dip the lobster in butter. Makes it easier for him to swallow. Slorah swears she melted the butter. Atchison says Cecile was here and can confirm the butter was melted. But we found him at the bottom of the cage amidst his own regurgitation. Go get dressed. Your grandmother wants a funeral."

"A funeral? I have friends coming over for a game of doubles."

"Let 'em play with their own balls. Your grandmother needs a family moment."

Chet wraps her arms around their grandfather. "Poor Poochie."

"There, there, lass. It's a tragedy, but he lived a king's life. Better to go by lobster than smashing into a window. That's rough on the glass."

A tragedy? Graham refrains from shaking his head. For all that his grandfather has experienced, for all that he's done and is doing—he doesn't actually care about a parakeet that ate itself to death, does he? The parallels to his father are concerning and hard to ignore.

"Granddad." Graham sets a hand on his grandfather's shoulder. "I know you're trying to console Granny." His voice lowers to a whisper. "But there's something you might want to know. Chet, can you leave us? I'd like to speak to Gramps privately."

Chet releases Gramps from the hug and heads back to the corner of the sitting room.

"What is it?" asks Gramps.

"I was at the newspaper, picking up my check, and I heard something. A guy came into Hogan's office and said that one of their cub reporters says he's onto something big in Grosse Pointe."

Gramps's jaw twitches. "I see. What could he be onto?"

"It wasn't about your situation. He said it's something about Bonafante."

Gramps shakes his head, his mouth tightens. "Godforsaken media . . . Ford's right. They're skunks. Everyone knows what happens when you get close to a skunk—you end up sprayed! Those blasted story grubbers. Well, you tell Hogan that you're sorry, but you can't write death salutes for him anymore."

"Wait, why?"

"It's all getting too close."

"This has nothing to do with Hogan. I just asked for a raise."

"For God's sake, Graham. We don't play games with folks who buy ink by the barrel. We need distance. I know how to handle this."

"I understand your apprehension, but this isn't about us. It's about Bonafante."

"Go get dressed, lad. We've a funeral to attend."

. . .

Graham falls in beside Chet on the way to the back garden near the summerhouse.

Chet lifts the black veil from her hat. "What did Gramps say about the reporter?"

"It didn't quite go as expected. Gramps was livid that the paper was sniffing around Bonafante. I know that telling Gramps about the reporter was your idea, but he was more furious than I anticipated."

"Displacement. He feels bad about Granny losing Poochie, so he's overreacting."

"No. This has nothing to do with Poochie. He despises the newspapers. Hates their probing. He insisted . . ." Graham takes a breath. "Chet, Gramps insisted that I quit the newspaper and the obituaries."

Chet halts mid-stride. "What are you talking about?"

"Just what I said. Gramps won't let me work for Hogan anymore."

"You're not working for Hogan. I am. And I love my job. You're not taking this away from me."

"It's not me. I'm not taking anything. Gramps—"

"Stop! We're not quitting. I won't let you. Do you know what was in that envelope with the check? The Houdini séance assignment. It's officially happening."

"It's not happening." Graham shoots a quick glance toward his family on the lawn. "Chet, you know this is complicated. And now Hogan wants me to work from the office. Gramps doesn't know about our plan."

"And Gramps doesn't know that I'm the one honoring people's lives and legacies. You're lying to Gramps about that, and you'll continue. You keep my secret and I'll continue to keep yours." Chet turns and marches down to the lower lawns, toward the group of family members clustered in black.

Graham walks slowly toward his mourning family as the sun lowers in the late afternoon sky.

His grandparents are there.

His father and Lilah are there.

Atchison and Slorah are there, along with a few of the servants.

Graham can't help but wonder: Is it really Poochie they're mourning, or is this a convenient outlet for everyone to mourn the chaos that is the life of Lennox?

"Graham, hurry on," calls their grandfather.

Graham jogs to the graveside, next to Granny's favorite rosebushes. Granny steadies herself in the grass with her umbrella Napoleon, the other hand balancing a sterling ice bucket.

"What's with the ice?" Graham whispers to his father. "Cocktailing graveside?"

"It's the coffin, you idiot."

Gramps turns to them. "You're the idiot, Duncan."

"Stop!" shrieks Granny. "I will not have you ruining this sacred moment with your arguments. Poochie loved a good Scottish whisky on ice. I've layered his casket bucket so he'll be infused for the deep sleep." Granny begins to whimper and cry. Chet moves and sets an arm around her.

"I just . . . he's been with us for years. How can I put sweet Poochie in a hole and never see him again? No. I can't. *I can't!*" weeps Granny. She thumps Napoleon.

"Would you prefer to embalm him or consult a taxidermist?" asks Chet.

"Oh, my dear girl. You're so compassionate. Yes, that's what we'll do. That way, Poochie will be with us forever."

Chet nods. "Of course. And Graham will write a death notice for the paper."

"Oh, yes!" says their grandmother. "My fortune teller had one for Mario, her blind cat that ran beneath the lawnmower. You did such a lovely job with that obituary, Graham, and I know you'll do the same for Poochie."

Graham stares at Chet. His sister's talents are of endless scale, a symphony of the supernatural.

Their grandmother looks to the ice bucket. "And this service just doesn't feel right. Cecile and Lou aren't here, and neither is Marjorie. Marjorie loved Poochie."

Lilah steps toward their grandmother and extends a hand. "We can delay the service if you want. Duncan has sent word to Cecile and Lou. And I've contacted Marjorie."

Graham and Chet lock eyes.

"I'm sure the telegram has already reached Marjorie at the cottage," says Lilah.

20

THE SCREAMING

Marjorie carefully wraps each item in a sheet of paper from her sketch pad and ties it with a ribbon.

She not only loves sewing, she loves gift-giving. And giving gifts is a wonderful and welcoming way to begin the residency and express her talents with the small remnants. A red satin bandeau headwrap for Ivy, a jersey knit scarf for the playwright, a canvas tool belt for Bernice, and a linen bow tie for Dock. And a special present, for some time in the future.

Marjorie extends her arms, stretching, then pulls her curtains closed. She's spent all day working and her eyes are bleary. The day departed, the light faded, and darkness has dipped over her sewing machine. She'll need to position a lamp there. But now she's finished and the fabric is gone, so she can request more. She takes her keys, exits the apartment, and locks the door. She loops the ribboned bundles over each door handle. She's placing Dock's gift at the top of the stairs when the gray door opens and Bernice appears, cigarettes saluting behind both ears.

"Hello there! Was gonna step out back for a smoke before calling it a night. Care to join me?"

"Yes, that would be lovely!"

Bernice closes and locks her door. She notices the bundle in Marjorie's hands. "Whatcha got there?"

"Just a little gift for you. The fabric provided was too small to make clothing, so instead I got creative and made a gift for everyone. You can open it later."

Bernice snatches the package. "I'll open it right now, thank you very much. I don't get many gifts. This is exciting."

She rips away the ribbon and the paper. "Well, I'll be damned! A real tool belt?" She immediately ties it around her waist.

"Your white jacket is lovely, but this might give you more pockets?"

"That jacket is crap. I swiped it from a cranky druggist. But this is the real deal. Canvas. That's gotta be difficult to sew?"

"Well, I've stitched leather and flesh before, so canvas felt easier."

"Thank you, Marjie, I love it! I just may sleep in it tonight."

"Oh, your happiness makes me so happy," beams Marjorie.

Bernice unbolts the large back door. "I smoke out here. Not safe to light matches around my wood and varnish."

They step outside, and Marjorie's hope deflates. Bonafante's car is gone.

Bernice plops down on a slatted iron bench beneath her apartment window. "They need another light back here. It's kinda dark." She extends a cigarette to Marjorie and lights it for her. Marjorie inhales on the cigarette and exhales a small puff of smoke.

"You're so dainty. You even smoke like a princess."

"Thank you."

Bernice strikes another match and lights her own cigarette. "See that other door? That's his door," she says, pointing along the back wall of the building.

Marjorie walks over to the door. It has the same decorative ironwork as the windows. She peers through and sees a narrow, lighted stairway ascending. She steps back to look at the building. It appears that lights are on throughout the upper floors, but she can't see in the windows. Marjorie returns to the bench and sits down.

"He was here earlier," says Bernice. "He comes and goes, but you know what's strange?"

"What?"

"He arrives and leaves alone. Sometimes there's a dog. He's affectionate with the pup, but I've never heard him speak. So that made me wonder. Think he's mute? Or maybe he's got one of those strange high-pitched voices. You know, a castrato."

"A what?" asks Marjorie.

"A eunuch. A fella who's been castrated."

"Oh, my, no. Why on earth would he be castrated?"

"I read that throughout history, some men who were appointed guardians of women had their stuff cut off. Occupational distraction, I guess. Since Bonafante provides these creative residencies to women, I put the hammer with the nail that maybe he was castrated. He's dead gorgeous, but his voice is shrill and that's why he doesn't speak."

"Bernice!" laughs Marjorie. "That sounds ridiculous. You should be the playwright."

"I know. Too many long nights in a lighthouse, right?"

They both laugh. Marjorie leans back on the bench and looks up at the sky. Even with the city light pollution of Detroit, she can see there are stars. She squints to make them out.

Marjorie tells everyone everything. Why is it, she wonders, that she's not inclined to tell Bernice that she *has* heard Bonafante speak. It was only a few words, but she knows that his voice is rich, certainly indicative that he's still in possession of his parts.

"That old artist beau you mentioned. Are you still pining for him?" asks Bernice.

"Peter? No, I'm not pining, but I was upset for a while. I reached out many times after the incident and he ignored me. I suspect that women aren't his first choice, but we were so compatible on other levels. We were dear friends and I was hurt that he just dropped me. I heard that he's working for a design firm on East Lafayette, near the cemetery. I drove by once but didn't go in. I knew if I did, my father would be furious." Marjorie sighs. "My family's complicated, Bernice."

"Everyone's family is complicated. So, tell me about your family's house. What type of architecture?" Bernice asks.

"Glen Arden? It's Scottish baronial. It was built by my grandparents. They're lovely and very hardworking people."

"And very rich people. Speaking of rich, you said Bonafante has a mansion near yours in Grosse Pointe. What style?"

"French. Château-style."

"Oh, Lord, imagine his chairs. The varnish. Boy, I'd love to pop out and see some of the incredible estates around here. That's the one disadvantage of this residency—not being able to leave. Well, that and the screaming. Did you hear it last night?"

Marjorie turns to look at Bernice. "Screaming? No. I heard some knocking. The playwright slipped a note under my door informing me that the Nightingale is haunted. Do you believe that?"

Bernice doesn't respond. Instead she says, "You met the gal behind the red door?"

"Not exactly. I tried to introduce myself through the doorframe yesterday before I came to see you. When I came back to my apartment, I found the note under the door."

Bernice inhales slowly on her cigarette, silent for a beat. "You sure it was from her?"

"Yes, she referenced my greeting at her door. A haunting—I'm not sure how I feel about that. I might enjoy meeting a ghost, as long as they're cordial. I have questions about their wardrobe. But if the building truly is haunted, maybe it's taking the playwright a while to get comfortable."

Bernice looks at Marjorie. "Wait. Say that again."

"Say what? That it's taking a while to get comfortable?"

Bernice jumps to her feet and begins pacing. "Sitting on that bench—I just had an idea. The banana chair is great, but I've realized that it doesn't suit all body types. Dock looked like a baby in it, and Ivy said she couldn't get comfortable. What if I made a version that's split in two pieces? Still molded wood, but with an opening at the rear that would allow everyone to position their backside where it's comfortable for them. I think I could do it in a couple of simple pieces." Bernice throws her cigarette to the ground and stamps it out. "Sorry to cut this short. I gotta sketch this. Lock up when you come in."

"Of course, go!" says Marjorie.

Bernice disappears through the back door. How wonderful to be among such creative people who have bursts of ideas and inspiration. Yes, an artistic community suits her quite well.

But the screaming that Bernice mentioned—she's from a rural community and probably isn't used to city noise. If there was screaming, Marjorie would have heard it.

Wouldn't she?

21

NO FIRE

Marjorie finishes the last of her cigarette and lies on the bench, staring at the square patch of dark sky above her.

Beyond the bench she hears engines, horns, voices, music. At this time of night, the Scots are probably singing at St. Andrew's, while the Irish gather in Corktown. Detroit's quilt of cultures includes German, Jewish, Italian, Polish, Lebanese, Greek, and others. And the city's factory-fired skies hold a myriad of industrial sounds and smells. She pictures the gray smokestacks puffing sooty clouds, the Detroit River aglow beneath the Canadian Club distillery sign, and the lights of Canada blinking less than a mile across the water.

Detroit. The Motor City. What do the stars see if they're looking down upon it all? She visualizes the city as a large set and the people as paper dolls. They're wearing brightly colored suits, ties, scarves, hats with feathers.

The light dims.

"Good evening."

Marjorie jumps. She sits up with a snap. "Hello," she whispers in reply.

Standing before her is Charles Bonafante, framed beneath a halo of weak light. Marjorie can barely breathe. Dark, glistening hair, parted to the side. A pale linen summer suit and a lovely plum tie. He holds a crate of what appears to be champagne.

"I didn't mean to frighten you."

"Oh, I wasn't frightened, just surprised." She stands and attempts to smooth her dress. "I'm Marjorie Lennox."

The side of his mouth lifts, almost a smile. "Yes."

His voice is so quiet, it pulls Marjorie closer. She looks at him. "You're taller than I remember. Which is odd, because I was younger the last time we met. And now I'm probably a bit taller, so you should appear smaller. But you don't. Isn't that interesting?"

The other side of his mouth lifts. Yes, a smile.

"Where did you come from?" she asks.

His brow bends.

"Oh, I'm not asking where you were born; I mean, where did you come from right now? I don't see your car."

"I parked alongside the building."

Marjorie nods, taking in his crisp shirt and silver cuff links peeking out from beneath the beautiful suit jacket.

"It's not safe for you to be alone in the dark."

"I was looking at the stars," says Marjorie. "I love the stars. And I was imagining what they might see if they were looking down at us."

He stares at her. Silent.

Marjorie's heart is suddenly pounding. She can feel it in her ears. And she's absolutely certain he can hear it, or perhaps even see it, thumping beneath her dress. And she's trembling. How embarrassing. She's making a fool of herself, as her father often says, chattering about nothing. And probably earning another demerit. "Well, I guess I should head inside. You have your door"—she points across the back of the building—"and I have mine." Marjorie turns the handle and pulls it open. "I won't forget to lock it."

He nods and walks toward his door. He easily shifts the crate of champagne onto one arm and puts a key in his lock. He opens the door and looks across, waiting for Marjorie to go inside.

"Well, good night," she says.

He nods.

She's about to shut the door when she hears his voice. "Miss Lennox . . ."

She peeks out and looks toward him.

"It's nice to see you again."

Marjorie's chest blooms with heat. "It's nice to see you too. No fire this time."

"No?" he asks. And then the slightest hint of a smile returns to his gorgeous face.

She can't breathe. She positively cannot breathe. "Good night," she manages to squeak.

Marjorie quickly shuts the door and locks it.

22

SOMETHING COLD

Marjorie stands with her back pressed against the door. Her heart is galloping. She feels a bit drunk.

What in the world is wrong with her? She didn't thank him for the residency. She didn't thank him for the supplies. Instead, she chattered a bit of nonsense and then ran away. So juvenile.

And "no fire this time."

Did she really say that? No fire? She was engulfed in flames. Her body lit like a furnace the moment she saw him. She never had that reaction with Peter, not even when he kissed her. And Bonafante's quiet, simple reply. Was he flirting? Of course not. Maybe? Oh, she made a complete hash of it all and came across as a first-class imbecile. Is this the type of silly, enchanted behavior that has sent daughters of other families to medical wards? If so, do people not understand that muddled behaviors might be confusion of the heart, not of the head?

Her mind races. She can remedy this.

Marjorie takes a few steps and stops. She turns and promptly bolts the back door. It's all so new. But she is learning. She dashes toward the green door of her apartment.

The tick-tock of the wall clock swings its steady rhythm. Marjorie barely heard it while she was working, but now it's somehow unsettling. Annoyingly loud, louder than the sinister metronome that Chet uses for God knows what. If Bernice's apartment is bewitched by screams, hers is bewitched by the clock and its ever-present reminder that time is a hunter.

The opportunity is now. She stares at the small bundle on the edge of her sewing-machine cabinet. The fifth special item she made today. The gift.

For Charles Bonafante.

But it's three minutes after nine o'clock. Past curfew. Marjorie paces in front of her sewing machine. The doors will be bolted, but they're always bolted. Surely a quick errand out back wouldn't count as breaking the lease, would it? The curfew just means that they can't leave to go anywhere. Dock said that if they needed air, the limit was thirty minutes. This errand won't take even five minutes. Yes, it should be okay.

Of course, she must find a way to keep the back door open if Dock tries to lock it. She knows that Chet and Graham have a technique using a playing card. But what does she have that she can slide within the door to keep it open and unlocked? Her suitcase is too big. Perhaps one of her fashion magazines? Goodness, the business of a lease is odious. And, as Ivy said, rules really are tedious.

And something else pecks at her. Is what she wrote in her short note to Bonafante acceptable? And, to that end, what's more important—to be acceptable or to be oneself? Oh, she wishes that Chet and Graham were here to comment.

But they're not. She is alone. And she can do this. She takes a breath, closes her eyes, and makes a proclamation, the type that annoys and embarrasses her father:

"Let me be true to my heart, lest I be a traitor to my soul."

Marjorie grabs the gift and the magazine, and heads out the door. She stops, turns around, and grabs her keys.

The rear door is heavy, probably four inches thick. She places the magazine in the bottom of the door to wedge it open a crack. Will that work? Doubtful. Best to hurry. She tiptoes along the back of the building. A smash of glass echoes from down the street, and somewhere in the darkness a dog barks. She quickens her pace. She turns the corner and, beneath a glowing light of the building, she sees it.

Bonafante's car. A Rolls-Royce Silver Ghost Playboy Roadster.

It's elegant, quietly unattainable, just like the man himself. And just like fashion, cars are expressions of style. They have a voice and make a statement. How grateful she is for the designers who were brave enough to insist that there could be more, should be more, than Ford's Model T.

She approaches the car. The long, sleek lines of the lustrous, sterling body mimic Bonafante's own tall frame. Since it's summer, the top is down, with the rich charcoal leather interior freshly oiled and buffed. Should she leave her gift on the seat? But Graham said there are burglars. What if it's stolen? She puts her hand upon the door and gently caresses the handle. It yields with a life of its own. A gasp escapes her lips.

She pauses, considering. An open door is an invitation. She accepts it and slides into the driver's seat of Bonafante's Ghost. The car smells beautiful. A mix of cedarwood aftershave and leathery interior. She runs her hands over the black steering wheel and the front bench. It feels warm, like a body giving off heat. Marjorie lies across the long front seat and sighs, looking up at the sky. Perfection. She could sleep here. But the top is down, which means that Bonafante might soon return. She certainly can't be found in his car.

And then she hears it.

Music.

The beautiful cascade of a harp. It's heavenly. She looks up at the building. There are only two windows on this side of the Nightingale. Both on the second floor. And they're illuminated. Is that where the celestial music is coming from? Is that where Charles Bonafante lives? She feels beautifully, inexplicably at home lying in his car. If only she had a glass of champagne.

But again, rules are on her mind. She sits up and looks around the dash. Where should she leave his gift? Perhaps under the seat? She runs her hand across the floor beneath the bench, and her fingers brush against something cold. She pulls it out and lifts it. It's quite heavy. An automobile component? But as the moonlight splashes across her hand, she sees it's not a car component that she's holding. It's a gun.

23

GLOBE FINIALS

Marjorie's so startled that she nearly drops the revolver. She quickly places it back beneath the seat. She loops her ribboned package over the gear shifter and promptly exits the car.

A loud horn blares in the distance. Marjorie scurries around the building to the back door. Why on earth would an elegant gentleman like Charles Bonafante have a gun in his car? As she approaches the door, she sees the magazine is still in place, wedging it open. She gives a quick sigh of relief, yanks on the door, and smacks right into him.

Dock.

Lips tight. Eyes narrowed. Clipboard clenched in a white-knuckled grip. Long-dried spittle crusts at the edges of his mouth. "Miss Marjorie Lennox. What a disappointment. What a dereliction. Will you be a premature washout?"

Marjorie stands in the doorway, fingers still on the handle. "I . . . I needed a bit of air."

"What you need is to remember that you signed a lease and agreed to obey the rules."

"Yes, if we could speak about that, Dock. Might I have a copy of the document I signed so I can reference it? Just as I was unclear about drinking tea from the cupboard, I'm unclear about some of the details regarding the lease."

"But you signed the lease, acknowledging that you had read and understood all of its contents, including those in fine print. You are now bound by the lease. And you have now earned your second demerit." Dock's anger fades to disappointment. "Oh, I had such high hopes for you, Marjorie Lennox. You're so delightful and struck me as a true creative, not some wayward, fanciful girl who needs disciplining."

Marjorie steps forward, giving Dock no choice but to step back or be pushed over.

"I am creative. And, yes, I am also fanciful. And I'll admit, I'm likely a bit spoiled and sheltered. But I am not wayward, nor do I mean any disrespect. All I'm saying is that I'd like a bit of clarity on some things here."

"Do you have a temper, Miss Marjorie Lennox?"

"What I have is self-respect and frustration, Dock. I'm so excited and grateful to take part in this program. It's a dream. Truly. But there are things I don't understand. If I'm expected to figure them out on my own, I'll inevitably make missteps. And instead of providing demerits, perhaps you could provide some clarity? If I have more information, I can better adhere to the rules and also better support the other women here."

"There, there. Don't upset yourself." Dock retrieves the magazine. He locks and bolts the door and leads Marjorie down the hardwood hallway toward her apartment. "Detroit City is a very dangerous place. We must ensure your safety. And if you cannot obey the rules of the lease, there will be consequences."

They arrive at Marjorie's door. "What sort of consequences?" she asks.

Dock lowers his voice. "Opportunity consequences. Opportunity is not something to be squandered."

"I agree. And with that in mind, might I request an alarm clock to ensure that I'm awake each morning to distribute the papers?"

"I'm afraid not. You have a wall clock to help you keep track of time. You best get some rest in order to be prepared for tomorrow."

"I've used all of the fabric you provided."

"Oh!" quips Dock, readying his clipboard. "You need more supplies?"

"Large bolts of fabric, please. Preferably silks."

"I'll see what I can do. Let us hope you fare better tomorrow. Good night."

Marjorie unlocks her apartment. "Good night, Dock." She shuts the door and locks it.

Oh, my. It's uncomfortable, yet necessary, to stand one's ground. She hopes Dock understands that. But she must not make any more mistakes. She can't. If she does, she'll be sent home and will miss out on opportunities. Once-in-a-lifetime opportunities. A few moments later a knock sounds at the door.

"Who is it?"

"It's Harry Houdini, darling. I'm back from the grave."

Marjorie opens the door to find Ivy standing barefoot in a short, sheer negligee that conceals nothing. She holds a cigarette in one hand and a small alarm clock in the other.

"Here, take it. I'll never use it. I hate the concept of time. And poor you, having to be awake at the crack of dark."

She hands Marjorie the clock. Had she heard their whole conversation?

"Thank you. But I'm not sure if I can accept it. We're not supposed to remove anything from our apartments. Would loaning me the clock be removing it?"

"No, silly. We're just not supposed to remove anything from the building. Don't let Dock rattle you. He's wound too tight. He needs a stiff drink and a good lay. If he put on a Santa suit, I'd give him a sleigh ride he'd never forget."

"Ivy!" gasps Marjorie, shooting a glance toward the basement steps.

Ivy gives a dismissive wave. "They expect me to be crass. I'm an artist. And good for you, speaking your mind to Dock. It helps all of us."

"Might I ask—what is your job here?"

"I have to sweep the front stoop. Bernice has to sweep the back. Boring."

"And what about the playwright?"

"I think she mops the hallway. But she must do it in the middle of the night, because the floors are always shiny in the morning but we never see her. Well, sleep tight, darling."

"Good night, Ivy. Thank you for the reassurance and the clock. And I have to say, now that I see you without clothes and makeup, it's apparent how truly stunning you are. And you're right—red and green would flatter you."

"Of course they would. Just like the gorgeous headwrap you made for me. Thanks, sweetheart." Ivy leaves the apartment, a trail of cigarette ash fluttering behind her.

Marjorie locks the door and heads into the bedroom to place the alarm clock next to her bed. Despite the mishap with Dock, her mission was accomplished. She left her gift in the Ghost, and Charles Bonafante will soon have her personal note and the present she made for him. She suddenly feels giddy and dances around the bedroom. She swings herself from the metal bed frame, and the globe finial comes off in her hand and thuds lightly to the floor.

She reaches down to pick up the large ornamental ball. It's hollow but not empty.

It's stuffed with hundred-dollar bills.

24

TOO RISKY

"Where are you heading so late?" asks their father.

"To pickle our livers," replies Chet.

He nods and raises his crystal tumbler in solidarity. "I'd come with you, but your mother insists I stay home tonight."

"Lilah's not our mother," says Chet. "She's Marjorie's mother. Our mother died, remember?"

"Watch your mouth, young lady." Their father belches, then grimaces.

"Still under the weather, old sport?" asks Graham.

"I'm not under the weather, just gas and the squirts."

"Lovely," says Chet.

"Think it's something you ate? I heard that a virus ran through the entire General Motors executive suite last week."

"Really? Tell Lilah that. She insists it's the Coney dogs from the joint on West Lafayette. Anyway, I'm enjoying the quiet without Marjorie and her godforsaken chatter. It's nice to have her out of the house."

"I miss her," says Graham. "It's too quiet."

"Are you joking? It's finally quiet because we're not worrying about what calamity she might cause. She's bad for business."

"*She's* bad for business?" Graham stares at their father, a man who lies, cheats, steals, uses violence, and extorts others to get what he wants. And he thinks their whimsical sister is bad for business?

"Yeah. Old Man Hardwick ribbed me recently, asking about my youngest, who pretends she's a tree. What the hell does that even mean? Cecile tells me what people say about Marjorie." He belches again. "Say, could Henry Ford be responsible for a virus, or whatever you called it? Maybe he's sabotaging me."

Chet's fingers ball into fists. "You know, Dad, perhaps you have worms."

"Worms?"

"Yes. They're quite invasive," nods Chet.

"Ask the cook to make you some broth. And maybe lay off the booze for a while," says Graham. They exit the room while their father's still speaking.

"Did Ford give me worms?" he calls after them.

Graham steers the Packard northwest down Woodward Avenue, passing the J. L. Hudson store that recently launched a Thanksgiving Day parade. He crosses Gratiot Avenue and sails by Sallan Jewelers. He shakes his head, thinking of his father's comment. Ever since Henry Ford opened his own glass plant, their father has espoused betrayal and conspiracy theories.

Graham looks to Chet. "You're quiet."

"I'm stewing."

"Oh, yeah? What's in the pot?"

"All the things I don't understand about our father. His feud with Gramps, whatever he's concocting with Cecile and Lou, and the fact that he never mentions our mother."

"That was a long time ago."

"You were just an infant, but I remember. It's not something you forget, Graham. When I was at the police station with Marjorie, the officer even mentioned it. Said he was new on the force when our father's first wife died and it was a 'tragic puzzler.' Again, it's not something you forget. But you know what someone did forget? To write an obituary for our dear mother. To honor her life and investigate her death."

Graham looks at the road, unsure what to say. Yes, Chet is telegraphing the importance of her obituary job, but she's also expressing something more nuanced and weighted. She was the one who found their mother. Chet was climbing trees near the edge of the yard and spotted her, splayed at the side of the road, tire tracks across her silk dress. She was a little girl at the time and didn't speak for nearly a year afterward. Each time she'd run away from home, they'd find her at the cemetery, curled up by their mother's grave, clutching her little suitcase.

Whenever Graham tries to speak with Chet about it, she shuts him down or loses control. So he waits for her to bring it up and then treads very carefully.

"Slorah says it was Gramps who wanted our father to remarry quickly," says Chet.

"Sure, he wanted us to have a mother."

"But don't you think it's odd? If what they say is true, Lilah dated Uncle Jamie. Your wife dies, so you steal your younger brother's girlfriend? Isn't that cracked?"

"Gramps says we're crooked and you can't bend a crooked straight."

"Well, he's right about that," sighs Chet. She looks at the road. "At least there's no traffic."

"Of course there's no traffic. Who else would be hoofing to the rural lake region of Oakland County after ten o'clock at night? We pick up the telegram at the cottage and then what?"

"We have to send a telegram back to Lilah," says Chet. "She'll expect a reply from Marjorie. So will Granny."

"We have several schemes, but this particular ruse to protect Marjorie is becoming very time-consuming," says Graham.

"It's temporary. The housewarming party is definitely an opportunity."

"Yeah. I've heard Dad talking about it. Sounds like they're planning a spectacle akin to New Year's Eve. Two hundred people. Fireworks, the whole shebang. Our father has to be plotting something. He seemed too excited about Cecile and Lou moving, and then this party."

"It's a shame about the timing. By the sounds of it, Marjorie would have loved the party."

"Of course Marjorie would have loved the party. She would have sewn outfits for the entire family. But it's too risky," says Graham. "Let's see what Gramps gets on this cub reporter and Bonafante. But I think we're okay. He's slowed down. The poor guy is suffering something awful."

"The poor guy?" scoffs Chet. "Our father? Let's get something straight." Chet grabs the steering wheel and jerks the car to the side of the road.

Graham skids to a stop. He speaks low and slowly. "Calm down. You're not yourself when you get worked up."

Chet's eyes flare. "Of course I'm worked up! I'm worried and so sick of putting up with everything. He's awful. Put a handle on him and he could be one of Granny's umbrellas. What if our sister's life is in danger? We can't let him run over Marjorie." Chet glares at him. "Like he ran over our mother."

"That's your *theory*. You don't have proof."

"There was blood on the windshield! That's not family metaphor. She died on the road, Graham, but the truth doesn't have to."

25

NEAR TOLEDO

The kettle whistles on the hot plate. Today Marjorie will perfect making her own morning coffee.

Who placed the cash in the globe finials of the bed frame, and why? After discovering the money, Marjorie inspected the other globes, and each one was full of a different denomination. More than four hundred dollars in cash. She could buy a Model T with that. Did it belong to the ballerina? Like her mother's secret stash, is it someone's "play fund"? Should she tell Dock, in case one of the previous residents reported it missing?

It's 7:00 A.M. and Marjorie is awake, dressed, and ready. The sounds of morning traffic percolate through the window screen.

But the papers haven't arrived. She paces in front of her worktable with the cup of coffee. Thanks to the shrill drill of Ivy's alarm clock, she woke early. After dressing, she arranged everything in her apartment. She still hates the wall clock and the decrepit rocking chair, but the room looks more interesting now. The ferns, lamps, and the rabbit-fur rug are a strong improvement. And the mahogany fainting swan has captured her particular affection. But it's still so very hot. She should have requested a fan.

She checked the stoop twice, but there were no papers. If the papers aren't at the doorsteps by seven-thirty, she'll get another demerit. She can't afford that. But she has a plan. If the papers don't arrive in time, she'll simply go downstairs to the basement and tell Dock. But at that moment the familiar face appears at her window.

"Oh, good morning, Hank! I was beginning to get worried. I have to distribute the papers by seven-thirty, no later."

"Sorry about that. This route is new for me. I overslept. Now we have something in common, right?" He smiles.

"Indeed. I'll be right out."

Marjorie locks her door and opens the front door.

Hank is now standing across the sidewalk, looking up at the structure. "Beautiful old building, isn't it?" he says. "The Nightingale . . . huh. Lots of character. Love the gas lamps."

"Yes, I do as well."

"And this is Bonafante's place?"

He asks so casually—too casually. The tops of her arms prickle with warning, just as they do when someone asks about her father's first wife.

"Bonafante?" she says innocently. Sweat beads on her neck.

"Yeah, I hear that's who owns this place."

"Oh, I wasn't aware. Who is that?"

Hank stares at her.

"I just arrived," adds Marjorie. "I'm only here temporarily."

"Oh, yeah? Why's that?" asks Hank.

Goodness, why is he asking so many questions? Could this be the reporter that Graham mentioned is sniffing around about Bonafante? She thinks of the gun beneath the seat of his car. There has to be an explanation.

Hank presses her. "Why are you here temporarily?"

"Because . . . I'm moving to Paris," says Marjorie.

"Are you a dancing girl?"

"No. I'm—" She pauses. "A seamstress."

"You don't say. You said you just arrived. Where'd you come in from?"

This young man is definitely the reporter. "From Perrysburg. Near Toledo," she replies.

"Wow. Didn't know Toledo had lookers like you."

"Thank you," says Marjorie. "I'll take those papers from you now. I don't want to be late."

"Yeah, I heard the gal who used to live in your apartment was worried about the same thing. She disappeared. What happened to her?"

Marjorie smiles at Hank. The lie comes out so easily this time.

"I'm told she got married and moved to Canada. Isn't that wonderful? Have a good day, Hank!"

Marjorie shuts the door. She locks it. She pauses, staring down the hallway, holding the stack of papers. Hank said the girl in her apartment disappeared. She looks at her green door.

Could that be true?

Dear Coco,

I cherish your notes.
And your honesty.
Please don't be frightened.
This will all be over soon.

26

SILVER KEY

For the next two days, Marjorie dutifully collects the papers and avoids being seen by Hank. The headlines are intentionally salacious. As Graham said, she doesn't want to become one of them.

Jewels Pinched by Bandits

Night Tide of Rum Crime Rising

Ford Remains Secretive About New Car

Demented Woman Escapes Eloise Asylum

Detroit Heat Wave Claims Lives

She scans the lead stories while standing at the top of the stairs to Dock's basement apartment. Does he have a window or is it terribly dark? She places the newspaper at the top of the stairway and realizes that she's missing one. She looks back, confirming a single newspaper at the three doors and the one for Dock. But that's only four. She doesn't have a paper for Bernice.

The red door opens and Dock emerges from the playwright's apartment. He quickly locks it up. He stoops to retrieve the newspaper and spots Marjorie by the stairs.

"Good morning, Miss Marjorie Lennox."

"Good morning, Dock. I was just dropping the newspapers. But I seem to be one short."

"No, you have the correct amount." He steps forward and hands her the playwright's newspaper. "This is Miss Tessin's."

"Does our playwright no longer want a newspaper?"

"Our playwright is no longer with us."

Marjorie pauses with confusion. "What do you mean?"

"Her lease has ended."

"Ended? She finished her play?"

"In a sense."

Bernice pops her head out the door. "What's news?"

"The playwright's gone. Her lease has ended," says Marjorie.

"I thought I heard some commotion last night," Bernice says.

"I'm hearing commotion right now!" booms Ivy from down the hall. "Unless there are presents under the tree, there's no reason to be awake this early."

Dock adjusts the pencil behind his ear. "Ladies, I am *very* busy this morning."

"Carry on, Dock. We're not keepin' you," says Bernice.

"But where has the playwright gone?" asks Marjorie.

"She's moved on," says Dock. He looks from Bernice to Marjorie. "Well, it's time for all of us to get to work," he says. And with that he heads to the stairway and descends to his apartment.

Bernice walks into the hall in her pajamas. "So, it's curtains for the playwright, huh?"

"We never even got to meet her," says Marjorie.

Ivy pads down the hall in a satin robe and hair rollers, cigarette dangling from the crotch of her fingers. She takes a drag. "Let's look in her apartment."

"Wouldn't that be an invasion of privacy?" asks Bernice.

"No, she's gone. We all want a glimpse into the lives of others, don't we? Voyeurism is natural, darling. Besides, maybe she's got something good inside."

"Dock locked the door," says Marjorie.

"It opens with a silver key," replies Ivy.

Bernice and Marjorie look to her. "How do you know that?"

"Because I'm dutifully curious. We each have a key ring with a gold and silver key. Didn't you wonder what the silver key was for?"

"We did," said Bernice. "But we couldn't figure it out."

"Well, I put that key in every hole I could find. Mine opens Marjorie's door. The playwright's key opened Bernice's door."

"It did?" gasps Bernice.

"Yes, I spied her trying it one night. At least I thought it was her. So, if my key opens Marjorie's door and the playwright's opened your door, your silver key opens her door or my door. Try it, darling."

Bernice steps forward with her silver key. She puts the key in the lock and turns. A click sounds and she opens the door.

"I don't understand," says Marjorie. "Why on earth would our keys open each other's doors?"

"Probably in case of emergency," says Ivy. "Artists are expected to look out for one another. Speaking of, you now have a key to my room. A passkey to adventure, Marjorie."

"I'd prefer that we continue to knock, please," she replies.

"Agreed," says Bernice. She knocks on the playwright's open door. "Hurry," she says, waving them inside. They laugh, scurry into the apartment, and shut the door behind them.

Their laughter ceases. The apartment looks like the spartan male counterpart to Marjorie's. A lonely kitchen with an enamel table; a metal chair behind a scuffed wooden desk holding a typewriter. A large glass ashtray next to a plain black armchair. Ivy saunters through, rifling through things. "Kinda reminds me of the Wayne County police precinct."

Marjorie and Bernice stand, staring across the room. Just as in Bernice's apartment, the windows face the back parking area. But above the desk, pinned to the wall, is a sprawling mosaic of note cards with typewritten words in black ink. Red yarn extends from each, connecting the dozens of cards into a frightening tangle of a web.

"Is that how someone creates a play?" asks Bernice.

"It's how writers track characters and the plot," calls Ivy from the bedroom.

Marjorie looks through the cards. They're names. Statements. Questions. Some just nouns and verbs.

Bernice grabs Marjorie's arm. She points to a card:

A castrato.

They look at each other. The red yarn extends from the card to another that says:

Charles Bonafante.

Marjorie gasps and points to the window. "She was eavesdropping!"

Bernice bursts into laughter. She tumbles into Marjorie, who swats at her to stop but then begins laughing herself. Soon they're both laughing so uncontrollably that they must cling to hold each other up.

Ivy emerges from the bedroom with a bundle of items. "What's so funny?"

Bernice says nothing, just points to the cards.

Ivy steps forward to inspect. She reads aloud in a dramatic stage voice. *"Whittle. Bang. Look here, Mary Jane. Too many long nights in a lighthouse. What a wise guy. Charles Bonafante. A castrato."* Ivy stops and puts a hand to her chest. "Bonafante as a castrato? Oh, my, this is a fun play." She turns to the other women. "I've solved the case, girls." Ivy puts the cigarette in her mouth and pulls a book from beneath her arm. She opens the cover and points to a handwritten name inside. She then displays a small article and reads aloud, expelling a plume of smoke from her nose.

"Georgina Godlin's one-act play, titled Alone, *has received second prize in the Bay City theater competition. Godlin is the daughter of a local shipbuilder and began writing plays as a child during summers."*

"That sounds nice," says Marjorie.

Ivy shrugs. "She was a bore. Never introduced herself. Wasn't even curious about us. It's not even eight A.M. and we're howling with laughter. What's not to love? Let's take her stuff."

"Does she have any gin?" asks Bernice.

"I'd love a saucer for my cup," says Marjorie.

"I want her red door," says Ivy.

27

MISS JOHNSON

The days pass, all without incident or demerit.

And all without a single sighting of Charles Bonafante. Graham stopped by her window to share that Poochie, her grandmother's beloved parakeet, aspirated its own vomit and died. He also informed her that her mother sent a telegram to the cottage, but he and Chet drove out and intercepted it. They replied on her behalf.

How lucky she is to have such wonderful and loving siblings.

Each evening, Marjorie shares a cigarette with Bernice in back of the building, hopeful that Bonafante might return. But he hasn't. They've seen others in and out of his door, always entertainers or delivery staff: a man in a tuxedo, carrying a bouquet of flowers; two gentlemen balancing an ice sculpture of a butterfly; and a string quartet tuning mid-step on the stairs.

"I wish we'd get invited to one of the parties," Marjorie said to Bernice one evening.

"I bet you do." Bernice lowered her voice. "Miss Lennox . . . it's nice to see you again." She grinned and broke into a laugh.

"You were eavesdropping too?"

"I wasn't eavesdropping. It's hotter than Hades and my window was open. The bench is right beneath. And you're right, he's definitely not a castrato."

"Oh, Bernice, stop."

"And he clearly thinks you're a doll—I could hear it in his voice. And yours. So, you got a crush on Bonafante?"

Marjorie shook her head sadly. "No, I don't have a crush."

The word "crush" doesn't begin to describe it. What she has is a complete fascination and infatuation with Bonafante, bordering on the ridiculous. They've seen each other only twice, but each time there was a connection for her. A soul-stirring connection.

"It's probably good that you don't," said Bernice. "You can focus on your work. I love the designs you've shown me so far. They're daring but elegant. Kinda like my chairs."

Marjorie thinks back on the conversation. Daring but elegant. Yes, that's exactly what she'd like her fashion line to be. She now sits at the sewing machine, finishing a dress. The wax mannequin finally arrived, and Marjorie promptly named her Miss Johnson. She's made great use of her already.

This morning she slipped notes under each of the women's doors, inviting them to her apartment to try on some of the samples she's made. She measured them a week ago and unlike Ivy, Bernice is flat-chested, which is perfect for some of the designs in Marjorie's new line of clothing. A knock sounds at her door.

"Who is it?"

"Good afternoon, Miss Marjorie Lennox!" calls Dock.

Marjorie opens the door and sees, instead of Dock's face, a large basket of white roses and a bottle of champagne.

"An unscheduled delivery," says Dock, shuffling into the apartment. He looks for a place to put the basket amidst the chaos.

"Set it on the worktable, please. Next to Miss Johnson."

"You've named your lifelike human made of wax?"

"Why, yes, many designers name their dress forms."

"I see. Well, this is an unscheduled delivery, and unscheduled deliveries are frowned upon. You haven't shared this address with anyone, have you?"

"No. Well, except with my brother. You met Graham the day I arrived. Oh, and Hank the newspaper reporter has the address, of course. But he doesn't know my name."

"Newspaper reporter? You mean the newspaper delivery boy."

"I believe he's a reporter posing as a newsboy. He asks so many questions."

Dock's mouth pinches. "What sort of questions?"

"Questions that require me to fib, Dock. The lease stipulates that I will not speak of this residency to anyone. So I've made up a story that I'm from Perrysburg, on my way to Paris. But I hate lying, so now I just try to avoid him."

Dock removes the clipboard from beneath his arm and begins to scribble.

"But each time he spots me, he asks questions about Mr. Bonafante, and I assure him that I know nothing."

"He's been asking about Mr. Bonafante?"

"Yes, he seems to know that Bonafante owns the building. Speaking of the building, I found the most curious thing in the bed—"

"Has this young man spoken to the other women?"

"I don't know." Marjorie gently picks through the basket. "What a lovely gift! But no note? It must be from my sister Chet. She knows I adore flowers and champagne. And it's chilled. Can I offer you a glass? Oh, but I don't have any stemware. You don't have a set of champagne coupes, do you?"

"No. I don't drink alcohol."

"Are you a Prohibitionist?"

"I'm a health enthusiast. You made the right decision diverting the questions from the newsboy. You won't be troubled by that anymore, Miss Marjorie Lennox."

"Oh, here's the note!" Marjorie opens the small cream envelope and removes a card.

"From your sister?" asks Dock.

Marjorie pauses, staring at the card.

"From your sister?" he repeats.

"Yes," she finally whispers. "From my sister."

28

AT GLENCOE

"Where is everyone?" asks Graham.

"Your grandmother requested that cocktail hour take place in the garden," replies Atchison.

Graham joins his family amidst a tumble of pink hydrangeas on the lawn. Beneath the trees is a glass bar cart on wheels with a full complement of illegal liquor and a new sterling ice bucket. An ornate birdcage has been brought outside and towers next to his grandmother. Inside is Lally, Granny's new, and very slim, parakeet.

"When will Poochie be back from the taxidermist?" asks Graham.

"It could be a year," sighs their grandmother. "Chet informs me that animal artistry is time-consuming."

"The whisky bath complicated things," mutters Chet.

Graham turns to Cecile, who is bejeweled and dressed to the nines. "I'm surprised to see you here," he says, helping himself to a drink. "I thought you'd be at the new house, preparing for the big party tomorrow."

"Dad and Lou are there. They requested I leave. Apparently they want to surprise me."

"A surprise? Will Delphine Dodge jump out of a cake?" asks Granny.

"She'll have to swim her way out of a bottle first," says Gramps.

"I hate surprises," says Chet.

Graham notices Lilah gazing away from the group. "Everything okay with Lilah?"

"Look at her face," says Cecile. "She's black and blue."

"From tennis," adds Chet.

Graham makes his way over to his stepmother. Cecile is right. A large purple knot sprouts from Lilah's forehead. "What happened?"

Lilah takes a generous sip of gin and gives a weak smile. "It's the silliest thing. I hit my head with my own tennis racket. But I've told Cecile not to worry. I have a feathered headwrap that will cover it for the party tomorrow."

"Did you see Dr. Boyce? You might have a concussion."

"Concussions can lead to sleepwalking," says Chet.

"That's a myth," scoffs Cecile. "Lou's had plenty of concussions after fights. He vomits, then sleeps like a baby. Never even has a headache."

"Wow, I bet you're jealous," says Chet.

"Why? I don't have headaches."

The family turns and looks at Cecile.

"What?" she sneers. "Why are you always making up stories about me? I have ringing in my ears. Tinnitus."

Graham sits down in the grass next to his grandfather.

"Good evening, laddie."

"Hello, Gramps. Any updates?"

"The reporter," he whispers. "Bit of a wee complication. He's the son of the chief editor. Desperate to prove himself, and his father's keen to give him the chance."

"But why Bonafante? The guy's never around. He's practically a ghost."

"Bonafante's a man of influence."

"In what way?"

"In a way that makes people nose around. And the poor lad's so bonny, it draws attention."

Poor lad. Graham notes the description. Interesting.

"Do you know him well?" he asks.

"I'm acquainted," says Gramps. "But it's best we keep our distance from all this now."

Graham sees Chet staring him down. She will not lose the job. But is she really going to write an obituary for Poochie the parakeet?

"Well, I had a thought," says Graham. "Keeping our distance might be the obvious thing to do. But what if instead of stepping away, we get closer? If anyone was ever suspicious about the family, they might expect that you'd distance yourself from a newspaper, as you always have, just like you've distanced yourself from the Scottish clubs in Detroit."

"Ach, by now—and at my age—they've bought the story that I prefer to assimilate."

Graham pauses. The secret he shares with his grandfather is entirely different from the secrets he shares with Chet.

"But could it help to have an inside track at the newspaper? The obituaries are a bit removed from the headline news, but being there gave me the tip that someone was sniffing around Grosse Pointe." Graham can practically feel Chet boring holes through him, pleading, insisting, on keeping her job. He tries another angle.

"Think of the Campbells, who were hosted by the MacDonalds at Glencoe. They dined together, sang together, bunked together. And then the Campbells massacred every last one of them. And they could do it because they were close."

His grandfather looks directly at him. "I'll give you the historical reference, but you're cocky to use it on me. What's in this for you?"

"I like having something, anything, that distances me from my father. Something he can't take credit for."

"That's fair enough. I'll think about it."

Graham glances at Chet and raises his one eyebrow. Lilah slumps over and falls headfirst into the grass.

29

POL ROGER

Marjorie arranges the white roses in the largest glass she can find. They're beautiful and deserve a vase, but she doesn't have one. And the champagne—Pol Roger. Very French. Very sublime. And nearly impossible to get in Detroit. Especially amidst Prohibition.

She grasps the small envelope, examining the thick cream bond and the expensive cardstock inside. Just two typewritten words.

THANK YOU.

There are a few possibilities:

* The gift is from Chet. Chet knows she loves flowers, any type of flowers, and will even bring her a fistful of wildflowers from the side of the road. And the *Thank you.* Yes, it could be a *Thank you for being a good sister* message. But the champagne? Unless Chet is mingling with a French undertaker, she would never have access to Pol Roger.

* The gift is from Hank, the newspaper reporter. A guise to impress her, lure her closer for information, or perhaps even get her to secretly let him into the building. An undercover reporter has access to many things, but could an undercover reporter really afford such champagne?

* The gift is from Bonafante. He's thanking her for the present she left in his car. This strikes her as telepathic, because the night she crawled into his car, she felt that all she needed was a glass of champagne. If Bonafante has access to a mannequin from Paris, he would have access to Pol Roger. And the night she saw him, he had a case of champagne. Yes. This makes the most sense—or is she simply hoping that it makes the most sense? But if the gift is from Bonafante, Dock would have known about it. It would not have been an "unscheduled delivery."

And, most important, if the gift is from Bonafante, is he implying that they should drink it together?

Banging sounds at her door. "Hurry up, I'm holding chairs!" calls Bernice.

Marjorie opens the door. "Oh! They're beautiful!"

Bernice extends her arm. "Here. You take this one. The varnish is perfect." Bernice enters the apartment, still wearing her canvas tool belt. "Wow, quite a lair you've got here, Marjie. Will we have room for chairs?"

"Of course. Set them across from Miss Johnson, please."

A flutter of knocks sounds and Marjorie scurries to the door. "Goodness, this is fun!" She opens the door to find Ivy wearing nothing but perfume and red lipstick. She has a newspaper tucked under her arm and extends an empty glass.

"Oh, my. Are you quite alright, Ivy?"

"Oh, I'm jolly, darling. You said we'd be trying on clothes, so I figured I'd save us all time and attend as a blank canvas. It's the painter in me. And I just knew a wealthy gal from Grosse Pointe would be serving cocktails, but these apartments have limited supplies, so I brought my own glass." She saunters past Marjorie, straight toward Bernice and her chair.

Bernice's eyes expand.

Ivy pats her shoulder. "This is an important study, Bernice darling. What everyone *really* wants to know about a chair is how it feels when you sit upon it naked."

"Really?" asks Bernice.

"Of course." Ivy slides onto the molded-wood chair. "Oh, sweetheart, the varnish on this one is perfect against my hind end. Very slippery." Ivy looks at the two women. "What? You're both looking at me like you've never seen a naked woman before."

"Never seen one that looks like you," laughs Bernice. "The loggers up where I live would lose their minds."

"Do they have Santa beards?"

"Hundreds of Kris Kringles."

Ivy closes her eyes and bites her lip.

"Well," says Marjorie, "I thought we'd have a toast before we get started."

"Please!" shouts Ivy.

Marjorie puts the bottle of champagne on her worktable and proceeds to pop the cork.

"Pol Roger," says Bernice, whistling. "Where'd you get that?"

Marjorie smiles. "You're familiar with it?"

"Who, me?" Bernice gives an awkward laugh. "No, um, not at all. Was just reading the name on the label. I prefer the good stuff."

Marjorie pours Bernice a froth of champagne.

Ivy extends her glass. "I don't care if it's Paul, Roger, Peter, or whomever. I'd trade my ovaries for some eggnog. Just pour me a giggle so we can discuss this very pressing and important news." Ivy lifts the newspaper and flutters it.

"You want a blanket?" Bernice asks.

"Does my nudity make you uncomfortable, Bernice?"

"Not uncomfortable, just a bit cold."

"Well, lucky that I made you just the thing," says Marjorie. She grabs a bundle and billows a red satin blanket over Ivy.

"Oh, holy night!" purrs Ivy. "I owe you, Marjie dearest. Anything. Anytime. You name it."

"So what's the big news?" asks Bernice.

Ivy slithers in the red satin throw. It takes a moment for her to compose herself. "Am I the only one who reads the paper that our poor dear Marjie works so valiantly to deliver each morning?"

"It's nothing but heists and car stuff," says Bernice.

"And advertisements for sad skirts at Kern's," nods Marjorie.

Ivy clears her throat. "From today's society page . . ."

> Also on Friday, Mr. and Mrs. Louis Fletcher (née Cecile Lennox) will unveil their new estate in the Detroit Golf Club at a house-warming party that is predicted to rival the Dodge wedding at Rose Terrace. The exclusive and private guest list is reported to number more than two hundred and will include Detroit's most elite families to celebrate the unveiling of a triumphant feat of Albert Kahn's architecture.

Ivy drops the paper and lifts her glass. "Cheers, darling."

"A triumphant feat of architecture?" gasps Bernice.

A party? Exclusive and private, thinks Marjorie. Was Bonafante invited?

"*Née Lennox.* That's your sister. Are you thinking what I'm thinking?" says Ivy.

"Of course!" bellows Bernice. "The chairs. The varnish. I gotta see 'em. I gotta see one of these big estates. Do you think Albert Kahn will actually be there?"

"No. But Graham—Marjorie's handsome husband of a brother—will be there, in all his one-eyed splendor," whispers Ivy.

"Your brother's missing an eye?" asks Bernice.

"Yes," replies Marjorie. "An unfortunate accident with an errant champagne cork. That's why I opened this bottle so carefully. Are we ready to try on the clothes now?"

Ivy shakes her head with dismay. "Did you not hear what I just said, darling? We must go to your family party. The Detroit Golf Club isn't far from here. We can take the streetcar."

"And thanks to you, we'll have some jazzy new outfits to wear," adds Bernice.

The two women hoot with delight.

Marjorie looks at them, confused. "But the lease. We all signed the lease. We can't blatantly disregard the lease . . . can we?"

30

NEW COMPLICATION

Chet, Graham, and Cecile wait outside Lilah's bedroom while the doctor tends to her.

"I hope she's okay. I haven't paid much attention to her since I came home for the summer," says Graham. "I've been more worried about our father."

"Why would you be worried about our father?" snaps Cecile.

"Let's see, maybe because he's a bloated alcoholic who can't catch his breath and is covered in sores that are leaking snot?"

Chet laughs, and without warning, Cecile slaps her across the face. Hard. The crack echoes through the hallway.

Graham grabs Cecile by the arm. "What's wrong with you?"

"What's wrong with me? What's wrong with you! Can't you see that I'm stressed? Something you two can't relate to. I have responsibilities. This party tomorrow night is important. And unlike the two of you, I want to make our father proud." Cecile looks past Graham to Chet. "Well, aren't you going to slap me back?"

Chet stands still, a patch of scarlet blooming across her left cheek. Her reply is barely audible. "Oh, don't worry. I'm going to slap you back."

Cecile swallows, then yanks herself from her brother's grip. "What's going on with this family? You're all deranged."

"We're not the ones assaulting people," says Graham.

The door opens and Dr. Boyce steps out into the hallway. He puts a finger to his lips and closes the door.

"She's alert and stable. She's asked Slorah to remain with her this evening. She needs to rest. That's quite a head wound."

"From a tennis racket," says Chet.

"A tennis racket? Oh, yes," says the doctor.

"Is that what she told you?" asks Graham.

Dr. Boyce changes the subject and turns to Cecile. "How are your headaches, dear?"

"Better. The tablets are helping," says Cecile.

Graham throws up his hands.

"And you, Graham? I'd be happy to take a look at your eye."

"Thank you, but I'd prefer that we focus on Lilah right now. What does she need?"

"I've given her something to reduce the swelling. Where is your father?"

"Yes," asks Graham, with exaggerated concern. "Where on earth is our father when his wife is suffering?"

"He's very busy," says Cecile, "preparing for an event tomorrow."

"Your stepmother mentioned your housewarming party. She insists she must go," says the doctor.

"Yes, she must go," says Cecile. "If she's not there, everyone will be talking about Lilah instead of our new house."

Chet turns to the doctor. "Of course, Lilah's well-being is more important than a party. Head wounds can be fatal. Perhaps it's best if we cancel or postpone the housewarming?"

Cecile's nostrils flare.

"Let's hold off on that decision until tomorrow. I'll return in the morning. In the meantime, you all get some rest too. I can see you're worried, Chet. You have a patch of rosacea on your cheek."

"It's not rosacea," says Chet, staring at Cecile. "My sister likes to pat my cheek." She smiles and swats the air.

"Speaking of sisters, how is Marjorie?" asks the doctor.

"Oh, she's swell," laughs Graham. "You know, in love with everyone and everything."

"Please assure Lilah of that. She seems concerned about Marjorie, and I'd rather she not be fretful right now."

Dr. Boyce heads down the hallway. Cecile trails him, chattering about her infernal headaches and the importance of the party.

Chet's voice is a whisper. "The party. Their stupid party. I don't know about you, Graham, but I can hardly wait." Chet storms off to her room and slams the door.

Graham slides down the wall and slumps on the floor next to Lilah's door. He takes a breath and tries to keep track of all that's living in his brain.

He and Gramps have a secret. Chet doesn't know about their secret.

He has a secret. No one knows his secret.

He and Chet have a secret. No one knows about their secret.

He and Chet are trying to keep Marjorie's residency a secret.

His father is up to something with Lou and Cecile.

Of all the rotten luck, why is a reporter suddenly fishing around? And which secret is he trying to catch?

And now a new complication.

Why is Lilah concerned about Marjorie? Does she not buy the story about the cottage? Did she not believe the response they sent via telegram? Cecile can be a grenade, but he never anticipated any issues with Lilah, always figured she'd be preoccupied with her "tennis outings." But what happened to her head? And was his father involved with the injury?

This is a snag. Marjorie, not Lilah, was supposed to be the problem. He and Chet worried that Marjorie might derail their plan and were delighted for her to be away as the critical days approached. But they may have miscalculated. Although Lilah is self-absorbed, Marjorie is her only child and she cares deeply for her. Of course her absence would be noticed. Lilah has always tried to shelter her daughter, and that's part of the reason Marjorie has such an innocently whimsical yet problematically honest disposition.

He needs to play a card with Lilah, to evaluate where things stand. But it's a dangerous move. He stands, gives a soft knock on the door, and enters. Slorah wears her usual black dress and sits guard next to Lilah's bed. Their whispers cease as he enters.

"Graham. Are you okay, dear?" asks Lilah.

"I'm fine. Just concerned about you. Dr. Boyce said that your head injury is severe."

"I'll be fine tomorrow. You'll see."

Graham takes a breath, ready to deal the hand. "I'm thinking I should go fetch Marjorie. She'd want to be here."

"No," says Lilah instantly. "Marjorie would be overly concerned and draw attention to me, which is entirely unnecessary. I'll be fine by tomorrow and will make sure I'm seen at the housewarming party. You can help me turn about the rooms, making multiple appearances, and I'll go home early. You'll help me, won't you, Graham?"

"Of course."

"Let Cecile and Lou have their big night. There's no need to worry Marjorie, so let's keep her out of this."

"If that's what you want, I agree," nods Graham. "Rest well."

He leaves the room and exhales.

Dear Coco,

Thank you for your idea.
You have so many ideas.
And so much courage.
But the darkness is upon us.

31

MOISTURE RISES

Marjorie lounges on the settee with her sketch pad and a cup of coffee. Morning sunlight glints through the front window. Last night's fittings went well, and she was able to finish the alterations before going to sleep. Now she just needs to design a matching headpiece for her dress.

But why? She can't really be considering going to Cecile's party, can she? It's patently against the rules of the lease. She told the girls that last night.

"Oh, don't be such a wet blanket," complained Ivy. "Shall we tell her, Bernice?"

Bernice looked to the floor.

"Tell me what?"

Ivy smiled. "Let's just say that we may have breached artistic captivity once or twice."

"Well, you, not me," said Bernice.

"But you were the accomplice. So, yes, it's 'we.' Anyway, I can't stand being cooped up here all night. So sometimes I go to Bernice's room."

Marjorie squinted. "But that's okay. Dock said we're free to socialize with one another."

"But we're not free to crawl out of the window," whispered Bernice.

Ivy rolled her eyes. "Bernice's room faces the back. The parking area is dark. I come and go."

"I just handle the window screen," said Bernice, lifting her hands in surrender. "Ivy's the one who put the bench beneath my window. I've never gone anywhere, but . . . I'd definitely bust out to see your family's new mansion. I've been dying to see the digs of some auto barons."

So, Ivy had long broken her oath to the lease. She comes and goes. Goes where?

"But isn't that disrespectful of the opportunity we've been given?" asked Marjorie.

Ivy shrugged. "I can paint all I want at home. I should probably crawl through Daddy's window. I'm sure he misses me."

"Then why are you here?" asked Marjorie.

"Because we thought it might inspire me to paint something on a different topic. I'm a bit focused on Christmas."

"A bit?" laughed Bernice.

"Well, I don't have the opportunity to create and design like this at home," said Marjorie. "I don't have Miss Johnson, for one thing. But you could go without me. Just tell them I learned of the party and extended the invitation to you. I'll give you a note. Besides, the newspaper said there will be two hundred guests. No one will know who was invited."

"Nope. That doesn't feel right," said Bernice. "I won't go unless you do, Marjie. But, man, how I'd love to see that house. I wonder if our program sponsor, Bonafante, will be there." Bernice raised an eyebrow at Marjorie.

"Of course he will," scoffed Ivy. "All the smashingly handsome Valentino sheiks will be there. Aren't you even curious? It's going to be the biggest dish of summer. By the sounds of it, the foyer alone could fit a sixteen-foot Christmas tree."

Bernice rolled her eyes.

Marjorie sits, reflecting on the conversation. Her new friends want to go to the party. But breaking the lease would prove that she can't adhere to discipline and structure, exactly what her father accuses her of. She can't let that happen. She must be successful at the residency, if only to prove to herself that her father is wrong about her.

Bernice said that it didn't feel right. Marjorie agrees. She looks to her lap. So why is she sketching a headband to match a new dress that she could wear to the party? Her charcoal pencil brushes against the page, creating a soft, slippered sound. But she hears something else. A voice.

Girleeee.

The sound is low, eerie, an unsettling singsong call. And then louder.

Girleeee.

She shudders, then sits up. "Who's there?"

Silence.

And then a deep laugh. "Come to the window."

Hank. Marjorie had purposely pulled her curtains, as she didn't want to be subjected to more of his queries.

"You can leave the papers on the stoop."

"I did. But I have a question for you."

Marjorie walks to the window and draws the curtain aside.

Hank's face is nearly pressed against the screen. He maneuvers his head, trying to get a glimpse into Marjorie's apartment.

"You know my name," he says. "But I don't know yours."

Marjorie refrains from rolling her eyes. Instead, she stares at the sewing machine. "Singer," she replies. "My name is Evelyn Singer. What's the news, Hank? I'm quite busy."

"Today's news? Big stuff. They're building an airline depot in Detroit, bandits stole a collection of Cartier from the senator's house, and someone from your building is trying to get me sacked." Hank narrows his gaze.

"Sounds like a very busy morning, indeed," nods Marjorie. She pulls the window curtain tighter around her face.

"You might want to teach your painter neighbor to draw her curtains like you do. She leaves nothing to the imagination. Remind me, what's her name?"

"I don't think I mentioned her name. Thank you for the papers." Marjorie snaps the curtains closed. His voice drifts through the screen.

"Big party tonight. Everyone's talking about it. Glamorous auto crowd meets rumrunner magnates at the unveiling of a new mansion. Want to go with me?"

Marjorie remains silent. Was Hank invited? Or is he crashing to cover it for the paper? Does he know that Cecile is her sister?

"Or maybe you're already going with Bonafante, your handsome landlord? Do you know what he's up to? Why are women disappearing from this building?" asks Hank.

Marjorie grabs her keys and steals to the hallway in her bare feet, leaving Hank speaking at her window. Bonafante won't be at the party. Will he? He never attends parties. She opens the front door, grabs the newspapers, shuts and locks the door.

She drops the newspapers at the doors along the hallway. She pauses at the top of the basement stairs. Dock needs to know about this. All of it. The money in the bed frame, her desire to attend the party, and Hank the reporter. She signed a lease. It's the right thing to do. It's disciplined behavior. The narrow stone steps press a cold silence against her bare feet as she flutters down the stairs to the basement.

Newspaper and keys clutched in her left hand, her right hand slides against the stone wall of the stairway. She didn't anticipate needing a candle. The basement stairwell certainly requires a lamp. How can Dock see where he's going? The temperature dips, but the moisture rises. Detroit is in the midst of a horrible heat wave. How fortunate Dock is to have naturally cooler quarters. Almost cave-like. She reaches the bottom of the stairs and peers around the corner. A glow of amber light curls around the edge of a door.

She approaches and knocks. "Good morning, Dock! I have your paper and some news." Marjorie pushes and peeks around the door. A small, dusty sitting room comes into view beneath the wobbly glow of a weak light hanging from the ceiling. Against the wall are stacks of nondescript boxes, clipboards, and bottles.

Dock appears from a door at the back of the sitting room. The wisps of his side hair are electrified, his shirtsleeves rolled at the elbow.

"Miss Marjorie Lennox. Is everything okay?"

"Yes, I have some information."

"I see. Unfortunately, I'm very busy at present." Dock absently swipes at his arm and what appears to be blood.

"Are you injured, Dock?"

"No, I'm just very busy. You may leave the paper."

"But I have information: I've found money in my apartment; my family is hosting a gathering that I'd like to attend; and Hank the newspaper reporter has been loitering at my window, asking about Mr. Bonafante."

The mention of Bonafante snaps Dock to attention.

"That newspaper boy—I was specific in my request. He should not be here."

"Well, he was. And he mentioned that someone was trying to get him sacked. He sounded a bit accusatory. And he seems to have a distinct curiosity about Mr. Bonafante."

Dock appears out of sorts, more than flustered.

"Are you quite alright, Dock? Have you heard all that I've said? I'd really like to go."

"Yes, yes. You may go."

"Oh! Thank you ever so much!" Dock flaps a dismissive wave at her and disappears once again through the door of the small sitting room. She hears the turn of the door lock.

You may go. That's what Dock had said. That meant to the party, didn't it? The wave of his hand, that didn't represent a "you may go" dismissal, did it?

Chet is the master of interpreting vaguery. Her rule is simple: Always interpret it to your own advantage. Marjorie decides to follow her sister's course. She asked and permission has been granted.

How exciting. She's going to the party.

32

PRETTY PERFECT

"Lilah is injured."

Graham stares at his father in disbelief. "Where have you been? Yes, she's been terribly unwell since yesterday. It's a serious head wound."

"From tennis," says Chet.

Their father reclines on the sofa, cradling a glass of whisky. "I've been with Lou, preparing for the party tonight."

"You're joining decorating committees now?" asks Chet.

"Well, I wasn't feeling great, so I decided to spend the night at their place."

Graham adjusts his eye patch. "Still not feeling well? Maybe you and Lilah should skip the housewarming."

"Hell no. We both have to be there. Graham, your pals from *The Detroit Times* called my office. They're sending a couple of reporters to the party."

"Reporters?" asks Chet.

"Yeah, one from the society page and some cub who begged to cover the event for the automotive news."

"I'm not sure we should allow press into the party," says Graham. "Gramps wouldn't like it."

"You think I care? I'm the boss of the company now. Things are going to be different. Look here, we'll each drive a different vehicle and park them all in the driveway, like an auto parade for Lennox windshields. I need my personal genius front and center for everyone to see." An audible gurgle comes from his stomach. "Oh, man."

"Take an extra pair of trousers," says Chet.

"Good idea," their father replies.

"But what about Lilah? Did you see her head? She's black and blue," says Graham. "It's not safe for her. And everyone will know something's wrong."

"The doctor cleared her to go, as long as she doesn't dance. She says she can cover it with makeup and some sort of headdress. And I came up with an idea . . ."

Graham braces himself.

"We'll have Slorah and Atchison dress in party clothes. They'll pretend they're a couple but will watch Lilah. If she looks unwell, they'll usher her out to Freddie and one of the cars."

"Slorah in party clothes?" laughs Chet. "That's your plan? The grim reaper in a flapper dress? What if they don't want to go to the party?"

"I pay them. They do what I want."

"Technically, Gramps pays them," says Graham. "Household staff is on his payroll."

"Well, do you have a better idea?" their father demands.

"Yes. Postpone the party until you both feel better," says Chet. "Your health is too important."

"This party is too important."

"Dad, just tell us," says Graham. "What's really going on here? What's the actual point of this party? If you tell us, we can support you."

"What do you mean?" he says unconvincingly. "It's just good timing. Perfect summer weather. A great guest list. I want to support Cecile and Lou."

"It's not good timing," Graham says. "Marjorie's not even here."

"Thank God," says their father. "Marjorie tries to steal attention. This is Cecile's night."

"Marjorie doesn't steal anything. Why do you hate her so much?" demands Chet. "What has she ever done to you?"

"She's a liability and an embarrassment!" roars their father. "Walking barefoot, reciting poetic bullshit, touching everyone's clothes, and asking the stupidest questions, like she's got a screw loose."

"Just like her mother?"

The question floats from behind. They turn to see Lilah, standing in a silk robe in the doorway, forehead bruised like a rotten apple. Slorah lurks in the shadows behind her.

"Oh, how are you feeling?" asks their father.

"At this moment? Like I wish *you'd* die of a head wound, Duncan."

"Don't blame me because you whacked yourself with a tennis racket."

"I don't blame you. I blame myself. For everything. So don't blame Marjorie. Don't you dare blame Marjorie!" yells Lilah. She turns and leaves.

Their father heaves a sigh. "See? Just the mention of Marjorie causes problems."

"You caused the problems!" says Graham. "You blamed Marjorie for being mentioned in the paper when Peter Howell was questioned about the jewel heist."

"Poor Peter," says Chet.

"Oh, don't 'poor Peter' me," says their father. "They're all bananas."

"What do you expect? They're artists!" says Chet.

"And what the hell does that mean?" he demands.

"You know—they're authentic spirits," shrugs Graham.

Their father roars with laughter. "Authentic spirits? Is that what I'm paying for at Yale? For you to become an authentic spirit? Jeez, you need to read a page from the book of reality. While you were off being authentic, Billy Durant's kid was sequestered up in Roscommon, creating the Detroit Special."

"You want Graham to be a race-car driver and a playboy?" says Chet.

"Why not?"

Graham shakes his head.

His father takes a slug of his drink and points at Graham. "Don't scoff at me. You're so thick. I hear you praising Chevrolet. Chevrolet will be dead in ten years, but Packard will be around a century from now. You're about as sharp as a butter knife."

"Maybe," says Graham. "Maybe I'm daft to think that slow and steady wins the race. Genuine relationships win the race. Respect wins the race."

"Stop talking stupid."

"I'm not talking stupid. And I'm worried about you. This illness seems to be lingering."

Their father sighs and shifts on the sofa. "I'm fine. Dr. Boyce gave me a charcoal compound that's supposed to dam all this up. Wonder how long it will take." He suddenly rises and hurries from the room.

Graham slowly lowers himself into a chair. He sits, silent, for several moments. "Hundreds of people, dancing, fireworks."

"And the press," whispers Chet. "Second thoughts?"

"No. Not yet." His voice quiets. "Were we convincing?"

"Very. It all felt pretty perfect."

Graham nods. "I know I complained about Marjorie's ruse being time-consuming, but after Dad's rant all I can think is—thank God she won't be at the party."

33

SMELLS TOO

Distant sounds of the city drift through Bernice's window. "Thank you for helping, Marjie. I've never worn a dress quite like this."

"Don't give it a second thought, Bernice! Designers love to dress their models."

Bernice runs her hands down the golden dress. "I do feel like a model. It's beautiful. But comfortable."

"I chose a blond gold for you. Like the finish on your beautiful chairs," says Marjorie. "Just think of it as living within a sparkling golden forest tonight."

"That's a nice thought. You're always so sweet. How's my hair looking?"

"Exquisite. Your brown hair is stunning with this gilded fabric." Marjorie leans over Bernice, designing her hair. Unlike most women, who now had bobbed styles, Bernice has long hair and no desire to cut it. So Marjorie has pulled it back into a flowering chignon, wrapped with a white ostrich-feather headband.

"Do I have to wear makeup?" asks Bernice.

"Not if you don't want to."

Bernice shrugs.

"Maybe just a dot of color on your cheeks and lips? To give you a healthy glow."

Marjorie reaches for her purse and her compact.

Bernice looks at Marjorie's opalescent dress, which dances as she moves.

"You always have a rosy glow. But I figure that comes from the inside, not from makeup?"

"What a lovely thing to say, Bernice! And thank you again for building the ladder. It will make it easier for us to get in and out of the window and to the taxi."

"Isn't a taxi expensive? I thought Ivy mentioned a streetcar."

"Yes, a taxi's more expensive, but actually, I wanted to tell you something." Marjorie turns to face Bernice. "It's the oddest thing. I found money in my apartment. More than four hundred dollars was hidden in the bed frame."

"Holy cow! What a payday!"

"Well, I tried to speak with Dock about it, but he said he was too busy. But what if the money belongs to the ballerina or someone from a prior residency? What if they need it?"

"You don't leave dough like that behind. Unless it's stolen."

Marjorie thinks of the ballerina and the playwright. Did they leave—or disappear, like Hank claims?

"I'm tellin' ya, something's odd about this building," says Bernice. "Strange sounds wake me up in the middle of the night. Smells too. But I haven't found any money. I scoured the apartment when I got here. All I found was a big knife and a matchbox full of toenail clippings."

"How repulsive. Is that some sort of artistic statement?"

"Dunno. Let's ask Ivy. So, are you almost done?"

"Yes, I think we're ready for the mirror. This is so exciting!" Marjorie covers Bernice's eyes and scoots her over to a full-length mirror. "Ta-da!" she exclaims, removing her hands.

Bernice stares at her reflection in the mirror. She says nothing. Her hand lifts, softly touching her face, as if to make sure it's real. Her lips part and, without warning, a single tear drops from her eye. "Thank you, Marjorie," she whispers.

Marjorie smiles, quietly moved by Bernice's emotion. She wraps an arm around her.

"I have to confess something," whispers Bernice. "I wasn't honest with you. I'm familiar with Pol Roger champagne."

"Oh?" smiles Marjorie.

Bernice nods.

"But I never felt like I deserved it." She gives a weak shrug. "I'll probably end up with an old logger or a miner. And sometimes that makes me sad. But right now, at this moment"—Bernice sniffs back tears—"I look so good, I think I could bag a duke."

They stand together, gazing in the mirror. Bernice is radiant in her deep gold with ostrich feathers. And Marjorie in her opal silk looks iridescent, with light shimmering off her dress and its overlay of sparkling organza. Instead of a flashy headpiece, she wears a single narrow band of small pearls.

Marjorie gently wipes the tear from Bernice's cheek. "I wasn't quite honest with you either," she says. She takes a breath and squares her shoulders. "I told you I don't have a crush on Bonafante."

"You don't," says Bernice. "You're in love with him."

Marjorie nods silently. Now she's the one who's crying. "For years," she whispers. "But, Bernice, it's more than an infatuation—though how is that possible? I feel like I know him, but of course I don't really know him."

"Maybe it's written in the stars."

"Oh, goodness," sighs Marjorie. "It feels so good to tell someone. Feels so wonderful to have a friend. How I wish we had some Pol Roger for a toast right now."

"Want to smell my new varnish? It's really gorgeous."

She wraps her arms around Bernice for a hug, just as a booming sounds at the door. They part, and Bernice scurries to the door and whips it open.

Ivy, wrapped in green satin, waltzes into the apartment. She extends her arms dramatically, and scalloped fabric hangs like branches. "It's the most marvelous hidden Christmas tree, darling. I might never take it off!"

"I'm so glad you like it. I didn't have time for ornate beading or flapper tunics, so I added a few rhinestones."

"It's divine. Speaking of divine: Bernice, you golden goddess. You're stunning!"

Bernice smiles, awkward beneath Ivy's compliment. "Aw, thanks. Say, Ivy, Marjie and I wanted to know something. How would you interpret toenail clippings in a matchbox?"

"As a metaphor, of course. Growth in captivity. Marjorie, I saw Dock at your door. I told him we're having a fashion show but not to intrude, as we might be undressing."

A knock sounds at the door. Ivy rolls her eyes.

Bernice jogs over to open the door. "Hiya, Dock."

Dock takes a step back, shocked by Bernice's appearance.

"What do you think of Marjorie's creation?" she asks.

"Impressive. Very inventive indeed. Transformative, in fact." He quickly makes a notation on his clipboard. "I'm so happy that you're making the most of your creative time here, but I'm afraid I can't stay for the fashion show this evening. Miss Marjorie Lennox, might I have a private word with you in the hallway?"

Marjorie's stomach plunges. She steps out into the hallway and closes the door.

"Yes, Dock?"

"Well, you see, in reflecting upon our earlier conversation, I realized that I made an error."

Marjorie nods. The party. Dock won't let her go. "I understand."

"You do? That's very gracious. It's only because I was so busy. But I do love it and am most grateful." Dock tugs proudly at the ends of his bow tie.

"Oh, the tie I made for you! Yes, you're most welcome. It looks quite dashing."

"I didn't want you to think me ungrateful. And in the future, don't ever bring the newspaper down to the basement, or you'll get another demerit. Leave it at the top of the stairs. The staircases are off-limits, as outlined in the lease. Well, you girls have a lovely time playing dress-up."

Marjorie smiles. "Oh, we will. Thank you, Dock. Have a good evening."

She watches Dock walk away. When he reaches the stairs, Marjorie slips back into Bernice's apartment and closes the door. Ivy's already halfway out the window.

34

TO DEBAUCH

The evening air blooms with the fertile scents of summer. There's no mistaking the house. It's lit up like a carnival and surrounded by endless rows of cars, parked three and four deep. Marjorie notes several of the family's vehicles positioned in choreographed sequence in front of the house, windshields gleaming on display. She scans the property for the Silver Ghost, but, as she expected, it's nowhere to be seen.

A tall line of flaming torches blazes a path down the drive, while a jazz band's rendition of "Sweet Georgia Brown" floats out onto the grass. Guests spill from the open arched doors onto the stone steps to congregate beneath the portico, cocktailing and dancing in the driveway.

"Wait," says Bernice. "I know this house. I saw it in *Michigan Architect and Engineer*. It's not Albert Kahn's. John Case was the architect. It's traditional English architecture." She points. "Natural stone, steep-pitched roof, lots of diamond mullioned windows."

"And lots of merrymakers," says Ivy. "It's perfect that we arrived late. Everyone's half in the bag. Oh, Marjie darling, I do wish you would have sewn me an eye patch to go with the dress. I want to impress your handsome husband of a brother."

Marjorie stops abruptly at the end of the drive.

"What's wrong?" asks Bernice.

"In my excitement to finish the dresses and get to the party, I forgot to come up with an excuse."

"You mean a plan? I thought the plan was to be quick and crawl back through my window," says Bernice.

Ivy begins to shimmy and dance in the drive. "Well, don't wait for me. I'm advising you both that I fully plan to debauch or be debauched. I might not come back for several hours. Maybe a day. Don't be concerned. Just put my newspaper and hampers in your room. Cover for me."

"No, I'm referring to my family. My parents have no idea that I'm taking part in the residency. They think I'm at the cottage. Graham didn't mention the party and I haven't told my siblings that I'll be attending. They've gone to great lengths to help me with my cover story, and I don't want them to get into trouble. It's probably best if I stay outside, mingling and blending with the others."

"Ha!" laughs Bernice. "You blend with nothing. You look like a little snow angel in that pearl outfit. All you need is wings."

"Bernice is right. You're jaw-droppingly gorgeous tonight, like a seductive fairy bride," says Ivy. "You'll turn every head. Wasn't that the point of these dresses?"

"Of course it's the point," says Bernice. "Daring and elegant. We're models for Marjorie, and we're going to make a statement for her line of dresses." She points a finger. "M. J. Lennox. That's what we'll call you. An air of mystery. People won't know if you're a man or a woman."

"It worked for Currer Bell," shrugs Ivy.

Marjorie looks to the broad stone manor pulsing with lights, guests, music, and laughter. Oh, how she'd love to see Chet and give her dear mother a kiss. But after all the trouble her siblings are going to, she'd be crushed to complicate things for them.

"No, it's too risky. You go in and I'll look through the windows."

"Ooh, Peeping Tom. Daddy likes to play that game," says Ivy. "Did you know that term originated with Lady Godiva? When she rode through the streets naked, all the men averted their eyes, except a man named Tom. Tom sounds like my type. I'm getting bored out here, darlings. Are we going inside?"

"I don't want to go without you, Marjie. In Copper Country we never leave someone alone in the woods. We always go in pairs."

"I'll be fine."

Bernice hesitates. "Well, I'll go in and just do a quick turn to see the chairs. I'll come right out, and we can head back to the Nightingale. Give me five minutes."

"Alright, meet me by that big tree at the edge of the yard," says Marjorie.

And with that, Bernice and Ivy scurry toward the house, instantly swallowed by the splash of guests and the dazzling display of music and lights.

Marjorie makes her way toward a front hedge, stepping over empty champagne bottles and orphaned shoes on the lawn. She peeks through a mullioned window.

And loses her breath.

35

PARTY CRASHERS

"So much for guest lists. There must be three hundred people here," Chet says to Graham.

"And quite the eclectic mix. Boxing coaches, the Hiram Walker heirs, even your new embalmer friend. I'm waiting for Edsel Ford to walk in."

"Edsel and Eleanor won't come. They're respectable," says Chet. "But isn't that Harry Bennett, Henry Ford's fixer? Who's he chatting with?"

"A bunch of goons. Legs Laman, serial kidnapper. Joe Adonis, dope king. Lefty Clark, gambling czar."

"Doesn't Lefty have a pet monkey?"

"Yeah, it's over there in the corner!" Graham shakes his head. "That reporter's gonna have a field day."

A couple lumbers by in a drunken dance, slurring along to "Ain't We Got Fun." The woman swings her long strand of pearls, smacking Graham in the face.

"Watch it!" shouts Chet. "You'll take his eye out. Hey, who's the man hovering near Lilah?"

"Ziggy Selbin. A Purple. Cut off a guy's finger because he liked his ring and the guy wouldn't give it to him."

"Cecile invited these criminals into her home? Where is Lou?"

"I haven't seen Lou. I'd wager that half the people here crashed. Speaking of party crashers, I'm surprised Myrtle Branley hasn't sashayed through to disapprove of everything."

"Oh," says Chet, turning to her brother. "I forgot to tell you. She's dead."

Graham spits a mouthful of illegal liquor back into the glass. "What?"

"Myrtle Branley's dead. Suffocated in her steam closet this morning."

"Stop. That's awful."

"It's what you wanted."

"Chet, are you joking?"

"I think you know how serious I am about death. Grosse Pointe police found her this morning."

"Were they responding to a call?"

"We can talk about Myrtle later. It's time someone else exited the party of life."

Graham nods, overwhelmed yet trying to focus. Was Chet joking about Mrs. Branley?

"It's tricky," says Chet. "He's been surrounded by crowds all night. I've watched people drink from the wrong glass this evening."

"It might not take much. He stayed in bed this afternoon. Do you think he knows?"

Chet shrugs. "That he's dying? Maybe." She leans toward her brother to whisper, "But does our father know that we're the ones killing him?" She shakes her head. "He doesn't have a clue."

Graham suddenly stiffens, grabbing Chet's arm. "That woman. The woman in the green dress talking to Lilah. I know her."

"The blond siren?" laughs Chet. "You know her from a sticky dream?"

"I know her from the Nightingale. She's part of Marjorie's residency."

Now Chet stiffens. "What's she doing here? And who's the pretty doll in gold with her? Look at their dresses. Those have to be Marjorie's. Aw, cripes, what's going on?"

Graham and Chet make their way over to Lilah, who's clearly trying to escape, with the help of Slorah and Atchison. Atchison gives Graham a nod as they lead Lilah away. Ivy spots Graham and breaks into a delighted smile.

"So good to see you, Graham darling. How's my favorite Captain

Kidd? I've just met your honey of a stepmother and her very sober companions."

"Yes, I see."

Chet steps forward to face Ivy. "Hello. I'm Graham's sister, Chet."

"Which rhymes with 'threat,' doesn't it?" says Ivy, smiling. "Charmed, I'm sure. This is my friend Bernice. She makes chairs and wanted to see your sister's. But we've decided that her chairs look uncomfortable to sit on naked."

Bernice looks as if she's swallowed the feathers from her headband. "We've heard a lot about you, Chet," whispers Bernice. "Marjorie adores you. She misses you."

"Yes, I miss her too. I long to see her."

"She'll be along any minute now," says Ivy.

"What?" snaps Chet.

"Marjorie's . . . here?" whispers Graham.

"Oh, Graham, I see your one eye has pulled wide with alarm. I'm so curious about the other. Maybe I'll find it in my Christmas stocking. Yes, Marjorie's here. But she prefers to mingle outside. Can someone point us to a bartender and a pair of highballs?"

"Marjorie told us that your parents don't support her residency," says Bernice.

"And your parents support both of yours?" Chet asks the women.

"Parental blessing is overrated, darling."

Graham stares at Ivy, transfixed.

"Graham, I think we should head outside and find our sister before Lilah does."

"I'll come with you," says Bernice.

"Will no one help me with the highballs!" exclaims Ivy.

Ziggy Selbin sidles up to her. "Hiya, doll. Sometimes I've got high balls."

Ivy throws her head back with laughter. "Oh, my, no. You look entirely too swarthy and dangerous, even for a vamp like me. But I'd be fascinated to know, what's on your Christmas list?"

36

WRECKING BALL

Music. Wobbling light. Peals of inebriated laughter. Marjorie stands next to a shrub, observing scenes through the window until the backside of a kissing couple smacks against the glass. She steps away and carefully walks through the front gardens toward the next window.

Her reaction—the feeling of nausea—perplexes her. Marjorie doesn't consider herself a prude. Just the opposite. She believes in revelry and the force of attraction without sexual prejudice. She's eager to explore her own internal furnace. But the scenes through the window were unraveling like a sloppy carnal sideshow—and an aggressive one at that. Drunken groping and a man stumbling around with a stuffed sock hanging from his open fly. A monkey performing lewd gestures with a banana. Aside from Cecile's stunning ruby necklace, nothing is even mildly interesting, certainly not the elegant housewarming reception she had hoped for.

She runs her hand along the window frame. It's a large home, powerfully strong in expression. If the house were an automobile, it would be what's known as an armored car. The gray stone exterior stands vault-like, and the dark paneling and chestnut floors combined with rose brocades give the interior a heavy closeness, like an aging womb or an Italian restaurant. But with Cecile's love of all things libidinous, thinks Marjorie, it might soon be brimming with the squeals of children, which will lighten the atmosphere considerably.

And the people she's observed—goodness, what a motley menagerie! Mostly her father's acquaintances, so it's no wonder she didn't spot her grandparents. But how wonderful that her father gave Slorah and Atchison the night off to attend the party. Slorah's ill-fitting dress is an injustice, but the overlength of sleeve covers her double thumb. Her mother's beaded gown is lovely, but something wasn't quite right with Lilah. Her headwrap must have slipped out of place while dancing. Marjorie could have fixed that for her. Seeing her mother out of sorts makes her regret that she's hiding from her.

But Bernice and Ivy—what an absolute triumph in their dresses. They turned every head. And she's so pleased that they have complete ease of movement in them, especially in such a tight crowd. But they've already lingered too long. They must get back to the Nightingale before anyone realizes they're gone.

Marjorie turns from the window and feels a clutch upon her arm.

"Miss Singer, I thought that was you. Wow, aren't you a knockout."

Marjorie recoils from the grip. "Oh, hello, Hank. I was just leaving."

"I didn't think you gals ever left the building. Bonafante seems to run a tight ship with his harem."

"I don't know what you're talking about."

"Lookers like you seem to congregate at the Nightingale. Changed your mind about the party, did ya? Why's that? And why are you peering in the window instead of going inside?"

"Because . . . I don't know the family. Do you?"

"Not personally, but they're a wrecking ball, from what I hear. Duncan, the father, is a bully of a lush, newly in business with his son-in-law, who's a Purple gangster. Oldest daughter thinks she's royalty, second daughter's a morbid maiden, brother's a vapid Yale dandy, and the youngest daughter, she's the most interesting."

"You've met her?"

"Not yet, but from what I hear, she nearly took down the dynasty."

Marjorie swallows. "Oh, really? How?"

"She's some artist nymph who pals with a bohemian crowd. Word is that her father can't stand her—or her friends. Thinks they're an embarrassment, not to mention a business risk. He's doing his best to get rid of them."

"Get rid of them?"

"Yeah, from what I heard, he fingered one of her chums for the jewel theft at the Institute of Arts and the fella disappeared."

"Peter Howell," whispers Marjorie.

"You know the guy?"

"No . . . I read about it in the paper."

"Well, there's a major war within the family. The grandfather, Cormac, is battling the swine of a son over plans for a new factory. Who knows which way the cards will fall."

"And you're here to investigate the family?"

"Me?" Hank pauses. "Oh, I'm just a newspaper delivery guy."

Marjorie spies Graham approaching with Chet and Bernice.

"Goodness, Hank!" she exclaims loudly. "For a newspaper delivery boy, you certainly have a lot of information. You sound more like a reporter. I'm surprised you're chatting with me instead of speaking with Mr. Bonafante himself."

"He's here?"

"Why, yes," says Marjorie. "I met him just this evening. He's in the backyard now, probably giving his regards before leaving. Perhaps you can catch him."

Hank tears off just as Graham approaches.

Marjorie runs to hug her sister. "Oh, Chet, I've missed you so!"

"I think I've missed you too." Chet pauses, then recovers. "What a little sneak you are, hiding out here. But I can see why. Your dress is beautiful; you would have turned every head and made Cecile insanely jealous."

"Who was that you were speaking with?" asks Graham.

"That's him—Hank! The reporter! Hurry, let's move before he sees me with you. It sounds like he's investigating the family. He said the most horrid things, Graham. And he knows about my ties to the Peter incident."

Bernice stands, eyes wide, unsure what to say. "We . . . should probably get going."

"How did you get here?" Chet asks her.

"We took a taxi."

"Well, that won't do." Graham fishes in his pocket and hands Marjorie a key. "Take the Packard back. I have an extra set of keys. I'll come by and pick it up tomorrow."

"Are you sure, Graham?"

"Yes, I'm sure. It's late. You girls should get going."

"And where did you send our reporter friend Hank?" asks Chet.

"To the back. I told him Bonafante was there."

"Nice to meet you, Bernice," says Chet. She gives Marjorie a quick hug and heads off in pursuit of Hank.

"Ivy wants to stay," says Marjorie. "Will you tell her that we've gone back?"

"Sure," says Graham. "I'll tell her."

"And maybe keep an eye on her," adds Bernice, then clasps a hand to her mouth when she realizes what she's said. "Oh, man, I'm sorry."

"It's fine," laughs Graham. "I'll keep my eye on her." He then shoos the women toward the car.

Marjorie looks back at her brother. Something isn't right. She knows her appearance was a surprise, but Graham and Chet weren't just startled to see her. They seemed deeply alarmed.

Why?

Dear Coco,

Did you hear the voices?
Why is it that family
Who should love us the most
Hurt us the worst?

37

MORAL LARCENIES

Marjorie drives along the dark slip of road, thinking about Chet and Graham's reaction. Also about what Hank said. Her father can't stand her? Yes, he often complains that she chatters too much, but many fathers probably have similar complaints. And Hank's comments about her friend Peter, they don't make sense. Her father was elated when Peter got into trouble, but her father had nothing to do with it. Hank's got the wrong end of the stick.

"You okay?" asks Bernice. "You're awful quiet."

"Oh, Bernice, I do apologize. Like I said before, my family's a bit complicated."

"All families are a mess. Especially the rich ones. Don't let it rattle you. Drive slowly, please. This is the only time I'll see this area, and I want a good gander. You're a solid driver, by the way."

"Well, I started driving quite young with my grandfather. You know, growing up in an automotive family and all."

"Sure. I ran my first wood splitter when I was five."

"I like being behind the wheel, managing my own direction. So, what did you think of Cecile's house and the chairs?"

"I liked the house. But why did they say that Albert Kahn was the architect when he wasn't?"

Marjorie takes a breath. "Albert Kahn is more well known. Again, my family—it's hard to explain, Bernice. They manufacture provenance. Sometimes they tell stories just to draw people in or see what they can get away with. They play wicked games, especially when trying to compete with others. I learned that young." Marjorie thinks of the many games her family has played, each contributing to a grand collection of moral larcenies. "Did you like Cecile's furniture?" she asks Bernice.

"Not so much. Nothing unique, just what's mainstream today. And I find mainstream boring. Is Detroit very different than Grosse Pointe?"

"Yes," replies Marjorie, trying to focus on the road. "Grosse Pointe is quiet. Some would say more refined. I'm not sure if you knew, but Mr. Joseph Berry built a mansion in Grosse Pointe."

Bernice slaps her hands on the dash. She turns to Marjorie in disbelief. "Stop the saws. Stop the saws! Joseph Berry, the late varnish tycoon?"

"Yes. His home—Edgemere—is on Lake Shore Drive."

"I gotta see it. I mean, we're already on this adventure and now we have a vehicle. Of course you understand, right, Marjie? If Erté lived nearby, you'd want to see his place. Is it close?"

"Not close. About six miles."

"But you know the area?"

"Of course. It's where I live."

Bernice falls back against the gray leather seat of the Packard, absorbing the information. "Hey, didn't you say that he has a house there too?"

"Who?"

Bernice gives Marjorie a dubious look. "The French château?"

"Oh, yes. Bonafante also has an estate in Grosse Pointe."

Bernice arrows her fingers toward the road. "Drive on, dear friend."

"Goodness," says Marjorie with concern. "It's nearly midnight. At this point, Ivy might make it back before we do. But I guess a little detour would be okay?"

Marjorie enjoys driving at night. Especially in Grosse Pointe. Sometimes it feels like she could drive forever. It's quiet, free from the noise of the city. And the evening air and soft breeze from Lake St. Clair feel clean and refreshing against her skin, washing away discomfort from the party. Bernice is a delightful passenger. She was so excited to see the estate of Joseph Berry, the varnish tycoon, that she insisted on stepping out of the car and bowing down in the street.

Marjorie tours Bernice by the house of baseball legend Ty Cobb; the estate of Charles Lindbergh's mother; the illustrious Moorings, owned by the Algers; and the estates of Henry Joy and Dodge, and the building site for the future Cotswold manor of Edsel Ford. She even parks the car so they can sneak down Lennox Drive to Glen Arden, her family home.

"It's a dream," gushes Bernice. "It's all a stinkin' dream."

"I agree," says Marjorie. "It is dreamy. Can you see why I feel so passionately inspired here? And it's not the wealth."

"It's the creative expression that the wealthy are playing with. Hell, I'm inspired just seeing the places from the outside. But let's be honest. The Grosse Pointe game is for the rich. Do you think you'd be a fashion designer if you grew up near the docks?"

"I hope so. My grandparents grew up humbly. Their fortune is self-made."

"Yeah, my grandfather made his lumber fortune through hard work. But that's a rare breed these days."

"That hard work, isn't there something beautiful and visionary about that?" asks Marjorie. "This is Windmill Pointe, by the way. Otto, the lighthouse keeper, just retired. I've heard they're trying to install an automated light of some sort."

"I have mixed feelings about that," says Bernice. "We don't have automated lights up north yet, and I don't think I want them."

Marjorie drives along the lakeside road. She pulls onto a patch of grass and turns off the engine.

"Wait," breathes Bernice. She looks out the window and laughs. "You're kidding me."

Marjorie smiles. Bonafante's château spreads out before them in all its splendor. Acres of perfectly manicured grass and sculpted gardens slope down and around the twinkling palatial structure, wrapping to a dock that peeks out the back and extends into Lake St. Clair. Unlike Cecile's new home, which is imposing and solid, Bonafante's beautiful estate is expressive and gentle, like a royal melody.

"He's got his own Eden. It really is a château," says Bernice. "What's that out back?"

"His yacht," says Marjorie. "But no one's ever been on it. He prefers to sail alone."

"Now I understand your confusion," says Bernice. "Why would he spend even one night at the Nightingale when he has this palace? I know you're smitten, but something doesn't add up here."

Marjorie sits, silent. Bernice is right. She hates to admit it, but she can't make sense of it. Bonafante, his secrecy, the Nightingale, the Silver Ghost, the gun, and this silent mansion that no one has ever been inside.

A car approaches, its headlights shining directly through the windshield onto their faces. "Uh-oh," says Bernice. "Is that the cops?"

Marjorie's stomach rises to her throat when the familiar vehicle rolls into view and up to the gates. It's not the cops.

It's the Silver Ghost.

It's Charles Bonafante.

38

THE STILLNESS

Marjorie and Bernice shrink down beneath the dash, trying to remain unseen.

"We're cooked," says Bernice. "Aw, we're cooked now!"

Marjorie attempts to start the car but fumbles in her nervousness. She drops the key and has to reach for it. The steward who opened the gates for Bonafante now approaches the car.

"The gatekeeper, he's coming!" gasps Marjorie.

"Well, it's been nice knowin' ya, Marjie. Thanks for making my dreams come true tonight."

A young man speaks through the open driver's side window.

"Excusez-moi. Little English. Monsieur Bonafante vous invitez à la maison."

"What's he saying?" asks Bernice.

"It's French. He's inviting us inside," whispers Marjorie. "Should we make a getaway?"

"Hell no," says Bernice, throwing open her door. "We could lose our residencies. If we're going home tomorrow, we're making a memory tonight." She exits and slams the door.

"Bernice, wait!"

Bernice leans in the passenger-side window.

"What are we doing?" gasps Marjorie.

"We're going inside the palace of the swanky guy you're in love with."

"Are you sure this is the right thing to do?"

"If you're asking whether it's safe, I'm not entirely sure," says Bernice, adjusting her ostrich headband. "Should we leave a breadcrumb trail for Graham and Chet in case we get murdered? You have anything in the trunk? I'm good with a tire iron. Even better with an ax."

"If we're contemplating weapons, we shouldn't be doing this," says Marjorie, gripping the steering wheel.

Bernice rolls her fingers against the top of the car, thinking. "You know what? I feel okay about this. If the little French guy's the type of muscle Bonafante's got around, I can take care of us."

"Alright. Thank you, Bernice." Marjorie opens a compact and inspects her appearance. She applies a sweep of rose lipstick and exits the car.

"Do I look okay?" whispers Marjorie.

"Like a dream. Really."

They link arms, and their heels echo in the darkness as they walk the long, cobbled drive to the front of the estate.

"Let him speak first," says Bernice. "That way we'll get a sense of what he's thinking and be a step ahead. But I need to know in case it comes up: Are you okay being alone with him?"

Marjorie looks to Bernice. All she's wanted is to be alone with Charles Bonafante. So why is she hesitating?

"We need a plan. In my lumber community, if a gal feels scared around a jack, she closes her fingers around her thumbs. If she feels safe, she clasps her hands together."

"Okay, that sounds good. You do the same."

Marjorie stands in front of the arched double doors. She takes a deep breath and exhales. She reaches for the door knocker, then stops.

"Bernice, look. His door knocker—it's a swallow. A beautiful swallow in flight. How unique!"

"Okay, this is good. Swallows are symbols of homecoming and family."

Marjorie smiles. "And also of loyalty." She grasps the wings of the bird and hits the knocker against the strike pad three times.

She grabs Bernice's hand. Marjorie can feel her pulse in her ears, her temples, even in her ankles. The clang of the steward locking the gate calls out from the darkness behind them.

The double doors part, opening together to reveal a gray-haired gentleman in a black tailcoat.

"Bonsoir, mesdemoiselles."

The women bob in greeting.

"Veuillez me suivre, s'il vous plaît." He gestures for the women to accompany him.

Marjorie's eyes instantly fill with the beauty of the foyer. Unlike Cecile's house, Bonafante's home is light, airy, and elegant. Ivory marble floors glisten with reflections and twinkles from a crystal chandelier overhead. The soaring walls are covered in opal jacquard silk accented with fleurs-de-lis. It's all so beautiful she can imagine a chorus of birds singing. They approach a cascading marble staircase with soft green carpets crawling up and over each step.

"Holy cow," whispers Bernice. "Did we crack up on the road? Is this some kind of heaven?" She stops to touch the willowy cast-iron banister. "Hector Guimard?" she asks.

The man in the tailcoat stops and smiles. "Oui, mademoiselle," he confirms with a nod.

Bernice squeezes Marjorie's hand, hard. "Guimard. Art Nouveau. Designed entrances to the Paris Métro. I might just faint right here."

They pass a room with a long dining table, shrouded in darkness.

"No lights or chandelier in the dining room? That's odd," comments Bernice.

The black tailcoat stops and turns. "Candlelight only. Plus romantique." They follow him and arrive at an alcove off the back of the house. He waves a welcoming arm toward an open door.

Marjorie steps into the room. It's a library. A massive, barrel-ceilinged two-story library, toe to top full of books. There must be thousands of them. Chairs, chaises, desks, and sofas dot the floor, accented by the honey glow of reading lamps. Marjorie squints, taking in the detail, and at the very end of the room, he stands. Bonafante, in a pale linen suit, his back to them, looking out the wall of windows toward the water. A sleek black Doberman sits dutifully by his side and quickly alerts as the women approach.

Marjorie spots their reflection in the windows. Bernice's gaze snaps from side to side, taking stock of everything. Bonafante turns, and Marjorie pulls in a breath. He's stunning.

And he's wearing her tie. The gift she left in his car.

They all stand, silent. Per Bernice's instruction, she and Marjorie say nothing. Bonafante looks from Marjorie to Bernice. The stillness extends. Stretching. Waiting.

"Good evening," he finally says.

Marjorie exhales, releasing the rush of breath she was holding. "Good evening."

Bernice takes a step forward. "Hello. I'm Bernice Tessin." She points to a chair. "And that's Émile Gallé. But holy smokes." Her voice drops to a whisper as she points to a glass side table. "Who is that?"

"Eileen Gray," says Bonafante. "It's a prototype."

"Eileen. A woman?"

He nods.

"A woman!" exclaims Bernice, running and kneeling at the small glass table to inspect it.

Bonafante watches as Bernice becomes transfixed by the table. His eyes shift to Marjorie, who is staring at him. He smiles.

"How are you, Miss Lennox?"

"I'm well, thank you."

Silence returns as their exchanged gaze intensifies. His head slowly cocks in query. "And may I ask how you both came to be here?"

"Well, that cat's out of the bag, isn't it," says Bernice. "We broke the lease. But it's not Marjorie's fault. We saw in the society page that her sister was having a housewarming, and we begged—no, insisted—that Marjorie take us."

"I see."

Marjorie wrings her hands. "I spoke to Dock about it and requested permission. But in all honesty, when Dock said, 'You may go,' I wasn't certain if he was referring to the party or implying that I should leave his apartment and—"

"You were in his apartment?"

Marjorie nods. "In the sitting room. I took the newspaper down to him. It's my job to deliver the newspapers."

Bonafante stands expressionless. His dog stiffens to attention. Did she upset him? Bonafante turns sharply to Bernice.

"Miss Tessin. Your enthusiasm about the furnishings—you're very kind. I have some drawings from Eileen and a few other designers. Would you like to see them?" Before waiting for a response, he opens a wide cabinet full of shallow drawers. He removes stacks of paper and brings them to a nearby desk. He switches on the desk lamp. "You're welcome to study the drawings." He points to paper and pencil on the table. "Feel free to take notes."

And then he turns to Marjorie. His eyes intensely upon her. "Miss Lennox, perhaps you'd like to accompany me to see the lake?"

The temperature in the room shifts. Marjorie's feeling hot and cold all at once. He's tense, suddenly rushing. What's wrong? And why is she hesitating? Bernice's eyes shoot from the sketches to Marjorie's hands, waiting for a signal.

"Or you could stay here," says Bernice cautiously. "To look at the drawings." She waits a beat. "These do look pretty interesting."

Marjorie's hands slowly join together, clasping in front of her.

"On second thought," says Bernice, "it's a gorgeous night. Have a look at the lake. I'll stay here with . . ." Bernice gestures to the dog.

"Daisy," replies Bonafante.

"Come here, sweet Daisy," says Bernice. The dog doesn't move.

Bonafante lifts a hand, and Daisy happily scampers to Bernice.

"Just don't leave us too long, now," smiles Bernice.

39

AND VIRIDIAN

Bonafante opens the glass door to the garden for Marjorie. The midnight air rests still, holding only the hum of cicadas and night birds. They fall into step across the large flagstone patio to a hillside stairway descending toward the lake.

"Lovely evening," he says.

"You're being very patient, but I do know that we're sidestepping the obvious."

He looks to her, expectant.

"We've broken the lease and our word, disrespected your generosity, and are trespassing upon you. You have every right to be angry."

He continues walking for several yards before the question emerges. "Why are you here?" he asks quietly.

"My father was throwing an enormous party to welcome Cecile and Lou into their new home in the golf club. Bernice and Ivy hoped—"

"Ivy?"

"The Christmas painter."

"Ah, yes."

"Were you invited to Cecile's party?" asks Marjorie.

"Perhaps." Bonafante pauses. "I don't go to many parties."

"Many parties?" Marjorie smiles. "Don't you mean *any* parties? Well, we went, but it was problematic from the start because my parents don't know or approve of me taking part in your residency program and I've had to dodge—no auto pun intended—my parents and allow them to think that I'm at our family cottage when really I've been having the most exquisite experience designing clothes and being part of an artistic community. It's raised all sorts of questions in me about my future and how I'd like to spend it. Time is precious, of course, and mustn't be wasted. But then this evening I ran into that horrid Hank, the newspaper reporter who poses as a delivery boy at the Nightingale. You're very astute, so I'm sure you know that he's intent on investigating you somehow."

"Yes," he says.

"Something about Hank—I get a shiver around him, and not the good kind of shiver. He feels menacing and said the most awful things about my family. He doesn't know who I am, of course. I told him that I'm from Perrysburg on a stopover in Detroit. But he proceeded to speak about my family and even tell stories about me, right in front of my face, and—"

Bonafante gently touches her arm.

"Don't worry about Hank."

"Oh. I'm sorry. I'm chattering nervously."

His eyes slide to her. "Why are you nervous?"

His glance, the low roll of his voice, it makes her pause. "It's . . . been an exciting evening. But my father complains that I chirp too much."

"No. And, as I said, you needn't worry about Hank."

During the course of Marjorie's monologue, they've walked all the way down the yard and across the dock. The waves lap softly against the edge of his yacht. Unlike some of the garish vessels belonging to the auto barons, this is tasteful, a gentlemanly craft of approximately one hundred feet. Navy blue and teak, with white accents. Gracing the back of the stern is a nameplate: *Laetitia*.

Laetitia.

Marjorie turns toward his palatial mansion, beautifully aglow in the dark. "Your estate, it's simply perfection. Every last detail seems to be intentional with personal meaning or significance."

"Thank you."

They stand, gazing at the beautiful, warm house. As Bernice said, it doesn't make sense. Things don't add up. She looks at the yacht's nameplate. She has to ask.

"Are you married, Mr. Bonafante?"

"No. I've never been married."

The air hums with the slow heat of summer. "Forgive my curiosity. Perhaps, like some artists I know . . . you prefer men?"

He gently shakes his head. "The estate was my mother's greatest dream. Thank you for noticing the tasteful details. They were all her doing."

Was. Were.

"I'm sorry for your loss."

A natural silence lingers, allowing them to breathe comfortably together. "Sometimes I prefer night to day," sighs Marjorie. "Daytime is so full of noise and expectation of answers, but at night the beautiful stillness allows us to live the questions."

Bonafante turns and looks at her.

"Do you ever wonder what life might be asking of us?" she says.

He studies her, then slowly nods in reply.

"Me too." Marjorie sighs. "What a beautiful spot this dock is, nestled between your house and the lake. All at once I can feel the warmth of your home, the cool of the grass, and the unknown depths of the water. It's all quite magical."

They stand, listening to the lap of the water and the hum of the night.

He glances at his watch. "We should get back to the house. But there's something I'd like— Maybe if we're quick about it." He extends his hand for hers and walks her toward the darkened, lowered gangway of his yacht. Marjorie's breath flutters. They enter the dim space and, still holding her hand, he guides her through the darkness toward the front deck. Once there, he releases her hand. "Let your eyes adjust to the darkness."

He points to a banquette on the teak sundeck. "It's getting late. Lie down quickly."

Marjorie looks to Bonafante, confused.

"Hurry, it's late." He points again to the banquette.

Alarm bells sound in her head. What is happening? Marjorie pauses, then slowly inches toward the banquette.

"Don't be afraid." Bonafante sits on a banquette opposite the one he's pointing to. He loosens his tie. "Close your eyes. Then lie down."

Is he going to kiss her? Marjorie slowly lowers to the banquette. She closes her eyes, then reclines.

His voice is deep, close. "Take a breath."

He's going to kiss her. Her body responds, flooding with heat. She breathes, parting her lips.

His whisper floats over her. "Okay. Open your eyes."

She opens her eyes to a slate sky dusted with twinkling stars. She gasps. The pinpricks of light flicker, as if winking secrets of the universe.

"You said you like the stars. Away from the house lights, you can see more of them out here on the water."

Marjorie takes a moment and drinks in the starlight. "Yes, and they feel so close." She reaches a hand toward the sky. "It's as if each one is some distant heartbeat, isn't it? I'd love to see what they can see." After a while she turns her face. Bonafante lies on the bench across, staring at her. She smiles.

"I was confused," says Marjorie. "I thought . . . Anyway, this is beautiful. Perfect."

He reaches inside his suit coat, removes a silver cigarette case, and passes it to her.

She takes the case with its beautiful LBC engraving, then changes her mind. "You know, I don't feel much like smoking." She passes the case back to him, and he returns it to his pocket.

After a few moments of weighted silence, he speaks. "We have to head back to the house."

His tone, it's definitive.

"Alright," she whispers.

He takes her by the hand, guiding, and the warmth of his fingers once again sets her body alight. But he releases her hand as soon as they're back on the dock.

They proceed up the planked walkway in silence.

"Miss Lennox. You're incredibly talented. But I fear you might be in over your head."

She nods. "I'm so disappointed. I loved my residency. And I threw it all away to go to a silly party. When do I have to leave?"

He doesn't respond.

In over her head. He was speaking of the residency, wasn't he?

"Maybe I can speak to Dock," he says.

"Oh, if you would, please. If there's anything I can do. Any way I can stay."

"Detroit is complicated right now."

"It's more than complicated. It's downright dangerous. And some of the hoodlums, they were at my sister's house this evening. I saw my father speaking with them. I'd love to stay away from all that. I'm so inspired and have many more designs I'd love to sew."

"The dresses you made are unique."

"Really? Do you mean it?"

He nods.

"And viridian." He stops on the lawn, lifting and admiring his tie. "It's one of my favorite colors."

Marjorie reaches out and runs her fingers across the tie. He catches her hand.

"Thank you," he says.

"You're welcome. Thank you for the residency opportunity, the gorgeous sewing machine, the supplies, the stars tonight, and . . ." She pauses. "Thank you for the special delivery. The Pol Roger—I'm so hoping it was you?"

The shadow of a smile emerges. Marjorie shivers.

"You're cold," he says, pulling her closer.

"Not really." Marjorie smiles. "That was the good kind of shiver." She looks up at him. "I have to confess something. I probably should have waited for you, but I drank the champagne."

"All of it?" he chuckles.

"No, I shared it with the girls during their fittings."

"Nice. Just like they do in Paris."

Marjorie can't ignore the stirring she feels between them. It leaves little to the imagination. She sighs. "Standing so close like this, I'm now quite confident that I could sketch you without clothes."

He remains silent.

Oh, dear, she said that aloud. Graham's always reprimanding her for saying such things. She pulls back and looks up at him. His face is indecipherable.

"Forgive me. I have the awful habit of speaking exactly what's on my mind. And I'm sorry I acted strangely on your boat. I was confused. I didn't think of the stars; I thought you were going to kiss me."

He stares at Marjorie. "Don't apologize. You speak your mind. You don't play games. It's brave, and I appreciate that."

"Thank you." Marjorie waits, but he doesn't take the bait.

Instead, he looks at his watch again, then releases her. "I'm so sorry, I have to leave for a meeting. My valet will see you and Bernice back to your car and follow you to the Nightingale. Good night, Miss Lennox."

"Please, call me Marjorie."

He pauses, running his finger across her delicate collarbone and dipping his face within her hair to whisper in her ear. "I'm sorry, Marjorie. I have to go."

And with that he disappears into the blackness.

40

BAD BEEF

Chet makes her way down the hallway, spotting Graham slumped against a wall. "Finally! There you are. What's wrong?"

Graham lifts his head, dazed. "Nothing's wrong. Believe me, it's all quite right."

"You have lipstick on your chin."

"Do I?"

"Wait, you've already defiled one of Cecile's new bedrooms?"

"No, I didn't defile. On the contrary. I've *been* defiled. By Christmas. And what a holiday it was. I can't feel my legs, Chet."

"Stop."

"She's so smart. No. More than smart. Ivy's clever. She's funny and clever and loves a good time without the cliché giggles of a flapper or a college girl at a petting party. She's different. Artistic." His voice lowers. "And so limber."

"How old is she?"

"She's mature."

"No. You can't do this. She's part of Marjorie's residency. Go to a brothel."

"I've been. Trust me, it's nothing like what I just experienced."

Chet looks to the door. "Is she still in there?"

"No, she returned to the party. It's taken me a while to recover." He shakes out his hands. "And talk about a curve—Marjorie showing up, as well as the reporter. Is our train completely off the tracks?"

Cecile storms down the hall. "Wait until you hear this!" she shrieks.

Graham sighs. "You're such fun, Cecile. Like water running cold in a bath."

"Or dead leaves littering a pool," says Chet.

"Oh, shut up," says Cecile. "The team from the *Times,* they're not here to report on our new home, not to feature Lou or me, but to report on our family! Some lippy reporter just asked me if I killed Granny's pig of a parakeet."

Chet and Graham exchange glances.

"What?" snaps Cecile. "It wasn't me. Slorah choked it with her thumbs." Cecile's nose suddenly lifts. She begins sniffing. She moves toward the bedroom door, running her hand across the wall. "Wait. I smell sex. Why do I smell sex?" She looks at her siblings. "Did one of you have sex in my new house?"

Chet looks at her shoes, stifling a laugh.

"You damn pigs. How dare you. Instead of fornicating in my hallway, you might want to help our father, who's comfortably numb and all too eager to answer questions about his wife's head wound."

Graham snaps to attention, stands, and takes off down the hall.

Cecile's head turns, like a dog following the scent. She clears her throat and returns her stare to Chet. "Did you speak to that cub reporter?"

"I did."

"What did you talk about?" she asks, casually toying with her ruby necklace.

"Well, I think we talked about Poochie's death. And we also talked about Myrtle Branley's unfortunate death." Chet feigns shock as she backs down the hallway. "Poor Myrtle Branley. We discussed the whispered suspicions that *you're* the one who killed her."

"What?"

"You haven't heard? You're to be questioned in the death of Myrtle Branley. Happy housewarming, Cecile." Chet turns and marches away.

Graham makes his way to the front drawing room, where Duncan holds court with a gaggle of bootlickers and late party freeloaders. Lou has finally appeared. He stands with Hank and an older reporter from the newspaper. Graham notes his father's appearance. Stable, but his face is ashen with random spots of pink, like beef going bad.

Hank turns to Graham. "Your eye patch. Were you in the war?"

"At war with a champagne bottle," smirks Duncan.

"The war?" sneers Graham. "No, I wasn't in the war. I wasn't old enough. I'm—" Graham turns to his father. "Dad, give Hank the ages of your children."

Duncan laughs and waves to someone across the room, pretending he didn't hear the question. The older reporter with Hank looks from Graham to their father. "Has the family discussed succession planning?"

"Our father is in his fifties," says Graham. "Much too early to speak of succession."

"That's what the Dodge brothers thought. The widows sold their company to some bank for 146 million."

"Cecile would never do that," says Duncan.

"Cecile? Don't you mean Lilah, your wife?" asks Hank. "Where did she go, anyway?"

Chet steps in beside Graham as he distracts with a question. "Say, did you fellas know that Lou here is a former boxing champ?"

Hank turns to Lou. "I followed your fights."

"Yeah? Thanks, buddy," says Lou.

"You're friends with Dempsey, right? Have you spoken with him recently? Where's his head since the murder and suicide?"

Lou takes a step toward Hank. "Jack Dempsey is family. I hate when newspapers get into a man's personal business. Those deaths, a real tragedy, see."

"Yes, death is very personal," says Graham.

"You don't say." Hank points his pencil at Graham. "But don't you work for Hogan in obituaries? You're digging into death all the time."

"Not digging," says Chet, raising a protesting finger. "Memorializing—"

"We're off track," interrupts their father. "Let's get back to my business."

The older reporter nods. "Sure, sure. Hank's just the curious sort. So, your son-in-law here has gone from boxing to glass manufacturing and you're celebrating his big new home. What department do you have him in?"

"Lou's in . . . our service bureau," replies their father.

"What about old man Lennox?" Hank asks.

"What about him?"

"Word is that you two had a falling-out. What's that about?"

"We have different work styles. So do Henry and Edsel. It's not uncommon. Look, wait till you gentlemen see the plans for our new factory. Lots of improvements and product expansions."

Hank doesn't appear interested in the factory. Or improvements. He's interested in the family. His eyes scan the room, making note of everything.

"Where's your youngest daughter?" asks Hank.

"She's right there. Charlotte. We call her Chet," says their father.

Awkwardness worms in. "Oh, but isn't there . . ."

Chet laughs. "He does that all the time. Actually, the youngest is out of town."

"When will she return? We'd love to speak with her for the profile piece. She's the one who was tangled with the theft from the Institute of Arts, right?"

"No," says Graham. "You must have her confused with someone else. Any last questions?"

"Yeah. I heard that Bonafante was here earlier."

"Excuse me, gotta hit the john," says their father. He makes a quick exit.

"Thanks for coming, gentlemen," says Lou, herding the group toward the door. "I'll show you out."

Chet pulls Graham aside. "I'm torn," she whispers. "It's all progressing so well. Did you see his coloring? At this point it might be safer to just let nature take its course. Anything additional might be overkill."

"Overkill. Very funny, Chet. Hey, have you seen Ivy?"

Chet looks at her brother. "Uh . . . nope. Haven't seen her."

41

HARDWOOD CRIMINALS

Marjorie stares at the ceiling. She's awake because she never went to sleep. She lies on the chaise in her apartment, wrapped in a silk caftan.

What exactly happened last night? Did she really throw away her residency to go to Cecile's party? If she hadn't broken the lease, though, would she have had the opportunity to visit Bonafante's home, spend time alone with him, and look at the stars with him? But she doesn't want to leave the Nightingale. Has he already informed Dock that they broke the lease?

The smack of the newspapers out front claps through the window. She peeks through the curtains and spots the delivery boy. It's not Hank. She doesn't care that she's not properly dressed. Marjorie takes her keys and retrieves the papers from the front door in her caftan. The morning hampers have been delivered. Except Ivy's. Is Ivy already back and awake? Marjorie taps on her door. No answer.

"Psst!"

Bernice leans out of her gray door, waving Marjorie toward her. Marjorie quickly drops the newspapers at the doors and joins Bernice.

Bernice drags the hamper into her room, shuts her door, and locks it. "Have you slept?"

"Not a wink," says Marjorie.

"Me neither."

"There's no hamper at Ivy's door. I knocked, but she didn't answer." Marjorie wrings her hands. "Oh, Bernice, have we been terribly foolish?"

Bernice paces the floor. "Here's how I see it. Bonafante knows we broke the lease, so yeah, we're getting sacked early, but that's okay. We've made progress and had an incredible experience." Bernice points to her chairs. "I created several different prototypes."

"But if I had refused the party, you'd still be working."

"If you refused, I wouldn't have seen my hero's home. I wouldn't have seen a world outside my own. And, most important, I might not have learned of Eileen Gray. Marjie, the sketches that Bonafante showed me, they're incredible and reveal a design horizon I didn't know existed. I'm gonna find her. I'm gonna write to her. And whatever it takes, I'm gonna beg her to take me on as an apprentice."

"That's a wonderful idea!" Marjorie's smile fades. "But, Bernice, things don't look as promising for me. Yes, I pursued the residency because I wanted time with Bonafante, but I also wanted to prove to my family that I could be structured and disciplined. That I could make something of myself so my father won't send me to a convent."

"A convent?" says Bernice. "No way. You saw people's eyes pop for your dresses, didn't you? Like Dock said, they were transformative. I've never had people look at me that way. I always thought that to look pretty I'd have to be uncomfortable. But I could've cut a cord of poplar in your dress."

Marjorie smiles. "Well, that does make me happy."

"It should. And, hey, you finally got to see your prince charming's house and spend time with him."

"Yes, but I can't stop thinking about what you've said. Something's odd."

"What do I know? I don't live with auto barons. I live in a lighthouse near a bunch of miners and loggers. But I trust my gut, and I want you to be safe and smart. Something's not right about Bonafante. I believe in ghosts, and at first I thought this place was haunted and—no foolin'—that he might actually be some kind of phantom. But he's definitely real. And I think he might be a gangster. Look, there were some genuine hardwood criminals at your sister's party. But this type can be even more dangerous. They hide behind manners and nice clothes and big houses. And they can get away with—buy their way with—everything," says Bernice.

Marjorie nods. "Something was definitely off. He seemed in such a hurry to leave last night. What type of meeting could he have at such an hour?"

"He came back here."

"He did?"

"Yes, around four A.M. And he wasn't alone. Sit down."

Marjorie sits, bracing herself.

"He had Chaplin with him."

"What?"

"Yes. Bonafante was with Charlie Chaplin. I saw it with my own eyes. They went upstairs and left again at five-thirty."

Marjorie looks suspicious. "Bernice, I adore you. But like your castrato theory, that makes no sense. Chaplin lives in Hollywood."

"I'm just telling you what I saw! Anyway, don't feel bad if we get kicked out today. I've learned a lot and you've given me something much more valuable than a residency."

"What's that?"

"Clarity." Bernice smiles and steps forward to take both of Marjorie's hands in her own. "And friendship. If you ever need to escape, just ride the rails up to Copper Country. Walk up the hill and look for the lighthouse. You're a loyal friend, Marjorie Lennox. And you'll always have a loyal friend in me."

Dear Coco,

Please stop.
The idea is a bad one.
This will not work.
And now I'm truly frightened.

42

SICKENING CREEP

Marjorie wakes on the chaise to the sound of rain splashing against the sidewalk. How long has she been asleep?

After a bath, she alters one of the new dresses she's made. If she's going to be asked to leave, she must get as much work done, finish as many pieces, as possible. She's organizing the fabric and creating a task list when male voices sound from the hallway. She leaves her list and peeks outside the door.

Men in uniformed coveralls are carrying things out of Ivy's apartment. Her easels, paints, and clothes. Dock stands by, making notations on his clipboard.

"Dock, what's happening?"

"Go back into your apartment, Miss Marjorie Lennox." He closes Ivy's door and locks it.

"But where's Ivy?"

"I'm afraid her lease has been terminated. Miss Tessin's too. Bernice left an hour ago. I must request that you return to your apartment while we complete some administrative details."

"I wasn't allowed to say goodbye? And this is unfair. If their leases are terminated, mine should be as well."

"I'm awaiting determination," says Dock. "Please, go back into your apartment."

The sickening creep of guilt crawls over Marjorie. This is her fault.

Why didn't she insist that they abide by the lease? She didn't need to go to Cecile's house. If she had refused, Ivy and Bernice would still have their residencies. Infatuation has blighted her common sense. She's seen it happen to others but is somehow ashamed that it could happen to her. She's heard snickers in Grosse Pointe about young people who have pursued fixations to the point of distraction. They're dismissed as "whimsical" and "of dreamy, unstable temperament." Thank goodness her parents don't know about the residency. Her father has such little patience with her, and this would make things much worse.

But most upsetting, Bernice and Ivy are gone. She's lost her friends without so much as a forwarding address.

Marjorie spends the day sewing, trying to soothe her sadness and finish as many pieces as possible. The gray day and spatter of rain outside the window are the perfect backdrop to accompany her mood. Afternoon gives way to the arrival of late-day sun. And also to Graham at her window. He stands, holding a beautiful bouquet of flowers.

"Hi there, Marjie. Just wanted to tell you that I'm picking up the car."

"Oh, hello, Graham." She smiles. "What a sweetheart you are to bring me flowers. I really need some brightness today."

Her brother bites his lip, sheepish. "Actually, I brought these for Ivy."

"For Ivy?"

Graham smiles. "Yeah. Boy, she's something, isn't she? We really hit it off. But her curtains are closed, so I thought she might be in your apartment?"

Marjorie looks at her brother, and her lower lip begins to tremble.

"Marjie, what is it?"

"Rules," she replies. "We weren't supposed to leave for an extended period. We went to the party and we got caught. My residency will probably be terminated," says Marjorie. "Ivy and Bernice were already sent home. Oh, Graham, I've been such a fool. This is the first real opportunity I've had, and I've thrown it all away. I imagine they'll turn me out at any minute."

"Don't come home," Graham says quickly.

"I don't want to come home."

"No, I mean, you can't come home."

"Why?" asks Marjorie.

Graham stiffens. "There's a lot going on. The newspaper is doing some sort of profile on the family. Our father's in a foul mood. It's best for you to go to the cottage. That aligns with our original story anyway. You don't know when you'll be turned out?"

Marjorie shakes her head.

Graham looks down the sidewalk, thinking. "See here. I'll leave the car so you can head to the cottage. Do you have any money? Enough for gas?"

Marjorie thinks of the money she found in the bed finials. It's not right for her to drain it. But she still has some money from her mother's play fund. "I have a bit that I brought from home." Marjorie looks at her brother, his expression of concern. "Graham, what are you not telling me?"

"Nothing. I'm just . . . When did you last see Ivy? Do you know if she made it back?"

"Well, I'm not sure."

"What do you mean you're not sure?"

"Graham, last night was complicated."

"So complicated that you didn't check on your friend?" he exclaims.

"Calm yourself. Ivy warned us that she might be out late. And you assured us that you'd watch over her. I assumed you'd drive her back."

"Do you know where her family lives?"

Marjorie thinks. "She mentioned that her family is in rubber. Tires. I think she said Palmer Woods? Graham, it's very kind of you, but why are you so concerned about Ivy?"

"Because . . ." He pauses, adjusting his hat. "Detroit's a dangerous place. That's why I gave you and Bernice the car. And Cecile's party, well, some pretty rough characters were there."

"That's an understatement. It was an underworld orgy. Even I could see that through the window."

"What time did you and Bernice return? Did you come right back?"

Marjorie pauses. She doesn't want to tell Graham that she went to Bonafante's. She knows he'll just scold her, and she couldn't bear if he let it slip to the family. "I drove Bernice around a bit before we returned. She wanted to see the area."

"Alright. I'm sorry I overreacted. But Ivy and I had some great . . . conversation, and then I couldn't find her. Tires. Palmer Woods. Do you know her last name?"

"No. Both Ivy and Bernice were dismissed before I could get forwarding addresses."

"Okay, I'll hit Palmer Woods. Aw, man, what a mess. If they kick you out, go to the cottage, okay?"

"Alright, Graham."

And with that, Graham and the flowers disappear from her window. It's a few moments later when the thought occurs to her.

The silver key. Her key opens Ivy's apartment. Maybe her last name and address are somewhere inside, just as the playwright's were?

43

HOLIDAY HORIZONS

Marjorie locks her apartment. She walks across to Ivy's blue door, holding the silver key. Are the silver keys really an artistic security measure, as Ivy suggested? The playwright's silver key opened Bernice's apartment, and vice versa. Ivy said that her silver key opened Marjorie's apartment, so yes, it would make sense that Marjorie's silver key would have a reciprocal function. But why? It doesn't make sense. Especially because it wasn't outlined in the lease.

Marjorie slips her silver key into the lock of Ivy's blue door and turns it. Sure enough, it opens. She closes the door and locks it behind her. And she's immediately smacked by the silence of abandon.

The apartment space is dead, ominously quiet, and flat without Ivy in it. Marjorie inhales a breath through her nose, hoping for a hint of Ivy's Guerlain scent, but gets nothing but dry nicotine. A large glass ashtray, crowded with lipstick-printed butts, sits next to the sofa. Marjorie remembers Ivy marching through the playwright's apartment, gathering an armload of leftover items, and at the time, that felt so uncomfortable. But that's exactly what she's inclined to do now.

She walks through the bedroom and bathroom, taking a jeweled hairpin, a tube of lipstick the color of a crime scene, and the red satin blanket. In the corner, as she's flipping through extra supplies and blank canvases, she finds a legal pad with what must be Ivy's handwriting.

She sits down to read.

Dearest Daddy,

I hope business is booming and that you're deliriously happy amidst all things rubber. I'm delighted to report that I am inspired in my residency. I've now made two friends, fellow creative residents, who you'll be thrilled to know have opened my head and heart to new holiday horizons.

One of my new friends is from up north but instead of Christmas makes me think of all things pilgrim and Thanksgiving: cold nights, smoky fires, fresh-hewn logs, and a laughing family gathered together. She's steadying, like a guiding glow from a lighthouse. The newest arrival is from one of the most notorious, eccentric auto families, which everyone has heard of. She is naïve in the best of ways. Can't we all remember ourselves at that twinkling dawn of our awakening? So many of us struggle to return to that beautiful place of unknowing. Despite her ill-famed ragbag of a family, this young woman aspires to the greatest vision of what a heart might be capable of. And in turn, she inspires me to pursue expressing the meaning of love and "Valentine." So you see, you have nothing to worry about! Thanksgiving and Valentine's Day shall be new subjects.

And yes, Daddy, I will try to sell my paintings for as much as possible. But in the meantime—again—please don't worry. I am well behaved and well cared for by my new friends.

The letter ends there, unsigned and unsent. Marjorie clutches the pad of paper, overcome with emotion.

Gorgeous, glamorous, and artistic Ivy. She says things that others dare not, drinks deeply and unashamedly from the cup of life in a way most could never dream of. No wonder Graham is smitten with her. And the way she spoke of Bernice is perfection. Bernice as a roaring wood fire of Thanksgiving, a glow in the lighthouse giving direction to boats that might be struggling in a storm.

Ivy said many nice things, but this in particular pierces Marjorie's heart:

I am well behaved and well cared for by my new friends.

Marjorie left Ivy at the party. Yes, Ivy said she was going to stay out late. But with all that Marjorie saw through the windows and Bernice's confirmation that the guests were a bunch of hardwood criminals, why didn't she and Bernice insist that they all leave together?

How could she have left Ivy behind?

44

FAMILY SUCCESSION

Graham eyes his father.

The main course of roasted lamb with cherry glaze is served. Atchison orbits the table, pouring red wine from a glass decanter. Chet arrives and takes her seat.

"Sorry I'm late," she says.

Their father shovels food into his mouth.

"Feeling better, Dad?" asks Graham.

"Ravenous."

"I was looking for my dictionary," says Chet. "Has anyone seen it?"

"I think your father ate it," says Lilah.

"Yeah, after your lover smacked you in the head with it," grumbles their father.

Lilah pounds her fist on the table. Everyone looks to her. "Excuse me," she says, and leaves the room.

"Good to see that everyone's feeling better," says Granny. "Graham, I read the most wonderful thing in the paper. There was a baseball pitcher, a Mr. Jim Manning, who lost his eyesight. For four years, he prayed before an image of St. Theresa in his home."

"If he was blind, how did he know it was St. Theresa?" asks Gramps.

"Don't interrupt. Well, recently, he saw a red flash, then a blue flash, and a booming voice called, 'Behold!' He saw St. Theresa with a rosary in her hand, and he fell over. When he regained consciousness, he could see.

I've called the church to order a framed icon. It should be here in a week. I want you to pray to it daily, dear. Remember, my fortune teller predicted that you won't wear an eye patch forever."

"We haven't seen your psychic lady in a while," says Chet.

"No. Poor dear was committed to Eloise Asylum. Such an injustice," says Granny.

"Bet she didn't see that in her crystal ball," laughs Gramps.

Lally, the slim new parakeet, squawks from down the hall.

Their father suddenly stops eating and sways uncomfortably in his chair.

"Is that the boiler gurgling?" asks Granny.

"It's Dad's intestines," says Chet.

"Aw, man, I thought this was over with," groans their father.

"Are you still taking the charcoal tablets?" asks Graham. He shoots a look to Chet.

Their father stands and hurries from the room.

"Let me know if my missing cuff link comes out!" shouts Gramps.

Gramps turns his attention to Chet and Graham. "I haven't heard from either of you. How was Cecile's party last night?"

"Entertaining," laughs Chet. "Graham spilled his glass in one of Cecile's new bedrooms."

"Shut up, Chet."

She looks at him. "What's eating you?"

"Nothing." Graham turns toward his grandfather. "The party was awful, Gramps." He looks to the doorway to make sure his father is out of earshot. "The attendees were all hoodlums. I've seen better clientele at a bawdy house. Not a single reputable auto chief was there. Dad was sauced, and in his usual quest for attention, he decided to hold court with a newspaperman and that annoying cub sidekick."

"What the hell for?" says Gramps.

"Let's see, maybe to embarrass our entire family?" says Graham. "No wonder we're notorious. The older reporter wasn't interested in anything he had to say but instead wanted to talk about your rift and family succession. But the cub had a list of prepared questions that he fired off, which included queries about everything from murder to Marjorie."

Granny's lips tighten. "Graham dear, which bawdy house do you frequent?"

"Imagine Cecile running a bordello," says Chet.

Color rises on Gramps's cheeks. "Those reporters. I'll fix them."

Chet leans over her plate. "What's your saying, Gramps? Never wage war . . ."

"With someone who buys ink by the barrel," finishes Graham.

"Yes," says their grandmother. "But someone clearly wants to wage war with the Lennox family through their stories. At the club today, they said there are whispers circulating that Cecile had something to do with Myrtle Branley's death and that she'll be questioned by the police."

Chet dons an expression of shock.

"Yes, isn't that ridiculous? Cecile was a great help to Myrtle, helped her organize the valuables after Harold died." Granny sighs. "Poochie, Myrtle Branley—death comes in threes, you know. I wonder who will be next."

Their grandfather looks from Chet to Graham. "Yes, I too wonder. Who will be next?"

Silence sits, awkward, until Chet coughs and reaches for her glass.

Granny stands with the help of Napoleon. "Well, we'll do what we can, won't we? Graham darling, you must write a nice obituary for Myrtle."

"Oh, yes," agrees Chet. "Write a nice obituary."

45

TANGLED SHADOWS

Marjorie sits alone on the bench out back. She crushes the dying cigarette, missing her evening smoke breaks with Bernice. In a few hours the door will be locked for the night, and who knows if she'll be able to get back in. She hasn't seen Dock since the morning. Is he avoiding her? And where is Bonafante? Is his car parked on the side street? She looks down the length of the building, and something pulls her gaze.

His door. Is it ajar?

She makes her way over and confirms that, yes, the door isn't closed. Through the decorative metal, something catches her eye. A long string of pearls lies at the bottom of the stairs. Goodness, someone will be missing those. She opens the door and bends to pick them up, and that's when the melodic sounds begin. The soft, celestial strumming of a harp swirls from upstairs. It's the same sound she heard when she was lying in Bonafante's car.

It's so lovely. And so beautifully peaceful. Marjorie ascends the stairs toward the sound and reaches a landing. To her right is yet another flight of stairs. But to her left is a black door, with the same swallow door knocker she saw at Bonafante's. The heavenly music comes from behind the door.

Marjorie looks to the pearls in her hand. She could hang them on the door handle. But instead she steps forward, grasps the swallow in her palm, and knocks.

The music stops. No sound comes from inside. Marjorie knocks again. Perhaps she's disturbing a lesson or a rehearsal? And then a voice emerges.

"Yes?" The word from behind the door is muffled. A woman's voice.

"Oh, good evening. I found a lovely string of pearls at the bottom of the stairs and wanted to leave them with you to return to their rightful owner."

She hears the sound of multiple locks turning, and then the heavy door opens a crack. The face of a middle-aged woman appears. "Thank you, dear. That's very honest of you." The woman looks at Marjorie. "My, aren't you lovely. Were you delivering?" she asks.

"Oh, no, I'm not a courier. I'm Marjorie Lennox, from downstairs."

The door closes. Marjorie stands, still holding the pearls. She waits a moment, then turns to leave. And then the door opens once again.

"Come in, Marjorie."

"Oh, thank you." Marjorie steps inside. The woman closes the door and turns the multiple locks.

Unlike the lower floor, which is divided by a hallway and four apartments, this floor is situated as one large spacious home. Marjorie stands in the entry area. To one side, she sees a large mahogany desk with two chairs in front of it. The other side is arranged as a sitting area with a small table, chairs, and a settee. Next to the settee stands a gold harp and a chair. The woman waves a hand, inviting Marjorie to take a seat.

"Forgive me, I didn't mean to intrude. The door was ajar. It's never been ajar, so I was concerned. I saw the pearls and my first thought was that someone might be looking for them. I didn't mean to disturb your lovely playing."

The woman gives a gentle smile and nods. She looks at Marjorie but offers no introduction.

"Do you live here?" asks Marjorie.

"Yes, I own the building."

"Oh. You're the owner? I understood that Mr. Bonafante owned the building."

"My brother spends time here, but he doesn't own the building."

Her brother. Marjorie nods slowly. The woman is older than Bonafante, attractive, with a hint of resemblance, but her elegant face carries a fatigue of sadness and life mileage, a look that's older than her years.

"I'm Marjorie Lennox." She repeats her introduction in hopes of learning the woman's name.

"How do you do, Marjorie. You're the fashion designer. I hope you're enjoying your residency?"

She knows of the residency and speaks as if it's intact. Marjorie nods quickly. "Yes," she whispers. "Very much. But I'm afraid that I'm not an ideal candidate."

"And why is that?"

"Well, a few reasons. First, I often find that amidst the excitement of a new experience, my heart and mind are consumed with anticipation, leaving little room for retention. I was so excited to be here that I signed the paperwork without fully reading the fine print and, as such, I was quick to break the rules. The second reason is that my father doesn't approve of women in the arts, so I've had to hide the residency from my parents. Dishonesty is always problematic—in this case, not only morally but logistically. And hiding the residency means I'm also hiding an aspect of myself, which feels . . . well, awful. Does that make sense?"

"It does. My father hated the idea of women in artistic pursuits."

"Were you raised here?"

"No, we were raised in Canada. I was schooled at home, my brother at Bishop's College in Quebec."

"So your family has nothing to do with the automotive industry?"

"Oh, I didn't say that," she laughs. "Most people here are connected in one way or another, aren't they?"

"Of course. Perhaps that's why I have no interest in it," says Marjorie.

"Your dress is beautiful. Did you create that during your residency?"

"Thank you, yes. Bernice, the furniture designer—she's so wise. She encouraged me to explore my own line of garments."

The woman looks at her, examining the dress. "That pale shade of blue suits you. I believe it's from the bolt of Mantero silk imported from Como. I've always loved Italian silks. The sheer drape of fabric off the shoulder, I'd describe it as ethereal. Does that feel accurate to you?"

"Yes. I know the popular style these days is heavy beading, and I thought I was interested in that. But once I began sketching after I arrived, I drew nothing of the sort. I felt as if I wanted to design things that represented nature. Isn't that curious? I once created a controversial dress that represented a tree, but with this I was trying to represent a breeze." Marjorie leans over, looking at the willowing fall of the dress over her legs. "I'm wearing stockings and shoes, of course, but I think it would best represent with bare legs and painted toes." She looks up and smiles. The woman smiles in return.

Curiosity presses in. "May I ask your name?" says Marjorie.

The woman pauses. "Juliette," she finally replies.

"Enchanting! Your name alone has been the inspiration of many writers, poets, and even architects. And most important, it was the inspiration of your mother, I imagine."

A soft sadness washes over Juliette's face. She neither confirms nor denies the comment about her mother. Instead, she takes a breath. "You strike me as a very honest person, Miss Lennox."

"That's a lovely compliment. Thank you. I've tried to share as much as I could with Dock while I've been here, with mixed success," Marjorie laughs. "But I did manage to tell him about the suspicious newspaper delivery boy and the money I found in the bed frame."

"Are you in love with my brother?" she asks.

The question lands like a punch. Juliette stares at her, unblinking.

The walls of the room suddenly compress, shrink, and push in around Marjorie. An invisible weight presses on her chest and, without warning, up through her neck. She nods, silent.

Noise sounds from the area of the foyer, and a low voice emerges. "I thought you'd be practicing by now." The door closes, followed by clicks of fastening locks.

Charles Bonafante appears in the room. He wears a gray suit with matching vest, complemented by the viridian tie. He removes his hat and runs a quick hand through his sleek black hair. He looks from Marjorie to his sister. His mouth pulls with concern.

"Why is she upstairs?" he asks Juliette. He turns to Marjorie. "You shouldn't be here."

A creeping tension grips the room, as if the air itself is holding its breath. Marjorie stands.

"I . . . I was just leaving." She lifts her hand, still clutching the string of pearls. "The door was ajar. These were at the bottom of the stairs. I only wanted to return them." She hands the pearls to Juliette. "It's late. Forgive me for disturbing you."

Marjorie flees from the room toward the door. She unfastens the latches, turns the locks, and hurries down the steps. But the door at the base of the stairs is bolted.

It's locked from the inside and requires a key.

She grabs the ornamental metal and shakes it. Marjorie turns and sees the dark silhouette of Charles Bonafante at the top of the stairs. Her breath quickens as, step by step, he slowly descends toward her. She stands, hand gripping the locked door, still trying to turn the knob.

Bonafante arrives in front of her. Moonlight sifts through the iron latticework, casting tangled shadows on his face. Marjorie releases the handle and faces him, her back pressed against the door.

He leans in, close. So close that she can feel the heat of his body and his breath on her ear. So close that she wants him closer.

"You have to stop. You have no idea what you're doing," he whispers.

She shivers but doesn't move, just grasps his lapels and pulls him against her. She knows exactly what she's doing. She wants to dissolve into the feel and smell of him. The impulse is overpowering. She can envision, and feel, exactly what waits beneath his expensive clothing.

"You don't understand," he says.

"I do," whispers Marjorie. "I don't want to go home. And I certainly don't want to go to a convent." Without warning, she stands on her toes, lifts her face, and runs her parted mouth across his chin, her tongue grazing his lips. Her hand reaches up, slowly looping her thumb beneath the knot of his tie to loosen it.

"Marjorie . . ." he whispers.

Her mouth swallows his words. She kisses him. And kisses him again. He momentarily pulls away, then suddenly leans forward, settling his mouth on hers without hesitation. She drops her hands to his waist, grasping his belt loops, tugging him tighter against her. He threads a leg between hers to gently prop her higher and holds her face, kissing her slowly.

"I think that's enough."

The voice sounds from above. Marjorie pulls from his lips and sees his sister, standing ominously at the top of the stairs.

Bonafante drops his head to Marjorie's neck. His uneven breaths pulse against her ear.

He pauses, then pulls away and exhales. He removes a ring of keys from his pocket and swiftly unlocks the door. He opens it and stands aside for Marjorie to exit. She takes a step out the door and turns to look at him, to say something. They were just getting started.

He shakes his head slowly. "I was trying to help you, Marjorie."

He closes and locks the door. And walks back upstairs.

46

LIVELY RAGTIME

Marjorie reclines on the chaise, watching dust particles dance in a beam of morning sunlight.

She kissed Charles Bonafante.

And for a few glorious moments, he kissed her back and lit her up from head to toe. The feeling lingers and the whisper of him still floats around her, all over her. She waited for hours last night, imagining that he might come to her apartment to continue what she had started. But no one knocked, and she eventually padded her way to the bedroom and fell into a short and fitful sleep.

He said he was trying to help her. He was referring to her clothing designs, wasn't he? And, yes, he did help her. So why did he sound distraught?

A thump on the stoop signals the morning delivery of newspapers. She draws back the curtain slightly to confirm it's not Hank. Should she really keep up the obligations of the lease when she's the only one left? Marjorie goes through the ritual of locking her apartment and fetching the two newspapers from the front stoop. She drops a paper at the top of the basement stairs for Dock and returns to her door. Her hamper has been delivered, so she pulls that inside, closes her door, and locks it.

The morning headlines shout with the typical murder, jewel thievery, and auto news. But her gaze is drawn to an article at the bottom of the front page.

WOMAN IN SEARCH OF CHRISTMAS ARRESTED

A woman claiming she was a Christmas tree was apprehended on Friday night on a roof in Palmer Woods, shouting down a chimney. The glamorous blonde was dressed in a green satin gown when police answered a call and found her perched atop the domicile.

The fire brigade was called to help the woman descend safely. Upon climbing down the ladder, the woman introduced herself as Ivy Boughs and claimed she was alerting her daddy that Santa would soon be arriving at the chimney.

Authorities consulted with the homeowner, who informed them that he was, in fact, her husband. He cooperated fully and shared that the woman's real name was Winifred Dixon, that they had been married for many years, and that his wife was an artist and occasionally suffered bouts of dissociation, which he believed stemmed from childhood trauma.

The woman was taken to Eloise Asylum for further evaluation by alienists.

Marjorie's hands tremble, fluttering the paper. A rush of cold shoots up the back of her neck. She sits down at her sewing machine. She reads the article again.

"Ivy," she breathes. "Oh, Ivy, no."

She stands quickly. She must do something to help. But Bernice is gone. She's the only one left on the floor. Dock. She must alert Dock.

Still clasping the paper, Marjorie swings open her apartment door and runs to the basement stairs. She sweeps up the copy of the paper for Dock and flies down the dark staircase. When her knock is unanswered, she turns the door handle and enters the front room of Dock's apartment.

"Dock!" she calls. "Dock, come quickly, it's about Ivy."

Her call is swallowed by the tight, airless space.

"Dock?" she calls again, louder this time.

Silence.

She slowly proceeds through the door at the back of the sitting room and finds herself in what looks like an office. A lamp throws weak light on the scene. There's a desk, a chair, and, hanging from the wall, a slotted metal contraption with rows of file folders.

"Dock?" Her voice cracks. "It's Marjorie. I must speak to you. It's urgent."

The word RESIDENCY appears above the first vertical row of names on the wall file. She recognizes them. Georgina Godlin. Bernice Tessin. Marjorie Lennox. And then she sees the file.

Winifred Dixon.

Marjorie grabs the file and opens it. It's a typewritten form.

Name: Winifred Dixon
Age: 30
Artistic Discipline: Painter
Alleged Diagnosis: Delusional Insanity

Marjorie goes cold. She grabs the other files from the wall.

Name: Georgina Godlin
Age: 27
Artistic Discipline: Playwright
Alleged Diagnosis: Aggressive Agoraphobia

Name: Bernice Tessin
Age: 23
Artistic Discipline: Furniture Architect
Alleged Diagnosis: Inhalant Addict

And this one:

Name: Marjorie Lennox
Age: 20
Artistic Discipline: Clothing Designer
Alleged Diagnosis: Chronic Imaginative Derangement.

Marjorie clutches the file folders to her chest. *Derangement? Alleged diagnosis?*

She opens her mouth to speak, but it's as if she's spinning in a nightmare and can't project her voice. "Dock?" she whispers. But no one answers. "Dock, are you here?"

At the back of the dim room is yet another large door, this one bolted from the inside. She turns the bolt and pulls open the door. It creaks with complaint, revealing an ascending staircase. Does it lead to Juliette's apartment? Is that where Dock is? She makes her way up the stairs and stops. There are too many steps. She's already climbed two flights. And it's so dark. She reaches a door with another turn bolt. She hears something. A tinkling of music. Marjorie turns the lock and opens the door.

A man in a tuxedo and top hat sits at a piano, playing a lively ragtime. A woman in a flapper dress dances the Charleston barefoot around the piano, holding a glass of champagne. A pretty redhead in a green day dress clutches a legless doll and sways to the music. Marjorie takes a step forward, and the woman thrusts the doll at her. "Would you like to kiss Betty Jo?" Marjorie pauses with alarm, to which the woman replies, "Hazel's under the table, sweetheart. We're all gone, gone, goners."

Marjorie begins to tremble. She makes her way farther into the space and spots Dock trying to calm a woman in a raincoat who's backed into a corner, swatting at him. He pulls a stethoscope from his pocket and hands it to the woman, which subdues her. She puts on the stethoscope, adopts a serious expression, and puts the silver metal disc to Dock's bald head.

"I do declare, Doctor, you're insane!" she bellows. She giggles, and Dock joins her in laughter. He lifts his clipboard and makes a note.

There's a swift pull at Marjorie's arm, and she turns to find Juliette Bonafante leading her across the floor.

"Come with me," she says. "This instant."

47

NO SAINT

Juliette closes the door and points to a Queen Anne wing chair.

"N-no," stammers Marjorie.

"Have a seat. I won't hurt you."

Marjorie looks around the room. It appears to be a woman's private parlor. Elegant wallpaper, gilt-framed paintings of the sea. Two chairs and a settee grace a rose-adorned Aubusson rug. Next to the seating area is a wheeled cart with a porcelain teapot and a tiered stand that holds what appear to be pastries and breakfast sandwiches.

"May I offer you some refreshment?" asks Juliette.

Refreshment? What is she talking about? Marjorie grips the newspaper and speaks slowly, enunciating each and every word to keep herself from screaming. Her voice quakes with emotion. "What you may offer me is an explanation. An explanation of what's going on here."

"You've been staying on the bottom floor. As you know, I live on the second floor. This top floor is a residential unit," replies Juliette. "For women who might need additional assistance."

"What kind of assistance?"

"Assistance coping with disorders and the exhaustion of nerves."

Marjorie stares at her. "I've been in an asylum?" she whispers.

"You've been in an evaluation program."

Marjorie shakes her head, "Please help me understand. You suspect that I'm out of my mind?"

"Your father does. Mine did too. Please, have a seat."

Juliette pulls her chair closer to Marjorie. Her voice drops in volume. "I was fifteen years old when my parents noticed that my behavior was changing, becoming unpredictable. My mother was consumed with concern, and my father was consumed with embarrassment. He locked me in my room, Marjorie. For three years. He claimed I was possessed by the devil. When my mother or brother tried to help me, he attacked them, physically and emotionally.

"My brother and I would exchange notes secretly through the bottom of the door. He was young but tried to help me. If we spoke through my window, he'd report things he saw to our mother. He noticed that I habitually pressed my hand to my jaw. One day, while my father was out of town, my mother and brother came up with a plan. They risked their own safety to take me to a dentist. It was discovered that I had an impacted tooth pressing on a nerve. The tooth was pulled and we stayed in a hotel, evaluating my condition. The behavior subsided, but of course other damage was done. I was forever changed."

Marjorie stares at Juliette, absorbing the unwelcome story.

"I could have been sent away," says Juliette. "Locked up for the rest of my life . . . because of an impacted tooth. I was eighteen when the tooth was pulled. My brother was thirteen. Recovery was complicated and music was part of my healing, but that doesn't matter here. What matters is that each year many healthy, sane women are institutionalized without proper evaluation, exiled by annoyed husbands or embarrassed families. The residency program is a quiet and dignified way to protect women and make determinations."

"Dignified?" Marjorie pushes back in her chair. "You are misleading women that you already know to be vulnerable. Ivy and Bernice are ambitious, with talents. As female artists they're subjected to an already manipulative world, and you've taken further advantage of that. By lying and pretending that this is an artistic residency, are you not toying with people's sanity? Not to mention the myriad of other swindles you're probably running. I'm sure you're paid handsomely by family members to hide away their lunatics. Am I right?"

"The program downstairs is an artist residency. It's not pretend. And the residency program is free, with only select candidates taking part in it.

We've had several residents go on to great success in the arts. The extended residence on this floor, however—yes, we are paid handsomely to provide an extremely high quality of living for the women."

"Oh, please," scoffs Marjorie.

"You're angry. I understand. I'm not the person I once was, and I too am angry about that. But our objective on this floor is always to get the resident back to her home. We have a very high success rate up here. That's why we have low occupancy. Only four or five women at a time. There are some wonderful family members who truly care about the women. But believe it or not, Marjorie, some families don't want the women back in their homes."

Marjorie pauses, trying to calm her breathing. "Bernice?" she asks quietly.

"Some creatives partake in substance abuse. Van Gogh liked absinthe, Baudelaire opium, Edgar Allan Poe used laudanum. At home, Bernice often inhaled varnish. But I believe she was bored, devoid of challenge, and needed a sense of direction with her creativity. Dock reported that she found inspiration being away from her rural community. Her mental acuity was sharp here."

"The rules of the lease and everything involved," says Marjorie, shaking her head. "The silver keys, the jobs, the curfew. It's all a test."

"In a way. But we've also found that those pursuing a creative project tend to thrive when sequestered with other artists. It provides a sense of belonging. Did you experience that?"

Marjorie nods but feels humiliated and desperately angry. She felt a deep belonging among women that the world deemed unworthy. Heat flares upon her neck, and her face brims with emotion. "Bernice and Ivy not only made the world less lonely for me, they were mentors," she whispers.

"Bernice does not know about the evaluation program, and I ask that you not tell her. Like many women who made it through successfully, she believes it was simply an artistic residency. In her exit interview with Dock, she cited you as opening her eyes to the world and putting her within reach of old and new heroes."

"Eileen Gray."

"Yes, I hope to facilitate a meeting."

Marjorie lifts the newspaper from her lap. "And what about dear Ivy? We have to help her. It says she's been taken to Eloise. Why is she not up here?"

"Our program focuses on rest and temporary rehabilitation to get the resident back home." Juliette clears her throat, but her voice cracks with emotion. "Ivy's husband claims he has tried hard enough. He doesn't want her at home."

Marjorie's throat tightens. "He doesn't . . . want her?" Tears well, clouding her eyes. Ivy is unwanted? The question must be asked.

"And my family?" she whispers.

"Your father, your family—they're complicated."

"I'm aware of that. But . . . do they want me back home?" whispers Marjorie.

"Those who might know you're here—I don't believe they understand the true nature of the residency." She stands and pours herself a cup of tea from the pot. "My brother is an extremely private person. He supports my endeavor, but I'm in charge of the program and the lease. People hear the name Bonafante and automatically assume it's his program. It's mine, and I've worked hard on it. But my brother has been inspired by you for some time. He has businesses of his own that connect him with people and places. He heard rumblings, your father's claims of imaginative derangement."

"My father wants to send me to a convent."

"No, his plan was to send you to the state psychiatric facility. Eloise Asylum."

Marjorie's face pales.

"Make no mistake, my brother—Charles, as many refer to him—is no saint. He's involved with several ventures, and just like this one, they're all confidential. But he felt inspired to help you, so he saw to it that your family stumbled on the brochure for the residency."

"I see," says Marjorie through clenched teeth. "Well, I'm happy I could provide him a charitable opportunity." She wipes her eyes and rises from the chair.

"Marjorie." Juliette stands and sets a hand on her shoulder. "You're incredibly creative and talented. And it's also clear that your father is mistaken. Our evaluations and Dock's reports indicate that you absolutely have your wits about you."

"Of course I do. You had no right to keep me here."

"We didn't bring you here. You yourself applied. You came voluntarily. And I'd like your discretion on behalf of the women involved. This is very confidential."

Marjorie pauses, pulling a slow breath. "I'm trying very hard to be understanding, to extend grace and compassion to you because of the personal things you've shared." She looks Juliette straight in the eye.

"But I'm sorry. I cannot. And I will not guarantee anything."

And with that, Marjorie turns and exits the room.

Dear Coco,

I told you.
I warned you.
But you wouldn't listen.
And now, because of you, I pay the price.

48

SCORCHING SCREAM

Marjorie parks the Packard outside the front door, two wheels on the sidewalk. She races through the apartment, gathering things to leave. She throws the dresses, supplies, and sketch pads atop the rabbit-fur rug. She'll roll it up and put it in the back seat of the car. She'll have to leave the sewing machine behind, but Miss Johnson is coming with her. She recalls Dock's comments:

You've named your lifelike human made of wax?
Do you have a temper, Miss Marjorie Lennox?

Her mind spools as she takes trips to and from the car. So, she's been a clinical study? And a charity case for Bonafante? Champagne and roses. The stars. Does he pity her? Why didn't he tell her what was really going on? What a manipulative monster. He's the one with a disorder. And Dock. Clever name. He's not a building manager. He's an actual doctor.

Are you a Prohibitionist?
I'm a health enthusiast.

He always said he was busy. Indeed he is, busy pretending innocent women are insane. Is she the only one to have gone upstairs and discovered their secret? The only one to have learned the truth about the Nightingale?

The Nightingale. Of course. Juliette considers herself Florence Nightingale, the lady of the lamp, a symbol of healing and devotion. Marjorie stops with her arms full of fabric. She kicks the rocking chair.

And why did she have to say that she wouldn't be discreet? There's nothing discreet about announcing you won't be discreet. Could that put her in danger? Will they try to silence her? And all this time she was annoyed with Hank. Hank was only trying to help her. How much does he know or suspect?

The scratches on the mirror, the money in the bed finials, the decorative metal over the windows and doors, Dock's clipboard, the jobs, the lease rules, the screams—it all makes sense now. But her own family. Does that make sense?

You can't come home, said Graham.

Her heart sinks. *Good sisters are understanding. Forgiving,* said Chet.

Forgiving—for sending her away? No wonder they were shocked to see her at the housewarming party. Are Graham and Chet in cahoots with her father on this? Did they know the truth about the residency? It's just too painful to believe. But if not, why did no one come directly to her to discuss it? She never told her siblings about her infatuation with Bonafante. If she had, would her family have sent her here?

Or maybe this is Cecile's doing? Her bizarre jealousy and desire to remain allied with their father? Or, worse, Granny and Gramps? Marjorie's stomach twists. No, she can't bear to imagine that her grandparents think she's lost her mind. And where is her mother in all of this? Or was she too busy exchanging love notes with her tennis partner to think about her daughter?

What a fool she is. She can bear her own naïveté, her silly infatuation, the bruise to her pride, but not the manipulation of Bernice and Ivy. No.

Marjorie lifts the fainting swan and looks at it. She shakes her head, winds up, and heaves it into the clock, releasing a scorching scream. She carries the rolled rug to the Packard and dumps it in the back seat.

You can't come home.

Yesterday Graham insisted that she go to the cottage. But, oh, no, she's not going to the cottage. She's going home. She's going to make them all squirm, and she'll enjoy every second while discerning exactly who knows what.

And something else.

Tomorrow she'll head straight to the newspaper and seek out Hank. What a willing partner he'll be to expose all of this. He was already on the scent.

But before heading home, she has important stops to make. Business to take care of.

Marjorie carries the last of the items out the door and to the car. She doesn't bother locking her apartment or the front door of the building. There's no "exit interview." And she takes the keys with her. Let them be afraid. Let them have to call a locksmith. She laughs.

The back seat of the car is overstuffed with the rug and Miss Johnson. She goes around to the rear and opens the trunk. It's empty except for a brown leather suitcase. She shoves aside the suitcase and drops the remainder of her items inside. She's about to close the trunk when curiosity gets the best of her. She pulls the suitcase forward and pops the latches.

It's filled with shoes. Baby's shoes. Of all sizes. They're darling, and some are quite beautiful. She lifts a lambskin booty, surprised to feel it heavy. She turns it over.

And just like a faucet, a stream of jewels pours out.

49

CLOSING IN

Graham rattles the door handle of Chet's room. He turns to leave when suddenly the hinges squeak.

"What do you want?"

"Have you been in there this whole time?" Graham whispers. He pushes past her into the room and closes the door. "I knocked an hour ago, but you didn't answer."

"I've been working on the tribute to Myrtle Branley. I'm trying to thread a needle that stabs Cecile. I'm gonna slap her back. It requires finesse, and I need to concentrate."

"You can't really believe that Cecile killed Myrtle Branley."

"Of course not. I made it up. But the story's grown legs, so I want it to trot."

"Well, put that aside. Something's happened."

Chet crosses her arms, impatient.

"An hour ago I was walking to the garage and I saw Gramps standing at the end of the drive."

"Taking his daily walk," says Chet.

"No. Talking to Charles Bonafante."

"What?"

"Yes!" whispers Graham.

"How do you know it was Bonafante?"

"He was in the Silver Ghost. He spotted me and left pretty quickly."

"Do you think Gramps knows about the residency?"

"I think Gramps may know more than we do. And given what Dad was considering for Marjorie, I thought the residency was a perfect solution. That the separation would protect her."

"And distance her from our own plan here."

"Exactly. But every time I visited her, it felt like there was more to it."

"More than designing clothes? Like what? Marjorie's an open book. If there was something more to it, she would have spilled it, made a proclamation."

"I think we're underestimating her."

"You think she knows that Dad was considering Eloise? You think she's running her own ruse? Boy, I'd be so proud of her!" says Chet. "What happened to her—the Peter incident—it was so unfair."

Graham leans against the wall. "I told you that when I went by to pick up the car, she thought she was getting sacked."

"Yeah. Why in the world did she bother going to Cecile's party?"

"I don't know. But while I was there, I stopped by to see Ivy and she was already gone."

"Ah, that's why you were so cranky at dinner last night. Couldn't get a second spoon of your Christmas pudding."

Graham shifts his eye patch and rubs the side of his face. "Well, when I was outside, I waited for Gramps to walk back up the drive and asked him about his conversation with Bonafante. He waved it off, but after I pestered him, he told me that the newspaper is closing in. They'll be running a story. An exposé, he called it."

"What exactly do they know?" says Chet.

"He didn't say, just said that he's relieved I'm not working in obituaries anymore and that he has another idea."

"You're not working in obituaries anymore? That's what he thinks?" Chet stares at him.

"Look, after you salute Myrtle Branley for smothering herself and ascending to join the fortune teller's lawnmowered cat, I'll need to resign."

"Like hell you will! We've been over this."

"Shh. Lilah and Dad have been screaming at each other all morning.

I'm developing one of Cecile's headaches. And enough already. It's time for the last hurrah. This shitting of cuff links and dictionaries, it's taking forever."

"That's because we didn't have enough. We were pinching it out too slowly. But I found a new supply."

"I hope you were careful about it."

"Of course I was. It's used in taxidermy."

"Well, we have enough to worry about. Set the obituaries aside. Just for a couple of months."

"No! I've already contacted Houdini's widow. I sent her a telegram. From you."

"From me? Chet!"

"Yes. Think how incredible this could be. A spirit returns to speak to the family, dictate his own obituary, and convey a final message."

Graham shakes his head with frustration. "Is this really about Houdini, or is this about Mom?"

Chet's face twists with offense. "What are you talking about?"

"Talk? We *don't* talk about it! About you finding Mom and your lingering anguish—*that's* what I'm talking about! It's derailed your entire existence." Graham gestures to the odd collection of mortality on her shelves. "You relate more to death than you do to life."

"That's not true."

"Chet . . ." Graham's voice thins with concern. He looks squarely at her, without his usual humor. "Don't explode or yell at me. That's how you deflect whenever I try to talk about this. You're my sister, my best friend." His voice drops to a whisper. "And I love you. I worry about you. Your bottomless grief has manifested into a bizarre obsession."

Chet turns toward the window. "You're exaggerating."

"Really? You spent nearly twenty minutes—on two separate occasions—waxing about some creepy paperweight with a dead beetle that you saw at the police station, how you can't stop thinking about it, how you have to have it. That's not normal. Your collection of dead stuff, that's not normal. Don't you realize? You're the beetle, Chet! What if you focused on living your life instead of being trapped beneath a bell jar of memento mori?"

Chet whirls to face him. "You weren't there! You didn't know her!"

Graham steps back. "You're right. I lost out. I didn't know our mother.

But surrounding yourself with souvenirs of death isn't going to bring her back."

"You think I don't know that?" Chet's eyes cloud with tears. "I've worked alongside you, Graham, because I know it's the right thing for everyone. And it's what Mom would want. When you were born, she would rock you, whisper that you'd be the man to finally steer us straight. And she was right."

She lowers her voice. "For our family and our business to survive, you have to take the reins. Uncle Jamie has his own fortune. He won't step in, because he doesn't have to. He probably anticipates that Dad will destroy everything. There will be nothing left by the time it gets to you. That's what this is about. And once it's over, an embalming has to happen straightaway to avoid an autopsy. We can't give anyone a chance to ask questions. Do you think I befriended an embalmer just for fun?"

"I kinda do."

A flicker of hurt shadows her face. She blinks it back. "You know what? Forget it. Just get out!" She opens the door, shoves Graham into the hallway, and slams the door. He nearly collides with Ina, the housekeeper, who carries a stack of towels.

"Oh, my. Everything okay in there?" asks Ina.

Graham looks at her, dazed. "I don't know. What do you think?" He points to Chet's door. "Is everything okay in there, Ina? There's a lot of dead stuff."

"Oh, yes. She's fine. Death décor is just a maudlin style these days. It doesn't foretell anything. Besides, if my memory hasn't rusted, I believe the servants' betting pool lists you as the first child in the family to die, not Chet. So she's okay. Enjoy your day, dear." Ina continues down the hall with the towels.

50

DOUBLE SHAMED

Why are there jewels in the baby booties, and to whom do they belong? When Graham told her to take the car home from the party, did he know they were in the trunk?

Marjorie pulls off the road into a filling station. The attendant jogs to her car.

"Good morning, pretty lady. What can I do ya for?"

"Top it off, please."

Marjorie removes the map that lives in the glove box and studies it. The attendant takes notice.

"Need directions? Where you headed?"

"I believe . . ." Marjorie traces her finger along the map. "To Nankin Township."

"Nankin Township? Ain't nothin' out that way."

"Oh, but there is," replies Marjorie.

The attendant looks at her. He adjusts his cap as if his head suddenly itches. "You mean the haunted hospital?"

"The hospital, yes. But what makes you say it's haunted?"

"Eloise? Well, between the poorhouse, the hospital, and the asylum, thousands have died there. And no one wants to be there in the first place. If you're sent out to Eloise, everyone knows something's not right and everyone also knows you're poor. You're double shamed. So the dead souls are disgruntled and take to haunting."

"I disagree," says Marjorie, lowering the map and looking at the young man. "Disgruntled souls wouldn't haunt the hospital; they'd seek out those who sent them there."

The attendant nods slowly and finishes topping off the gas. He collects the money from Marjorie.

"My pop had an old aunt who was sent out to Eloise. For a rest, they told us. Must have been a permanent rest. Never heard of her again. You have family folk at Eloise?"

Marjorie takes a breath and grips the steering wheel.

"Yes, I have family there."

Marjorie turns off Michigan Avenue into the entrance of the facility. She stops short of the main gate to take in the sprawling scene. Two red-brick pillars flank a small guardhouse beneath a wrought-iron sign with the letters ELOISE displayed in a delicate crescent. Intended to convey elegance, the spindly letters instead conjure something macabre, like the entrance to a ghostly laboratory.

Eloise appears to be a city unto itself. Countless buildings, a huffing brick smokestack, and pastures full of residents working in the fields, dairy barns, a piggery, and more. If what she's heard is true, there are two large cemeteries and the compound covers nearly a thousand acres, over a square mile. Albeit a bit custodial, Eloise seems much more straightforward and transparent than what she experienced at the Nightingale.

A guard steps from the gatehouse, holding a clipboard. He looks to the car. Marjorie takes a breath and rolls to the gate.

"Morning," nods the guard.

"I'm here for visitation," says Marjorie.

"Poorhouse, hospital, or asylum?"

Marjorie detests the word "asylum" and prefers the modern terminology. "The psychopathic facility, please."

"Building D. The big red one here in front. Parking is to the side." The guard peers into the rear of the Packard and spots Miss Johnson's wax face pressing against the side window. "Uh . . . male or female patient?"

"Female."

"Fourth floor."

Marjorie pulls around to the parking area. As she removes a few items from the Packard, she thinks of the comments made by the filling-station attendant. That being at Eloise is a double shame, that the patients are not only ill but poor. But Ivy's family is in the tire business. She said their home is in Palmer Woods, a wealthy new development with homes of more than five thousand square feet. They're certainly not low on funds.

But Marjorie knows the truth. For some women, Eloise isn't about funds.

It's a form of punishment.

Granny would recount grim stories from the Detroit newspapers—horrific cases of women being involuntary committed. In one instance, a group of a dozen Detroit women physically fought with police and Eloise ambulance drivers to free their neighbor, pleading that their friend was of sound mind. The women retained legal counsel and, at their own expense, provided evidence of wrongful imprisonment by the spouse. But the ornery judge ruled for the husband, a local businessman who had taken up with another woman and wanted to be rid of his wife. The judge cautioned the women not to meddle in the business of others and that it was a man's place to make decisions regarding "his chattel."

The episode issued an unwritten warning to women: Behave. Or we'll lock you away. Granny predicted women of the decade would take stock. And she was right. Marriage rates slowed, and women began to sow their oats and pursue new freedoms. But the threat remains.

The blocky red-brick building in front of her does not convey freedom. It conveys institution. The entrance comprises a portico of cast concrete with three arched openings. Staircases jut to both left and right of the entry—stone arms extending to pull you in.

Marjorie enters the building, taking in the stark white walls and shiny tile floors. A guard stands from a desk.

"I'm visiting a female patient on the fourth floor," she says.

"Is the patient permitted to have visitors?"

Marjorie pauses. She didn't think of that. Could Ivy be denied visitors? No. That seems plain cruel. "Yes," she smiles. "She enjoys visitors."

"You'll have to report to the floor and consult with the duty nurse."

Marjorie climbs the three flights of wide stairs to the women's ward, carrying her bundle. She arrives at the reception desk, winded.

"Hello. I'm here to visit a patient."

A nurse in a starched white uniform greets Marjorie with an equally starched expression.

"Patient name?"

"Iv— I . . . I've come to see Winifred Dixon."

"Are you family?"

"Yes," lies Marjorie. "A cousin."

"Your name?"

She hesitates, thinking, then gives a smile. "Sandra Claus."

"I don't see any restrictions with regard to the patient, but the items you're carrying will need to be inspected if you plan to give them to her. Hand them over to me. We'll bring them to you if they're approved; otherwise, you can collect them on your way out. You'll find Mrs. Dixon in the day hall at this time. Proceed through the door behind me and walk all the way to the very end of the long corridor. Please don't stop or communicate with patients. Go directly to Mrs. Dixon."

Mrs. Dixon.

Is she really married? And Marjorie can't adjust to the name. She's not Winifred. She's Ivy.

She pushes through the heavy swinging door and enters a long, shadowed hallway. A chemical odor slows her steps. The air is thick with disinfectant but also laced with something heavier, something unspoken. She tries to avoid stopping or staring, but every sound draws her attention. Yelling, crying, laughing, fists pounding upon doors. A young woman with matted black hair hugs the wall and slithers slowly down the corridor. Marjorie moves past dormitory-style rooms, each with neat rows of identical beds. She passes private and semi-private rooms and doors with industrial-sized locks and small viewing windows. She swallows, thinking of the woman dancing and drinking champagne on the top floor of the Nightingale. How many women exist behind the closed doors she's passing, their lives reduced to a hum of yellow lights and the click of a latch?

She arrives at the end of the corridor and peers through the square glass window on the door. The enormous day hall has the appearance of a sunroom. At the back is a bank of windows overlooking the rear grounds of the property. As she enters, a nurse nods and smiles kindly. Marjorie walks through clusters of women at tables working quietly on puzzles or drawings. She passes a curly-haired girl petting a stuffed cat and pauses at a woman balled on the floor in the fetal position, whimpering and rocking back and forth.

"She's alright. Just a bit of self-soothing," assures the nurse.

She spots a plume of platinum hair across the room, in front of the bank of windows. Marjorie approaches and quietly steps beside the chair.

Ivy's head lolls to the side on a rubbery neck. She's asleep.

Marjorie says nothing. She doesn't want to wake her. She kneels beside the chair and fights the impulse to throw her arms around her friend.

Ivy's face is pale, slackened with sleep. Her nails, normally glossy red, are now bald and hacked to the quick. Her hair is combed but hasn't been set. She wears a drab gray cotton dressing gown.

How does this happen? How does a beautiful, talented woman who embraces every aspect of freedom become imprisoned like this? A flicker of images plays through Marjorie's mind like a silent film strip: Ivy taping the Christmas sign to her door, stealing into the playwright's room, laughing and scattering snowfalls of cigarette ash, handing her alarm clock to Marjorie, and crawling through Bernice's window in the green satin dress.

Her chest burns with injustice. The emotion rises and she chokes back a sob.

And at that moment, Ivy's eyes slowly flutter open, revealing two glassy and tranquilized pools. She looks at Marjorie, blinks, and as she lifts her head, a single tear drops onto her cheek. Her voice is a whisper.

"Hello, darling."

51

BROKEN TOYS

Marjorie takes Ivy's hands, warming them between her own.

The dramatic flair is absent from Ivy's voice. "How on earth did you find me?"

Marjorie doesn't want to mention the story in the paper. "Let's just say I did some digging. Are you okay?"

Ivy sits up, clearing her throat and shaking her head to awaken her faculties. "Yes, just terribly sedated. Daddy's orders, I'm sure. He's probably convinced them that I'll scale the walls to the roof."

"Your father?"

"Well, that's what he demands to be called." She looks at Marjorie. "In truth, he's my husband."

Marjorie exhales, relieved that Ivy has a grasp on reality.

"Please tell me you have a cigarette, Marjie. A cigarette might clear this head fog."

Marjorie removes her cigarette case from her purse, then pauses.

"Are you allowed to smoke?"

"Oh. I should be careful. If I misbehave, they might send me to a nuthouse, right?" Ivy rolls her eyes. She then motions to the nurse and points to the cigarette. "I'm considered low security. I can smoke if there's a nurse in the room, but I can't have matches. Nothing scarier than a disgruntled wife with a fistful of flame. They'll inspect me before I leave the room to make sure I haven't stuffed my bra with puzzle pieces."

Marjorie lights her cigarette, and Ivy takes a deep drag. She closes her eyes, hostaging the smoke in her chest for a long beat before exhaling. "There. Oh, that's better."

Ivy leans forward, placing a hand on Marjorie's cheek. "Oh, darling, come sit next to me. Don't tell me they've frightened you with Luther's account of the evening. Luther's an evil father of a husband. I know I told you my family is in rubber, but the truth is that my real father worked as a laborer in my husband's rubber plant. When I was a young girl, Luther's pants would expand whenever he saw me. My mother died when I was little, and when my father fell ill, Luther claimed he'd care for me. He convinced my father to let him marry me. I was thirteen."

Marjorie turns with shock before taking the chair next to Ivy. "But that's illegal. You have to be sixteen to be married."

"Oh, trust me, I've looked for loopholes. You have to be sixteen in Michigan. But in fourteen states, you only have to be twelve. And here I thought we drove to Kentucky so I could get a pony. Of course, I wanted nothing to do with Luther, so he showered me with expensive gifts, told me of the grand life I'd live, and put the fear of God in me that I'd be sent to the poorhouse once my ailing father died. Well, it seems that's happened anyway. I'm sorry I wasn't transparent about everything. Sometimes it's easier . . . to pretend."

"Of course," nods Marjorie.

Ivy adjusts the tattered afghan around her shoulders. "You're probably wondering what on earth transpired. Well, the night of your sister's dubious party, I had such a wonderful time with your handsome brother that I finally decided I had endured enough. I went home to demand a divorce from Luther and, no surprise, he had a girl in the house. I went on the roof to hang my head over the bedroom window—catch them in the act and scare him. When he saw me, he berated me, taunted me to jump off the roof, said he'd love to be rid of me. He claimed I was crazy if I wanted to divorce him. He's very adept at manipulation and mind twisting.

"Well, I had no intention of flinging myself from the roof and ripping that fabulous Christmas tree dress you made for me. I had already snagged it climbing the tree and crawling across the shingles. Luther called the police and told them I was off my trolley, yelling for Santa."

"Were you?"

"Probably," shrugs Ivy. "I was loaded on highballs and the deliciousness of your brother." She flicks ash to the tiled floor. "How did you sneak out of the Nightingale? Does Bernice know you're here?"

Marjorie takes a breath. "We got sacked."

"No! Because of me?"

"Not because of you. We all snuck out. We broke the lease." Marjorie looks at Ivy, wondering if she suspects what's really transpiring at the Nightingale. "You know, I never asked. How did you hear of the residency?"

"A nurse I know once mentioned a 'creative retreat' program. The chance to get away sounded heavenly, so I badgered her to share the brochure and get me an invitation."

Marjorie looks at Ivy. So she didn't know the truth about the program. Did her husband put the nurse up to it?

"How does your husband feel about you painting?"

Ivy exhales smoke toward the ceiling. "He thinks creativity is a disorder. Luther accuses me of so many things. He claims I'm delusional and insane, but my actual diagnosis is 'mourning and melancholia.' Some days I feel so bereft and trapped in my life that I simply can't get out of bed. I'm melancholy and mourning my innocence that was lost to a pervert father of a husband. So I jumped on the chance to get away. Luther didn't care. It gave him the opportunity to bring in someone younger."

Marjorie sees a woman in a starched white cap approaching with the items she brought. She smiles at Ivy. "I brought you something that might lift your spirits."

"You smuggled in some gin?"

"Something better."

The woman arrives and hands Ivy the red satin blanket and the rug.

"My Christmas blanket!" gushes Ivy. She tosses the tatty afghan aside and coils herself in the red blanket.

Marjorie unfolds the rabbit-fur rug and lays it at Ivy's feet. The woman places an ashtray next to Ivy's chair and retrieves the afghan before walking away.

"See, darling," says Ivy, calling to the woman, "this is what I was telling you. All I need is a little holiday cheer. I feel so much better already." A bit of animation returns to Ivy's face.

Wrapped in red satin, she looks more like herself.

"Ivy . . . why Christmas?" asks Marjorie.

Ivy's gusto fades. She taps ash from the end of her cigarette, completely missing the ashtray. "It was my last memory with my mother. There was a fire at the rubber plant on Christmas Eve and my father was called in for a late shift. That night, there was a marvelous snowstorm. I spent a snowy Christmas morning alone with my mom. We opened presents from Santa and had tea and cookies all by ourselves. I sat in her lap next to our little Christmas tree while she read to me, and I fell asleep in her arms." She looks at Marjorie and pauses, gathering her memories. "It was the last time that I ever felt truly safe. Painting scenes of Christmas comforts me, reminds me of my darling mother. It brings me peace."

A stab of melancholy pierces Marjorie's heart. She judged Ivy's paintings as quaint, something from a dime-store holiday card. But they're so much more.

Ivy smiles. "You're such a doll for coming. Thank you, Marjie." She sighs. "Well, I tried so hard, but I guess Luther got the last laugh exiling me here, didn't he?"

"No! He didn't get the last laugh. But we'll be laughing when a good lawyer arranges a divorce and breaks you out of here."

"Lawyers cost money, sweetie. And didn't you hear what I said? I've got a medical diagnosis. Melancholia. Low spirits," she says dramatically. "I'm tarnished goods, broken. Broken toys are put in the trash. We're not even listed as patients on the paperwork here. Over at the hospital they're called patients and can be released. Here we're called inmates. We have to be paroled. And attorneys are expensive."

Marjorie looks at her friend, thinking of the jewels in the baby booties and the money she took from the bed finials. "I might have access to some funds."

Ivy's eyes well with tears. "Bless you." She sniffs and finishes the last of her cigarette. "You're such a loyal friend, Marjorie."

"Should I call you Winifred?"

"Good God, no. Ivy's been my artist name for years. When I'm old, with knockers at my knees, I can be a Winifred." She gazes away as she floats the question. "So, have you seen Graham?"

"He came to the Nightingale the morning after the party looking for you—with an enormous bouquet of flowers."

Her head turns swiftly. "Really?" Her eyes spark. "He's such a dream. I know he's your brother, so it's wildly inappropriate to say this, but he's fabulous in the sack. That was no silent night. Oh, Marjie, please get me out of here. I know I'm eccentric, but I'm not insane. I don't belong here. If I'm made to stay, I'll surely lose my reason."

Marjorie nods slowly. She doesn't want to believe that Graham knows the truth about the Nightingale. If he did, pursuing Ivy would be evil.

"Since we're hanging our lingerie on the line, there's something you should know," says Ivy.

Marjorie looks to her.

"The stunning ruby necklace that your sister Cecile was wearing at the party. Did you recognize it?"

Marjorie shakes her head.

"Of course you didn't. It belongs to my neighbor in Palmer Woods. It was stolen six months ago."

52

GET JACK

Marjorie drives back toward the city, thinking not only about Ivy but of the many other women who are unjustly institutionalized. Juliette claims it was her reason for establishing the Nightingale and the residency program. But if Bonafante knew that Marjorie was under evaluation, their episode in the stairwell was more untoward than she originally thought. Or maybe that's why he was hesitant and told her to stop?

And foremost on her mind is Ivy's last comment, about Cecile's necklace. Cecile's always been fixated on jewelry. Her jewelry armoire is nearly the size of her garment wardrobe. Are Cecile and Lou in business with a fence? Could that explain the baby booties in the suitcase? Each day, the papers report stories of jewel thefts and bandits who break into the homes of the wealthy in Detroit and Grosse Pointe. There are so many incidents that she doesn't even read the stories anymore unless she recognizes the name in the headline.

But everyone has their particular obsessions. Her father's obsessed with food and power, Ivy's obsessed with Christmas, Chet's obsessed with death, and Cecile is obsessed with jewelry. Although she loves fashion, Marjorie isn't infatuated by jewelry. She prefers fake glass gems, because they come in a wider array of colors to match the fabrics she works with.

A bolt of knowing hits Marjorie. She swerves, whips the car to the side of the road, and slams on the brakes. Adrenaline surges through her body. Her fingertips go cold.

She prefers fake gems.

Fake glass gems . . .

How could she be so thick?

When her grandfather retired, her father took over the windshield business. Which meant he also took over the factory. Lou now works for her father—in their glass factory. Of course: Who would have the talent and resources to make fake glass gems?

Marjorie sucks in a breath.

"No," she exhales. "No, they didn't!"

She hits the gas and peels back onto the road, amidst a flurry of honks and yells from other drivers.

The afternoon is cooling as the Packard pulls to a stop in front of a small building. Marjorie checks the name on the sign before exiting and locking the car. She smooths her skirt and takes deep breaths, trying to calm herself. Is this a huge mistake?

She pulls on the door and enters the building. A handsome, diamond-tiled floor leads to a reception area and a desk flanked by two potted palms. A small sofa and two chairs sit in front of a coffee table scattered with magazines. The receptionist finishes a call and looks up at Marjorie.

"Good afternoon, may I help you?"

"Yes, please. I'm here to see Peter Howell."

The woman appears confused. "Peter Howell? Do you mean Jack Howell?"

Jack? Marjorie's mind ticks. Did she once hear Peter's father refer to him as J.P.? Perhaps his first name is Jack? She smiles at the woman. "Yes, silly me. Jack Howell."

"And who may I say is here?"

Marjorie pauses. Peter's been avoiding her. Maybe he'll try that again.

"Tell him Winifred Dixon is here to see him."

"Do you have an appointment?"

"No," says Marjorie. She sees the advertising magazines on the coffee table. "It's regarding a new clothing campaign."

"Alright." The woman stands. "We're a small company and don't have a switchboard, just a telephone for incoming calls. I'll go get Jack."

She'll go get . . . Jack. Peter always wished his name was Pierre. If he changed his name, he certainly wouldn't choose Jack, would he? And Howell is a common last name. What if it's the wrong person entirely? What will she say then? No, she's certain this is the company she heard that he was working for. She drove by the building once.

Marjorie stands, too nervous to sit. She paces the floor. The door behind the desk opens and the receptionist returns to the lobby, followed by a man.

He freezes. His expression is one of shock.

Marjorie smiles, taking on a role. "Hello, Mr. Howell. I'm so sorry to bother you without an appointment. I'll take only a minute. Perhaps we can speak outside?"

He nods slowly, raising his hand and then pointing absently to the door behind him. "Sure, I'll get my hat." He disappears through the door. Marjorie waits a moment and then realizes. She dashes out the front and runs to the back of the building just as he's trying to escape. She blocks his path.

"Hello, Peter."

53

SOME FIXER

Peter walks the perimeter of the building, making sure they're alone. They sit on a bench out back. His hair is shorter than usual, with a pedestrian cut. His bland navy suit could be from any department store, and his hands appear pale and lonely without his usual complement of rings.

"I'm working, Marjorie. It's the middle of my workday."

"This won't take long."

"You shouldn't be here at all. I wish you'd just leave."

"Five minutes. I won't tell a soul that we spoke."

Peter drops his head in his hands.

"I was so confused," says Marjorie. "I couldn't figure it out. My father forbade me to see you, and even when I tried, you didn't respond. Yes, you had been questioned about the jewel heist, but you weren't formally accused. It felt like my family overreacted. But now I've put it together."

Marjorie's voice drops in volume. "My family was responsible for the heist at the Detroit Institute of Arts, and you helped them. My father made the glass replicas and you swapped them for the originals."

"Shh! It wasn't like that! See, you've got the wrong end of the stick. No one will understand."

"Then tell me what happened."

"I can't," says Peter, his voice cracking with emotion. "My family's been through too much already."

"Your family? What happened to your family?"

Peter looks at her in earnest. "You really don't know? Swear to me that you don't know."

"I swear!" says Marjorie. "We were close, Peter. You were one of my dearest friends! You were questioned after the heist and I never heard from you again. But today it suddenly dawned on me that my family could be making fake gems and, because you collected glass shards at the factory, that you were involved with them."

"No, it's not nearly that straightforward."

"Peter, I have no illusion that my family, especially my father, is on the right side of business . . . or life, for that matter. He lies, cheats—"

"And blackmails people," whispers Peter.

"He blackmailed you?"

Peter nods and again checks to make sure they're alone. "I had come across a few tiny imitation gems in the floor sweeps. I loved them and asked your father if I could have them. He shrugged, said sure, and acted like he didn't know what they were. But a week later, Cecile's husband, Lou, showed up at my house to drop off a package."

"Lou?"

"Yeah. I had a friend . . . who will remain unnamed. He was a great guy, and our relationship evolved to, well, more than friends." Peter looks to Marjorie for a reaction.

She nods and places her hand on his.

Peter grips her hand, gathering courage. "Well, Lou showed up with two thugs and an envelope of photographs of me with my friend." Peter glances around. "The pictures showed us sharing an intimate moment. Lou said that if I didn't help him with a job, your father would release the photos to the newspaper, plaster them at my father's factory, and mail them to the entire congregation at our church."

"What? How evil!"

"Yes, Lou made sure to show me that he had our church directory. Trust me, your dad didn't lose any sleep over it. He's known for stunts like this, and he's always been in competition with my father."

"And the job was to swap a couple of jewels at the DIA with glass replicas?"

"Not just a couple of jewels—the entire Frederick K. Stearns collection. A twelve-foot case. The swap went unnoticed for months, but then your dad and his thugs wanted more." Peter begins to cry. "Of course they did. How could I have been so naïve! But the next time, they blackmailed not only me but my friend in the photos as well."

Tears spill down Peter's face, pressing a quiet ache to Marjorie's heart. She wraps her arms around him.

"My . . . my friend was so terrified, the whole thing got botched. Word leaked and the papers briefly picked up the story. I had no choice"—his voice breaks with sobs—"but to tell my parents. And I crumbled and confessed to them about what was in the photos. My parents decided that I should accept a diagnosis of mental illness. That if I was ever charged with the crime at the DIA, I could claim insanity. They sent me to a psychiatric facility at University of Michigan to get well. And in the meantime, my father found some fixer to bury the whole thing, make it all go away."

"An attorney?"

Peter chuckles, wiping his nose. "You're still so sweet, Marjie. No, not a lawyer. Some fixer, a high-level blackhander. It probably killed my father to resort to such tactics. After my stays at the psychiatric facility, it was agreed that I should use a different name."

"Jack?"

"I know. Of course I wanted Pierre but didn't dare mention that to my parents. We settled on Jack because it's my legal first name and it sounds brawny. My friend moved to New York. As soon as I can save up some money, I'll be joining him. I have to get out of here."

Peter blows out a breath and peers around. "Marjorie, I can't be seen with you. Please don't ever contact me again. I've been through hell because of your family, and I live in fear that your father's thugs are still following me. When the blackhander fixed things for my family, I was told that I could never speak with you again."

"Because I'm a bad influence," says Marjorie, looking to her lap.

"No," says Peter. "Because you're in such danger."

Marjorie looks up at Peter, confused. "I'm in danger?"

He nods. "That's what the blackhander said."

"Did you ever meet this blackhander fixer person?"

"No. All I know is that he's some swish guy from Grosse Pointe."

54

NO POSTMARK

Evil.

How could her father and Lou be capable of such evil? How can the blood running through her veins be connected to such cruelty? And of course Cecile was in on it; that's why she always reacted so negatively to Peter. But who else in the family was involved?

Marjorie pulls off the road before reaching Glen Arden. She dumps the jewels from the baby booties into her own suitcase and fills the little shoes in the brown valise with rocks from the side of the road. If she must escape from her family, she'll inspect the jewels. If they're real, she'll sell them for cash. But what if they're fakes?

The wind stirs uneasy clouds, echoing her storm of emotion as she pulls down the long front drive to Glen Arden. The mansion she's always loved now appears slightly askew beneath the graying light. She parks and the entrance doors swing open. Marjorie takes a breath and exits the car.

"Welcome back, Miss," says Atchison from the front steps.

"Hello, Atch. Could I trouble you to send everything to my room? I'd be so grateful."

"Certainly, Miss Lennox."

"Oh, except the small brown valise in the trunk. I'll take my suitcase, though." She nods to him and walks toward the house, lugging her bag. Each step across the gravel toward the doorway prickles with the sensation of ascending a gritty tongue into an open mouth.

Her grandfather spots her in the foyer.

"Well, hello there, lassie!" booms Gramps. "So happy you're finally back. Things just weren't the same without you. Your granny has a bonny new parakeet. You must come and meet Lally." He waves her forward and heads toward the sitting room. Atchison follows, handing an armload from the car to Ina. He reaches for Marjorie's suitcase to assist, but she gently pulls it toward her.

"Thank you, Atchison," she smiles. "But I could use the exercise." She enters the sitting room and sets the case beside the sofa.

"Marjorie! I'm so delighted you're back," says her grandmother. "The house lost its sparkle without you, my dear." The parakeet chirps, and Granny beams. "Oh! And Lally agrees. See, he already loves you."

Marjorie sits next to her grandmother and puts a hand upon hers. "I'm so sorry about Poochie, Granny."

"Yes, such a tragedy. And such a violent death. It just doesn't make sense. I'm still having terrible sympathy dreams where I'm flapping my arms and projectile-vomiting lobster. My poor Poochie. Dead. And Myrtle Branley too."

"Myrtle Branley?" gasps Marjorie. "That woman had the constitution of a bull."

"But apparently not the lungs of a bull," says Gramps. "The poor gal suffocated."

"What?"

"Yes, in her vapor bath," says Granny. "She was quite partial to heat therapy, claimed some Scandinavian theory that it cleared the toxins. But I can't imagine what toxins she was trying to clear. I hate to speak ill of the dead, but she wasn't very exciting. Her sole vice was sweet cream sodas from Sanders."

"Those can be hard to sweat out," says Gramps.

"Yes," agrees her grandmother. "In other news, I have a new umbrella—Genghis Khan. Cecile and Lou have moved into a new home. Your father threw a large party for them, but we didn't go. Best to leave the partying to the young people."

"I heard it was grotesque," grumbles Gramps. "A mix of rapscallions and miscreants. Such a blight to the Lennox family name and business."

"Well, Cormac," sighs her grandmother. "Different generations have a different approach. Speaking of different generations, your friends Judith and Helen arrived at the flower show more lit than Electric Park, Graham's been frequenting a bordello, and your mother smacked herself in the head with a tennis racket and collapsed in the garden. But tell us, how are things at the cottage? How are my purple coneflowers?"

Marjorie, generally able to follow her grandmother and even match her speed, struggles to keep up.

"Oh, everything is wonderful," she says. She takes a breath but doesn't continue. She can't. Things aren't wonderful. Her heart is broken. Shattered. Her vision of the world forever changed. She looks at her beloved grandparents, confused.

"You okay, love?" asks Gramps. His expression—he's studying her.

"Yes, just a bit tired from the drive. I think I'll head up to my room to rest."

"Yes, you do that, dear," says Granny, patting Marjorie's hand.

"It's great to have you home, sweetheart," Gramps reiterates. "Your grandmother's right. Glen Arden lacked a certain twinkle while you were gone."

Marjorie gives them each a hug and leaves them to read their newspaper. She picks up the suitcase and heads up the tartan-carpeted staircase. Her father always claims that her grandparents are wily. But they seem so sincere. Can she believe them? How awful that she even has to question. It's infuriating.

Marjorie trudges across the upper gallery and enters her bedroom. She quickly closes and locks the door. Habit now. She stands, fingers trembling, trying to grasp her suitcase in one hand and her future in the other. She sees her familiar four-poster bed, her dressing screen, and the full-length mirror, side-slung with her long strands of pearls. Her bedroom window is open, allowing the brooding air to seduce the pale-ivory curtains into a gentle dance. Ina has brought up her things, and Miss Johnson now stands sentry in the corner.

Her body wilts with exhaustion, and myriad emotions cascade over her. She begins to cry. She misses her frowsy apartment with the moss drapes, the enamel butcher table, the crusty kettle, and her narrow convent bed. She misses the chug of the Singer sewing machine and the bustling noise of the city beyond her window. And, most of all, she misses

Bernice and Ivy. Bernice in her braids and canvas tool belt. Ivy in absolutely nothing but perfume and red lipstick.

The first days of the residency, she felt a curious intimacy with loneliness, but this is different. It never occurred to her until this moment that it's entirely possible to feel alone and misplaced even when surrounded by family. Even in the bedroom of your own home.

A soft knock sounds at her door. "Hey, kid."

It's Graham.

"Please go away, Graham. I'm terribly tired and need to rest. I'll find you and Chet later."

"Alright. We're here if you need us to take you to the cottage."

Again, the cottage. Does everyone want to get rid of her? What does Graham know?

She sets down the suitcase and removes her hat. A small stack of mail sits upon her dressing table. She sifts through it, uninterested. A postcard from a friend who's summering in Les Cheneaux. A catalog of French tulle she had sent away for. But sitting in the center of the stack is an envelope with no postmark, simply her name. She doesn't have a letter opener, so she uses a large hairpin to slice through the flap of the envelope.

PLEASE JOIN ME FOR DINNER TOMORROW
8:00 P.M. WINDMILL POINTE

Marjorie examines the envelope. When did this arrive and how did it get into her bedroom?

Fear crawls onto her shoulder, whispering in her ear.

Some fixer, a high-level blackhander . . . some swish guy from Grosse Pointe.

She shakes off the shiver. Her eyes narrow. Is it really from him? She used to find delight and excitement in absolutely everything. She detests this new skeptical version of herself. And there's something she hates even more: Despite everything, there's still a large part of her that wants to see Bonafante, to be with him. What is wrong with her? *Chronic imaginative derangement,* the file said.

Marjorie opens the drawer of her dressing table, retrieves a cigarette, and lights it. The brochure for the residency peeks out from beneath a compact and comb. She takes it and walks over to sit in the window, smoking and looking out onto the front drive and gardens of Glen Arden. She inhales, thinking, and exhales a long ribbon of smoke through the open window.

The brochure briefly describes the residency, the fact that it's by invitation only, and the application process. Nowhere does the name "Charles" or the title of "Mr." appear. Juliette was right. People make assumptions. Marjorie certainly did, not because she doubted the ability of women, purely because she was naïve and single-minded, desperate to get to know Charles Bonafante. She's so relieved that she never told her family or siblings about her interest in him. Bernice is the only one who knows the truth, and by now that secret is long safe, up in a lighthouse. Marjorie frowns. Just the thought of Bernice hurts her heart.

It's easy and convenient to fall in love with a man of means, isn't it? And a handsome, mysterious man on top of it. That makes her such a cliché. But isn't it also clichéd for a man of means to be attracted to a little bird with broken wings? She felt a true connection with Bonafante the very first time she saw him at the Pontchartrain. Yes, he's easy on the eyes, but she's always believed there's more to it.

If he's a true louse, wouldn't he be seen somewhere—anywhere—drinking, gambling, with women on each arm or in his car? Wouldn't there be whispers of his doings? But just like his car, he's an elegant ghost. Bernice's warning filters back to her upon the tendrils of cigarette smoke.

This type can be even more dangerous. They hide behind manners and nice clothes and big houses. And they can get away with—buy their way with—everything.

Is Bernice right?

Of course she is.

But it doesn't matter. Marjorie will accept the invitation and undress Bonafante.

Metaphorically. And literally.

55

NEW HEIGHTS

Marjorie pulls the chair away from her bed. The idea came to her while perched in the window.

Each end of her four-poster bed is capped with a finial carved into the shape of a large acorn. Upon inspection, she found that the caps were removable—the perfect place to hide the jewels that she took from the suitcase. The echo of experience from her residency produces a smile, a quiet contentment to have secrets of her own.

The jewels are exquisite. She tried to examine them more discerningly beneath the light of her window but needed a magnifier. One large sapphire is particularly stunning. She's no gemologist, but if the jewels were left in the trunk, they can't be real. Which is a shame, because if she wants to escape from her family and help Ivy and Peter, she'll need additional funds besides the stash she found in her apartment at the Nightingale.

She thinks of the "play fund," the secret bank in her mother's vanity. It's nearing five o'clock. Marjorie's mother was out when she came home. She can't waste any time. If she's going to pilfer from the play fund, best to sneak in now, before she returns.

Marjorie peeks out of her bedroom door to make sure no one's around and steals across the upper landing to her mother's suite of rooms. She passes through the bedroom, opens and closes the door to the boudoir, and quickly heads to her mother's dressing table. She pulls open the top left drawer, removes the false bottom, and takes several bills. Interesting—

the stack of cash is larger than usual, and in addition to the cash, there are now several envelopes in the drawer. Marjorie lifts one. It's addressed to Slorah. She looks at the other envelopes. They're all addressed to Slorah. And they've all been opened.

Why on earth would her mother have Slorah's mail?

Marjorie peeks inside one of the envelopes, only to find another envelope, this one with her mother's name on it. Someone is communicating with her mother through Slorah. She lifts the flap of the internal envelope and sees a letter in a masculine scrawl that begins with *My darling angel . . .*

Oh, dear. More letters from her tennis partner.

The bedroom door handle rattles.

Marjorie quickly stuffs the cash and the letter into her bra and replaces the false bottom of the drawer. She jumps onto her mother's fainting couch and closes her eyes.

Muffled voices sound from the bedroom, and the door to the boudoir opens.

"It was just too soon," says her mother. "I— Marjorie! Heavens, what are you doing here, dear?"

Marjorie stretches and fakes a yawn. "I'm home from the cottage and wanted to see you. I was waiting and must have dozed off."

Slorah stands next to her mother. She drills Marjorie with a stare.

"Hello, Slorah," smiles Marjorie.

"Welcome back, sweetheart," says her mother, wedging in next to Marjorie. "I'm so happy to have you home," she says, wrapping her in a hug. Marjorie feels the envelope crinkle against her breast. "You must tell me all about the cottage and the equestrian series."

Marjorie eases back and looks at her mother. Is she being genuine? She no longer knows what to believe.

Her mother turns. "Thank you, Slorah. Can you return in a few minutes to help me dress for dinner? I'd like to catch up with Marjorie."

Slorah exits without a word.

"Mother, Granny said you injured yourself?" asks Marjorie.

"Injured?" Her mother laughs. "That's an understatement." She quickly pulls off her stylish headscarf. "Look at this! And it was all my doing." A sweep of yellowing-green bruises paints her forehead.

"Oh, Mother, that must have been quite bad."

"It was bad, but the bruise to my pride was probably worse. I made the mistake of going to a party at Cecile's. I remember very little of it, honestly, except vomiting in the sink of her pristine new powder room. Your father had the grand idea of dressing Slorah and Atchison as guests to accompany me. Can you imagine? Slorah hasn't worn anything but black for decades. She looked like a corpse in periwinkle blue. After an hour they became enchanted with their stage roles and deserted me. I was so exhausted I could barely put a sentence together. I have no idea what I might have mumbled or to whom I mumbled it. It was all a dark comedy."

Marjorie nods, recalling Slorah's ill-fitting dress. "Goodness, that sounds like an ordeal. And how are you now, Mother?"

Lilah pauses, gathering words. "I'm grateful to be okay, and I'm grateful that you're home. The house has been oddly still without you. Your father and I have been disagreeing a lot lately. More than our usual bickering. We're of different minds on things. So many things." She sighs.

"I imagine it's normal for married couples to be of different minds on things."

"Perhaps. But it can't be ignored that marriage truly is a legal and contractual partnership. Do you know that I can't even travel on my own without his permission?"

Marjorie thinks of Ivy and the stories of women from the newspapers.

"Women—we're scandalized over the smallest things. That pressure forces our hand and directs our behaviors. It certainly has mine. At the birthday dinner at the club, I said your dress was too revealing. But in truth I loved it. And I loved your courage in wearing it." She meets Marjorie's eyes. "But I couldn't say that in public."

Marjorie nods. It's common for women to stifle their true feelings. But she's never been able to.

"I know this might sound hard to believe, but I do understand you, sweetheart, more than you might imagine. I want you to make good decisions. Decisions that are freeing, that allow you to pursue life in all its complicated splendor, wherever that may be."

"Thank you, Mother."

"I often think back to when my parents and I moved here from Cleveland and I first met your father's family. I adored them and, at the time, there was a match. When my father passed unexpectedly, my mother and I were left quite vulnerable. I convinced myself that financial security was most important and that the glass business could provide a stable adventure. But the marriage was . . . Well, I've aged, and there are decisions I deeply regret. Things that now bother me in an inexplicable way."

Like his syphilis and weeping sores? His desire to condemn his daughter to an asylum? Marjorie keeps the thoughts to herself, nodding and patting her mother's hand. "Relationships are complicated," she says, thinking of the envelope pressing against her chest.

"Yes, especially with family members, aren't they? So we have to be a step ahead. Outplay them."

Outplay them? Is that a tennis metaphor?

"When we're in the marriage contract, yes, we try to satisfy our spouse. But what's most important is to honor the vision we have of ourselves."

"And what is that vision of yourself, Mother?"

Lilah looks toward her vanity with longing. "My vision? I want to be someone who can grow, explore new heights yet plumb old experiences. One day I'll explain it all."

"But you said, 'a stable adventure.' That's an oxymoron. Any adventure worth having is far from stable. And men, please. We're smarter than men, Mother."

Lilah looks at her. "Oh, Marjorie, it feels like you've grown up overnight. Yes, that's exactly it. And no one would understand my situation, so I don't even bother. I no longer care what people think of me. And when did that happen? But I'll tell you something, it's liberating."

"Good," says Marjorie.

"But, Marjorie, please believe me when I say that regret is a ghost of the worst kind. Oh, my dear, might you consider something that will allow you to take flight? A degree or a pursuit that will guarantee your independence and engage both your head and your heart? Something that allows you to travel? Your sense of adventure and creativity—you've inherited the strongest parts of us."

Marjorie studies her mother. She doesn't want to be hurtful, but "creative" is hardly how she'd describe her father's ventures. Does her mother know about the jewel racket?

"You look beautiful but tired," says her mother, caressing Marjorie's cheek. "Are you alright? I'm sorry, I've done all the talking and haven't really asked about you."

"I'm fine. Just tired. I'll skip dinner and—"

"No, please don't skip dinner. I've endured too many dinners without you. It won't be too taxing. Cecile is coming, and she'll command the conversation. Wait until you see the new house she and Lou have moved into. I don't want to hurt her feelings but, between us, the interior's a bit garish. Imagine a speakeasy nested within a velvet theater box." Her mother laughs, then rises from the couch and opens a closet.

Marjorie seizes the opportunity to leave. "Alright, I'll see you at dinner."

She hurries back to her own room and quickly closes and locks the door. Her mother's frustration was palpable. How would she react if she knew that her husband had planned to send their daughter to an asylum? She said no one would understand her situation. She didn't admit that she's having an affair or that she's the darling angel of her tennis partner. But the weight of regret was evident.

Marjorie sits on her bed, pulling the cash and folded envelope addressed to Slorah from her bra. And that's when she notices the postmark. It's not local.

The postmark on the envelope reads: BARBADOS. She gasps.

The family knows only one person in Barbados.

Her mother is not the darling angel of a tennis partner in Grosse Pointe.

No.

Her mother is the darling angel of someone much closer to the family.

Her father's younger brother. Uncle Jamie.

56

DECEITFUL WILES

Graham paces the drawing room, his dress shirt soaked with a blend of evening heat and nerves.

"Calm down, would you?" Chet leans toward Lally's cage, smiling at the parakeet.

Graham pauses to catch the breeze at the large open window. He lifts his eye patch slightly and fans beneath. "I find it extremely unsettling that you can be so calm amidst all that's going on, Chet." He swallows, looking at the whisky decanter next to his father's favorite chair. It's risky. It would've been more natural at the party.

"Something else I find unsettling," says Graham. "Ina informed me that the servants have a betting pool predicting our fates."

"You're just learning of it? Yeah, they're pretty sharp with their odds too. Atch nailed the pot that I would leave Rockford after only one semester."

Marjorie enters the drawing room, wearing a shimmering dress of champagne silk with an asymmetrical hemline.

"Well, hello!" Chet strides over and hugs her. "Graham said you were back. And wow, look at that dress. Your creation, I assume?"

Marjorie gives a small nod.

Chet looks at her. "You okay?"

"Yes. Just a bit tired."

Graham evaluates Marjorie as she walks toward the bar tray. Her response to Chet: It's tepid. No smile. Something's different.

"Well, we were tired too." Chet lowers her voice. "We hoofed it all the way to Oakland County to send that telegram back to Lilah."

Marjorie stops mid-step and looks from Chet to Graham. "Oh, that's right. Thank you both."

"Say, any word from Ivy?" asks Graham. "Any chance she'll be at the dinner dance at the yacht club tomorrow?"

Chet rolls her eyes.

"What? I just want to make sure she surfaced, that's she's okay."

"Are you okay? You were the one who couldn't feel his legs," says Chet.

"Thank you, Graham," says Marjorie. "Yes, she surfaced." She reaches for the decanter. "But she won't be at—"

In the blink of a beat, Graham grabs the decanter and throws it out the open window.

Marjorie looks from the window back to her brother. "Graham, what on earth? You just tossed a full decanter."

"It's whisky. Since when do you drink whisky?" asks Chet.

"I didn't see the gin," replies Marjorie.

"They put it away," says Graham. "They're milling in the dining room. It's cooler in there."

"He tossed the decanter because Dad's been sick. It's contagious," says Chet.

"He's been shitting himself something awful," says Graham.

"Oh, that does sound unpleasant," says Marjorie.

"Well, look who's back," says Cecile, waltzing into the drawing room. "So, our little goldfish returns. Nice dress, where'd you get it?"

"I made it," says Marjorie.

"You made it or stole it?" laughs Cecile. "I mean, you *were* hauled into the police station for a dress incident."

Marjorie returns the laugh. "Stole it? A member of the Lennox family, stealing? Oh, my. Really, where *do* people get their stories?"

"Are you denying being at the police station?"

"Shh . . . I'm secretly dating a cop." Marjorie winks and grins.

Cecile pauses, unable to ascertain if Marjorie is being truthful.

"One point for Marjorie," whispers Graham.

"Maybe two," nods Chet.

Cecile steps forward, challenging. She lowers her voice. "I also heard that you were at my party." She gives a smug look. "Why be so secretive about it?"

"Oh, because my cop boyfriend came too—dressed in plain clothes, of course."

Cecile stiffens. "You brought a cop to my house?"

"He was so anxious to see it and have a look around. And someone brought a newspaper reporter too!" gasps Marjorie. "Is that where you're pinching your stories from, Cecile? They're almost as unique as that new necklace you're wearing."

Cecile's mouth drops open. She quickly smiles to regain her footing. "Very funny. As usual, you're being so weird. You're disturbed."

Marjorie employs Lou's method of diversion and, instead of replying, just laughs.

"Well, if you really made that dress, then make one for me," says Cecile.

"I'd be happy to!" beams Marjorie. "With tree titties?" She laughs again.

"What is going on here?" whispers Chet.

"No clue," says Graham.

"Shall we head in to dinner?" suggests Marjorie.

They enter the dining room. Their father stands at the window, next to Granny, who leans on Ivan the Terrible, one of her dinner umbrellas.

"Finally! It's about time," says their father. Everyone drifts to their usual spot.

"It's not our fault," replies Chet. "We were waiting for Cecile."

"Don't blame me," snaps Cecile. "You and Graham were fawning over Marjorie."

Their father looks to Marjorie. His shoulders fall as disappointment rises. "Did the cottage bore you?"

"It's nice to see you too," smiles Marjorie. "Are you alright, Dad? You look a bit peaked."

Gramps laughs. "If his face looks peaked, imagine what the other end looks like. If Agatha Christie hadn't been found, I would've sworn she'd pop out next."

Lilah laughs. Loudly. More gin than tonic.

The family takes their seats, and the servants step forward with a first course of chilled shrimp.

"Dad's fine compared to your mother," says Cecile. "Look at her head. She somehow whacked herself."

"At tennis," adds Chet.

"Yes," says Marjorie, looking to her mother with compassion. "Poor darling angel."

Lilah's brow bends.

Their father sets his forearms on the table. "Well, Marjorie, while you've been gallivanting God-knows-where doing God-knows-what, I've been fighting a terrible illness. We're pretty sure Henry Ford planted it on me."

"I'm sorry. That sounds awful. What are your symptoms?" asks Marjorie.

"Like I told you, shitting his brains out," says Graham.

"C'mon," says Gramps. "We're at the dinner table now."

"Andrew Saks died at the dinner table," nods Chet.

"The new Saks Fifth Avenue is lovely," says Granny. "Speaking of death and business ventures, your grandfather and I have noticed something interesting."

Graham's fork stops midair.

"As you know, for the past half century it's been our custom to read the newspaper together. Lately we've observed a terrible degradation in the quality of reporting and stories."

"Really?" asks Chet.

"Yes," insists Granny. "Ridiculous yarns, like the cock-and-bull about Cecile and Myrtle Branley. I won't have people messing with my family. Since your grandfather is still so virile—"

Graham grimaces.

"Excuse me, since your grandfather is still so *vibrant* and you all seem to be very ambitious with your own ventures and won't need any money, we've decided that your grandfather will come out of retirement and put in an offer to buy a newspaper. Maybe the *Detroit Gazette.*"

"Yes!" yells Chet.

"No!" booms Duncan.

"What?" says Graham.

Their grandfather turns to Graham. "It was your idea."

"My idea?"

"Yes, the Campbells at Glencoe. Get inside their house and slaughter them all. Great historical reference. And very fitting here. Newspapers have too much power."

"Damn you, Graham. We're not buying a blasted newspaper!" bellows Duncan. "We need that money for the new factory and the glass-coffin business I'm planning."

"A company in Altoona already makes glass coffins," says Chet.

"Wait, what's happening?" asks Lilah.

"We're plotting to take down an empire, dear," smiles Granny.

"We need that money!" yells Duncan.

"Dad, don't get so worked up," says Cecile.

"Britannicus, son of Claudius, also died at the dinner table," smiles Chet.

"Actually, owning a newspaper might be convenient," says Graham.

"Of course you think so. You could have more pretend writing jobs," says Cecile.

"Better than pretend headaches," says Chet.

"Actually, I agree," nods Marjorie. "Think of it, Dad. If you ever need to blackmail someone, you won't have to pay a conglomerate to run incriminating photos."

All heads turn to Marjorie. One by one, she carefully surveys the faces. She then grasps the wine decanter in one hand, lifts her glass with the other, and stands with a tight smile. "I have something I'd like to share. From William Blake."

"Oh, for Christ's sake," says their father.

"The truth fairy has returned!" says Granny.

"In such a lovely new dress," notes Lilah.

Marjorie clears her throat and begins to recite.

> I was angry with my friend;
> I told my wrath, my wrath did end.
> I was angry with my foe;
> I told it not, my wrath did grow.

Marjorie takes a breath. Her voice dips, accelerating and becoming progressively more ominous.

And I watered it in fears,
Night and morning with my tears;
And I sunned it with smiles,
And with soft deceitful wiles.
And it grew both day and night,
Till it bore an apple bright;
And my foe beheld it shine,
And he knew that it was mine.
And into my garden stole
When the night had veiled the pole:
In the morning glad I see
My foe outstretched beneath the tree.

Marjorie makes a small curtsy, turns on her heel, and heads toward the grand staircase with the wine.

Everyone sits. Silent for a moment.

"Am I the only one who sees it? She's just not right," says Cecile.

"Yeah, what the hell did that even mean?" says their father.

Granny laughs, brandishing Ivan.

"I think it means you're all fucked."

Dear Coco,

The pain is so great.
So loud.
Is there any last hope
For you to save me?

57

SOLE BENEFICIARY

A summer squall blew through overnight. Instead of shutting the windows against the storm, Marjorie lay on the wood floor beneath her bedroom window, allowing the rain to pelt her nightdress and skin, imagining she was on the deck of a boat amidst a tempest.

Her family is a tempest. A whirling tempest of deceit, treachery, and betrayal. And despite her desire to love her family, she has no illusions. The tempest will throw her overboard. The tempest will grip her by the ankles. The tempest will pull her down until her lungs fill with mud and the world slips to black.

So with the floor planks pressing against her back and rain spraying across her nightgown, she made several decisions. It's useless to mourn an idealized version of what she wishes her family could be. That's not who or what they are. She must gather her own tools, chart her own course, and become the author of her own destiny.

For a moment, fear crept in. So to confront her fear, she allowed herself to posit the most terrifying possibilities about her family, every awful fictional scenario she could imagine, from farcical to downright probable. The mental list included planting defective parts in the vehicles of rival suppliers to cause fatalities, grave-robbing for glass eyes, false identities, forcing accomplices to swallow stolen jewels for transport, creating fake Tiffany-glass lamps, and even impaling enemies with poison umbrellas.

Goodness, the mind is also a tempest.

She thought about it long and hard overnight. And the fictional scenarios led her to this morning's truthful conclusions and declarations:

Her father will not commit her.

Her siblings will not manipulate her.

No one shall pity her.

She will stand her ground. She will make her own plans. She'll get answers, and if she doesn't, she'll go straight to Hank and the newspaper.

She'll make a meal out of them all.

A knock sounds at her door.

"Marjorie?"

Her mother. Marjorie walks to the door and opens it a crack.

"I know the stockings tied to your door handle are a request for privacy. But you skipped breakfast, so I had Slorah prepare a tray. I can leave it here on the floor or I can bring it in, dear."

Marjorie opens the door. "Thank you, Mother. That's very sweet. You can put the tray on my vanity. Be careful, the floor might still be wet."

Lilah sets the tray on the vanity and examines the soaked drapes. "Is the window malfunctioning?"

"Not at all. It was a metaphorical study."

Her mother admires the lavender dress displayed near the window. "That's gorgeous. Will you be wearing that to the dinner dance tonight?"

The dinner dance. Marjorie pauses. "Oh, yes. But actually . . . I won't be riding with the family to the yacht club. I'll be going with Helen Hardwick." Marjorie swallows the truth. She won't be going to the dinner dance at all.

"Alright, sweetheart." Her mother heads to the door. She stops and turns before opening it. "I must say, that's a lovely dress form. Very lifelike. European, I assume? Didn't know you could get those at the cottage." She gives a wink and exits the room before Marjorie can reply.

Miss Johnson. Her dress is displayed on Miss Johnson. How did she not think of that? Of course her family would wonder where the mannequin came from. Was her mother teasing or telegraphing?

She lifts a plate of triangle sandwiches from the tray and brings them to her bed. She retrieves Uncle Jamie's letter from beneath her pillow and reads it. Then reads it again. She can ascertain quite a bit.

Jamie and her mother clearly have a deep bond through a prior relationship. He refers to events of more than twenty years ago.

Her mother is full of regret. Jamie mentions her decisions, grief, and responsibilities.

Her father has learned that Lilah and Jamie have been communicating. Jamie discusses the potential impact, Duncan's revenge, and not wanting to endanger *their beautiful secret.*

She sets the letter aside and leans back against her pillows. Although her father's sister, Finny, has visited a few times, she's met Uncle Jamie only once—very briefly, at Cecile's wedding. He's adored. Her grandparents have taken trips over the years to visit Jamie. Graham once spent an entire summer in Barbados with him. She remembers how her grandparents and the staff simmered with excitement prior to his arrival for the wedding.

Marjorie's first impressions of Uncle Jamie: He was dazzlingly suntanned; his cream linen suit was expertly cut; his smiles were beautifully genuine—and he was nothing like her father. He had the relaxed Caribbean ease of a self-made man. When he spoke, his speech had an intriguing rhythm, an ever-subtle salting of Bajan Creole and calypso. Unlike her father, Jamie was tall and slender. His facial features appeared more carved and aristocratic, resembling Granny. Granny and Gramps doted on him entirely, but, for some reason, Uncle Jamie didn't stay in the guest wing at Glen Arden. And she has no recollection of suspicious interactions—or any interactions—between her mother and Uncle Jamie. But there's one thing she now thinks back on.

She had mentioned to Uncle Jamie that she'd love to visit Barbados, that Graham's historical tales of pirates and treasure hunters intrigued her. She asked him if he'd discovered any buried treasure. He shook his head and smiled.

"I don't need to dig for treasure, Marjorie. My treasure is here in Detroit."

At the time, she thought he was referring to the Lennox family fortune, the fortune that her father would inherit as the eldest son. But what if he was referring to her mother?

Or . . . what if he was implying something else?

Your sense of adventure and creativity—you've inherited the strongest parts of us.

Those were her mother's words. And Jamie's letter mentions *Duncan's revenge* and their *beautiful secret.* Could she be the secret he's referring to? It's far-fetched but would certainly fill in some blanks. Her father's attitude toward her, for one thing. The Eloise Asylum plan as revenge, for another. And—interestingly—the possibility of being Jamie's daughter intrigues her more than upsets her. As she finishes the sandwich, a typewritten sheet of paper swishes beneath her door. She walks over to retrieve it.

> LENNOX, Charlotte: Aged 24 years. Died of shame in her bedroom last evening while ruminating on the words of William Blake. Known to many as "Chet," the young Lennox was considered the misunderstood member of the family, with rebellious hair, who often felt so awkward around humans that she preferred the solitary company of a metronome, decayed keepsakes, and a typewriter through which she searched for redemption within the lives of others. Contributing factors to her demise included unresolved maternal grief and the underestimation of a younger sister whom she adored and wanted desperately to protect from institutional banishment. Too shy to donate her naked cadaver to science, Miss Lennox will instead be interred within the plot originally reserved for Poochie the Parakeet on the rear grounds of the sinister family sinkhole, Glen Arden (glass casket patent pending). Notorious Knödel, former chef to Kaiser Wilhelm, will travel in from Zurich and use every pot and pan to cater the funerary luncheon. Faded blooms only. In lieu of cards, please send generous quantities of cash to the deceased's sole beneficiary, Miss Marjorie Lennox.

Marjorie smiles. Of course this is how Chet would apologize. She finds a pencil and makes an edit to Chet's obituary so the beneficiary of the cash reads:

~~Miss Marjorie Lennox~~

`Peter Howell. Poor Peter.`

So Chet and Graham knew of their father's plans to send her to Eloise? Marjorie sits on the edge of her bed. There's still something that concerns her. Peter said that she was in danger.

If her father wants to commit her, how far would he actually go to get rid of her?

A breeze stirs the lavender dress draped on Miss Johnson. Marjorie won't be going to the yacht club tonight. Just as her mother said, she must be a step ahead and outplay them. Very wise of her. She thinks of her mother's wink and starts with a realization.

It wasn't Chet who left the brochure in her room. Her mother left the brochure in her room.

She's known about the residency all along.

58

INVISIBLE CURTAIN

Marjorie drives down Kercheval and turns. By the time she crosses Jefferson Avenue and approaches Windmill Pointe, her palms begin to sweat. What if the invitation wasn't actually from Bonafante? Could someone be following her? Lou has a special mirror on his windshield that provides a view through the rear window. He calls it a "cop spotter." She wishes the Nash had one. What if her father is luring her into some kind of trap? In thinking overnight about her father, the word she continually returned to was "resentment." At times it feels like he resents her. If what she suspects about her mother and Uncle Jamie is true, that would make sense.

The warm road rolls beneath the tires of the car. She simply walked into the garage this evening and took the Nash, with no explanation to Freddie, the family's auto steward.

"Jeepers, you're a sight for sore eyes, Miss Marjorie. That's some dress. Going to the dance at the yacht club?"

The old Marjorie would have chattered and spilled every bit of information about the dress she made and the dinner she was attending. But instead of responding, she just thanked him and smiled.

"Would you like me to put the top down?"

"No, thank you, Freddie."

And that was the extent of the exchange.

It's now eight o'clock, and the summer sky surrenders its bright light to softer hues of evening. She takes a breath. She can do this. And of course she'll be polite with the gatekeeper and the butler. None of this is their fault. But as she pulls up to the estate, it's not the watchman at the gates.

It's Bonafante.

He stands within the golden light on the drive, wearing an ivory summer suit, mist-blue tie, and gray suede side-buckle loafers. His dark hair gleams against his sunlit face. Oh, dear. Does he have to look so delicious? And the majestic grandeur of his home creates such a dreamlike backdrop. Marjorie's heart begins to race. He unlocks and opens one side of the gate, then approaches her driver's side window. He looks at her, silent. The evening air spins between them atop a soft buzz of cicadas.

"Hello," he finally says.

"Hello," she replies.

"I've opened one of the garage bays for you."

But before she can reply, he returns to the gate. Marjorie looks at Bonafante and then back to the open garage stall. He's having her park in the garage. He doesn't want the car to be visible from the street. Does he want the car to disappear?

Some fixer . . . a high-level blackhander.

She takes a breath, proceeds through the gate, and drives down the cobblestones and into the garage. She throws a glance over her shoulder. He's already walking back down the drive. She quickly checks her face and lipstick, snaps her compact shut, and tosses it in her purse. She exits the car.

"We'll head out the back of the garage," he instructs. "I'll close up and meet you on the side patio." The large wooden bay doors groan on their hinges as he pulls them shut. Marjorie walks through the back of the dark garage and onto a side terrace, waiting for Bonafante.

She ticks through her list. She will resist any and all urges. She will remain focused. This is a game, and she will play it well.

Marjorie hears his footfalls and turns. She stands, a vision in lavender silk with pale-opal stockings and matching shoes. Her bobbed brown hair is held not by a headwrap but by a slender headband adorned with pale amethysts. He stops abruptly.

"Your dress, it's beautiful. Did you create that during the residency?"

Marjorie smiles, then regroups. "Yes. But, please, let's not pretend it was an artistic residency."

He nods, extending a guiding hand toward the stone walkway leading to the rear of the estate. The back veranda stretches across the entire expanse of the house. In the center, a table dressed in white damask is set for two. Beside the dinner table is a sparkling bar cart loaded with an array of bottles, glasses, and a sterling chiller with a foiled champagne cork peeking out from a bath of ice.

Marjorie's mind flashes to the gun in his car. Her nerves begin to percolate. Instead of walking to the table, she walks straight to the railing of the veranda. She takes a deep breath, absorbing the carpet of green lawn that cascades down to the wooden decking, his yacht, and the shimmering blue waters of Lake St. Clair. Towering evergreens on each side of the property create a natural privacy fence. Marjorie looks to the lake and suppresses her instinct to peel off her shoes and stockings and race toward the water. And then she feels Bonafante at her side. He leans in, resting his elbows on the stone top rail.

"At sunrise, I always swear the morning light is the most beautiful. But then evening sets a scene like this to change my mind."

"It's breathtaking," she replies. "So serene and peaceful. When I stand here, it's hard to believe there's a coal-smoked, crime-filled city nearby. I couldn't see this in the dark when I was last here." She turns and looks at Bonafante. He's staring at her. He straightens.

"May I offer you something to drink?"

She nods and follows him to the bar cart. Why does life have to be so cruel? Under any other circumstance she would positively bathe in the delight of the atmosphere, the alchemy of the evening, and the beautiful man in front of her. A large part of her wants to put it all aside, just for the night.

But she cannot.

He opens a bottle of Pol Roger and pours a hiss of effervescence into two delicate glass flutes. Each is shaped like a calla lily blossom. He hands one to Marjorie.

"What a beautiful champagne glass."

"Thank you. It was created by a young glassblower in Quebec."

"Your sister mentioned that your family has French roots."

"Well, like many, they traveled from France to Canada and then to Detroit. My mother was related to the Rivards and the Campeaus. It's sometimes difficult to think of Detroit as a French settlement, though, isn't it?"

"Yes. It's so American industrial." Marjorie takes a sip of champagne, feeling awkward and trying to figure out how to segue from the distracted small talk. Thankfully, she doesn't have to.

"You're angry."

Her eyes snap to his. "Furious. I'm so furious and I hate it. It's such an awful feeling."

"What would you like to know?"

"Where do I begin?"

"Let's have a seat." Bonafante pulls out a chair for her.

Marjorie looks toward the house. The gatekeeper, the butler—she's seen no one.

"Where is the staff?" she asks.

"I've given them the evening off."

Marjorie nods warily. "And Daisy?"

"With my sister."

A few days ago, Marjorie would have thought nothing of it. In fact, she would have delighted at the prospect of being alone with Bonafante. But the lens through which the world once looked so lovely is cracked. She can still see and appreciate beauty, but she is now keenly aware of potential hidden layers and threats that lurk beneath the surface. Secret liquor tunnels, hidden stairways to asylums, beautiful people full of lies and manipulations. The layers in Detroit are elusive and deeply stacked. She now understands what Ivy referred to in her letter—that heartfelt wish to return to a *beautiful place of unknowing.*

But right now she can't allow herself to be distracted by all that's in front of her and all that she's feeling. She needs information. Answers. At what cost, though? There's always a cost.

Yes, she's finally alone with Charles Bonafante. But despite her past wishes and dreams, her heart knows there's an invisible curtain. And behind the curtain lives the truth.

It could all be a trap.

59

INSIDE JOB

Marjorie takes a seat. Bonafante also sits and waits expectantly.

"You duped me," she says.

"I was trying to help you."

"Why would you want to help me?"

He looks at her. "Why would you leave gifts in my car?"

She takes a sip of champagne. "Dock was always scribbling on a clipboard. He has a file on me. I want to see it. All of it. And don't you dare remove anything."

"Fine. I'll get the file from Juliette."

Marjorie's mind travels through the list she compiled while lying awake the night prior.

She asks her questions, and he seems to have patently convenient answers for everything. The program is Juliette's, a passion born from their father's confinement of her. Only one other resident ever discovered the truth about the program—a novelist who was granted a residency a few years ago. She's threatened to write a book about it.

The discussion becomes more interesting when Marjorie probes about his own work and the ventures his sister mentioned. "Your sister commented that you're no saint, that you have several businesses of your own, but that you're not part of the residency."

"I'm not a principal, no. The residency, that's her endeavor."

"What sort of work do you do?"

"A bit of this and that. Import, export. Art patronage. And I assist people with delicate matters. But only certain people."

Import, export. Marjorie looks to the sparkling bar cart loaded with champagne, cognac, and expensive French products. All illegal and highly prized during Prohibition. He has shipping routes through the Atlantic to Canada.

"Alright. You said you 'assist people with delicate matters.' That's quite vague. What type of matters?"

"Things that could unfairly impact their family, their businesses' solvency, or their reputation. I try to protect people."

"Like Chaplin? It's no secret. The media has long reported that his beloved mother suffers a mental condition and was nearly deported. You were helping him."

He remains silent and takes a drink.

"You protect people . . . like Harry Bennett protects Henry Ford? Like Lou protects my father?" asks Marjorie.

"No. Harry's a personnel director, and Lou's an actual business partner with your father."

Marjorie nods. "Protecting people. So you're a gangster."

"No. 'Gangster' implies belonging to a gang."

"Have you ever used the gun that lives beneath the seat of your car?"

His reaction of surprise holds for a beat, then he answers. "I have. Unfortunately, Detroit is a precarious place. Do you have a moral objection to men with ventures that live in the gray area of the law?"

Marjorie laughs. A sincere laugh. "Isn't that the whole of Detroit? What I have objection to are those who manipulate women under the guise of helping them."

"That's fair."

"Are you celibate?"

His brows arch with the direction shift. "No. But it's been a while since I've seen anyone."

Marjorie relaxes slightly, taking a sip of champagne. "Your yacht is named *Laetitia*—who is she?"

"A Roman goddess of joy."

"That's lovely. Have you ever had a steady girlfriend?"

"Two. They lived in Windsor. As we grew older, we had different views of the world." He takes a drink and volleys back. "You've had boyfriends."

"Only one, really. Peter Howell. An artist. He's a lovely person and a dear friend, but I'm fairly certain that he prefers men." She looks at him. "And he somehow got caught up in the jewel heist from the Detroit Institute of Arts."

"If I remember correctly," says Bonafante, "the news reported that his confession claimed the robbery involved a girl in Grosse Pointe."

Marjorie rolls her eyes. "As if I was involved. It was ludicrous but sent my family into a tailspin. I was put under house arrest while they tried to control the news accounts. They refer to it in our house as 'the incident.' Poor Peter, they claimed he had lost his mind to do such a thing."

"And what do you think?"

"He hadn't lost his mind. My father blackmailed him to swap the jewels with threats of exposing pictures to the paper."

"You knew that at the time?"

"Of course not. I put it together later, along with the fact that you saved his family." Marjorie takes another sip of her champagne. "You said you assist people with delicate matters. I'd like you to assist me."

Bonafante's gaze narrows. "You're in trouble?"

"Not yet. But I'll probably create some." She reaches down the neckline of her dress and retrieves something from her bra. A flicker of intrigue glints across his face. She slides a handkerchief across the table.

He opens the handkerchief and finds the large sapphire.

"Very nice."

"It can't be real. Not where I found it."

"Are you sure?" he says.

"See, it's quite convincing. My grandfather used to enjoy glass gem cutting," says Marjorie. She gestures to her jeweled headband. "He made these. Everyone believes they're amethysts, but they're just purple glass. He taught my father, but they eventually got in a huge fight about it. I now realize that it's part of their permanent rift. Gramps says my father ruined his hobby."

"It's one thing to make glass replicas. It's another to swap out the entire Frederick K. Stearns collection at the DIA," he says.

"Of course," she agrees. "My father needed someone to do it. He despised Peter. Called him a two-cylinder boy but mainly felt intimidated because Peter's father was so successful in steel and was threatening to expand into glass. My father and Lou—they have a racket swapping fakes and stealing the real gems. My older sister Cecile benefits greatly. She probably has half the collections of Detroit in her drawers. But she's no gemologist."

He looks at the sapphire. "And?"

"They're greedy. And worse than hurting me, they hurt my friend. I can't abide people who harm those dear to me. So, in order to help Peter, I have to make them pay—literally. I want them to buy this fake jewel, thinking that it's real."

"They don't buy jewels. They just steal them."

"Sometimes Cecile does buy things, for herself. I imagine she needs some sort of paper trail for the amount of jewelry she wears. We'll set up a fake scenario. A Cartier consultant from Paris passing through on his way to Chicago."

Bonafante nods, intrigued.

"He'll act like he's enchanted with Cecile, fawn over her, ask if she wants to see a few pieces. Of course he'll make a big fuss about one sapphire, swear her to secrecy because it has a unique provenance and he already has a buyer for it at the Yondotega Club. Cecile will ask how much the Yon member is paying and then offer him more. She'll also ask to see others."

His gaze holds a quiet grin. "You're going to sell your family their own fake jewels."

"Exactly!" She smiles and sips her champagne.

His brow lifts with curiosity. "Do you have others tucked into your dress?"

"No, but there are more in my bedroom," says Marjorie. "We'll give the money from the sale of the sapphire to Peter Howell. After all that my family has put him through, he deserves it. He desperately wants to move to New York, and this would give him what he wants."

Bonafante studies her. "And what do you want?"

Marjorie glances at his mouth, then looks away. "An attorney. I want to help Ivy. She needs a divorce and a way out of Eloise."

"I can assist with that."

"Wonderful. The other thing I want—the missing pieces of this puzzle. Who knows what, exactly."

He leans forward. The way he looks at her, he's pressing, telegraphing something.

"Your father. He's a dangerous man, Marjorie."

She nods. "To be truthful, I'm not actually certain that he's my father. I've discovered that my mother has had a long attachment with my father's younger brother. Their letters indicate that they've been hiding something more than their feelings, that my father is suspicious, and they fear his revenge. If what I suspect is true, it would certainly explain his resentment toward me."

His click of sudden comprehension, it's visible.

"So, yes, that makes everything more dangerous, doesn't it? Right now I can't trust anyone."

"Do you want to?" he asks.

She pauses, her brain starting to hum. It's a fair question. She's so angry. And what hurts more than the way she's been treated is the wound to her whimsy. "I know what I don't want. I don't want to lose my sense of enchantment. I don't want to be bitter. That's not who I am. But I don't want to live in fear, so I have to be a step ahead."

"You're nearly there."

"Nearly?" she asks.

"Yes, it's impressive. You've brought clarity, even to me." He sits back in his chair. "Like you, I can't abide harm to things I care about. I keep mainly to myself to stay ahead."

She stares at the tiny lines of bubbles traveling north in her champagne. "Do you know my uncle Jamie?"

He pauses before replying. "Yes. We do a bit of rum business. Jamie stayed here during your sister's wedding. He's nothing like Duncan." His brow softens. "My mother socialized with very few people, but she was close with your grandparents. They often visited when we were building the estate and helped when my mother fell ill, so I've known them for quite some time. I consider your grandfather a friend, Marjorie. He quietly came to me after the heist at the Institute of Arts."

Marjorie nods. "Because he feared for the business and the family name."

"No, because he loves you. And he feared that your father, if we call him that, might try to silence you. Permanently."

Permanently? She stares at Bonafante.

"Think about your father, how he approaches things."

Marjorie looks out at the water. The sun has surrendered to the oncoming darkness. Her father's a blowhard and a bully, she thinks. He'll stop at nothing to get what he wants. He'd betray Lilah or Gramps. He took his son's eye out with a champagne cork. Whispers have long circulated that his first wife's death was suspicious. She thinks back to her conversation with Graham while driving to the Nightingale. *He's ruthless, competitive, and greedy, not to mention shallow. Our family business is windshields, Marjorie. Glass. An entire fortune built on sand. There's a deep irony there.*

"If he suspects you've figured out the truth about his gem racket, you'll be in grave danger," says Bonafante. "The Detroit game is big money, Marjorie. Art heists, jewel theft, liquor, gambling, kidnapping for ransom. There are a lot of people involved. When children of wealthy families disappear in the snatch racket, do you know what I often discover? That the kidnappings are arranged from *within* the families themselves. They don't want their secrets getting out. And something else to consider—sometimes parties with huge guest lists are nothing more than diversions to complete a job elsewhere."

Marjorie gasps.

Cecile's party wasn't a housewarming. It was a distraction for another heist.

Her mouth slowly opens. Her cracked lens is suddenly perfectly sharp. How could she have missed that?

Marjorie stands, pushing her chair back against the flagstones. "Whose home did they rob?"

"A widowed jeweler that Cecile flirts with. It was planned as a double grab. He likes his liquor, so they invited him to the party. With him distracted, they hit not only his jewelry store but also his home. But it didn't go as planned. Apparently his elderly mother was in the house. They tried to tie her up, but she gave them quite a fight."

Marjorie is too stunned to speak. An elderly woman? Cecile would allow Lou and his thugs to batter someone like Granny?

Bonafante rises and walks around the table to her. He takes her hands in his. "There's danger around your family now, Marjorie. Specifically around your father. And the enemy's inside."

"Yes, he's rotting of syphilis."

"No, I think his liquor's being poisoned. An inside job."

"How do you know that?"

"I get reports. One of my sources confirmed poison being purchased on two separate occasions."

Marjorie thinks of the decanter that Graham pitched out the window. Poisoning their own father? Could that even be possible? It wasn't one of the ludicrous scenarios she concocted. So, Graham and Chet—how much do they know about their father's doings?

She gazes up at the sky. Stars are beginning to wink from above. She looks at Bonafante, understanding. "It's a sick, evil game, and for what? For more money? Because they each feel threatened by the other? I've been so thick. You told me I was in over my head. I'm embarrassed that I didn't put it together when it was all right in front of me."

Danger, poison, parties, competition, the jewels she put in her bed finials. She doesn't know what to think. Doesn't know what's real. How is she supposed to make sense of this?

Bonafante lifts her chin. "You're extraordinary. Although members of your family each know something different—I think you know it all. And I also know that's difficult. I'm sorry, Marjorie."

She nods and chuckles awkwardly. It's not the correct reaction or response. It's an odd, nervous laughter. A frightened awareness that bats in her throat like a moth trying to escape. She wants to make it stop, but she can't. She's attracted to the intense man in front of her, but she's also a bit frightened. Can she believe him? Her breaths suddenly come faster, less like laughter, more akin to stifled sobs. Bonafante pulls her close.

"Slow your breathing," he says gently. "Match my breaths." He takes slow and deep breaths, gently laying a hand to the back of her head while circling beneath her shoulders with the other. "Match my breaths," he repeats.

She slips her arms beneath his suit coat, clasping him, breathing with him. Heat radiates through his beautiful starched shirt, warming her arms. She inhales deeply, her palms tracing the ridges of his back. Her hands move slowly, synchronized with their breaths.

"I'm sorry, Marjorie," he repeats.

Her breathing eventually quiets, but the moment lingers. They stand for several minutes, intertwined within the darkness. She isn't inclined to move.

"I admire your loyalty to Peter and Ivy. And I want you to be able to trust me," he says.

She waits, listening.

"To earn your trust, I'll make . . . a suggestion." He pauses, cautious with his words. "I don't have a personal life in public. I don't attend parties or events, just business meetings. Socializing is against my self-governance."

"And why is that?" whispers Marjorie.

"Because sharing personal information—letting the outside inside—it compromises security."

He was betrayed once. Badly, thinks Marjorie.

"But I'm willing to make a statement to secure your safety and also your trust."

She lifts her eyes to him.

He takes a breath. "You look beautiful. Let's go out. We'll go to the event at the yacht club. Together."

Marjorie's face lights with guile and mischief, thinking of her family's reaction when they see her with Bonafante. "Really?"

He nods. "Besides, if I don't get you out of here, you might try to seduce me like you did in the stairwell." He leans to whisper in her ear. "Don't want anyone to say I took advantage of you after a bit of champagne."

Marjorie sighs. "As they say, it's like drinking stars, isn't it?"

"It is. But I think you'll need to eat," says Bonafante.

"I think I'll need to kiss you," replies Marjorie.

"Oh, that'll happen. After we take care of business."

60

NEVER SURRENDER

The evening heat of summer simmers beneath the tires. From Jefferson Avenue, they cross the small bridge link over the Detroit River to Belle Isle. Marjorie extends her hand from the window to feel the rush of air as they roll along the shore to the small private island on the banks of Belle Isle Park. Bonafante slows and pulls into the shallow curving drive in front of the Detroit Yacht Club. The sidewalk and entrance glisten with twinkling lights.

"Oh, how I wish Bernice could see this," says Marjorie.

The yacht club was founded after the Civil War, and the stucco Mediterranean-style villa in front of them is newly designed. It's not only the largest yacht club in the country, it's an anchor of Detroit society. The Dodge family yachts, *Miss Syndicate* and *Sister Syn,* have raced under the colors of the Detroit Yacht Club when winning their national titles.

A young man in a white jacket sprints to the Silver Ghost.

"Good evening, Mr. Bonafante. You'll park it yourself as usual?"

"Yes. Thanks, Bobby." He hands the valet a folded bill and pulls around to a reserved spot. "Never surrender your keys or your car," he tells Marjorie.

She nods, then scowls. "Oh, goodness, that's Mr. Hardwick among the crowd near the entrance. He and his wife called the police about the dress

I made to cheer up their daughter. By the way, thank you for bailing me out at the police station."

"You knew?"

"I saw you. You're quite memorable."

"I heard the dress they hauled you in for was pretty memorable. Quite forward facing."

"It was a tree trunk. Nature can be imposing and forward facing, can't it?"

"Definitely. I'll show you later." He lifts her hand and kisses it.

Marjorie turns to him. "I should know, for this evening—do you dance?"

"Yes, but not where people might know me. Reveals too much. Ready to head in?"

"Absolutely."

Bonafante steps out and walks to Marjorie's side of the car. The knot of onlookers at the entrance watches, tittering like a crowd at the Egyptian Theatre on opening night. Whispers of shock and breaths of scandal scurry into the shadows of the lighted trees, because they've spotted the elusive Bonafante and—wait—does he have someone with him?

He opens Marjorie's door and offers his hand. She takes it, extending a lovely, slender leg from the car to the pavement. She exits the Ghost in her lavender dress, and the world drops into slow motion as they stroll, hand in hand, down the illuminated pathway to the revolving wooden door beneath the stone lintel sculpture of Neptune.

Mr. Hardwick steps forward, eager to establish himself and meet Bonafante while others look on. "Miss Lennox, so nice to see you. And this particular dress—now, this one is lovely."

"They're all lovely," says Bonafante.

"Yes, of course." Hardwick sticks out a hand to Bonafante. "Pleasure to finally meet you."

Rather than drop Marjorie's hand to shake Hardwick's, Bonafante simply nods. "How do you do."

Hardwick retracts his hand. "Would love to have you over next week to discuss a bit of Rolls-Royce business."

"Sorry. I'm not available. Sailing next week."

"Ah, wonderful," says Hardwick, hungry for the gossip. "Where are you going?"

"We're going inside," replies Marjorie, smiling brightly. "Have a good evening, Mr. Hardwick."

They walk through the door, leaving Hardwick and the group behind.

61

JUST PRICELESS

Graham leans back in his chair. The massive three-story ballroom glitters with merriment, both grand and intimate. Across the length of the room, multitiered chandeliers descend from hand-painted beams beneath a vaulted wooden ceiling. The gleaming floors reflect the light, freckling the hardwoods with glowing orbs. The band plays from a jester's balcony perched above the arched doors at the end of the room, while discreet bartenders serve illegal cocktails.

Chet leans over to Graham and whispers, "You can relax. This is even better than Cecile's party. More people, and Dad's already juiced. We'll wait until most people are in their flasks."

Cecile is in her element, feigning friendship and humility each time an acquaintance stops at the table to tell her how radiant she looks. Granny and Gramps sit at a separate table with the Alger family, at the opposite end of the ballroom.

"Haven't seen much of Lou lately," says Graham.

"He's working," says Cecile.

"Unlike you," laughs their father.

"I saw Mrs. Lindbergh in the ladies' room," says Cecile. "She was mobbed."

"Of course she was," says Lilah. "Her son just completed the first solo transatlantic flight. That's an incredible accomplishment."

"So," shrugs their father.

"So, flying is wondrous," says Lilah. "He worked as a mail pilot, served in the military, and then set a world record. He'll be awarded the medal of honor by President Coolidge."

"How do you know so much about him?" asks Duncan.

"We all know about him," says Chet. "I'm sure Cecile has sucked his new postage stamp by now."

Graham laughs, but Cecile glares.

"His mother is incredibly accomplished," says Lilah. "She has degrees from the University of Michigan and Columbia. She's a teacher."

"Does she play tennis?" asks Chet.

"She doesn't need a hobby," replies Lilah with a smile. "She lives separately from her husband."

"Well," says Cecile, "Mrs. Lindbergh said Charles has been elected an honorary member here at the yacht club."

"What the hell for?" grouses their father. "He's a pilot, not a sea captain. Christ, I guess I'm the only one in this family who can do anything impressive."

"What have you done?" asks Lilah.

"I saw him eat an entire napkin once," says Graham.

"I forgot about that," replies their father. "I was pretty lit."

"Myrtle Branley had a college degree," says Chet.

"Most college women are unattractive," nods Cecile.

"You're unattractive for thinking that," snorts Graham.

"Look," says Chet. "There's Hank, the reporter from the newspaper."

"He's a phony!" bellows their father. "He wasted my time, claimed he was running a feature about my plans for a new factory, but he never ran a damn thing. Where's the waiter with my gin rickey?"

"Hank just wanted to see my new house, same as everyone else," says Cecile.

"Maybe he's the one who vomited in your powder room," laughs Lilah.

"Wait, how do you know about that?" asks Cecile.

And suddenly the cacophony of crowd noise dims.

"What now, another announcement?" says their father. "I need my drink."

There is an announcement, but of a different sort. The crowd parts, silenced, as a couple enters the ballroom. They're elegant. Blindingly gorgeous. And they're entirely rapt, lost in conversation with each other, indifferent to the hundreds of eyes upon them.

Graham sits up with a snap. "Is that Bonafante?"

"No, he's a recluse," says Cecile, not bothering to look and instead studying her bracelet.

"It *is* Bonafante," Lilah gasps. "With Marjorie!"

"What?" Cecile turns. "How would Marjorie know Bonafante? She's such a liar."

"Has it ever occurred to you, Cecile, that Marjorie just might know a lot of things?" says Lilah.

They watch with the rest of the crowd, stunned, as Bonafante and Marjorie walk casually across the ballroom to the table with Granny, Gramps, and the Algers.

"A pity date. So what?" says their father. He swallows. Hard.

Marjorie hugs Granny, while Bonafante shakes the hands of both Gramps and Mr. Alger. Bonafante then whispers something in Marjorie's ear. She laughs and reaches up to stroke his cheek. He catches her hand, kisses it, then pulls out the chair for her to take a seat. The room pulses with a collective intake of breath.

"Holy hell," mutters Graham.

"That doesn't look like a charity date," says Lilah.

"She told me she was dating a cop," says Cecile.

Their father's head turns. "She told you what?"

Graham can't process what he's seeing. No. How is this possible?

Chet starts to laugh. Softly at first, then escalating to a howl.

"What's so funny?" demands their father.

Chet is doubled over. She pulls a breath and sets a bracing hand on the table. "It's just . . ." She's laughing so hard she can barely speak. "It's just priceless. Marjorie's brilliant. She's stinkin' brilliant! Brava. BRAVA!" yells Chet, drawing attention to their table.

Graham shifts in his chair and adjusts his eye patch, shocked by the turn of events. His stomach churns with the sickly, sinking feeling that Granny was right.

They're all fucked.

Dear Coco,

No one will believe us.
But it doesn't matter.
Nothing matters now.
Because I've traded my fear
For anger.

62

BACK OFF

Palms and flowers. Horns blaring high notes. Hickson suits, pinstripes and windowpanes. Silks, crepes, drop waists, and high heels on hardwood. Marjorie recognizes designs by Hattie Carnegie, House of Lucile, and display window offerings from B.Siegel and Hudson's.

She does her best to appear casual and relaxed. Bonafante drapes his arm across the back of her chair, which helps. Granny gives her a delighted, mischievous smile from across the table, subtly saluting in approval with the gilded handle of Leopold.

Marjorie's been to countless balls and events. But this feels entirely different. Different because of the swell of voyeuristic energy toward their table. She's relieved they're not sitting with her father, where guests feel comfortable and curious enough to approach—only to later snicker "vulgar," "crass," and "nouveau riche." But with statesmen like her grandfather and Mr. Alger as barrier buoys, the average attendee knows better than to swim too close. So instead they hover behind an invisible line, hoping to make eye contact.

"You okay?" asks Bonafante.

"I'm fine," she whispers. "I'm more concerned about you. You're a phantom in the flesh that everyone wants to see with their own eyes. I'm sorry, I didn't consider this fully."

A bespectacled man hesitantly approaches the table. "Good evening, madam. Forgive me for disturbing you, but I'm completely taken with your dress and had to tell you so. I'm with Himelhoch's."

Himelhoch's.

The exclusive retailer known for bringing Fifth Avenue to Detroit. Marjorie stands and takes a step from the table to shield Bonafante. "Such an honor to meet you! I'm Marjorie Lennox."

"The pleasure is mine. The fabric, the cut, the fall of your dress—is it a French design?"

Marjorie leans in. "French, wouldn't that be lovely? No, I designed and created it myself. So I guess we'll have to call it a Detroit design?"

A stunned silence, the thrill of the impossible, pulls across his face. "My word! Do you have others?"

"Yes. I've completed a few designs that represent a thematic line I'm working on."

"Incredible. As you can see, there's nothing like it here in the ballroom."

"Oh, but I did spot a gorgeous creation beneath the balcony."

"Yes, we brought that in from Paris for Mrs. Schlotman. It's an experimental from a new designer, House of Schiaparelli. But of course Paris is quite a distance, and the idea of a new designer right here in Detroit is very exciting. Might I have the pleasure of giving you my card?"

"Certainly." Marjorie accepts his business card, admiring the embossed design. "Himelhoch. German descent, correct?"

"Latvian, actually. Well, it's certainly been a pleasure, Miss Lennox. Forgive me for disturbing you and your party. I do hope you'll contact me. As you know, there's great demand here for bespoke design."

Marjorie sits down, clutching the business card. Bonafante places a hand upon hers.

"Well done."

She smiles at him. "I'm sorry I didn't introduce you. I wanted to respect your privacy."

"I know the Himelhochs. Juliette buys from them. Lovely family. And very considerate—that's why he didn't acknowledge me."

"Oh."

Marjorie thinks on it. When is ignoring someone's presence considerate instead of inconsiderate? And then she spots him approaching. Hank, the newspaper reporter. She looks to Granny with frantic eyes.

"Leave us be," says Granny, gripping Leopold. "Get rid of him, Cormac."

"Back off! We're in a conversation here," bellows Gramps. Alger laughs.

Hank shrinks away to the perimeter near the dance floor.

Bonafante's left knee bobs slightly. She can tell that he hates being on display, hates witnessing those who try to use familiarity as currency. He hasn't touched the drink that someone wormed in to give him. Suddenly Marjorie sees it through his eyes, how people leech on, sucking for favor and position, and how revealing the slightest bit of information can be dangerous. She doesn't want anyone touching him or bothering him. She can feel his discomfort in her own body. He's not antisocial; he's private. There's a difference. And he's only doing this for her. To protect her from her father—as he's apparently done for some time now.

She makes a show of looking around on the table. "Silly me. I forgot my purse in the car. Can we pop back out and get it?" she says.

"Of course. Excuse us."

He takes her hand and guides her through the crowd of dancers and diners in the ballroom. Whispers mingle with shadows of cigarette smoke and silent judgment. As they approach one of the doors, an older woman reaches out to stop them. "Mr. Bonafante! Bonita Bergel. So good to see you. We met years ago in Grosse Pointe. You had the most beautiful furry companion. I'm sorry, I can't remember the name of your dog."

"Oh, don't feel bad about that," says Marjorie sweetly. "We all have so much to keep track of." They glide past the woman, subtly quickening their pace toward the exit.

"Smooth. You're good at this," he says.

"At what?"

"Caring about what's important to people and protecting them. And you're sweet with your deflections to others. You don't hurt their feelings."

"Poor Daisy. She's probably used often as a conversation starter."

"Oh, don't feel bad for Daisy. Dobermans have great instincts."

They reach the car, and after seeing Marjorie into the Ghost, Bonafante wastes no time in pulling out of the club parking lot. As they cross the bridge, he glances over at her and smiles.

"So, where in that small dress did you hide your purse?"

"I didn't. I purposely left it beneath the seat in case we needed an excuse to escape."

He nods, impressed.

"I didn't want to look. Was the rest of my family there?"

"Yes, seated clear across the ballroom, with a myriad of expressions. Chet seemed particularly pleased."

Marjorie takes a deep breath. She slides across the bench seat to be close to him. They drive in silence, and instead of being awkward, the quiet feels easy and familiar. When they cross over the city limit from Detroit into Grosse Pointe, he pierces the silence with a question.

"Are you hungry?"

"Starving."

"Our dinner's still in the warmer. Might be a little dry but still edible."

"Anything will be grand."

As they head back toward his estate, Marjorie studies the card from Himelhoch's. She would have sold the dress right off her back there in the ballroom for cash to help Ivy and Peter. If she can get the fabric, she'll create more and sell the store an exclusive line, as she discussed with Bernice. But if she can sell the fake sapphire back to her family, she won't have to rush and can thoughtfully map out her clothing venture. Temptation hangs close. After all, as Ivy said, rules can be tedious. In the Motor City, men build empires out of loopholes and lies. Legitimate business is for those who can afford to wait.

She looks out the window into the darkness. But if she cons her family with their own fake sapphire and sinks to their level, is she no different from them? She doesn't want to hurt Chet or Graham. She doesn't want to hurt anyone. But she does want to protect herself.

Her grandfather is a lovely man. Could she go to him with her plight? But if Uncle Jamie actually is her father, her grandfather must know. Granny and Gramps know everything. They had the opportunity over many years to be honest with her, for her own protection, and they didn't. She has no illusion that her grandfather's a saint. Few titans of industry are, especially in Detroit. And she knows that Granny is fierce about protecting the family as a unit. But protecting the whole sometimes means sacrificing a piece or a part.

The thought is frightening. Marjorie stares at the dark roll of road beneath the headlights.

"Fear," she says aloud. "I often wonder, what is the fear that shapes me most?"

He remains quiet.

She turns to him. "If we voice our fears aloud, we face them. Disempower them," she says.

Silence.

"You don't agree?"

His reply is soft in volume but firm in certitude. "It can be dangerous to dance with demons. Acknowledging their existence grants them unnecessary power."

"So it's better to ignore them?"

"No," he says. "Protect all that you are and all that you love. Stamp them out. Immediately."

They drive on, silent for a spell, until he speaks. "I'm sorry if that sounds harsh. Unfortunately, I've been acquainted with the darker side of the human spirit."

She glances over at Bonafante's strong profile. His conviction. From what Juliette shared, that conviction was hard-fought and likely hard-won.

Protect all that you are and all that you love. Stamp them out. Immediately.

She reaches over to the steering wheel and peels his hand off into hers. He slowly exhales.

Despite all that's transpired, she's still besotted with him.

Some fixer . . . a high-level blackhander.

There are bad men and there are worse men.

Which one is he?

63

SMOKE SCREEN

Bonafante lifts Marjorie and sits her on the counter in the broad, steel-and-tile kitchen. She softly grasps the knot of his tie to loosen it and releases the top button of his shirt.

"Are you going to dazzle me with your culinary prowess?" she asks.

"Hardly. I'm terrible in the kitchen." He walks to an adjacent counter, where elements for their planned meal had been staged. A bottle of wine, two glasses, and a basket covered with crisp linen.

He brings over the wine, opens it, and pours them each a glass. "Juliette cooks and studies nutrition. She oversees the kitchen staff and meal planning for the third-floor residents at the Nightingale. It's important to her that they eat well."

Marjorie thinks of the daily meal hampers during the residency, how thoughtfully they were prepared and packaged for each resident, even including maraschino cherries for Ivy because she longed for something red.

Bonafante returns with the basket and a tray containing olives and a variety of fresh cheeses. He opens the envelope of linen over the basket to reveal fresh bread. He chuckles.

"What?"

"Your eyes just popped, like a kid spotting a bowl of candy."

"I'm sorry, I'm hungry."

"No need to be sorry." He stands in front of her, glides a layer of butter on the bread, and lifts it to her lips.

"If I swallow the whole thing without chewing, will you be repulsed?" she says, accepting the bread into her mouth.

"No, but I'd rather you not choke." He hands her the glass of wine. She waits for him to take a piece of bread and lift his own glass, softly touching hers in a private toast. They eat silently for several moments, watching each other.

"I'm grateful you took me to the club, but I'm sorry you had to endure the scrutiny."

"I'm used to it."

"Really? I felt you were a bit anxious. You have a tic."

He nods. "My knee."

"Exactly. Thank goodness poor Myrtle Branley wasn't there. She would have marched right over and started peppering us with questions."

He takes a sip of wine and nods, with an odd expression.

"You haven't heard? Mrs. Branley passed away."

He takes another sip of wine. "Oh, did she?" he says.

"Yes, she suffocated in her steam closet."

He looks to the floor, concealing his face. Is he laughing?

"It's not funny."

"No, of course not."

He turns his back, and she sees his shoulders shake with laughter. Is he that evil?

He rotates back to her. "I'm sorry. But is that what they're saying about her death? That she suffocated in her steam closet?" His eyes dance with amusement.

"Stop, you're scaring me. How can you find that amusing?"

His face immediately sobers. "I'm sorry. I didn't mean to scare you. Since we're building trust, I'll share this with you, but you can't breathe a word of it to anyone." His expression darkens. "Not to anyone."

Marjorie nods slowly.

"Myrtle Branley isn't dead."

"What?"

He shakes his head. "Battle-ax Branley is part of a sting operation. She was so incensed about the wave of home invasions and heists in Grosse Pointe that she tried to recruit a citizen patrol force. When that failed, she went to the cops and suggested she disappear like Agatha Christie, in hopes that thieves would try to rob her home and they'd catch the ring of bandits."

"No!"

He nods. "Quite a scheme. She's always fancied herself a community sleuth. But I didn't know the smoke screen was that the old bird suffocated in her steam closet."

"I believed it!"

He starts to laugh again, hard. And Marjorie laughs with him, and soon they're both laughing and smiling.

And he looks beautiful.

"So, where is she?" asks Marjorie, catching her breath.

"At some health spa—in French Lick, Indiana."

"What a name," says Marjorie.

Once the laughter dies, he moves to stand closer. "I'm sorry I scared you."

Sitting on the high counter, Marjorie is at eye level with him. "You're gorgeous when you laugh."

"As are you. It's been a while since I've laughed that hard. In my business, you have to truly trust someone to be able to laugh with them."

He can't even laugh freely? How sad. And he said, "in my business." What exactly does that mean, she wonders. She examines his handsome face. "Well, I love to laugh and I love to see you smile, so we'll have to laugh often. Is there a time or place where you can truly relax?"

"On the water."

"Oh, are you quite different on your yacht?"

He edges closer. "Sail with me. You decide."

"Well, there is a lighthouse in the Upper Peninsula that I'm longing to see."

She reaches out and traces a soft finger across his hairline, down along his temple to his brow, curious to feel the shape of the bone beneath. She takes a sip of wine.

As she swallows and shifts the glass from her mouth, he slowly runs his thumb across her bottom lip. His brows arrow, studying her. She sits, comfortable within his gaze, and gently pulls him closer until the insides of her knees are at his hips. She slips her arms around his neck and threads her fingers up the back of his hair. He closes his eyes and breathes for several moments.

He opens his eyes. "I'm glad you're here," he says.

She nods, silent.

His face drops forward until their foreheads are touching. She feels the warmth of his breath and the sensation of dissolving, drowning in him envelops her, just as it did that night in the stairwell. She slides her hands from the back of his hair to his chin, lifting her lips to be level with his. They hover there, breathing together, until she takes his hand and places it upon her chest.

He looks at her, acknowledging the intense gallop of her heart. He gently frames her face in his hands and stares at her with a mix of fascination and longing. She smiles, shifts to the end of the counter, and pulls him against her. He presses in, holding her, his body offering its response. Her eyes flutter shut and he kisses her in a way she's never been kissed, deep, with building intention, instantly sending a magnetized swell from her mouth through the rest of her body. Waves of light flash behind her closed eyes. She shivers as he dips within her hair to whisper in her ear.

"I dream about you, Marjorie."

She trembles, brushes her mouth against his lips, then slowly slides her dress up her thighs, revealing her opal lavender stockings and the dainty clasps of her garter ribbons. He shudders, then kisses her again. She pulls him closer. Then nearer still. The world narrows to their kiss, and she grasps him with an audible summons. He draws back, takes a steadying breath, kisses her nose, her ear, her neck, and slides her hips slightly off the counter to press against him until she's nearly beyond herself.

And then he lifts her off the counter entirely. And carries her upstairs.

64

BROKEN GLASS

A soft knocking sounds at Graham's door. He ignores it and rolls over in bed. There's no stripe of light around the curtains, so it's much too early for anyone to be bothering him.

The knocking sounds again. Louder.

"What?" he calls.

No reply. Just more knocking. He rises from the bed in his undershorts and pauses at the door. "Who is it?"

"It's Ina. Your grandfather asks that you come downstairs. It's most . . ." Emotion snags her voice. "It's most urgent."

He pauses, suddenly alert. "I'll be right down."

Graham stands with his back against the door. The hands of the clock point to 5:45 A.M.

It's done. It's finally over.

He shakes his head, scarcely able to grasp how he's feeling. He's confused. It's a cocktail of finality with a sickly splash of dread. Suddenly he doesn't feel prepared. Is this how Victoria felt when her uncle died and she ascended to the throne?

He races around the room, dressing quickly. Should he wake Chet? They didn't discuss this part. No, probably best to be with Gramps and then go to Chet's room so she can call the embalmer.

Who found him? And where? Graham fastens a few buttons of his shirt and hastily dons his eye patch. He runs out the door and down the stairs in his bare feet. He finds his grandfather alone in the sitting room with his head in his hands.

"Gramps?"

His grandfather looks up at him, his face red and sweaty beneath the shock of gray hair. "Sit down, Graham."

Graham closes the door to the sitting room and takes a seat next to his grandfather on the sofa. Gramps reaches for a newspaper on the coffee table. He hands it to Graham and points to something above the fold in the "Auto News" section.

DEEPENING CRACKS OF A DETROIT DYNASTY

While most are trying to withstand the heat of summer amidst speculation about Ford's secret new car, others are throwing soirees that epitomize the clichéd nouveau riche behavior and hyperbole that this decade has long been criticized for. Materialism and moral decay were on full display last week at an auto-family fete that felt like a desperate overreach to compete with the Vanderbilt–Cecil reception at Biltmore House. The event fell embarrassingly short in both pedigree and poise. The result was a gathering of unrefined unsavories, all eager to dole out information on one another. Music, gossip, and illegal liquor flowed freely, and as the night waned, so did the loyalties.

Among the attendees was a dotty woman who had been concussed the day prior when she crashed a plane trying to get a pilot's license; an in-law who whispered that a relative wears an eye patch with no injury; a morbid woman who secretly pens obituaries under the guise of her brother as the author; and a satin siren asking male guests for their Christmas lists while offering to stuff their stockings.

Whispered sightings at the event included members of the Purple Gang and the Lizard Gang, as well as gambling czar Lefty Clark and suspected serial kidnapper Legs Laman. The extremely attractive hostess was overheard lamenting that a vile circus had invaded her home, defiling her powder room and bedrooms.

One has to feel sorry for Detroit's old guard and men of the Pontch, who must be turning in the dirt seeing their once-dignified industry now smashed and scattered like broken glass. The city of Detroit has reached a new benchmark, not only for corruption but for a stunning role reversal—a city where the living haunt the dead.

Graham stares at the newspaper. He swallows. Tries to hide his panic over the unexpected reveals. He clears his throat. "Bastards. Calling us nouveau riche. What else is new. But Lilah's been taking flying lessons? We thought she was at tennis," says Graham.

Gramps's face turns a deep shade of plum. He stands, clenching his fists. "That's all you can say after reading that? An eye patch with no injury and a woman writing under the guise of her brother? You assured me, promised me, that you'd save the family business, Graham. Not destroy it further."

"It's that young newspaper reporter, Hank. He's telling lies, trying to ruin our family."

"You've been telling lies! Chet's been telling lies! Do you think I didn't know what you were up to?" Gramps walks in a huff to the window. He stares through the glass, unable to look at Graham. "You're a shite executioner. I was onto your scheme early. I swapped out your 'inheritance dust' with laxative powder, and you never noticed."

Graham's mouth falls open.

"You thought I was too stupid to catch on? Well, think again. I've played the game from every seat at the table. And you know I've got eyes and ears in this town. If you buy a stick of chewing gum, I know about it. I planned on confronting you right away, but your father's rear-end rainstorm was too amusing. I appreciate that you were trying to protect the family fortune, but you're a bloody amateur."

Graham sits in stunned silence.

Gramps shakes his head. "You had your granny fooled with the eye patch. But why in God's name would you do it?"

Graham sinks into the sofa.

"It wasn't an accident. He tried to take my eye out on purpose, Gramps. I know it."

"You sound like a four-year-old."

Graham takes a breath. "When it first happened, I needed the patch. Everyone was mad at him, just like I was. And that made me happy. When Uncle Jamie heard about it, he sent me a congratulatory letter with cash, saying I was officially a pirate, like the stories he shared when I was in Barbados. And as strange as this sounds, I came to love the patch, because it was a constant reminder to the world of how awful he is. I didn't want people to forget. So I continued wearing it, as a badge of his dishonor."

Gramps stares out the window. "But you—you know the truth. Our name is a badge of dishonor. I shared that with you because you'll be the one to protect the family."

"More than fifty years have passed, Gramps. If something was going to happen, it would have already transpired."

"Never assume you're in the clear. It's just when you breathe easy that ghosts of the past return to press their fingers to your throat. You understand that? The bones of the real Lennox lie in a shallow garden behind a house in Scotland, but they haunt this family—and this house—as if I buried them just yesterday. Delphine Dodge was right. Our walls whisper. Christ, Slorah will tell you that. But stealing the Lennox name all those years ago—that's my sin, not yours. I confided in you, not only about our family name but about your father's jewel racket, because I know you'll have to navigate it in the future." His fingers flex and clench again.

"I know you've told Chet things but not everything. Don't. Not yet. But enough with this godforsaken death plot! You have enough 'sins of the father,' so don't go creating sins of your own." He turns to face Graham, his eyes ablaze with ferocity. "Is that understood?"

Graham nods.

"You're a decent lad, Graham. You could bring grace to the family name, like Edsel has done for Henry. But I've gotta train you, and that can't happen overnight. So, in the meantime, tell your granny you want the framed icon she mentioned that restored the baseball player's sight. We'll have a quiet miracle."

Graham sits, bewildered. "And what about Marjorie's appearance last night? Are you shocked?"

"Not at all. Brains and beauty, just like her father."

Graham sneers. "What's that supposed to mean?"

"It means she'll be an important ally. Trust me when I say you've done well trying to protect your sister. Bonafante won't forget that. But watch yourself. Beneath his quiet exterior is a beast, barely leashed. Power and influence—that's his bloodline. The Bonafantes don't bow; they make others kneel. Don't cross him, Graham. Ever."

"Should we be concerned for Marjorie?"

"Not at all. But if anyone hurts her, even slightly . . ." Gramps shakes his head.

Graham feels sick with uncertainty. Does Bonafante know what their father had planned for Marjorie? He scans the article again . . . *an in-law who whispered that a relative wears an eye patch with no injury.* That makes no sense. His only in-law is Lou. How would Cecile and Lou know about the eye patch?

"Say, this article—it doesn't mention you, Gramps."

"It doesn't directly mention your father either. How convenient."

"Wait, you're right. Dad was practically holding court with Hank at the party. But I didn't hear him say any of this to that reporter. He was just waxing on about wanting to build a new plant. So where did the reporter get his information?"

"What have I been telling you? Newspapers are dangerous animals. With all that I've done, all that I've given, and all the information that I've shared with you. You think you've kept me in the dark about my very own family this whole time?" says Gramps. His anger rises. "Does everyone think I've become some retired, silent witness? Does everyone in this house think me a fool? Well, think again."

Graham hears the utter disgust in his voice. But for a split second he sees the shadow of something else. A sly smile curling across his grandfather's face.

Wait. Where, indeed, did the reporter get his information?

65

FRANCE PERHAPS

Bonafante walks across the terrace to the breakfast table. He leans over and gives Marjorie a lingering kiss. "Good morning."

"Good morning." She smiles, wrapped in his dress shirt. "Hope you don't mind. I've borrowed your shirt."

"Looks good on you. Are you tired?"

"Actually, I feel quite invigorated. I wonder why?"

He laughs and pours her a glass of orange juice from the neighboring bar cart.

Marjorie gazes at him, recalling the way he shared himself last night—unguarded, ashamed of nothing, allowing her fingers to trace the collection of violent scars storied across his body. He would have explained had she asked. The past was there, waiting, but she didn't want it to invade the present.

She waves an expressive hand. "I've made an aesthetic decision. I've decided that you need a gaggle of swans here."

"Really? And I had my heart set on peacocks," says Bonafante.

Her face flares with delight. "Peacocks! Oh, yes, even better."

He takes a seat. "Our discussion about your family. Have you thought about it?"

"Of course. I'm just so blisteringly mad about everything. And . . . a death plot in my own family? To be honest, I'm ashamed and embarrassed—of my family, but also of myself. Did I really not see everything? Or did I not *want* to see everything?"

"Juliette said she told you about our father. He was diabolical. I saw what was happening in our family, but it took me two years of careful planning to deal with it."

"You were a little boy."

"Not so little. My mother had family money, but when we left him, everything was frozen. I needed to provide for us quickly. I was lucky to have a mother and sister who were strong and could endure. Juliette can be . . . complicated. Her experience left fractures. But she trusted me. Speaking of trust." He hands her a folded newspaper. "The paper ran something about the party. Have a read."

Bonafante watches as Marjorie reads the article, her brows lifting in surprise.

"Oh, my. Broken glass, indeed. Cecile's anger about the nouveau riche comment will be eclipsed by the fact it says she's attractive. I do feel bad for Chet, though. She loves her obituary job, and I want her to keep it." She looks up from the paper.

"But, wait, Graham's eye patch is phony? Oh, poor Graham, that's surprising. But not as surprising as my mother taking flying lessons. Is that true? She said she wanted to explore new heights, but I didn't realize she meant literally. Again, was I not listening or did I not want to hear? But good for her. Perhaps she's planning an escape to the West Indies. Wouldn't that be exciting?"

Marjorie falls silent. She looks up and locks eyes with Bonafante. "Goodness, this exposé, it seems to involve nearly everyone—except myself and Gramps." A gentle curve of her mouth emerges. "How interesting."

"Isn't it, though?"

She sighs and smiles widely and freely for the first time in days. Bonafante leans back in his chair, staring.

"What?" she asks. "Why are you looking at me like that?"

"You don't feel it?"

"Oh, I feel it. I felt it years ago. And I certainly felt it last night."

He nods. "When I'm near you, it's almost overwhelming."

"Does that frighten you?"

"No. But it's different. You're fearless in your authenticity. When I first met you, several years ago at the Pontch, you were walking straight toward that enormous fire, didn't even pause. For a moment, I actually thought you were going to dive in. So I stepped forward, and then I truly saw you. It's hard to describe."

"I know," sighs Marjorie. "I tried to deny it with Bernice. She heard us through her window that first night in back of the Nightingale and knew immediately. She could hear something in our voices."

He pauses, reflecting. "But we didn't say much."

"Apparently we didn't have to."

They sit, taking in the quiet of the morning together, listening to the lap of the lake onto the shore. Marjorie reads the article again, processing it all.

"I'm sending you with a few things today. Hope that's okay." Bonafante smiles. "And the decorative item you requested, I found one in the attic."

"Thank you. My brain is still cataloging it all. It seems Cecile is in cahoots with my father so she'll inherit the business instead of Graham?"

"Correct. But your grandfather tells me that the way the trust is worded, if something happens to your father, the business returns to the ownership of your grandfather and he would choose a successor."

"Right. And he'd choose Graham, of course. Well, Cecile doesn't need the windshield business. From what I gather, Lou and my father have been quite busy. Cecile probably has the entire jewel collection of Detroit in her drawers. Oh, those poor women. They have no idea they're wearing glass replicas and that their originals were stolen?"

He shakes his head. "What are you going to do?"

"I'm not entirely sure yet," she says, plucking a cluster of cherries from a small basket on the table. "There's something so poetic about them paying for their own fake jewels. What does one do when their family is a nest of secrets within a carnival of cons?"

"Watch quietly from afar. Hide your aces."

"Like you hide your name?"

He looks at her. A dust of surprise shifts to admiration.

"That was an easy hand. Your cigarette case. The initials were clearly visible. LBC. 'C' is your middle initial. And Juliette referred to the fact that people call you Charles."

He nods slowly. "Well done."

"What does Juliette call you?"

He pauses. "Coco. A nickname from when I was a small boy."

"How adorable! Shall I call you Coco?"

"No, please don't."

"What is your given name?"

"Luke. But with the French spelling—Luc."

Marjorie looks up, twirling her hands, digesting and allowing the name to wash over her. "Luc. It's fitting. I approve."

He laughs. "I'm glad." He puts the napkin on his lap and surveys the breakfast table. "I pulled the Nash out for you, and I've put the top down. Give me a list and I'll pick up whatever you need while I'm out."

"Well, as agreed, my file from Dock. Some clothes and"—Marjorie looks to him—"the sewing machine?"

"Of course."

"I have a few designs to complete to finish my line."

"It's going to be a nice evening. When you come back, we'll go for a sail and a swim."

"That sounds lovely." Marjorie stretches, then leans across the table. "I'm still terribly angry about everything. But last night was transcendent. I predict many more such evenings."

"Really?" he says, buttering a piece of toast. "I predict an intimate elopement."

Marjorie grimaces. "That's not funny."

"I'm not trying to be funny. I think we understand each other. Deeply. We're both intensely loyal people. I'm a very private person and I trust you. That's rare. We appreciate nature and the arts, which we can parlay into successful ventures. We'll travel. It's not wise to stay in one place too long. We share a philosophy of individualism, but we're equals. We'd be a wonderful team, in many ways."

Does he not grasp the whole of the situation? Perhaps he doesn't understand her as well as he thinks. "Let me be clear. After all that's happened, I'm more than wary."

"That's understandable."

She looks at him squarely, plainly honest with her proclamation. "I'm not interested in becoming anyone's chattel, being lorded over and saddled with restrictions. I'll earn my own way, and I'd rather be low on funds but long on independence. And, yes, this is a wonderfully adventurous decade. I might allude to pleasing my body, but you're mistaken if you think I'll discount my heart."

He leans toward her. "Your heart, your body. You forgot to mention your mind and spirit. What if I want that too?"

Marjorie folds her arms and leans in close. "My, you're ambitious, aren't you. How's your work ethic, Luc?"

"Patiently strong," he says, giving her a kiss. "Some might even say old-fashioned. Give it some thought, so when your anger lifts and I eventually ask properly, you'll be prepared. France perhaps? I still have family there."

She gives a shrug. "Or maybe Barbados. I might have family there too."

"For what it's worth, I did request your grandfather's permission to invite you to dinner last night."

"Really? And how—and when—did you decide you'd slip an invitation into my room?"

The side of his mouth lifts with amusement. "That first night, after we spoke near the back door of the Nightingale and I found your gift in my car. Your note—*Not so close.* It killed me."

Marjorie smiles. "I wondered if you'd understand it."

"Oh, I understood it. It's what I said to you that very first night, around the fire at the Pontch. And when I got your gift and the note, it confirmed what I had long suspected—we were connected. Juliette objected to my plan, of course. But I knew you'd be leaving the Nightingale, so I simply put 'tomorrow' on the invitation, figuring we'd meet the first evening after you left. After requesting your grandfather's permission, I asked him to put the invitation in your room."

"And how did you plant the brochure for the residency?"

"Let's just say I made sure your mother stumbled upon it. Your mother truly loves you and could see what your father was planning."

"And she outplayed him." Marjorie smiles. Her mother put the brochure in her room, just as she suspected. "But did my mother know the true nature of the residency?"

"No. But I knew that Dock's report of your sanity would be important to protect you from your father, and I wanted you to have that protection."

Marjorie nods. She won't deny it: She loves that her family has no idea what's she's up to or what she might know. She also loves imagining their shock last night when they saw her with Bonafante. The family's glass lens will soon sharpen.

Everyone will know she's untouchable.

She will be the author of her own destiny.

There will be new rules. A new lease.

And she's going to write it.

Dear Coco,

Detroit
Is a city of secrets.
Some ghosts remain buried,
Others rise when called.
And let's not forget,
They recognize my voice too.

66

A CHOICE

Marjorie drives the Nash to the gates.

Bonafante leans in, resting his forearms on the open driver's side window. "What have you decided?" he asks.

"Nothing yet. I'll let the spirit move me along the way."

He shifts, uncertain. "Let me come with you."

"No. Everyone has their secrets." She eyes him temptingly. "Let's keep all of ours a little longer. And speaking of secrets, remind me to tell you about the bed finials in my room."

"Maybe you should show me." He smiles.

"I'll see you this evening for our sail. I can't wait." She leans in, gives him a slow kiss, then pulls away from the gates and onto the road. She doesn't have to look back to know that he stands watching as she drives off. There's a tethering presence between them now, an anchor at each end despite any distance.

How quickly the world can change, thinks Marjorie. The earth shifts on its axis and the person you were yesterday is but a whisper of who you are today. And it's not just the Lennox family. It's happening with countless families. The city's population is skyrocketing. The swell brings even more glamour, grift, and greed.

This twisted game with her family, it began long ago and will continue long into the future. But right now she has a choice. She can go straight to Glen Arden, rejoin her family while holding the cards of truth. As she slowly reveals her hand, they'll all wonder what else she knows and how she knows it. She smiles. The crooked crown of Lennox glass could be hers. But why would she ever want it? No throne stands firm on a fortune of sand.

And what is the fate of Detroit? Who gets to make the rules and who gets to break them? Will her inventive, luminous city rise and regain the best possible version of itself or forever be shackled to the guiles and fortunes of the auto industry?

Marjorie arrives at the cross street and pauses at the new yellow stop sign. The flexibility of options eases the weight of uncertainty. How broad the horizon feels when you're able to choose your own direction.

It's wonderful that Luc lives so close. A right turn and Glen Arden is only a mile away. Just one right turn—a short distance—to confront each family member with all she knows. Or she can leave the family be. She can sell Cecile the fake gem and focus on her business venture and building a new family all her own.

He said he was sending her with a few things. Marjorie reaches beneath the seat, and her fingers brush against something cold. Recognition flickers to a smile—trust, partnership.

The man she calls her father: Would he even be happy to see her? Does he truly need her?

Who needs her?

She lifts the long silver strand from the passenger seat and spools it around her neck. She looks to the right toward Glen Arden. One right turn to choose the family she knows. She takes a breath and smiles contentedly.

And then she makes a left.

"Santa's coming, Ivy. The sleigh is on the way!"

Marjorie hits the gas and rolls down the road, tinsel scarf fluttering in the wind. An echo of jingle bells chimes in the distance.

Mystery of the Detroit Museum's Stolen Gems

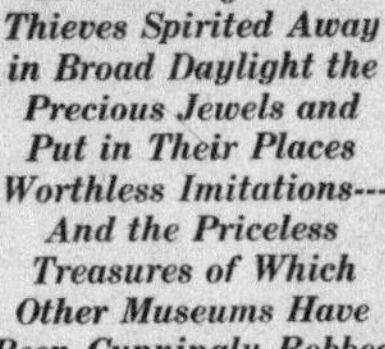

How the Ingenious Thieves Spirited Away in Broad Daylight the Precious Jewels and Put in Their Places Worthless Imitations--- And the Priceless Treasures of Which Other Museums Have Been Cunningly Robbed

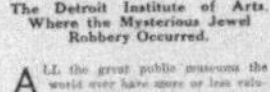

The Detroit Institute of Arts, Where the Mysterious Jewel Robbery Occurred.

ALL the great public museums the world over have more or less valuable collections of jewels and rare stones. They are usually in glass cases where visitors can approach and examine them and they seldom seem to be closely watched by museum attendants.

Why does it seldom happen that the valuable gems in the public museums are stolen?

At last this very thing has happened.

The Detroit Institute of Arts has been robbed of one of its rarest and most costly collections of gems, on which a police department valuation of $25,000 has been placed, though their real worth is far greater.

It was one of the many rare collections that have lain unguarded in the big museum for years. The theft is believed to have taken place more than two months

Some of the Imita-

DETROIT MILLIONAIRE MYSTERIOUS

Had Girl Accomplice.

Howard's sweetheart, a Grosse Pointe girl, whose name he would not divulge.

ACCUSES HUSBAND OF PUTTING HER IN ELOISE ASYLUM

Infected Molars Play in Health Cause of "Mental Delusions"

DETROIT, MICHIGAN, SUNDAY, JUNE

FORMER WRITER IS INSANE

Death Rings Down Curtain on Houdini

Alleged Purple Gangster Jailed

Parakeet Prodigy Passes

Wealthy Widow Suffocates

SAYS SIGHT HAS BEEN RESTORED WITH PRAYER

Jim Manning, Former Major League Pitcher, Able to See Agin After Four Years.

Reporter Gets 'Eyeful' On How Rum-Runners Work

OPENING CHAMPAGNE BOTTLE, STRUCK IN OPTIC.

DETROIT RUMMER ADMITS BUSINESS OF $5,000,000

Woman Crashes Plane

Prominent Grosse Pointe Girl Engaged

JEWEL THIEVES HOLD SEVEN AT BAY, TAKE GEMS

WORE EYE-PATCH

BRAVO, LINDBERGH!

Yankee Airman Arrives in France

NEW HOSPITAL AVERTS MENTAL BREAKDOWNS

Daughter Poisons Father

They hated to say so, but they thought that she was growing eccentric and someday might do something irrational that would dissipate the whole fortune.

SCHOOL DYNAMITER FIRST SLEW WIFE

Charred Body of Mrs. Kehoe Is Found in Ruins at Home That Michigan Maniac Blew Up.

HOTEL PASSES

Pontchartrain Closes Doors; All Service Ends Saturday at Midnight.

HOTEL PONTCHARTRAIN, CADILLAC SQUARE

STEALS GEM TREASURE
OF DETROIT INSTITUTE
the robbery, he told the police. He refused to divulge names but declared he had been blackmailed to help on the job.
BULK OF DODGE'S
FORTUNE TO WIDOW
Himelhochs
The Detroit Times
ADMITS STEALING
$25,000 IN GEMS
FROM MUSEUM
The Fine Luggage of
Louis Vuitton of Paris
at The J. L. Hudson Company
MAY DEPORT
CHAPLIN'S MOTHER
Woman Believes
in Santa Claus
JUDGE THE CAR
BY THE PEOPLE AROUND IT
ELOISE
AGATHA CHRISTIE FOUND ALIVE

AUTHOR'S NOTE

Detroit during its Golden Age was a city of ambition, contradiction, and reinvention—a place where fortunes were built and broken overnight. Although the Lennox family is fictional, the 1920s world they inhabit is entirely real. The events and details impacting their lives are drawn from long-forgotten stories I unearthed during a decade of research, some of which are included in clippings on the preceding pages.

As a novelist born in Detroit, I found this project to be a wonderful opportunity to examine not only an eccentric microcosm of American ambition but also to share the underrepresented history of a legendary city at war with itself. While certain locations have long dominated our cultural imagination as epicenters of glamour and crime, Detroit remains a unique, uncombed historical wilderness.

Like many who grew up near the Motor City in the twentieth century, I have a family with ties to the automotive industry. My grandfathers both worked for Ford, and my father owned a design firm that contributed art to many automotive campaigns. It was an era defined by the personalities of cars and their creators, and also a period when newspapers and radio reigned all-powerful in the city.

I was nine years old when the fashion writer for *The Detroit News* invited our family to visit her mysterious and storied 1926 estate in the Detroit Golf Club. It was during that visit I first learned that a selection of homes in Detroit and Grosse Pointe had hidden speakeasies and underground tunnels. My grandparents' house, where we often stayed, was in a humble enclave near the intersection of Woodward and Six Mile. But the homes in Palmer Woods, the Detroit Golf Club, and Grosse Pointe made such a shocking and lasting impression on me—as did Detroit's legacy of glamour and grift—that they sparked a lifelong curiosity for the untold history of my birthplace.

While tracking footprints through the past, I came upon a trail of breadcrumbs and discovered that, in 1925, a collection of valuable jewels was stolen from the Detroit Institute of Arts and replaced with glass replicas. It was part of a crime wave and two related heists, which also involved items donated to the museum by Edsel Ford. I researched and collected countless documents on the events from a century ago.

Despite the magnitude of the heist, it had all but vanished from memory. Even the staff members at the DIA had no knowledge of it. The reports claimed a girl from Grosse Pointe as an accomplice and revealed that a young man involved was the target of blackmail. It was a story that somehow slipped behind the dresser of history and went dormant, alongside stories of mysterious millionaires, mental-health struggles, family-dynasty wars, rumrunners, con artists, and local gangs.

Research is often a team effort, and I was fortunate to meet and consult with many brilliant people, as well as to reference prior works.

Gina Tecos, archivist and historian for both the Grosse Pointe Historical Society and the Ford House, assisted in my exploration of the 1920s period. Maria Ketcham and James Hanks in the Research Library Archives and Collections department of the Detroit Institute of Arts welcomed my inquiries. They allowed me to access the DIA's wonderful historical holdings for supporting information amidst my continued attempts to track down the current location of the missing jewels. Betsy Alexander, Historic Research and Education Coordinator for the Grosse Pointe War Memorial, is a fellow research enthusiast and author. The famous Italian Renaissance home of the Alger family—formerly the Moorings, now the War Memorial—is a centerpiece of Grosse Pointe history. Betsy gave me an immersive tour of the legendary property. She spent an enormous amount of time discussing leads and research avenues, and helped bring the period to life for me.

I'm grateful to the Windmill Pointe community; the Grosse Pointe Public Library; the supportive teams and guides at Ford House (the historic estate of Edsel and Eleanor Ford); the guides at Meadowbrook Hall, built by Matilda Dodge Wilson; the team at the Detroit Yacht Club; and the staff at the Henry Ford, Greenfield Village, and Ford's winter estate in

Fort Myers. I hold a heart of gratitude for Kris Kornmeier, a dear friend and Grosse Pointe resident who provided sources and encouragement over many years.

The archives of the *Detroit Free Press*, *The Detroit News*, *The Detroit Times,* and other Michigan newspapers provided a strikingly clear window into the daily life of Detroit in the 1920s, and I'm so grateful to have had access to them. The Detroit Police Department and the Law Department of the City of Detroit provided supplemental information for specific events, and former FBI special agent Tom Vinton helped me interpret details to build characters. In reading through countless news reports, police reports, and oral histories from a century past, I marveled at how much has changed yet mourned the echoes of many things that have remained the same.

I often referenced the work of Katie Doelle, whose book, research, and wonderful writings for Higbie Maxon Agney helped familiarize me with many historic estates of the period. Historical fiction sits on the shoulders of nonfiction, and I'm grateful to all of the sources that helped me explore Rose Terrace I and II, owned by Anna Dodge; Clairview, owned by the Eleanor Ford Torrey family; Harbor Hill, owned by the John Dodge family; Fair Acres, owned by the Henry Joy family; Stonehurst, owned by the Joseph Schlotman family; Gaukler Pointe, owned by the Edsel Ford family; Drybrook, owned by the Truman Newberry family; the Fisher House, owned by Charles T. Fisher; and the Bishop Mansion, designed by McGinnis & Walsh.

I returned time and again to *Detroit Is My Own Home Town* by Malcolm W. Bingay, a colorful retrospective published in the 1940s, and also to the first edition of *We Never Called Him Henry,* a wealth of underworld information shared by Henry Ford's longtime head of security, Harry Bennett, as told to Paul Marcus, published in 1951.

The licensed photos and illustrations in the historical collages are courtesy of The Grosse Pointe Historical Society, The Westland Historical Commission, and Wikimedia Commons.

The yachts of the auto barons and the many private clubs in Detroit and Grosse Pointe were fascinating to research. They could be a suite of novels all their own, as could the architecture and design culture of the city.

Fellow Michiganders might recall whispers of Eloise Hospital—at the time called Eloise Asylum—and the tragic, cold shadow of secrecy it cast upon many Midwestern families. At the height of its operation, Eloise housed more than ten thousand patients and two thousand staff members. This was also a time when wealthy families dabbled in secret and shocking experimental options for mental-health evaluation and treatment. During my research, I came upon tragic stories of misdiagnosis, revenge, and involuntary commitment, but there were also success stories of rest, rehabilitation, and patients who triumphed.

Eloise deserves many retrospectives to examine its long history and honor the thousands of souls who passed through its gates, and I'm grateful to the Westland Historical Commission and the Wayne Historical Society for their preservation efforts. Three books I referenced were *Annie's Ghosts: A Journey into a Family Secret,* by Steve Luxenberg; *A History of the Wayne County Infirmary, Psychiatric, and General Hospital Complex at Eloise, Michigan 1832–1982,* by Alvin C. Clark; and *Eloise: Poorhouse, Farm, Asylum and Hospital 1839–1984,* by Patricia Ibbotson.

Regarding Eloise and the time period in general: In keeping with the historical authenticity of the 1920s, some characters in the novel use vocabulary and terms that were widely accepted at the time but are no longer appropriate in modern discourse. I'm grateful that we now approach topics and conversations with greater respect and compassion.

History is often shaped by those who held power. But it lingers in the lives of those who lived it—in the stories tucked away in the attics of memory or within the echoes of old houses and city buildings. And on that note:

For Detroit, Michigan, and anyone who has lived or worked there:

You are part of an incredible, unique legacy of immigration, ingenuity, and fortitude. Something nuanced and complex for others to comprehend. But you understand creating something from nothing. You understand the honor in relentless hard work—never given a break, but never giving up. You exemplify a braided, multicultural community that believes in miracles.

So, for the creative, fighting spirit of all those who came before us and paved the way, may we honor them by uncovering and giving voice to their stories and also—

By sharing our own.

ACKNOWLEDGMENTS

This novel materialized through the encouragement of many extraordinary people.

Steven Malk, my incredible literary agent at Writers House, has guided my steps since 2007. I couldn't ask for a better creative copilot, mentor, and friend.

Hilary Teeman, my spectacular editor at Ballantine, deeply and immediately understood what I was aiming for and helped me build the book into something beyond what I imagined. Other invaluable champions include Elsa Richardson-Bach in editorial, my copy editor Kathy Lord, my publicists Kathleen Carter, Karen Fink, and Emily Isayeff, Kelly Chian in production editorial, Jessie Bright in the art department, as well as rockstars Taylor Noel and Rachel Taylor in marketing and Pam Alders and Saige Francis in managing editorial. A deep bow of gratitude to the wonderful team at Ballantine—Kara Cesare, Jennifer Hershey, Kim Hovey, and Kara Welsh. The physical beauty of the book is all thanks to interior designer Ralph Fowler and cover designer Molly von Bortsel at Faceout Books.

I must also salute the extended teams at Random House, as well as all of the Penguin Random House field reps.

Jeffrey Kirkland manages my days and events with love and laughter. I am blessed to work with him. My writing partner—and general partner in crime—Sharon Cameron, has stood beside me for more than twenty years encouraging me to write this Detroit story, as have Court Stevens, Amy Eytchison, Angelika Stegmann, and Howard Shirley.

Courtney Donovan, Kristina Sepetys, Aristéa Santoro, Kacie Wheeler, and Steve Sheinkin all gave thoughtful, comprehensive reads and feedback that helped shape the book, and the Fortescue family provided a beautiful and historic place to work.

My longtime Penguin Young Readers family—Ken Wright, Jen Loja, Jill Santopolo, Shanta Newlin, and Kim Ryan—all blessed me on this journey of writing an adult novel, as did the ever-inspiring Ann Patchett and Rae Ann Parker with my local indie, Parnassus Books.

Heartfelt thanks to Writers House, Sean Marks at Marks Law Group, Sylvie Rabineau at WME, and all of my wonderful international publishers, sub-agents, and translators who share my stories globally.

Deepest gratitude to educators, librarians, and booksellers. And most of all—the readers. I appreciate each and every one of you.

My creative family—The Rockets, Steve Vai, Niels Bye Nielsen, Yvonne Seivertson, Marius Markevicius, JW and Kaci Scott, Heather Napier, Noah & Andrew Faber, Mary Tucker, the Baysons, the Peales, the Smiths, the Myers, and the Schefskys have all supported me on my journey of writing and fuel my dedication to research and history.

What a gift to be raised within an environment of incredibly strong women, and men who appreciated them. A toast of Pol Roger to Meta Sepetys, our very own Detroit designer who created my bespoke dress for a special event at the Detroit Yacht Club, my incredible mother and father who always stressed the importance of self-determination, and my current cohort of Sepetys women—Aunt Ruta, Kristina, and Jennifer—who hold the torch of independence high. Thank you for lighting the way.

No one could possibly understand the devotion to Detroit, the eccentricities, or the raucous rhythm of the family in this novel—except Kristina and John Sepetys, my siblings and very best friends. Thank you for your loving support of your whimsical youngest sister. How lucky we are to be a family on the dance floor of life with memories of such unique and wonderful parents. *C'mon, we're at the dinner table! Death comes in threes, you know.*

And of course my loving husband, Michael, whose brave and beautiful heart gives me the courage and the wings. He is my everything.

ABOUT THE AUTHOR

RUTA SEPETYS is an internationally acclaimed, #1 *New York Times* bestselling author of historical fiction published in over sixty countries and forty languages. Considered a "Seeker of Lost Stories," her books are read by both adults and students worldwide. Winner of the Carnegie Medal and honored by the American Academy of Arts and Letters, Sepetys is renowned for giving voice to underrepresented history and those who experienced it. Her books have won or been shortlisted for more than fifty book prizes, appear on over forty state reading lists, and are currently in development for film and television.

Sepetys is the daughter of a mother who hailed from Detroit and a father who fled from Lithuania as a refugee. Born in Michigan and raised in a family of artists, readers, and music lovers, she spent more than twenty years working in the music industry prior to becoming a novelist. Whether writing about the oppressive weight of communism or the intoxicating allure of legendary cities, she traces how power, secrecy, and corruption compromise the lives of ordinary people, revealing human patterns that echo across past and present. Her research and writing on human resilience have earned her invitations to speak at NATO, European Parliament, the U.S. Capitol, the Library of Congress, and embassies worldwide. She has been awarded fellowships from the University of Oxford in England and the Rockefeller Foundation's Bellagio Center in Italy.

The New York Times Book Review declared, "Ruta Sepetys acts as champion of the interstitial people so often ignored—whole populations lost in the cracks of history."

Sepetys was bestowed the Cross of the Knight of the Order by the President of Lithuania for her contributions to education and memory preservation and was honored with a postage stamp containing her image. She is deeply grateful for her Baltic heritage—even if it means she has a name that no one can pronounce.

Ruta Sepetys lives with her family in the hills of Tennessee.

rutasepetys.com

ABOUT THE TYPE

This book was set in Garamond, a typeface originally designed by the Parisian type cutter Claude Garamond (c. 1500–61). This version of Garamond was modeled on a 1592 specimen sheet from the Egenolff-Berner foundry, which was produced from types assumed to have been brought to Frankfurt by the punch cutter Jacques Sabon (c. 1520–80).

Claude Garamond's distinguished romans and italics first appeared in *Opera Ciceronis* in 1543–44. The Garamond types are clear, open, and elegant.